# The Sipsey Swamp Stories

## Wendell Wiggins

Outskirts Press, Inc.
Denver, Colorado

Cover picture: The path through Grimsley's farm to the swamp.

The Sipsey Swamp Stories
All Rights Reserved.
Copyright © 2008 Wendell Wiggins
V2.0

Outskirts Press, Inc.
http://www.outskirtspress.com

ISBN: 978-1-4327-2860-1

Library of Congress Control Number: 2008932617

Outskirts Press and the "OP" logo are trademarks belonging to Outskirts Press, Inc.

PRINTED IN THE UNITED STATES OF AMERICA

# Preface

When I was a kid, I made up stories to entertain other kids and myself. Sometimes at school, when the teacher was exhausted at the end of the day, she would let me concoct some on-the-spot tale to fill the last few minutes while she collapsed in a desk at the back of the room. It gave my first indication I could fabricate stuff that others would find engaging. I favored ghost stories and mysteries, and sometimes the tale might be just a thinly disguised version of a book I had read. I hereby apologize to the many authors I plagiarized without remorse back then.

I gave up imagining stories as an adult until my daughters, Lucy and Rebecca, came along. I regret I didn't spend more time creating fantasies for such an appreciative young audience, but the days and years flew by as I realized and lived out my childhood fantasies as a scientist. They had to make do with a whistling mouse.

These Sipsey Swamp stories were originally recalled especially for my very precocious young friends, Carly and James Reilly, when they were five to ten years old, and my career had begun to wind down. Their good reviews encouraged me to put the stories on paper. Throughout these tales, my aim has been to give my young audience a true glimpse of another world that existed long ago and far away. For older readers, a bit of fun and nostalgia is nice.

The stories wouldn't be possible but for the amazing people that inhabited Frog Level as I grew up, because I am not creative enough to have fabricated some of the unusual characters. Even though I have changed their names, stirred them together, and squeezed them into these stories, I thank all the real Frog Levelians for being my inspiration.

Chief among the Frog Level characters who made the adventures possible is my brother, Kavanaugh.

To all my muses, I dedicate these stories.

They would still be floating around the back of my mind if it were not for my wife and forty-five year long friend, Joan. She provided the comfortable, supportive home and family that gave me the freedom to find the memories back there in my head.

Near the end of this book, when I was about to leave Frog Level, one of the Sipsey Swamp characters gives me the advice, "Take some good friends with you." I wouldn't have accomplished that goal without Joan. I've spent too much of my time thinking science and too little thinking about the people around me. On the other hand, one can hardly see Joan go off to the grocery store without allowing that she may bring someone home with her. I am most grateful that some of them hung around long enough to see that though her husband is odd, he has some redeeming qualities.

My daughter, Rebecca, recorded one of the stories, encouraged me to transcribe it, and thus the book was begun. Several of my friends and family reviewed and edited it. They are Pat Hartman, Ellen Picard, Erin Reilly (Carly's and James' mother), Davia Sacks, Joan Wiggins, and Lucy Wiggins. To the extent that it is readable, they deserve much of the credit. All the wordiness and incomprehensibility is my fault.

# Table of Contents

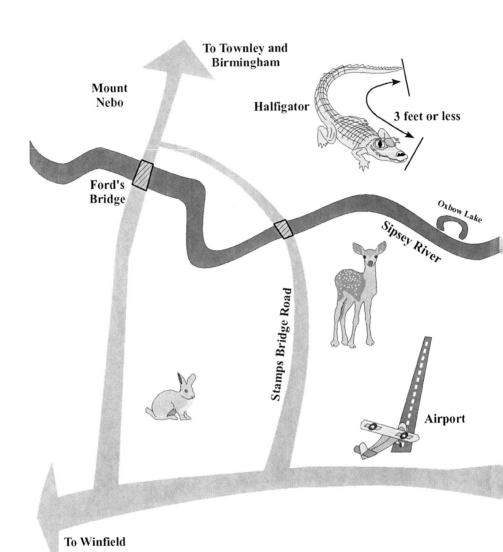

To Townley and Birmingham

Mount Nebo

Halfigator

3 feet or less

Ford's Bridge

Sipsey River

Oxbow Lake

Stamps Bridge Road

Airport

To Winfield

## Map of Frog Level and the Sipsey Swamp

Homeless but happy
Luxapalilla Turtle

To Vernon

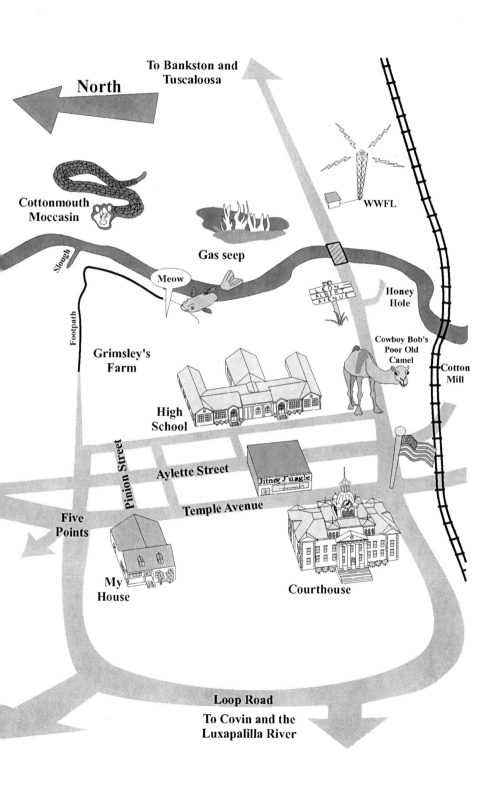

# An Introduction to the Swamp

Imagination is more important than knowledge. Knowledge is limited, imagination encircles the world.

Albert Einstein, from an interview with G.S.Viereck, Saturday Evening Post, Oct 26, 1929

I grew up in Frog Level, Alabama, on the west side of the Sipsey River and swamp. The place is called Fayette now, but it was Frog Level then. Well, some people had already begun to call it Fayette, but I always thought of it as Frog Level. The name comes from the fact that the town sits at the edge of the swamp—right down on the level with the frogs.

The river rather than the inhabitants of Frog Level long ago defined and still regularly enforces the eastern boundary of the town. Anything built closer to the river will be flooded. You may count on that. It tolerates any encroachment by man-made structures beyond the flood line only temporarily or on isolated mounds of dirt, but it is friendly so long as you respect it. The land slopes up slowly as you enter town, so no part of the town ever floods.

As you pass the main street of the business area, Temple Avenue, the land slopes up more steeply and makes a decent hill and then flattens out around the loop road at the western edge of town. Past the loop road on the way to Covin, the land eventually slopes down again into the Luxapalilla River valley. I've heard that Luxapalilla means "floating turtle" in the local Indian dialect. This valley no longer floods since the river was channelized; that is, it has been dredged out into an absolutely straight channel where the water flows swiftly and never escapes its banks. While it made the Luxapalilla valley a great place to farm, it destroyed the lush, mysterious swamp that had been there. The turtles no longer have any place to float in the fast flowing water. Most fortunately, the Sipsey River has not been channelized. They thought about it once, but the guy who made the plans died before he could bring in his dredges.

The main intersection in town is where Temple Avenue crosses Columbus Street. In the 1950s, a flagpole stood there, and from the flagpole, you could survey most of the important institutions of Frog Level: the Courthouse, the Citizens and First National Banks, Freeman's and Central drugstores, the railroad yard, and most importantly, my father's grocery store, the Jitney Jungle.

Temple Avenue was so named because of the several churches located on it. You passed the First Methodist Church, the First Baptist Church, and the Church of Christ as you drove north from downtown. At one time, maybe around the 1920s, Temple Avenue had been the most prestigious residential address, but it had been replaced before the 1950s by the loop road where our most prominent businessmen and doctors lived in large, fine houses: colonial or ante-bellum mansions, classic American brick houses, and one post-Frank-Lloyd-Wright object of art. The finest and oldest homes on Temple Avenue still seemed stately if not so modern.

My home in Frog Level was on Temple Avenue about a mile north of the business area, just opposite Pinion Street, and a few houses south of Five Points and the Garrison Brothers' General Stores. It was not one of the fine homes. It was too small and had been built too late and too far from downtown. It had only two bedrooms, but a beautiful fireplace stood on one wall of the living room, and a front porch with chairs and a swing would seat six people for a summer-night conversation. It cost all of three thousand dollars to build during the Great Depression. From our front porch, I could see the horse barn at the Grimsley's farm. Grimsley's was the last outpost of civilization before the Sipsey Swamp took over.

The highway to Bankston, Berry, and Tuscaloosa ran almost directly east from town and served as one access way to the swamp. It was usually just called "the Tuscaloosa highway." About five miles to the north, the road to Townley and Jasper crossed the Sipsey on Ford's Bridge. Earlier a bridge had crossed the river in between the major highways on Stamps Bridge Road; but in the 1940s and 1950s, vehicles could not cross since the wooden deck was missing, yet it remained intact enough that adventurous kids could climb across its triangulated skeleton of steel beams and rods. Unofficial, private, rudimentary roads or trails had appeared wherever someone wanted to go fishing or swimming or picnicking, and they all just ended near the river. We used the dirt road through Grimsley's farm.

The Sipsey Swamp consists of a swath of flat land varying from less than a mile to a few miles in width. To the north of Frog Level, the river runs more swiftly as you head toward its origins in the Appalachian foothills. In a rare show of good sense, the federal government declared the upper part of the Sipsey to be a "Wild and Scenic River" and conveyed legal protection from pollution and development on it. In Fayette County, it is slow, lazy, and populated by several species of fish, but above all else, catfish. Several types of mussels and a few clams also call it home. In some places, dense cypress groves enclose the river, while in other places, cultivated fields run right up to the water's edge—if the farmer is willing to lose his field periodically to the floods.

Cottonmouth moccasins, a species of pit viper, find the swamp a nice place to live, and they have been fruitful and multiplied. This snake is called a cottonmouth because the inside of its mouth is white. It's a nasty creature. I know that all God's creatures are beautiful in their own way, but my opinion is that a cottonmouth is ugly. It will bite you if provoked, and the bite will be painful and take a long time to heal. It could kill you. It requires medical attention in any case, and treatments of antivenin are needed if the snake injected much venom. Often the snake infects the wound and it has to be treated with antibiotics. If you go into the swamp at all, you seriously risk being bitten by a cottonmouth, or even a rattlesnake or copperhead. Don't say you weren't warned!

On the other hand, almost anyone who doesn't go to the swamp regularly will overestimate the likelihood of encountering a cottonmouth. Not that they're scarce; they're just happy to stay away from you as you're happy to stay away from them. Swamp novices probably think the cottonmouth is aggressive, but in fact, it simply defends its territory. If you encounter a cottonmouth and give it a chance to leave you alone, it will. I advise giving it that chance.

Because of its connection to the Gulf Coast, the swamp is home to other slightly larger reptiles. The Sipsey flows into the Tombigbee River, the Tombigbee flows into the Alabama River, and the Alabama runs into Mobile Bay. Like all places on the Gulf of Mexico, alligators inhabit Mobile Bay. The alligators procreate and must find new nesting places, so some of them swim upstream into the Alabama River. As they move away from the Gulf, the winters become colder, and the overall semitropical environment becomes more semi and less tropical. Those that have lived up the river for a few generations are smaller than their ancestors due to the hardships and sparser foodstuffs. Those Daniel-Boone-type alligators that go so far as the Tombigbee evolve to yet smaller sizes. Some have even made it into the Sipsey.

While the Gulf Coast alligators grow to six feet long or more, the ones in the Sipsey measure less than three feet long. The Frog Level natives, recognizing that the Gulf Coast beasts are called *all*igators, ages ago began to refer to the smaller local reptiles as *half*igators.

Be careful to avoid both cottonmouth moccasins and halfigators in the swamp, but the snakes are the most dangerous. I think the halfigators somehow must remember when their ancestors were bigger, and they have an inferiority complex now. They're mostly a nuisance; usually not life-threatening. The prospect of snacks or freshly caught fish attracts them to humans, and given half a chance, they'll steal your catfish or your lunch. If seriously provoked, they might bite off a finger or two or leave a nasty wound on your leg. The best and the traditional weapon to ward off halfigators is a good stick. Whack the beast right between the eyes and he'll turn tail. If you've got a good, strong pine limb, you'll be okay. Sipsey Swamp regulars know these tricks.

Of course, the swamp has the usual complement of white-tailed deer, skunks, raccoons, opossums, bobcats, and other small mammals, amphibians, and reptiles; and it has lots of insects. The natives also have a special name for the mosquitoes. Remarking on their phenomenal size and ferocity, they are called *most*quitoes.

So I was born into the small Alabama town I just described in 1942. Kavanaugh, my brother, had arrived three years earlier. Unlike me, he is musically and artistically talented and, as a boy, performed well at sports. Unlike him, I'm interested in science, technology, and mathematics. Both of us have vivid imaginations. As we grew older, we developed very different interests, but in the early 1950s, we were mostly interested in playing out grownup adventures.

My parents had unusual attitudes about protecting Kavanaugh and me. On the one hand, they protected us closely. We were taken to the doctor whenever we exhibited the mildest symptoms. And, of course, they warned us about "strangers." On the other hand, they allowed us to be quite adventurous if they thought it prepared us for adult life. Fortunately for us, wandering around in the Sipsey swamp was considered such preparation. My father grew up on a farm near Andalusia, Alabama, and was never more comfortable than when he rummaged about in the woods. He held the view that we should be prepared to "live off the land," and he taught us hunting and tracking skills. I once overheard my father explain to one of his friends:

"If they're not down in the swamp, they're going to be running around the streets on their bicycles or roller skates. I think they're safer chasing water moccasins and halfigators than bouncing off bumpers."

Some of these stories involve what parents of today, especially ones living in the very structured society of large cities and wealthy communities, may think of as risky and dangerous behavior. I am obliged, therefore, to offer the following observation to those parents. You're absolutely right!

Maybe I don't remember everything in great clarity after all this time. I was not a particularly perceptive youth, and many things that were obvious to some of my friends as they occurred, only dawned on me years or decades later. And finally, even though I try to get it right, I am just a bad reporter sometimes. There's one exception to these caveats; if I mention anything about burning or exploding something, it is the gospel truth.

In several situations, I mention that my family was dedicated to the Church of Christ. It was a very important part of my young life, so it will come up in some of these stories. Don't confuse it with The United Church of Christ or other similar sounding denomination. The Church of Christ is a deeply fundamentalist, Bible-believing, mostly southern denomination. I'll explain its theology as needed when it comes up in the stories.

One last note to avoid confusion: the radio station in Frog Level had the call sign, WWFL. A station near Orlando, Florida picked up this call sign in 1971 after Frog Level became Fayette. The Florida WWFL has nothing to do with this story or the Sipsey Swamp. They have only Disney World in which to live out their fantasies.

# Grandmother and Aunt Brazzie Take Us to the Swamp, 1951

> Yes, we'll gather at the river,
> The beautiful, the beautiful river,
> Gather with the saints at the river
> That flows by the throne of God.
>
> From a favorite church hymn by Robert
> Wadsworth Lowry

## Things you see in the swamp

As I turned nine years old in 1951, the swamp was a mystery to me. I'd seen the river from our car as we rode to Tuscaloosa, or Birmingham, or just went across the river to visit my father's friend, Storey Lufkin, and his family; but I'd never been into the swamp itself. Most of all, I really, really wanted to go fishing, to catch a couple of big catfish and have Mother cook them for supper.

We ate breakfast, dinner, and supper; not breakfast, lunch, and dinner. Breakfast was always a big meal. It usually consisted of eggs, bacon, hot, strongly-seasoned sausage, or ham, or all three, and freshly made buttermilk biscuits. The midday meal was the biggest of the day. Cooking it began as soon as the breakfast dishes were cleaned up. It consisted of meat, several vegetables, and often, fresh hot cornbread or leftover biscuits. Supper was usually leftovers from dinner, maybe with something added if the leftovers were sparse, or maybe just cereal and peanut butter.

I thought it would be quite grown up and praiseworthy to bring home a huge catfish or two to feed the whole family. My father hunted for squirrels, doves, quail, and deer; but I was not yet old enough, or patient enough, to go with him. I loved the occasion when he returned home with a bag full of squirrels or a quarter of a deer. I helped my father skin the squirrels with my pocketknife[1] and then we handed them off to my mother to cut up and put in our freezer. I thought that I was now old enough to go fishing and be the one who "brought home the bacon."

Though my father loved—yes, loved is the right word—hunting, he didn't care for fishing at all. Too boring, he said. He thought it was interesting to stand perfectly still in the woods waiting for a squirrel to show itself or to sit for hours waiting for a deer to run by, but it bored him to watch a cork bob in the water. This distinction seemed silly to me. I eventually developed a preference for staring at a cork over hunting, which is, I admit, equally silly.

Anyway, given his opinion of fishing, my begging him to take me down to the river was fruitless. After several attempts made with pathetic whining and persistent wheedling, he agreed to take me to the State Lake. We didn't have a boat, so I had to fish from the shore where the water measured only one or two feet deep. Large fish simply do not hang around in warm, shallow water. I didn't know that at the time, but after about thirty minutes of absolutely no action, I wanted to go home. I think he planned the trip to convince me that his opinion was right rather than to assist me in reducing our grocery bill.

My brother, Kavanaugh, also keenly wanted to go to the swamp, although he was motivated more by the general sense of adventure than by wanting to fish. It seemed like the wild territory we saw in cowboy movies. We imagined that we might encounter bad guys or wild animals there.

---

[1] Many of my readers won't know the details of skinning a squirrel. There's nothing elegant or uplifting about it. It's downright gross, so if you don't already know, I leave it to your imagination.

After I gave up on getting my father to take us to the swamp, I tried my mother. She knew the territory well since she picnicked there in her youth. But now she said she was too busy, and she didn't like fishing either. I almost decided to give up on her too when my grandmother intervened.

My mother's mother lived with us, and we called her simply Grandmother. My grandfather had died before I was born; so following the custom of the time, when she no longer needed a separate household nor could afford it, she moved in with one of her children. My parents welcomed her in, and she became an integral part of the household, especially as far as I was concerned. Grandmother cooked sometimes; she tended the "victory garden" in our backyard during and for a couple of years after the war; she sewed, quilted, and braided rugs. Braiding rugs was her favorite pastime. They covered the floor of every room in our house except the bathroom and kitchen.

As much as we all loved her, just one aspect of having Grandmother around was a little icky: she dipped snuff: powdered tobacco that is held in the mouth. Women of my grandmother's generation and social environment dipped snuff as commonly as men smoked cigarettes. The main problem with it is that the strong taste makes the mouth produce lots of saliva, and it has to be spit out. It requires, therefore, that the user keep a spittoon around. The most common type of spittoon, the kind Grandmother had, was a Toby. A Toby is a ceramic jug usually shaped like a fat man. He has a hat with an upturned brim that forms the rim and spout of the jug, and there's a handle on his back. Toby was usually found wherever Grandmother was last sitting. She couldn't carry it with her walking stick in one hand and anything else in the other hand, so she called on me to carry it for her several times a day, or worse, to empty it in one of the flower beds. They said it had a pesticidal effect. I don't doubt it.

My parents apparently didn't anticipate Grandmother moving in with us when they built the house. Since our house had only two bedrooms, Grandmother slept in one and Mother, Daddy, Kavanaugh, and I slept in the other. We desperately needed another bedroom. We would get it in a few years, but for now, Kavanaugh and I had never known any other arrangement, and Mother and

Daddy couldn't afford expansion, so we all lived with it.

My grandmother's given name was Elizabeth Armenia. Her sister, my Great Aunt Brazilia, lived directly across Temple Avenue from us. They both got nicknames early in life, and were generally known to everyone as Lizzie and Brazzie. She called my grandmother Wizzie, a name she concocted in childhood as a pet name for her sister. Even though she was Kavanaugh's and my great aunt, we called her "Aunt Brazzie."

Grandmother Lizzie was an authority on The Bible, which she had read and studied several times, cover to cover. She could quote long sections of the Bible that dealt with events and doctrinal questions of importance from memory. She studied the weekly Sunday School lessons with the dedication of a university scholar. She read The Complete Works of Flavius Josephus[2] when she was over eighty years old just to add its history to her biblical knowledge. Other women often consulted her as an expert on religious matters.

Growing up and living most of her life on a farm gave her what is sometimes called "the pioneer spirit." She simply did whatever was required by her circumstances. She had the built-in drive and a large grab-bag of skills with which to do it.

For example, when my uncle, Herman, was young, and they had moved from the farm near Sterling to Tuscaloosa, Grandmother gave him a quarter and sent him to buy a loaf of bread. As he bounded down the wooden steps of the house, he dropped the quarter; it fell between two steps; and the family rooster pecked at the shiny disc and swallowed it.

It was a significant sum of money back then. When Herman came back in the house with his sad news, Grandmother ordered him to catch the wrongdoer and carry it to the wooden bench in the backyard where odd jobs were done: corn was shucked, peas were shelled, and chickens were beheaded.

They needed the rooster more, however, to tend the many hens than

---

[2]    Flavius Josephus was a renowned first century Jewish historian.

10

for a pot of dumplings. Grandmother came out of the house not with an axe, but with a pair of scissors, a knife, sewing thread, and a needle. While Herman held the patient down on the table and a couple of neighborhood kids looked on, she cut open the rooster's gizzard, extracted the quarter, and sewed him up again. The rooster lived a long life afterward, and Grandmother continued to take care of the needs of the day, whatever they were.

Aside from the surgical procedure by Grandmother, Brazzie was the medical expert. Many people consulted her for what to do to cure various ailments. Once she prescribed a remedy for Lizzie's digestive problems. The remedy required a large number of ingredients, including a sizable quantity of burned wooden matches. Mother placed a tin can by the kitchen stove, another one by the heater in the hallway, and one by the fireplace in the living room. Brazzie and a couple of her friends also collected burned match stems. After several weeks of collecting, the match sticks were ground together with figs, sulfur, and some other ingredients, rolled into one-inch balls, and stored in our refrigerator for Lizzie to use. She ate one a day and recommended them highly to anyone who had the same symptoms.

Medical instinct ran in the family. Though he had no medical training at all, one of Lizzie's and Brazzie's brothers, O.C. Dobbs, invented a truss to relieve abdominal hernias. He named it *The Dobbs Truss* and manufactured and sold it all over the world until surgical treatments were developed.

One of Brazzie's compounds, an ointment for aches, pains, and minor wounds, was also commercialized. Dewey Michaels liked it so much that he began to manufacture it at home and sell it as Dewey's Ointment. All the drugstores for some distance around Frog Level carried it in stock and it sold consistently, and Brazzie received a small royalty from Mr. Michaels.

You should see by now that Lizzie, in particular, was not afraid of any mortal being nor did she hesitate to do something new. Thus, when she heard my pleas to go fishing fall on deaf ears, she stepped into the breach and volunteered herself and Brazzie to take Kavanaugh and me to the swamp to fish.

11

# Wendell Wiggins

When Grandmother announced that my begging could end and we could prepare to go, Mother pitched a fit. Her mother was too old; she needed a walking stick wherever she went; Brazzie was no better off; she didn't know anything about the swamp; there were cottonmouth moccasins and halfigators down there, and on and on. Grandmother countered that it was June, warm and sunny, but not too hot yet; and reminded Mother in no uncertain terms that she still was not completely over the hill.

When Grandmother told me she and Brazzie would take us fishing and Mother finally gave in and consented, Kavanaugh and I were overjoyed. We lavished praise on Grandmother, asked if we could do any favors for her, and began to prepare our cowboy outfits for the trip.

Like most Frog Level boys of that time, we were avid cowboy fans, so of course, we had to go to the swamp with our guns and hats!

We played cowboy in our back yard several days a week. We might get two or three other boys from the neighborhood to join us. With enough kids, we divided into good guys and bad guys. The bad guys would declare that they had pulled off some crime—a bank or stagecoach robbery, cattle rustling, or whatever—and the chasing and gunfighting began.

The backyard was less than a half acre of land, but it included a garage, a scuppernong[3] arbor, lots of bushes, several big trees, and an old chicken-roosting house in it. We found lots of places to hide. If Jamie Wilson, our next-door neighbor, joined us, then we would have his yard too. On the other side of our house lived the Stonecrofts, an older couple who were nice enough, but who didn't relate to kids at all. We could use their territory only if we remained unseen.

The favorite site for gun battles was the garage and the scuppernong arbor behind it. We could climb up the arbor, jump to the storage

---

[3] A scuppernong is a wild grape that grows throughout the southeast United States. It turns a rich golden color when it ripens and it is not sour like most wild grapes. It tastes so good that many people cultivate the vines. A single vine covered a twenty-foot square arbor behind our garage.

room and workshop that made up the back side of the garage, then step up onto the higher main roof and jump across a drainage ditch head-first through a window in the attic of the Stonecroft's garage. From that attic, we could crawl through a hole formed by two loose boards onto the roof of what had once been a livestock shed and finally jump back down to the ground under the Stonecroft's apple tree. It thrilled us to climb up, over, and down. Better yet, it was completely hidden from the Stonecroft's house and from ours.

Our cowboy fantasies were fed regularly by the Saturday morning program at the Richards Theater, our local movie theater, or as we called it then, picture show. For twenty-five cents we could be entertained by two movies, two cartoons, a news reel, a chapter of a serial adventure, coming attractions, and a live country-music stage show that was broadcast on the local radio station, WWFL. At least one of the movies would be a western, and the other might be a western or a World War II adventure. The program ended at noon. A large popcorn cost ten cents, and a Coke or orange soda cost five cents.

We liked most of the cowboy stars. Roy Rogers and Gene Autry were our favorites of the cowboys who sang in their films. I liked *Broken Arrow* with Jimmy Stewart, but he wasn't really a cowboy: he played all sorts of roles. John Wayne made some good western pictures, but he also made other stuff, and we liked him better in the World War II movies. My overall favorite was Johnny Mack Brown. He was the real McCoy. No dallying around in other movies for him. And in addition to all his bravery, cleverness, and great adventures, he came from Alabama.

Johnny Mack Brown was a hero to me on several levels. Born and reared in Dothan, Alabama, he became a celebrity while playing football for the University of Alabama Crimson Tide. His running skill earned him the title, "The Dothan Antelope." He became nationally famous in 1926 when Alabama beat the Washington Huskies to win the Rose Bowl. Two of the three touchdowns that Alabama scored were made when Johnny Mack caught a long pass from Pooley Hubert and ran it into the end zone.

His fame, good looks, and pretty good acting talent led him into a movie career. He began in silent movies as a leading man to the biggest starlets of the time: Norma Shearer, Greta Garbo, Mary

Pickford, Mae West, and several others. But, because of his natural Southern accent, he was not invited to star in the new "talkies." The grownups lost him; we gained a hero. His smooth Southern drawl played perfectly in cowboy movies. He went on to make over a hundred and sixty movies, most of them as a cowboy. I was unaware of his first career in "grownup" picture shows. I knew only of his career in westerns and liked him for what I thought was his first true love.

Kavanaugh liked Lash LaRue best. He always wore a black hat, black shirt, black pants, black boots, and a black gun belt with shiny rivets along the top and bottom edges and all around the two gun holsters. His special gimmick, however, was that he always carried a bullwhip. At least once in every movie, he would use the bullwhip to pull the gun out of some bad guy's hand.

In his early pictures, Lash played The Cheyenne Kid. In a couple of them, he started out as a bad guy but had a change of heart and ended up the hero. In a later film, he became a lawman, Cheyenne Davis, U.S. Marshall, and eventually became so popular that he used his name, Lash LaRue, for his character. I think the combination of his handsome all-black clothes and accessories, his complex good/bad persona, and his heroic use of the bullwhip made him Kavanaugh's choice.

We had outfits to wear when we played cowboys. They changed from time to time as we acquired a new hat or new revolvers and wore them out. In 1951, my father had been given a choice of rewards for buying some number of cases of Kennel Ration dog food for his grocery store. He chose a complete Roy Rogers suit and guns for a kid. He got only one outfit, so when he brought it home, Kavanaugh and I launched into a vigorous fight for it.

I don't remember now what sort of promises and trades I made, but I got the outfit. It was beautiful. It had two pearl-handled revolvers with a picture of Trigger molded into each side of the handle, leather holsters for the pistols, a vest, a hat, and chaps. The chaps were made of cloth, but leather fringe trimmed the edges and leather rosettes and chrome stars decorated the front of each leg. After I outgrew the chaps, they hung in the garage. Kavanaugh eventually scavenged the trim from them to decorate a shoeshine box he made.

The Roy Rogers pistols were, of course, not real. I loaded them with rolls of red paper caps. Almost every cap gun we ever had would misfire most of the time. I could pull the trigger repeatedly and get click, click, pow, click, click, click. But not the Roy Rogers pistols. They fired almost every time until they were worn out.

Of course, I wanted a Johnny Mack Brown outfit, but I preferred the whole Roy Rogers set of paraphernalia to some makeshift collection that I would have to pretend made me look like Johnny Mack Brown.

Kavanaugh assembled his outfit from pieces. It was, in the end, a wonderful imitation of Lash LaRue. He didn't have a black shirt or pants, but he had a black cowboy hat. He used a pistol he picked up at Elmore's dime store. Some liquid shoe dye made the holster authentically black. A real, leather bullwhip he purchased by mail from an advertisement in a Lash LaRue comic book completed his outfit. He figured out a way to hang it on his gun belt so that a pistol hung on the right side and the bullwhip on the left.

Kavanaugh practiced using the bullwhip in our backyard. He lined up tin cans on the brick retaining wall between our house and the Wilson's and picked them off one at a time. He considered it a failure if he disturbed one he was not aiming at. He attached a cap pistol to a tree limb as it might be in a bad guy's hand and plucked it away with the whip. He was really good.

So you see we wouldn't think of going into the mysterious, dangerous swamp without wearing our cowboy outfits. Grandmother said she and Brazzie would chaperon us, and mother finally agreed on a Tuesday that we could go, but first, Grandmother had some quilting to do and some church duties, so Friday was set as the day of our fishing trip. This gave us time to refurbish a couple of cane poles that hung in the garage with new lines, hooks, and bobbers before we went.

Lizzie and Brazzie could not easily walk all the way to the river, so Mother agreed to drive us as far as an automobile could go on the dirt road that went through Grimsley's farm. We would have to walk the last third of a mile or so. Our family had only one car at the time, and neither Brazzie nor Grandmother could drive, so Mother would have to take Daddy to work and bring the car back home.

My father rose at 5:30 each morning. Mother prepared breakfast for the two of them, and he ate and left to open the grocery store before 6 o'clock. The rest of us ate breakfast regularly at 6:30 each morning. On the day of our trip, Kavanaugh and I were so excited we could hardly sit down and eat. We kept jumping up to do some preparation we'd forgotten. Grandmother didn't mind since it gave

16

her more time to eat leisurely. Finally at about 7:30, everyone was ready. Kavanaugh and I had our cowboy outfits on. Each of my pistols had a fresh roll of caps loaded in it, and four more rolls waited in my pants pocket.

We tied the fishing poles on top of our 1948 Chevrolet and dumped the other stuff in the trunk. We carried a can of worms, a burlap sack to put the catfish in, and a Thermos jug of cold water. The grownups decided we probably wouldn't have the patience to fish for long, so no dinner or snacks were packed, and Mother announced she would return to pick us up at the end of the dirt road at 11:45. That gave her time to dump us back at the house and pick up Daddy for dinner. Brazzie agreed to carry a pocket watch to keep us on time.

We picked up Aunt Brazzie across Temple Avenue at her house, and drove down Pinion Street past Barbara Rogers' with the cow peeking out of the shed as always, across Aylette Street and past the Grimsley's brick mansion. The car was crowded, and Kavanaugh and I irritated the adults with our inability to sit still and a constant narrative about bad guys ambushing us from the roadside ditches, or Indians firing flaming arrows at the gas tank.

Mother was glad to get us out of the car when we got to the end of the road, and Grandmother and Aunt Brazzie were already showing signs of being vexed with us. Mother lectured us sternly about how old and unstable Grandmother and Brazzie were and how we must hold their hands while we walked to the river and back. With a walking stick in one hand and a child in the other, Grandmother and Aunt Brazzie could not carry any of the paraphernalia. Kavanaugh had to carry the water jug and bamboo fishing poles in his free hand, and I carried the burlap bag with the can of worms inside.

We headed off to the river along the path so well trodden by decades of others going to the river to fish. Kavanaugh and I were impatient to get to the fishing spot, but we managed to take our duty to hold the old folks' hands seriously. We made pretty good progress until we came to a small creek, maybe just a drainage ditch. Grandmother told me it was named Adams Creek.

The ditch held water only a foot to two feet in width, just enough to require some method of crossing it. Someone had laid a pair of two-by-twelve rough-sawn oak boards across it to form a footbridge. Kavanaugh and I considered the bridge a luxury; we could easily jump over the water. On the other hand, it made a serious obstacle for Grandmother and Aunt Brazzie. On Grandmother's orders Kavanaugh and I carried the fishing equipment and water across and put them down. We made a big show of not using the board bridge to cross back, but rather ran and jumped over the ditch to show off our bravado. Then we held Grandmother's and Aunt Brazzie's hands as they inched across, and soon we ambled on down the path.

Even at our slow pace, we came to the river in less than a half hour. The underbrush in a large area was kept cleared back by the constant traffic, and about fifty yards of riverbank was mostly free of weeds. A couple of fallen trees made good places to sit.

A side arm of the river, maybe thirty feet wide and fifty yards long ran along the left edge of the clearing. As it passes Frog Level, the Sipsey is a meandering stream in geologic terminology. That means that the course of the river shifts over time due to flooding. In a big flood, the fast moving water carves away the riverbank in some places while it deposits mud in other places where the current is slower. After several floods have combined their effect, a new river channel can be cut open and a part of the old channel that no longer has a water current may be filled with mud at one or both ends. If it is filled at both ends, it forms an isolated oxbow lake. If the old channel is filled in at only one end, it forms an arm of the river where there is little or no current, generally called a slough.

Tall grass lined the slough on the side next to us and extended along the bank from the river almost to the end. It stood about three feet above the water level and came up to my waist as I stood on the bank. It grew so dense that I couldn't see the ground nor the water between the stalks. It was so green and even, it looked like someone had planted it, but I saw that it occurred naturally in many spots up and down the river. The end of the slough was shallow with a couple of fallen trees and some weeds. Steady usage kept a clearing on the far side just like the one we were in, but grass hadn't grown along the bank there.

The scene that morning was astonishingly beautiful, but of course, it was largely wasted on Kavanaugh and me at the time. We saw only places for bad guys to hide, trees to climb, and a river that we knew was just full of huge catfish. I can remember the tall grass, the sun filtering through the trees and filling the constant breeze with the smell of warm vegetation, and the endlessly varying texture of leaves—a hundred sizes, shapes, and shades of green.

Finally free of our duty to hold Grandmother's and Aunt Brazzie's hands, we ran to the river, along the bank, around the edge of the clearing. We climbed onto logs, jumped off them, and yelled and shouted a soundtrack to our imagined adventures.

I found an unexpected treat at the downstream end of the clearing. A very large oak tree sat right on the riverbank with its limbs hanging over halfway across the river. Someone had cut off two of the lowest limbs to expose a very large one and hung a heavy rope about two-thirds of the way to the end. It was instantly clear that you could grab the rope and swing out over the river. At the far end of your swing you could let go and plunge into the river. Wow!

Grandmother saw me looking at it and yelled an immediate warning to halt any ideas I might be forming.

After a while, it occurred to us to get to the fishing. We picked a spot at one end of a large log, a tree that had fallen into the river and lodged itself against the riverbank. People standing or sitting on it had worn the bark off. Kavanaugh and I wanted to sit on it, but Grandmother vetoed our plan instantly saying we would get our feet wet and probably fall in.

Since there was no place for Grandmother and Aunt Brazzie to sit right on the riverbank, Grandmother dictated that she and Brazzie would use a log about thirty feet back. Kavanaugh and I could stay on the riverbank to fish, but we could not cross a line that Grandmother drew in the dirt with the end of her walking cane.

Kavanaugh and I unwound our lines; each of us selected a worm and threaded it on our hook while Grandmother stood behind us and instructed us on how to perform this operation: so simple, so messy, and so horrible from the worm's perspective.

We each required two or three attempts to get our lines away from the bank. Grandmother barely sat down when my bobber disappeared with a blurp. Instinctively I jerked on the pole. Something that felt like it weighed a hundred pounds pulled on my line.

I jumped up and yelled, "What do I do?"

"Pull it in," Grandmother and Kavanaugh yelled in unison.

I pulled the pole up as I stepped back from the river, and a beautiful catfish, about a foot long, flopped up on the riverbank. I thought it looked huge, but my pride was punctured when Grandmother asked, "Do you want to keep that little one?"

"What do you mean? It's not little."

She had come over to where I was trying to figure out how to get hold of the flopping fish. "Just look, after you cut off his head and his tail, there's only about six inches of fish. You'll catch much bigger ones than that."

I insisted we keep it. "I'll throw it away if I catch bigger ones," I offered. Grandmother showed me how to grab and hold it. I tried to pull the hook out but couldn't manage it. After I tried a while, she reached into her apron pocket and pulled out a pair of pliers.

"Use this," she said.

I was surprised to discover she had made preparations we hadn't even thought of. "Thanks, Grandmother."

Indeed, in no more than thirty minutes, Kavanaugh and I caught three catfish that were at least eighteen inches long and tucked them in the burlap bag.

As we experimented with different depths for our hooks and different sitting or standing spots along the riverbank, Aunt Brazzie spoke up. "Look out there boys," she said. We looked up to see her pointing across the river with her walking cane.

"That's a halfigator," she said. "I suspect that it's smelled our fish, and it'll be over here before long."

We followed the aim of her cane, and, after a few moments, Kavanaugh and I both saw the eyes bulging out of the water and a small wake of ripples as it glided along.

"What'll we do if it comes after the fish," I asked.

"We'll whack it on the head," Brazzie answered. "All you need to deal with those critters is a good stick. I've got my walking cane. It'll do fine. You might want to look around and find a good strong stick for yourself."

"What would we do if we were swimming and one came after us?" I asked as I carefully tracked the halfigator.

"You shouldn't be in the river in the first place," she answered, ignoring my real question.

"But what if. What if I was out fishing in somebody's boat and it tipped over."

"If a halfigator bothers you in the water, just scream and thrash around. If you make lots of noise and splash enough water, he'll go away."

"Do you remember when old Josh Hollingshead jumped off the Hubbertville bridge right on top of one?" asked Brazzie, as spasms of laughter began to swell in her stomach and work their way up her body.

Grandmother turned and stared hard at her. The laugh evaporated.

"What happened?" Kavanaugh and I asked in unison.

Neither Brazzie nor Grandmother answered.

"What happened?" Kavanaugh insisted again.

"Brazzie just can't keep her mouth shut," Grandmother finally said. "You boys don't need to get any bad ideas. Josh Hollingshead, I reckon about sixteen years old, jumped off the Hubbertville bridge on top of a halfigator. Said he was going to ride him down to Mobile."

Aunt Brazzie's laugh started to percolate again, but it shut down after another glance from Grandmother... almost.

"It was funny," Brazzie offered in her defense.

"It wasn't funny when the halfigator bit off his thumb," Grandmother shot back.

Aunt Brazzie apparently thought it was, and small ripples still shook her every few seconds even though she looked down and bit her bottom lip. Without looking up, she said, "If you hadn't.... Owwh. Ouch." Her sentence was cut short this time by a hard rap on her shin from Grandmother's walking stick. The look that came with it prevented Brazzie from trying again.

Grandmother went on. "They're like I hear black bears are up in the Smoky Mountains. The bears are usually shy and harmless, but as people drive up that new parkway they're building on top of the mountains, the bears learn that there's food to be had, and some people get hurt. You leave the halfigators alone, don't have any food nearby, and they'll leave you alone."

The looks exchanged between Brazzie and Grandmother told us the halfigator discussion was over. With one eye on the halfigator, we continued fishing. In another half hour, we had a total of six catfish. One was two feet long. I now realized what Grandmother meant by saying the first one was "small."

I put my pole aside for a minute and went for a drink of water. As I opened the burlap bag to admire our catch, Kavanaugh called out, "Hey, there's a boat coming." We all looked up to see a flat-bottom, wooden boat with three young adults, a man and two women, coming down the river. I waved to them, and they waved back in an open, friendly way.

Instead of going by us, they turned into the slough to our left. The man paddled the boat until it began to drag bottom. Then he stood up, jumped to shore and pulled the boat up near the end of the slough on the far side.

Kavanaugh and I had both stopped fishing by now, fascinated by the appearance of these people who looked as if they had dressed for church services, the only regular occasion for dressing up in Frog Level.

Kavanaugh and I asked if we could go and see what they were doing. Grandmother and Brazzie speculated on what might be happening, and while they discussed it, several more people came down the path to the clearing on the far side of the slough.

"They're going to have a river baptism," Grandmother said. "I'll bet you boys have never seen one of those before."

"No, ma'am," we both said. "Can we go over there to watch?"

"You can go over there and say hello and ask what church they're from. Then come right back. I don't want you boys bothering them while they're holding a service. You understand? I'll come get you if you aren't back when the service starts."

"Yes, ma'am." We took off, running at top speed along our side of the slough and around the end to the other clearing.

We slowed down as we approached the gathering group. The crowd circled a man in a light brown suit who seemed to be in charge. He was too busy talking to the others for us to approach him. We just hung around for a minute or so, and then one of the young women who had arrived in the boat came up to us.

"Hi, cowboys. Lookin' for cattle rustlers?"

"Hi," I answered. "Ain't seen no rustlers this morning, ma'am."

Kavanaugh spoke up. "We're fishing, ma'am. My grandmother and Aunt Brazzie brought us down here today, and we've already caught six big catfish."

"That's a lot of fish for the middle of the morning. I like your cowboy outfits." She looked at me. "I can see you're Roy Rogers."

"Yes, ma'am." It wasn't hard to see I had on a Roy Rogers outfit since it had a picture of Trigger on the front of the hat and the name, "Roy Rogers," on one side of the vest.

"But who are you," she asked Kavanaugh.

"I'm Lash LaRue. Well, I'm obviously not Lash LaRue, but I like him. He's tough and smart. He uses a bullwhip to get the crooks without having to shoot them." He patted the bullwhip hanging on his belt.

I thought the young woman was very nice. She actually seemed to be interested in us even though we were so much younger than her. She had a pretty smile and wore a flowered dress that spread out from her waist like a large upside-down poppy. When she knelt down to look at the chrome stars on my chaps, I could smell her hair. It smelled really nice, like soap and flowers.

"You boys must be good fishermen," she said. "Can I come to supper with you tonight?"

We didn't know whether her question was serious or not. After neither of us replied for a few seconds, she said, "I'm just kidding. I'll bet your mother is a good cook though."

I could easily reply to that comment. "Yes, ma'am. She's a really good cook!"

I took the opportunity to ask our question. "Are you folks having a baptism?"

"Yes. Well, at least they are." She waved her arm at the rest of the crowd. "You see that girl in the yellow dress standing by Brother Kitchens, the man in the brown suit?

"She's Brother Kitchens' daughter, Barbara. The boy next to her in the white shirt and red tie is my brother, Dwight. They just got married last week. Dwight and me—Oh, I'm Jessie. What's your names?"

"I'm Kavanaugh and this is my brother, Wendell."

"Hi, Kavanaugh and Wendell! Kavanaugh is an unusual but very nice name. As I was saying, Dwight and me were raised in the Church of God. Brother Kitchens and his family are in the Church of Christ. Dwight promised he'd convert to the Church of Christ if she would marry him. He got rebaptised two weeks ago, just before the wedding."

"We go to the Church of Christ," Kavanaugh said. "My family goes to lots of gospel meetings in the summer, and Wendell and I have to go too, but I've never seen Brother Kitchens before."

Jessie seemed to think this was odd just as we did. There were lots of little Church of Christ congregations in Fayette County, and we thought we'd seen them all one time or another.

"Dwight wants to be a minister. He's already been preaching in the Church of God, but he's having a hard time learning how things are done in the Church of Christ. He's trying hard, but Brother Kitchens has had to correct him a lot this week during the gospel meeting. We're a lot more praisy and shouty in the Pentecostal churches."

For those of you who are not familiar with the Church of Christ or the Church of God, I'll explain briefly a few particulars about them so that you can understand what was about to happen.

The Church of Christ is a fundamentalist church. They believe in the literal truth of the Bible. They like to quote verses directly from the Bible to back up any religious stand they take. Of course, the many other fundamentalist denominations that take this view end up with different interpretations, so instead of a common belief in the literal truth of the Bible leading them all to the same set of customs, it gives rise to endless disagreements on the particulars of worship and policy. For example, most fundamentalist churches use a piano or organ, or even a guitar to aid their singing. Not the Church of Christ. It holds that since we have no biblical command to use a musical instrument and no example of people playing musical instruments in church worship in the New Testament, one cannot use any instrument in church. They have no pianos and no organs.

On the other hand, they consider other biblical statements to be irrelevant to the modern era. The gospel of Mark reports Jesus saying, "And these signs shall follow them that believe; in my name shall they cast out devils; they shall speak with new tongues. They shall take up serpents; and if they drink any deadly thing, it shall not hurt them; they shall lay hands on the sick, and they shall recover." The Church of Christ denies the present-day validity of this declaration. It is a rather straitlaced denomination.

The Church of God is also fundamentalist, but they find in the scriptures a full permission to use musical instruments in worshiping God, and they very strongly believe in current-day miracles including healing the sick. They believe that when spiritual ecstasy sweeps over them, they have the ability to speak in languages unknown to any humans: a practice called speaking in tongues. In general, people in the Church of God express their religious emotions spontaneously and freely. As Jessie had told us, they are "more praisy and shouty." Since the Bible describes several of their beliefs and practices as happening on the first Day of Pentecost after the death of Jesus, they are sometimes called Pentecostal churches. Their tendency to carry ecstatic praises to the extreme, including falling and rolling on the ground, has earned them the popular, but somewhat derogatory name, holyrollers.

The baptism service seemed about ready to begin, so Jessie said goodbye, wished us good fishing, and headed back to the group. Kavanaugh thought it would be okay to hang around until they actually started singing or some other definitely religious activity.

The crowd gathered along the slough. Brother Kitchens took off his suit coat, broke off a head-high limb of a small tree and hung the coat on the stub. Then he slowly began to wade into the water. As he went, he directed two middle-aged men to wade in, one on either side of him. Each of them carried a pole; I guessed it was to steady him. We noticed that they were the only two middle-aged men in the group. The remainder of the congregation was women, young children, and a few old men. We knew from attending the gospel meetings at our church that most men did not attend daytime services during gospel meetings because they would be at work. They attended the evening services with the women and children.

"Why do you think those two guys are out there in the water?" I asked Kavanaugh.

"They're the lookouts to keep halfigators away," he answered. "See, they've each got a stick to hit them if they get too close; just like Grandmother said."

Jessie's brother, Dwight, had stepped just a couple of feet into the water and faced the crowd. He began to lead the congregation in *Oh Happy Day*.

> Oh happy day,
> That fixed my choice
> On thee my Savior
> And my God.
> Happy day, happy day,
> When Jesus washed
> My sins away.

Kavanaugh and I decided it was time for us to leave, so we started back around the slough. We could hear the congregation beginning the second verse. They had no songbooks, but Dwight sang loudly enough so it didn't matter if some of them missed a word here and there. The congregation sang that song at every baptism we had ever witnessed.

Our church didn't go down to the river for baptisms. The Church of Christ believes that baptism means immersing the person completely under water, so it takes quite a bit of water to do it. Our church building had a baptistry right behind the pulpit. It was just wide enough for the preacher and the person being baptized to stand in the middle and long enough for the preacher to lean the repentant sinner back and under the water.

So we felt right at home as they sang *Oh Happy Day* but were very surprised when, as soon as the second verse ended, Dwight launched into loud shouts. It was our first clue that Dwight hadn't left his Church of God customs completely behind him.

"Praise the Lord! Thank you Lord for these sinners, they have heard the word, believed the word, repented from their evil ways, and they're gonna confess your Holy Name, and have their sins washed away. Praise God!"

Kavanaugh and I stopped in our tracks and looked back across the slough. Dwight's head was raised heavenward as he finished his oration. The crowd looked ill at ease. When no one else added to his hallelujahs, he turned to Brother Kitchens with a sheepish look on his face.

Brother Kitchens shook his head just barely noticeably. "Let everything be done decently and in order, Dwight. First Corinthians, 14:40" He paused for a moment, then added, "How many times I got to tell you, Dwight?"

"I'm just so happy, Brother Kitchens. Sorry."

Dwight took the first baptizee, a young girl, maybe thirteen, by the hand and helped her toward Brother Kitchens.

Back with Grandmother and Aunt Brazzie, we reported.

"It is a baptism. I guess you heard the singing and knew that."

"Who's the preacher?" asked Grandmother.

"Brother Kitchens," I said. "A lady told us he's a Church of Christ preacher. Do you know him?"

"Oh, I know him," she said with a look at Brazzie. "He's the preacher for that anti church up the Winfield highway."

"What's an antichurch," I interrupted.

Instead of answering, Grandmother asked us, "Who was doing all that praising the Lord stuff?"

"That was Dwight," Kavanaugh said. "He grew up in the Church of God and just married Brother Kitchens daughter."

"Well, that explains it." Aunt Brazzie shook her head. "A holyroller in an anti church. Lord be."

"We want to see the baptisms," I said. "I think they've got three or four baptizees. Can we go back and watch?"

"I told you not to say, 'baptizee.' It's irreverent," she answered.

"Yes, ma'am. They've got three or four people to baptize. Can we go back?"

Grandmother nodded. "Don't go back around the slough; just stand by the tall grass there on the bank. You'll see from there as good as anywhere."

"Do you want to go too," I asked, but both Brazzie and Grandmother declined.

"You can't see the people down in the river," I protested.

"I see just the tops of their heads over the grass and most of the congregation," she said. "That's enough. Now go, you're missing it."

Kavanaugh and I ran to the tall grass, maybe ten yards. The first baptism had just finished and the girl was wading back to shore, trying to push her wet hair out of her face.

Our newly made friend, Jessie, had taken a seat in the flat-bottom boat away from the congregation. We guessed that even though her brother converted to the Church of Christ, she didn't feel quite at ease in the crowd.

As the second baptizee, a boy Kavanaugh knew, was raised from the water, it seemed that Dwight's habits took over again, but he caught himself after a, "Praise the Lord!" Brother Kitchens clearly took note, but as he was about to admonish Dwight again, one of the really old men in the congregation let out a hearty "Amen!", so Brother Kitchens let it drop.

The third baptizee was a young woman named Faye, as we learned when Brother Kitchens called her to come to him. She seemed to be a friend of Barbara and Jessie because, as she stepped into the water, Jessie and Barbara both let out squeals of delight. Kavanaugh and I looked at each other; and I did a pretty good imitation of the squeal, "Eeeeeeeeh," but not loud enough, I thought, to be heard across the slough. Kavanaugh returned my squeal with a more prolonged one and we broke into giggling. Brother Kitchens did hear and turned around to stare at us with a stern frown on his face. We hushed until he turned away and then covered our giggles with our hands. He glanced back again but said nothing.

Jessie stood up in the flat-bottomed boat, perhaps to see the proceedings better. The shift of her weight raised the front of the boat off the slough bottom, and it lazily drifted away from the bank. She seemed not to notice or not to care since she was engrossed in the baptism.

Brother Kitchens wrung out a white handkerchief he used to cover the nose and mouth of each baptizee as he immersed them. He folded it, placed it in Faye's hands, and whispered instructions to her. Then he placed his left hand behind her neck and raised his right hand.

Aside from being in the river, the ceremony was familiar to us. We knew each step exactly. Brother Kitchens would ask if she believed that Jesus was the son of God. She would say yes. Brother Kitchens would say a standard speech, and then raise her hands and the handkerchief to cover her mouth and nose, tilt her backward under the water, then raise her back upright. Dwight would lead the congregation in another verse of *Oh Happy Day*. It has lots of verses.

Kavanaugh punched me in the ribs and pointed as unobviously as possible at Jessie. "See how she's floating toward Brother Kitchens?"

"Yeah. You think the boat's going to hit them?"

"No, but remember that Grandmother said she couldn't see anything but the heads of the people in the river?"

"Yeah. So what?"

I could tell from the expression on Kavanaugh's face that he was up to something. But, before he could make his move, Jessie began to shout just as her brother had done.

"Hallelujah! Praise God! Hallelujah! Praaaaise God!"

The shouts attracted Grandmother's and Brazzie's attention, and they looked intently at Jessie.

"Watch this," Kavanaugh whispered to me. He turned to Grandmother and Aunt Brazzie and, in a tone and volume of voice matched to Jessie's, he shouted, "She's walking on water!"

I let out an involuntary snort, and then, not wanting to give away the joke, I held my breath as long as I could to keep from laughing. Since the tall grass hid the boat, it had to seem to Grandmother and Aunt Brazzie exactly like she was walking on water.

Grandmother's eyes got big, but otherwise, she seemed calm. Aunt Brazzie's face showed real surprise and amazement. "Oh Lord, Wizzie. Look!"

When I had to breathe, I pointed my left arm at Jessie and waved my right arm as if trying to attract Grandmother's attention. "Look, Grandmother! Look! She's walking on water!" I hoped that my jumping up and down and waving disguised my laughing; that it all would be interpreted as excitement over seeing the miracle. Brother Kitchens turned his head a couple of times and glared at us to indicate his annoyance, but not knowing how the tall grass hid the boat and trying to concentrate on his baptism, he ignored any meaning in our shouts. He was simply mad at us for disturbing his ceremony.

Brother Kitchens had been irritated by Dwight's outbursts, then by Jessie's hallelujahs, and our giggles and shouts made it worse. We could see that he was almost at his limit of composure. Nevertheless, he tried to carry on with the baptism. Holding Faye's neck and hands and trying to prevent her from turning around to see what Jessie was doing, he began the speech. "By the authority invested in me as a minister of the Holy Gospel, and upon your confession of belief in Jesus Christ, I now baptize you in the name of the Father, the Son, and the Holy Ghost, for the remission of all your sins, that you may rise........."

Brother Kitchens didn't get to finish. Jessie had floated until she was directly behind Brother Kitchens and Faye. She began to speak in tongues. It was half talking and half singing with her head turned up to heaven. "Ooohh, Yasuuuuusea. Behina yow alawaw. Josinaia glef yessee. Mummmm yo mizzzziwaw. Glosia! Glosia!"

Well, that's the best I can do to reconstruct Jessie's outpouring. Her whole body moved along with the sounds in a harmonious, completely natural way. She was turned just enough so I could see the beautiful smile on her face.

Brother Kitchens gave up on the baptism and turned around to face Jessie. He was so perturbed by her that he didn't think to warn Faye, and she had already begun to lean on his hand at the back of her neck. When he abruptly removed his hand, Faye fell backward into the water with a surprised shriek. Jessie's interruption had distracted Brother Kitchens so badly that he didn't even notice Faye's splash and took her cry as part of the general commotion.

"This is the most outrageous thing I have ever seen or heard of," Brother Kitchens shouted at Jessie. "You people think you can come into this sacred worship service and just.... just......" he searched in vain for the right phrase to describe their Pentecostal habits. "That you can come in here and just do all your holy-roller stuff, perform miracles, speak in tongues. You think you can walk on water, don't you?" He called to the halfigator lookout nearest the rear of the boat, "Reuben, move her back!" and motioned with his head that the lookout should move Jessie away from the ceremony.

Kavanaugh and I stared wide-eyed at each other. Brother Kitchens had just verified Kavanaugh's claim that Jessie was walking on water. Of course, Brother Kitchens didn't know what Grandmother and Aunt Brazzie were seeing. He saw that Jessie was standing in the boat. "Just walk on water" was simple hyperbole for him, or maybe

Kavanaugh's shout had put the phrase in his mind. He used it the way people often do to remark on someone's overbearing actions. Anyway, at that moment, it was the best fairly common phrase he could think of to emphasize his frustration and anger at their unconstrained outpourings.

Nevertheless, to Grandmother and Brazzie his exclamation seemed actually to back up Kavanaugh's claim of a miracle. Grandmother had to take it seriously now and decided to investigate. She planted her walking stick in the dirt and started to get up. It took a little while and a push from Brazzie because the log was so low. Aunt Brazzie had just been staring in amazement at Jessie as she glided and testified. Now, she also decided it was time to get a better look.

"Oh, Wizzie. Is it really a miracle?"

"Of course not, Brazzie! The only question to settle is whether it's some of Brother Kitchens' mischief, those holyrollers, or those rascal boys behind it."

Jessie still sang softly and swayed in her ecstatic state and didn't hear anything Brother Kitchens said.

Unlike Brother Kitchens, it horrified Dwight to see Faye splash backward into the water. He leapt forward toward her like a racer clearing hurdles to help her regain her footing. As his feet splashed into the water with each stride, fountains of it sprayed out in all directions.

Out of the corner of his eye, Brother Kitchens saw Dwight bounding toward him with his arms extended to help his balance and to grab Faye. He simply failed to digest the multiple indignities that he and his ceremony were suffering. He began to rely on basic instincts and thought Dwight was going to attack him because of his outburst directed at Jessie.

Brother Kitchens, now completely beside himself, perhaps temporarily insane, lunged at Dwight to engage him. Dwight's new wife, Barbara, broke from the congregation and splashed into the water to try to separate her father and her husband, both of whom had disappeared under violently splashing water. Poor Faye was left to fend for herself.

Now Jessie recovered from her ecstatic outburst and wanted to do something to calm everyone down. More concerned about their well being than her own, she instinctively stepped toward Dwight and Brother Kitchens and caused the boat to tilt. At the same time, the halfigator lookout, Reuben, managed to grab the rope trailing from the boat, and he pulled on it to move it away as Brother Kitchens requested. While the tilt of the boat and the jerk on the rope might have been manageable for Jessie, the additional rocking generated by Brother Kitchens and Dwight wrestling overcame her ability to balance. She pitched over the side of the boat and landed almost on top of Brother Kitchens.

Maybe because of all the commotion in the water, or maybe by sheer coincidence, or because God has a sense of humor, just then the lookout posted nearest the main channel of the river spotted a halfigator that emerged from the tall grass where we were standing and swam out into the slough. The other lookout, Reuben, stood a little closer, but he was still holding the rope attached to the boat and seemed horrified at causing Jessie to fall in. He didn't see the halfigator, so the other lookout had to cover quite a distance to get to the halfigator. He didn't wait until he got in range, but rather, began to swing his stick over his head with each stride and bring it down as hard as he could on the river. A sheet of water sprayed from each side of the stick when it hit and part of it rained down on Faye, Dwight, Jessie and Brother Kitchens as they struggled to keep their mouths above the water. They didn't even notice it. Barbara had gotten wet only up to her waist as she waded toward Jessie and the wrestlers, but the deluge from the halfigator stick drenched her completely. Finally close enough, the lookout lifted the stick again and crashed it down on the hapless reptile's head.

Given the lesson Aunt Brazzie and Grandmother had given us, I figured the halfigator was trying to get away from all the commotion, but the lookout seemed to think otherwise. It was, of course, the first time I'd ever seen how to control a halfigator, and I tried to watch as carefully as I could while following the other action.

I punched Kavanaugh in the ribs and pointed to the retreating halfigator. "Wow, did you see that?"

"Yeah," he replied. "It didn't seem to injure him, but he sure is hightailing it!"

When Grandmother and Aunt Brazzie got up to where we were standing and could see the whole scene, they saw altogether seven people in the slough: Brother Kitchens, Dwight, the two lookouts, Faye, Jessie, and Barbara. The boat rested against the bank on our right. Dwight was fending off Brother Kitchens' attempt to hit him. Jessie had grabbed Brother Kitchens from behind to keep him off Dwight, so she was, more or less, riding him piggyback. One of the halfigator lookouts held the sputtering, weeping Faye, and the other one had intercepted Barbara and urged her back to the shore while keeping an eye on the halfigator.

Brother Kitchens turned away from Dwight to try to face Jessie, but she stayed on his back and turned as he did. When they spun far enough to place Jessie near Dwight, he grabbed her and lifted her off the preacher's back. The loving concern she had felt for Brother Kitchens had been lost in the churning water. She showed no signs of calming down and kicked at the preacher. Dwight turned and dropped Jessie behind him. As she sank in the water and it filled her mouth, she stopped kicking and waving her arms and concentrated on getting on her feet. Brother Kitchens regained his composure a bit, and all of the people in the water began wading toward the bank.

"I guess they don't baptize the same way we do," Kavanaugh said as he looked up at Grandmother and Brazzie with wide innocent eyes. He couldn't keep a straight face and we both started laughing with no chance of stopping.

Grandmother whacked Kavanaugh's leg using the side of her walking cane. "Church of God and Church of Christ just don't mix," Grandmother said, mostly to Brazzie. She turned to Kavanaugh and me. "God wants you to use your head. That's why he gave you some sense. Emotions are okay sometimes, but they lead people down strange roads most of the time. I still don't know what got these people into this mess, but I'm sure it wasn't because they used their heads. 'Study to show yourself approved unto God, a workman that needs not to be ashamed, rightly dividing the word of truth,' Second Timothy, 2:15. Remember that boys."

"Yes, ma'am," we said in unison.

She surveyed the scene a bit more, then asked Kavanaugh, "She was standing up in that boat wasn't she?"

"Yes, ma'am. I thought it was a good joke."

Grandmother looked at him intently. "You love pulling jokes on people, don't you. Just like your uncles, Herman and James. Mind your fooling around, boy. It'll get you in trouble some day."

The entire congregation had reached land now. Dwight said something to Brother Kitchens and put out his hand to shake, but brother Kitchens wasn't ready to make up yet, so he just nodded his head to acknowledge Dwight's offer. Barbara sobbed while Jessie tried to soothe her with a succession of dry handkerchiefs offered by the women of the congregation.

Grandmother and Aunt Brazzie went back to sit on their log. After a few more minutes, the congregation began to leave. We noticed Jessie looking at the boat wedged in the tall grass on our side of the slough.

"Want us to row it over to you?" I called out.

"That would be so nice! Would you?"

"Yes! We'll come straight over!" I pushed Kavanaugh toward the boat. "You pull it up on the bank. I'll ask Grandmother if we can take it to Jessie."

The answer was no. I pleaded a few times, then gave up.

"My grandmother won't let us bring the boat," I yelled back across the slough.

"Okay, that's alright," Jessie called back. "Dwight will come get it."

Kavanaugh held the boat until Dwight arrived. We continued to watch as he took it across the slough, and the girls climbed in as gracefully as their wet clothes allowed. As they moved way from shore and Dwight began to row toward the main channel, Jessie looked up at Kavanaugh and me on the bank and her face brightened. She waved and grinned.

"I guess you boys got quite a show," she called to us and seemed to laugh as she said it, but it made Barbara burst into tears again, and Jessie's face fell as soon as she noticed. It wasn't hard to figure out that Barbara was upset because her husband and her father had been fighting in the river. It made me a little happier to think Barbara would have Jessie to cheer her up. I'd taken a real liking to Jessie in the more or less one hour since we met, and I thought Barbara was lucky to have such a kind friend.

Kavanaugh and I didn't know what to say as Jessie hugged Barbara and Dwight rowed into the main channel, so we just waved back. Then, silently, we walked back to where Grandmother and Brazzie sat.

Grandmother looked at us without moving for a while. She shifted her eyes back and forth from one of us to the other, Her lips pursed a little and then, I think I saw just a slight side-to-side shaking of her head. "What time is it, Brazzie?"

While Aunt Brazzie dug the watch out of her apron pocket, Grandmother gave her appraisal of the morning's events. "I guess all that commotion wasn't your fault, but you certainly didn't help matters any."

"It's about ten after eleven," Brazzie said.

"You've been pretty good about staying out of the river," Grandmother said with a more positive nod of her head. She paused again; then, "Brazzie and I are too old to be doing this. If you want to keep on coming down here, you're going to have to do it on your own. I'll talk to your mother and daddy."

Aunt Brazzie agreed vigorously, "Amen, Wizzie. I can't do this again ever. Now, we better get going."

"Get your poles, boys. Dump the leftover worms in the river," Grandmother ordered.

We walked back along the path we'd used earlier. I had lots of questions to ask: some of them about fishing technique, but most of them about the strange baptism service and the partially familiar, partially strange people and customs.

"Grandmother, what's an antichurch?"

"It's not antichurch, one word, it's anti, space, church: two words. It's called that because the people are against one thing or another.

They're anti-Sunday-school or anti-orphan-homes, or something else."

"Why would somebody be against Sunday school or orphans' homes?"

"I'm against Sunday school," Kavanaugh said emphatically and sincerely. "It's boring. And then we have to sit through an hour long sermon."

"That's not why they're against it. And you wouldn't think it's boring if you paid attention." Grandmother swung her cane at Kavanaugh again, but missed. She went on. "The Bible doesn't mention Sunday school. It doesn't mention orphans' homes, but says good Christians should take in orphans and care for them."

"You mean that we're supposed to let an orphan live in our house?" I asked. "Boy, we don't have enough room now. He'll have to sleep in your room!"

"That's why we build orphans' homes like the one in Cullman. Very few members of the church have room where they live, so we all give money and other things they need to the orphans' home, and they take care of the orphans."

Brazzie had a bit to offer: a lesson for Kavanaugh and me. "We please God by doing anything the Bible teaches directly, anything that has an example in the Bible, or anything we necessarily infer from what the Bible teaches. We infer it's okay to have an orphans' home to take care of them. The anti-orphan-home people like Brother Kitchens just don't understand that you can infer that."

"What does infer mean," I asked.

"It means if the Bible tells you you're supposed to do one thing, then you can use your head, your common sense, to know you're supposed to do something else as well. If your mother tells you that if you lie down in the middle of Temple Avenue, then you'll get run over by a car, you can infer that if you lie down in the middle of Aylette Street you'll also get run over."

"But what if there weren't any cars on Aylette Street when you laid down? Maybe it was 2 o'clock in the morning." I never understood why lying down in the middle of the road was always the adults' example of behavior, all sorts of behavior, but it just was.

Grandmother took over the discussion. "Don't be a smart aleck with Aunt Brazzie, Wendell. You know what she means."

I wasn't sure I knew what she meant. I pondered it for a minute or so as we walked. "Then why can't we infer that if the Bible tells us to sing at church, then we can sing with a piano? That makes sense to me."

"No, when you bring in a piano, you've added something to what God said to do."

"Well, if we build an orphans' home to take care of the orphans, we added the orphans' home."

"It's too hot to argue with you, Wendell." Grandmother seemed to be getting really tired now. We walked the rest of the way in silence.

As soon as we sat down to dinner, Kavanaugh and I began to recount our exciting trip. Grandmother interrupted only when she thought we were exaggerating or otherwise too far off the truth. Daddy seemed to be very proud of us. He seemed just as proud as when he returned from a hunting trip.

We described the baptism service, but our narration was interrupted every few sentences by laughter. Mother and Daddy defended us when we told about pulling the trick on Grandmother and Aunt Brazzie. By the end of the story, even Grandmother began to see the humor in it.

Grandmother told how we behaved and said we observed the cautions she gave us. She ended by suggesting that it would be okay for us to go fishing without adults if we made solemn promises to be careful.

Mother objected vigorously. The discussion was warming up to a full-blown argument when Grandmother looked straight at her and asked, "How old were you when Herman began taking you down under the Northport bridge to fish?"

Daddy looked at her for the answer. Finally she just shrugged and said, "Okay."

The next day, Grandmother called Kavanaugh and me out to the back yard where she sat under one of the pecan trees, shelling black-eyed peas. We talked about our trip to the swamp with her, and she asked us when we would go back. We hadn't decided yet.

Then she added seriously, "You've got several years of growing up to do before you might go off somewhere else. I guess you'll be going down to the swamp pretty often. Remember to carry a stick to drive away halfigators."

She paused and appeared to be pondering her next advice, took a deep breath, and then shook her head as she let it out. "Lord, what I have started with you two. Listen to me carefully. Two things you especially need to remember. Don't forget this. One: things you see in the swamp are often not what they seem to be. Two: as soon as somebody gets in the river, things start to go wrong. Sometimes, bad wrong. Do your swimming somewhere else, Luxapalilla or the city pool. Stay out of the river. You hear me?"

"Yes ma'am."

## Flying solo

On Tuesday just over a week later, we asked to go fishing again. At first, Mother tried to renege on her agreement that we could go alone, but when she realized we would appeal to Grandmother and remembered that Daddy was in favor of us going, she gave up.

We went into a patch of woods over the hill behind our house and cut two saplings to make walking sticks as Grandmother told us to do. We stripped the bark off and carefully whittled down the knots where limbs had grown. We took them to Grandmother and showed her that we followed her instructions and violently demonstrated how we would club halfigators with them.

We put on our cowboy outfits and got the fishing gear. Mother wouldn't take us to the end of the dirt road as she had done on the first trip and reminded us that she did it the first time only because of Grandmother and Aunt Brazzie. We would have to ride our bicycles.

After we loaded the bikes with the fishing gear and walking sticks and started down the driveway, Kavanaugh discovered that with the poles strapped alongside his bike he couldn't turn the handlebars. I got my chaps tangled in the bicycle chain. While we eventually learned how to arrange things so that we could ride our bikes, for then, we unloaded the equipment and just walked.

Our walk to the river took about an hour with the equipment we carried and with several detours to see this or that. We were wild with happiness to be in the beautiful clearing at the river. We looked at the swing for a long time, then untied it from the limb that held it on the riverbank and worked up our courage to try it. Finally, we decided the risk was just too big. If we fell in the river on our first solo trip, we almost certainly wouldn't be allowed to come back. We ran, jumped, climbed, shot our cap pistols, hid from each other, and probably played for at least an hour before we decided to try fishing.

I settled down on the bank by the log where we sat the last time. As I threaded the worm on the hook, I felt an extraordinary surge of satisfaction. Like most children, more than anything, I wanted to be grown up, and doing what I thought of as an adult activity, fishing without my parents around, made me feel at least a little grown up.

I looked up at Kavanaugh. "Do you feel grown-up?"

He seemed to know what I meant. "Yeah, I guess so," and after a long while, "But, it's so long until we're really not kids anymore. Sometimes, I think I just can't wait. I'm twelve and going into the seventh grade, but I can't do what I want to do for another six years or more."

"What do you want to do?"

"I don't know. Maybe play in a big band like Harry James."

"I'd like to be an engineer." That wouldn't be news to Kavanaugh.

"Yeah, you already tear apart your electric train and make stuff with your chemistry set. You already do little science things. It seems to make you happier with being a kid than I am."

"I guess so, but don't you think going to the swamp alone is being a little grown up?"

"Yeah, but it won't strike you as so great when you're twelve. Quit talking and fish."

In almost no time, we had three nice catfish.

Over the years and many trips to the swamp, we found it quite rare to encounter people there during the week. On weekends, if the weather was at all decent, we would find people fishing at all the popular spots. But on this second trip, like the first, we were soon joined by adult company.

Two men arrived in the clearing just after the third catfish went into the burlap bag. They each nodded to us, and one of the men said, "Good morning, boys. How's the fishing this morning?"

"Pretty good," Kavanaugh answered.

"What are you using for bait?" the other man asked.

"Just worms," I said. "We've got three big catfish, so far."

"Well, let's see if we can do as well as you," the first man said with a small laugh.

The men picked the spot where the slough joined the main channel and began to set up. They had very fancy fishing rods with reels, two boxes full of lures and other professional-looking equipment. Our cane poles seemed pathetic in comparison.

One of the men wore a "fishing hat." It was the kind you see in magazine advertisements for cigarettes or beer with a floppy, full brim that immediately suggests fishing and nothing else. The other man had on a cowboy hat made of felt. It had a band around it that looked like an Indian design. They both wore blue jeans and plaid shirts. Just like Jessie, Barbara, and Dwight had appeared out-of-place in their church-going clothes, something about these men seemed too fashionable for the Sipsey Swamp.

We went back to minding our business, but we didn't catch anything except a small perch that we threw back. The presence of the men and the considerable commotion of their throwing first one and then another man-made lure into the water seemed to have spooked the fish.

I noticed Kavanaugh looking at one of the men intently. After a while, I leaned over and whispered, "What are you looking at?"

"See the man in the cowboy hat? Do you think he looks like Johnny Mack Brown?"

I began to study him for a while. "Yeah, he does look a little like Johnny Mack. What do you think?"

"That's Johnny Mack Brown!" Kavanaugh said with conviction.

"What's he doing here?" I asked skeptically. "What's he doing in Frog Level, in the Sipsey swamp? I think he's got other things to do."

"His wife is from Tuscaloosa. He played football for Alabama. Maybe he's just visiting some family and college friends."

I looked at him intently for a while, comparing him to the image I'd seen on the screen two Saturday mornings ago. Finally, I decided not only did his face look familiar, his movements were familiar. "Yep, that's him," I said excitedly.

Kavanaugh jumped up and dusted off his pants. "Let's go say hello."

I remained seated. "You can't just go up to a famous person like that. He'll just tell you to go away." The men seemed friendly enough when they arrived, but we'd been taught to not bother grownups when they were busy. Many adults would say hi to a kid, but they didn't want the kid to bother them after that.

"I don't care," Kavanaugh countered. "At least, I want to know for sure if it's him."

I put down my pole and got up too, and we slowly approached the men, being careful not to disturb their fishing.

They didn't seem to notice us until we were about ten feet behind them. The man in the fishing hat turned to us and said, "What's going on, boys? Tired of watching your lines?"

"Nosir,"[4] Kavanaugh answered. He didn't seem to know what to say next.

---

[4] Yessir and nosir are used here as single words because that's how we used them. There was no gap between yes and sir when they were pronounced. Sir and Ma'am were required of Frog Level kids when addressing anyone more than about five years older than the speaker. On the other hand, for some reason unknown to me, yes and ma'am were separate words.

Since we didn't know their names, we needed some way to address them. "That's a nice cowboy hat you've got," I said.

It worked. The cowboy hat turned to me and smiled. "Thanks," he said. "That's some pretty nice duds you boys have on. You're Roy Rogers and Lash LaRue. Fancy meeting you here in the swamp." They both broke into friendly laughter.

Kavanaugh seemed to relax. "You recognized the whip, I guess?"

"Yep, that and the black holster and hat."

Kavanaugh decided it was time for the big question, "Are you Johnny Mack Brown?"

I cringed and took a step backwards expecting some sort of humiliating answer. "Boy, are you a hick!" "Johnny Mack Brown? Don't bother me kid. Bob, how about that? He thinks I'm Johnny Mack Brown."

The actual answer came with a simple smile, "Why yes. You're a very observant young man. How did you recognize me?"

The other man, Fishing Hat, actually not named Bob, started to say something, but a big grin from Johnny Mack stopped him.

"Well, you just look like you do on the screen," Kavanaugh answered. "We go to the picture show every Saturday morning, and you're nearly always in one of the shows."

"Well, I'll be a suck-egg mule[5]. Most people don't recognize me. Good for you, sonny"

This down-home exclamation put us both at ease. We began to pepper him with questions about what it was like to make western adventure movies. He answered them all and seemed to enjoy the attention.

---

[5] A suck-egg mule is literally a mule that gets into the hen house and eats the eggs. It is used to indicate that the speaker feels worthless or that he is impressed by someone else's cleverness or ingenuity. When my father would beat Uncle Doc, Aunt Brazzie's husband, at checkers, Uncle Doc would say, "Well I'll be a suck-egg mule!" or "You bessie bug, you!" I still don't know what a bessie bug is.

The other man, Fishing Hat, just stood and listened. Johnny Mack would look at him occasionally and he would smile. He seemed to enjoy just hearing Johnny Mack talk about his adventures like we did.

When our questions began to slow down a bit, Fishing Hat spoke up, "Why don't you tell 'em about your football career?"

"Oh, these are cowboys," Johnny Mack said. "They're not football players."

"Oh, yes we are," Kavanaugh protested. "We play on the vacant lot by Jack Stonecipher's house all the time."

"Well, cowboys and football players, too," Johnny Mack laughed. "Men after my own heart."

I knew that he was a football hero, but I didn't know the details to ask about. Kavanaugh was full of questions, so I just listened for a while.

We had talked for maybe twenty minutes. Johnny Mack had put his fishing gear aside and knelt down on one knee. He picked up a stick and drew swirly lines in the bare dirt as he talked.

Finally, we'd run out of questions. Kavanaugh looked at me, and we decided it was time to excuse ourselves. "Mr. Brown, it's really nice to meet you," he said. "We'll be sure to see all your movies."

"Yes, we will. I'd wear a Johnny Mack Brown outfit if I had one," I explained, "But my daddy got this one free with some Kennel Ration dog food."

Both men laughed at this piece of information. Fishing Hat asked me about the connection between my outfit and the dog food, and I explained as best I could.

"Oh yeah, I nearly forgot; why are you in Frog Level?" I asked.

Johnny Mack pursed his lips as though the question was unexpected, so Fishing Hat spoke up. "Remember, he played football for Alabama. He's just down visiting and we heard how good the fishing is here."

"My wife is from Tuscaloosa," Johnny Mack added. "Did you know that?"

44

"Yes, I did" Kavanaugh said and flashed me a told-you-so grin. "My mother grew up in Tuscaloosa, and I think they knew each other. Mother said something about it one time."

"Well, I'll have to ask Connie if she remembers your mother," Johnny Mack said. "What are your names, and what's her name?"

Wow, I'd never heard this bit of information that Kavanaugh had. We were family friends of Johnny Mack Brown! Well, not quite. My mother knew his wife.

"I'm Kavanaugh Wiggins. My brother here is Wendell. My mother is Gene Wiggins."

"Gene Marle," I interrupted. "She was Alma Gene Marle before she got married."

"Yeah, of course," Kavanaugh shrugged.

"I'll ask her," Johnny Mack said. "Now, I've got a souvenir for each of you,"

Johnny Mack Brown reached in his jeans pocket and pulled out a handful of keys, change, and a few bullets. "Here," he said as he gave us each one of the bullets. "Those are for my revolvers. They're 44s. Now you boys be sure to let your dad know you've got them. And, be safe. No playing around!"

"Yessir! Thank you. Do you really use these in your picture shows?"

He laughed. "No! Think about it! Would I use real bullets in a movie? We fire blanks; no slugs in them."

"No, of course not. That's stupid. We know that."

"Anyway. Back to your question about why I'm here. I won't be making movies much longer. I've been at it for quite a while. My friend here is the Athletic Director at the University of Alabama."

"Don't tell them that!" Fishing Hat objected.

"Keep your shirt on, Paul." Johnny Mack put his hand up to stop Fishing Hat. "These boys can be trusted. Like I said boys, I won't be making movies forever. I'm thinking about moving back to Alabama and taking the coaching job when Coach Drew is ready to retire."

"You're going to get us in trouble," he objected again.

"These cowboys and football players can be trusted. Don't you worry."

Fishing Hat laughed a sarcastic laugh and shook his head. "Okay, Johnny."

Johnny Mack turned back to us. "The part about taking the coaching job is a secret," he said. "Just between us. That part can't go even to your parents. Okay?"

Yessir, we'll keep the secret," we both promised.

Fishing seemed too mundane for now. We picked up our poles and our bag with only three fish. We started home even though nearly an hour remained before we had to leave. We were bursting with our exciting news: we met Johnny Mack Brown! We had bullets to prove it! Barely out of sight of the clearing, we both pulled the bullets out of our pockets and examined them to see if they displayed Johnny Mack Brown's name. They didn't. They just had the usual labeling on the rear face of each: Hickok, .44 cal. Nonetheless, we thought they proved we met a special person with revolver bullets in his pocket to give away. Why would someone do that unless he was a cowboy hero? Everybody knew that the Lone Ranger always left a silver bullet behind at the end of each adventure. Some old codger would ask, "Who was that masked man?" and someone else would know from the silver bullet that the Lone Ranger had been there.

I thought of other ways to prove our claim of a famous encounter. "He told us about his wife being from Tuscaloosa. Not everybody knows that."

"I knew it," Kavanaugh reminded me, "Remember, we can't mention the coaching job."

"Don't worry," I assured him.

We told Mother and Grandmother the minute we came in the back door. We asked Mother about her friendship with Mrs. Johnny Mack Brown.

"Oh, I knew Connie casually," she said. "We went to the same school. I think she was a year younger than me."

Even after repeated questions, Mother never admitted to anything other than a casual acquaintance. That was enough. "My mother knows Johnny Mack Brown's wife," carried an air of importance. It was close enough to illuminate us with the flame of fame.

We brought out the bullets. Mother immediately took them and wouldn't give them back until Daddy had examined them and okayed it.

At dinner, we went through the whole story again. I almost slipped and mentioned the football business, but I caught myself in time. When Daddy asked who was the other man, we said truthfully that we didn't know his name. I remembered Johnny Mack had called him Paul once, but I considered that was too vague; I wasn't required to mention it.

Daddy examined the bullets. He turned them over in his hand and stared at the brass cartridges for a while. He tossed them gently to get a feel for their weight. Finally, he said that they were authentic; 44 caliber pistol bullets to be exact; just the kind used by the cowboys who civilized the West; just what Johnny Mack Brown would use. He questioned us in detail about why Johnny Mack Brown gave them to us. We explained that he said they were souvenirs.

After Daddy concluded we had told everything we knew about the bullets, he announced, "Did you notice they've already been fired?"

We hadn't. Daddy pointed out that the center of the back face of each bullet had a small, round dent in it. "That's where the pistol hammer hits the cartridge. An unfired bullet has a smooth domed center. I'll show you one after dinner."

He took his handkerchief from his pocket, grasped the lead slug at the front of the bullet in the handkerchief and the brass casing of the bullet in the other hand. After a couple of tugs, the slug came out of the cartridge. He looked into the open end of the cartridge, then held it toward us. "Empty," he announced. "It's empty. The bullet has already been fired and then someone has put an unused slug back in it. It's just for display. You can have them. Be careful, though. Every time you pick it up, check the back end for the hammer mark; and make sure you haven't confused it with a live bullet."

By the end of the afternoon, we had told our story to Jamie Wilson, Jack Stonecipher, Monty Baucus, Miles Starett, and several other neighborhood kids. I could hardly wait for school to start again so I could tell everyone about my new buddy, Johnny Mack Brown. When he took the job as coach, I would tell everybody that I'd known about it for a long time. I tried to think of some way to establish I knew it in advance, but I couldn't think how to do it without breaking the promise to keep it secret. I imagined that if I studied at the University of Alabama, I could drop in his office every now and then and say hello.

Given the way Kavanaugh and I spread our news, there really wouldn't be anyone in Frog Level that didn't know the story within a few more days. By Friday, when I went in Daddy's grocery store, Mr. Gibson asked me if he could see the bullet. I happily showed it since it stayed in my pocket all the time.

On Sunday afternoon, after his regular after-dinner nap, Daddy needed to go to town to get a fresh pack of cigarettes. He smoked over a pack of strong cigarettes each day: Picayunes, a Southern brand from New Orleans. Such heavy smoking was common then. It would have been easy for him to bring two or three packs home with him on Saturday night, but he brought only one. I think he was so attached to his grocery store and he worried about it so much that he couldn't stay away an entire day. Needing cigarettes provided an excuse to go check on the store on Sunday afternoon. Daddy always paid for the cigarettes and rang up the purchase on one of the cash registers or, sometimes, let me do it.

Just after we came out of the store, while Daddy locked up, I looked across Temple Avenue toward the post office. Coming down the steps was Johnny Mack Brown and Fishing Hat.

"Daddy, Daddy! Look at the post office. That's Johnny Mack Brown!"

He looked up and across the street.

"Who? Which one?"

"The man in the cowboy hat," I said urgently.

"Let's go meet him," Daddy said. "Come on before they drive away."

Cigarettes had their good uses; they slowed down the pace of life. Fishing Hat stopped to light up before he got in their car, so we got across the street while both men were standing beside a beautiful new blue and silver Buick Roadmaster. Johnny Mack Brown would drive that sort of elegant automobile.

"Good afternoon," Daddy said as we approached. Both men turned to face us and see who greeted them.

"I saw your demonstration out at Dorsey Young's lake," Daddy continued, looking at Johnny Mack. "That was impressive."

What did he say? Had he met Johnny Mack? Daddy's statement completely mystified me, and I furiously tried to discern what he meant. Why hadn't he told me? I started to reach out and grab his sleeve.

"Thank you," Johnny Mack responded. About the time he finished his thank you, he seemed to notice me for the first time. He glanced at me and then did what I knew from the movies is called a double take.

His face slowly developed a strange expression. He looked amused, and apprehensive, and maybe puzzled at the same time. He opened his mouth to speak, but then closed it.

Daddy noticed his strange look at me. "Do you fellows know each other?" he asked.

"Yes, I believe we do. Well, we've met. Is this your son?"

"Yes, it is. He says you're Johnny Mack Brown. That's a surprise to me."

Johnny Mack turned red. "I'm sorry. What's your name?"

I had Daddy's sleeve in my hand. I let go and just looked at the men. I had nothing to say.

"Wiggins. J.C. Wiggins. I run the Jitney Jungle over there." He gestured across the street.

"Mr. Wiggins, I'm afraid we pulled a joke on your son. I told him that I'm Johnny Mack Brown. Actually, I didn't just come out and say it. You've got two sons?"

"Yes, this one and an older one."

"I'm Fred Butler. I guess you know that from the demonstration. This is Paul Means. He's the Hickok Arms representative in Birmingham. We ran into your sons when we went fishing the other day. Your older son asked me if I was Johnny Mack Brown. It's not the first time. People are always telling me I look like him. It seemed like too good a joke to pass up, so I said yes. I hope it hasn't caused any trouble."

The truth slowly sunk into my mind. He wasn't Johnny Mack Brown. He had lied to us. He wasn't going to be the next Alabama football coach.

"Well, I think my son is seriously disappointed," Daddy said.

He looked down at me. He and the other men could easily see the disappointment in my face. I looked at the pavement to hide my expression. "It's not fair," appeared somewhere in my head and echoed around inside.

"I think you owe my son an apology," Daddy said.

I agree," Johnny Mack, no, Fred said. He came from the car door to the sidewalk and knelt down by me just as he had done in the swamp. "What's your name, son? I hate to say I don't remember it."

"Wendell," I replied without looking up.

"I'm really sorry for pulling your leg like that. I shouldn't have done it. I wouldn't have if your brother hadn't suggested it."

"He didn't tell you to lie about it," I pointed out.

"No. You're absolutely right. No excuses. I pulled a mean joke on you and I'm sorry. If it's any help, I promise I will never do it again; not to you, not to anyone. I didn't think about how you would feel if you found out, and I should have known you'd find out eventually. I'm sorry." He put out his hand to shake.

"Okay," I said. It wasn't, but what else could I say? "You're a rotten, no-good, stinking skunk, snake, pile of rotten frogs?" No, that wouldn't help. I shook his hand and looked up at him. "Why did you have bullets in your pocket?"

"My job is to promote Hickok Arms ammunition. I go around the country showing off our new products. I always carry display cartridges in my pocket to hand out. I had mostly the new magnum cartridge, but I remembered that I had a few of the regular ones."

"What were you doing out at Mr. Young's lake?" I asked Daddy.

Mr. Butler answered, "I fired several of the new magnums to show their penetrating power. I shot some steel plates and some really thick timbers. Your dad was there. That's how he knew I wasn't Johnny Mack Brown."

You can imagine how Kavanaugh reacted when we got home and told him the news. He first accused Daddy and me of trying to pull a joke on him. Then, as he realized we were telling the truth, and free of the need to be polite in front of strangers on the main street of town, he made no effort to hide his anger and said a few words that got him in trouble.

Finally we both were resigned to it. We started to tell all the people we had earlier told about Johnny Mack Brown that it had been a joke on us. We didn't have to confess to many people. The news spread faster than our original story had done.

About a month later, I arrived home from playing Monopoly at Monty Baucus' house to find a parcel-post package with my name on it. I didn't receive boxes addressed to me very often. Even a birthday present to me from an uncle or other family member would be addressed to my mother or father. And there was another one for Kavanaugh. His package and mine were not the same size, but they were wrapped in identical paper and tape and both had a return address to the Hickok Arms Company.

Kavanaugh was still out playing, but I didn't wait to open my box. It contained a brand-new Barlow pocketknife with Johnny Mack Brown's picture on the side and a note on Hickok Arms Company stationery. It said:

> Dear Wendell:
>
> I apologize again for pulling the joke on you.
>
> I hope this gift will make it up to you a little

and you won't always hold it against me and
Hickok.

Sincerely,

Fred Butler
Hickok Ammunition Development
Representative

Kavanaugh's package contained a similar note and an autographed picture of Johnny Mack Brown in almost the same pose as was shown on the side of my knife.

Grandmother and I were talking about it one afternoon on the front porch while she braided another rug.

"Remember what I told you," she said near the end of our talk. "Things you find in the swamp are not always what they seem to be."

## Feeling at home

The summer was moving on much too swiftly, and Mother began to get us ready for school. The afternoon sun had developed that rich yellow hue that lets you know the time of year without looking at a calendar. We'd been back to the swamp to fish several times since the Johnny Mack Brown episode, and we began to feel comfortable there.

We always went to the same clearing at the end of the path through Grimsley's farm. We had explored up and down the river for a short distance. We formed opinions on where to find the best fishing spots. We found great places to hide and jump out on each other and knew the best trees to climb. Pines rose very tall, but had no limbs anywhere near the ground. Sweet gum trees sprouted lots of limbs, but were often small. Oaks were overall the most fun to climb. One favorite oak could be climbed high enough to see just one corner of the roof of our house. We felt at home in the swamp.

We no longer wore our cowboy suits. My Roy Rogers vest and chaps always got in the way and the hats were too hot. The cap pistols weren't of much real use, and caps cost a lot. Now we carried more practical stuff like snacks and water, and I always had my Johnny Mack Brown Barlow knife in my pocket. Kavanaugh still carried his

Lash LaRue whip.

We had abandoned our walking sticks. They were just too much trouble. Anyway, I'd put mine down and lost it somewhere, and besides, it seemed unnecessary to carry a stick since it was so easy to find one lying most anywhere in the swamp.

One afternoon we embarked on what might be our last fishing expedition before school started. We knew that we'd be making far fewer trips after we had homework and other school activities.

At the river, as we began to set up for fishing, I decided to try a new location.

"Kavanaugh, I'm going to try this log that's stuck here. I can get my line a good three or four feet farther out from there." I referred to the very log that Grandmother had forbidden us to use on our first trip.

"I don't think it'll make much difference," Kavanaugh said. "Go on, but watch out. If you fall in, Mother and Daddy might not let you come back to the river."

"We've been down here maybe…, well, lots of times, and we haven't fallen in. If I fall in once, they're not going to make me stay home forever."

"Okay, it's your choice, but I'll tell them I warned you. I can come back without you; with Jack or somebody else."

The log had been stripped of its bark and worn smooth by repeated use, but it had a limb that stuck almost straight up and provided a convenient handhold. I moved about three feet down the trunk, far enough to avoid interfering with Kavanaugh's line, and sat facing along the log with my feet folded under me to keep them from going in the river.

Kavanaugh handed me a worm and we got down to business. Nothing took my line for two minutes or more. Not even a nibble. Perhaps sitting on the log wasn't such a great improvement after all. I pulled the pole up and moved the bobber down. I wanted to drop it in near the log and a few stalks of grass. It looked to me like a nice place for a catfish to hang out.

As soon as I dropped it in, the bobber disappeared. I pulled up hard and the line stretched out toward the middle of the river. I'd snagged a big one, and it was trying to get away from the bank. As I pulled the pole up, it bent so tightly that I was afraid it would break. I needed to stand up and drag it onto the riverbank without bending the bamboo cane too much, but I feared that if I let go of it with one hand, I might lose it. I tried to get up without using my hands. I could do a cross-legged stand-up from the floor easily, but on a smooth log, now wet from my struggling, it was not so easy. It became clear that I should have heeded Kavanaugh's warning.

As I struggled to stand up, I noticed that Kavanaugh, far from scrambling to my support, stood back a few feet on the riverbank and laughed at my predicament. "Oh, come on," I called out. "Help me get up."

He tried to stop laughing and stepped onto the log to steady me. I got up, but all my efforts to stand combined with the weight of his feet dislodged it from the riverbank, and it began to move; Kavanaugh almost lost his footing and had to jump back to the bank.

"Forget the fish," he urged. "Jump off the log!"

I ignored him. The fishing line had my full attention and I tried hard to pull it in. I made no headway at all, but the fish steadily pulled me out into the river. By the time Kavanaugh's calls and the laws of physics got my attention, it was too late. I couldn't jump back to dry ground even if I dropped the pole.

He and I just looked at each other helplessly for a minute. "What should we do?" I asked.

He replied without a pause, "What do you mean, 'we', paleface?"[6]

"It's not funny. Can you reach me?"

---

[6] This is a line from a joke every kid knew then. I''ll tell it as I would have told it then. The Lone Ranger and his Indian sidekick, Tonto, get into a battle with some hostile Indians. The Lone Ranger says, "It looks bad, Tonto. It looks like they're going to capture us and scalp us." Tonto replies, "What you mean, 'us,' paleface." If you don't believe me, watch the 1948 Bob Hope movie, *The Paleface*. American Indians generally don't use the term paleface now and probably didn't then, but the American motion picture industry used it and so did we. Given that we were just kids, I think our usage was more easily forgivable than the industry's.

"No!" he answered with a bit of irritation, "How can I reach you if it's too far to jump. I think you can do it."

"No, I can't. I'll fall in, for sure."

Kavanaugh got a bit more serious. "Okay, let's think."

I finally dropped the fishing pole, and the log slowed its speed away from the bank and down the river.

After about another minute and several bad ideas for getting to shore, I spotted the swing that hung out over the river just ahead. "The swing," I yelled. "Untie it and throw it out to me."

Kavanaugh's face lit up. He liked the idea as well, and he started along the riverbank toward the swing.

"Hurry," I yelled. "I'm going to pass it before you get there."

"Aw, keep your shirt on. I'll make it in plenty of time."

He got to the tree, untied the rope, and began to judge when he should throw it.

"I need to throw it once to judge how hard and when. Don't grab it."

"That's stupid," I replied. "If I can reach it, I'm going to catch it."

"Okay. Just don't lunge for it and halfway get it. If it ends up hanging out over the river and you don't have it, I won't be able to throw it again."

I saw the logic in his warning and waited anxiously. He threw the knotted rope hard. It swung out about five feet down-river from me, and then back. He caught it and froze for a moment, calculating his next attempt. He swung his arm back and made two false movements forward like a batter checking his swing. Then, he threw it a second time accurately enough that it hit me in the chest. I managed to wrap my left arm around it and held on, then let go of the upright limb I had been holding and grabbed the rope with both hands.

I pulled on the rope, expecting that I could get the log to drift over to the riverbank at least far enough that I could jump off. Instead of moving the log, I moved just myself, lost my balance, and, having no choice but to hold onto the rope or fall in the river, I pulled hard and lifted myself off the log.

The rope swung back toward the riverbank, but it didn't go far enough for me to drop onto the bank nor for Kavanaugh to catch me. I swung back out to nearly the middle of the river.

Beginning to panic, I yelled, "Catch me! Catch me now! I can't hold on!"

As I made my second approach to the bank, we saw that I didn't come as close as on the first time. I would swing less and less until the rope and I came to rest out over the river.

Faced now with pure necessity, I remembered our tree house in the back yard and how, if I jumped off and wrapped my legs around a knot in the rope, I could lock them in place and swing for a very long time.

The rope had a knot in it just below my hands, but not where I could lock my legs around it. If I had been on our tree-house swing, I wouldn't have gathered the strength to pull myself up, but propelled by the thought of falling in the river, I managed a couple of hand-over-hand grasps up the rope and latched my legs around the knot. Now I could hold on for a few minutes.

As I relaxed a little, I looked back at Kavanaugh. He showed absolutely no concern. He wasn't frantically looking for a way to rescue me. He sat on the ground, his legs stretched out in front of him, leaning back on his arms, and grinning from ear to ear.

Okay, he wasn't the one in trouble. He didn't have the motivation I had to solve this problem. But the relaxed pose, the self-satisfied grin got to me.

"Well, are you going to help me, or do you plan to just sit there, or go home and leave me hanging here? Just tell me, so I can figure out what to do."

"I'm going to help you," he said without moving a muscle.

I waited to see if he would get up, or at least tell me what he had in mind.

"How? What are you going to do?"

"Relax," he said. "It's all under control. Kavanaugh to the rescue." He yawned.

Again I waited. I didn't have the patience for more than a few seconds. "Then do it!" I yelled. I felt really frustrated and afraid. What if a halfigator came along, waiting for me to drop in the river? I remembered Josh Hollingshead and his missing thumb. I kicked my feet to spin around and survey the river. No beasts lurked—not right now. I could feel tears start to come, and I grimaced to hold them back. A whole list of dangers raced through my mind.

Cottonmouth moccasins can swim well and are completely at home in the water, but they don't just float around all the time like fish do. I didn't worry that a cottonmouth might be waiting below me.

I didn't swim very well, but I could keep my head above water and make slow headway. I could get to shore if I had to.

I knew little about halfigators and their habits except what Grandmother told us, and I remembered how one emerged from the tall grass just as the baptismal ceremony got noisy. Maybe all our shouting and my kicking the log around had attracted one's attention. That worried me. I decided if I had to drop in the river, I would look carefully first to make sure a halfigator wasn't around, then drop in and make a huge splashing commotion just for good measure.

But in spite of halfigators, cottonmouths and even having to swim for my life, I feared to return home wet more than anything. I would never be allowed to go to the swamp again. That's what made me feel like tears might come. That's what almost made me tremble. And to make matters worse, I suddenly thought I understood why Kavanaugh didn't seem so concerned. I suspected he would rather come to the swamp with Jack Stonecipher or some other of his friends who were nearer his age. His joke played back in my head, "What do you mean, 'we', Paleface?"

"You got a good hold on the rope?" Kavanaugh asked.

Thinking this was the opening part of my rescue, I answered calmly, "Yes, I'm sitting on the knot. I can hold on for a while."

"Good," he said. "First of all, if you hadn't hesitated to jump on the rope, you would have made it to the bank."

"Whaddya mean?" I objected. "I didn't plan to jump off the log at all."

"Then what did you plan to do?" he asked.

"I was going to hold onto the rope until.... I thought if I held onto the rope, the log would swing around and.... I'm not sure." I realized I had no idea what I'd planned to do.

"Well, I thought you would grab the swing, push off the log with your feet, and it would carry you back to the bank," Kavanaugh said with a shrug. "Never mind. Guess how I'm going to save you."

"What?"

"Guess how I'm going to save you. I'll give you three guesses. If you don't get it, I'll save you anyway."

His offer left me speechless for a few moments. We played the guessing game in a lot of situations, but never something like this. I considered just letting go, but decided I might as well play along first to see if it got me rescued.

"You're going to call a big yellow bird to swoop down and grab me and drop me on the river bank," I rattled off as fast as I could.

"Nope. Pretty fancy guess, but not very realistic. Your next two guesses have to be reasonable. Something that might really happen."

I said the first thing that came to mind. "You're going to swim out here, have me drop into the river and then you'll pull me to shore."

"Nope. It wouldn't help if I got wet too. Then we'd both get chewed out for getting wet and neither of us could come back to the swamp. Your third guess had better be a really good one or I'll make you keep guessing."

I couldn't think of anything to say. I think Kavanaugh sensed that I was near the end of my rope, figuratively as well as literally. He stood up. "Here's a hint," he said and wiggled his hips.

"What? What in the world does that mean?"

He turned his left side toward me and wiggled again. "Look, dummy!"

I finally got it. "The whip! You're going to use the whip!"

"Good guess, Paleface," he said as he took it off his belt.

"Hurry," I yelled. "Hurry!"

Kavanaugh stepped up as close to the riverbank as he could and swung the whip around his head a couple of times as he always did when he warmed up.

"Hurry," I said, more in anger than fear now.

Kavanaugh stared intently at me and the rope. He drew his arm back and paused, then lowered his arm. "I need to catch the bottom of the rope," he said. "Can you climb up a little?"

"No! I can't climb up. Catch my leg!"

He considered a moment. "Okay," he said, "It's your choice. It's gonna hurt!"

Again he raised his arm and threw the end of the whip back in the dirt. He didn't like the way it laid, so he pulled it forward and snapped it backwards again. Pleased with the way it trailed out behind him, he stared directly at my foot. "Ready?"

"Yes! Do it! Now!"

Kavanaugh pulled the whip forward. It spun around his head and flew straight out at me. When he threw it, it moved too fast to be really seen. A bullwhip makes a cracking sound when it is thrown and jerked back because the tip goes faster than the speed of sound. I winced when it wrapped around my right foot. The last inch of the whip popped against my ankle and, boy, did it hurt. If I hadn't been wearing thick socks, it would have made a blister for sure.

He pulled on the whip and I began to move toward the bank. I moved several feet toward Kavanaugh, but finally came to a stop about three feet from the bank.

"Pull harder!" I yelled.

"I can't pull any harder. I'll have to give you a swing," he said. "I'm going to let go and you'll swing out. Then, as you come back, while you're moving, I'm going to catch you again and pull as hard as I can. It's just like the tree-house swing. You'll have to drop off while you swing over the dry ground. Got it?"

Without waiting for me to answer, Kavanaugh gave the whip a quick jerk, and it uncoiled from my foot. I swung out over the river, past the middle, reversed and headed toward Kavanaugh again. As I glided past where I had hung motionless, he shot the whip out again and caught my foot almost exactly as he had done the first time. As soon as the whip tightened around my foot, he pulled on it and fell backward on the ground. The extra momentum his pull gave to the swing took me all the way to the riverbank. Just before I stopped moving, I let go of the rope and fell on the dirt, feet first and then on my butt.

We both lay there for a while. I breathed heavily and began to calm down while Kavanaugh delicately coiled up his whip and brushed away a few specks of mud that had stuck on it. He wore an expression of smug satisfaction. I pulled down my sock and examined the spot where the whip had popped. It was very red, but not bleeding. It would blister for sure. It looked like the socks hadn't been thick enough after all.

"Thanks," I said.

"Aw shucks, he ain't heavy Mister, he's my brother,"[7] Kavanaugh replied with his steady grin.

I understood his reference and took it as a "You're welcome."

"I could have done without the questions," I said.

"Aw, come on. I was going to help you. Just wanted to have a little fun."

"It wasn't fun," I said.

"Well, it was for me!"

---

[7] "He ain't heavy, Mister, he's my brother" was the motto of Boys Town, an organization to help abandoned and neglected boys. In their ads that appealed for donations, the motto accompanied a picture of one boy carrying another smaller boy on his back. We saw the ads so often, the phrase had become a cliché for brotherly love.

We told our tale at supper that evening. It featured me hiding and jumping out on Kavanaugh, climbing a tall oak tree, and other won't-get-us-in-trouble things. We told only the truth, but it didn't include my adventure on the log. Of course, I had to account for the missing fishing pole. "I caught a really big fish on it and he pulled it out of my hand," I offered as a simple explanation. It was true so far as it went. I just left out the details.

The next day, Grandmother called me from the front porch as I ran by. "Get Toby for me," she said. I fetched it, held it at arm's length, and carried it to her.

As I handed it too her, she asked, "You got any more to tell about your trip to the river yesterday?" and looked at me carefully.

"No ma'am."

"You remember what I told you about not getting in the river?"

"Yes, ma'am. I remember. I didn't get in the river."

"Not this time," she said.

# Cowboy Bob's Wild West Rodeo and International Livestock Exposition, 1952

Pride goeth before destruction, and an haughty spirit before a fall.

Proverbs 16:18

Never be haughty to the humble; never be humble to the haughty.

Jefferson Davis

**As close as I'll ever get**

In the 1950s, television had not become the centerpiece of American society that it is today. My family didn't get a television until 1955. We had a motion picture theater, but my parents rarely went to see a show. I would go to the theater on Saturday morning for the cowboy pictures and whenever a kid's feature came to town. Radio was a big part of our entertainment. We listened to news, comedy, music and drama on the radio every evening for an hour or maybe more.

Traveling shows fulfilled the desire for spectacular visual entertainment that our other options didn't satisfy. Frog Level was very small, but we were on the circuit of a couple of smaller circuses. The big circuses, of course, only came to Birmingham.

Occasionally, we got other traveling shows. I remember when a "minstrel show" came to town. I can't remember the exact title, but "minstrel show" was part of its name. This part of the title apparently brought back childhood memories for Daddy, and we all went to see it. It featured some dancing acts: tap dancing and routines like Fred Astaire did in the movies but not as fancy or elegantly done. I didn't really understand the comedians, and I gathered from the adult's reaction that it was naughty stuff. When some women came out in shiny tasseled outfits and began to shed parts of their clothes, we got up and left. The police ran them out of town the next day.

The show I remember best arrived in the summer of 1952. The traveling shows were announced by the sudden appearance of brightly colored signs on the utility poles in town. I hopped on my bicycle one day, took a right turn out of our driveway, and found an announcement on the pole at the corner. It announced that Cowboy Bob's Wild West Rodeo and International Livestock Exposition would make a one-day appearance in Frog Level next Friday. There would be a matinée and an evening show.

The red and yellow lettering covered a background picture that showed cowboys, Indians, cattle, horses, stagecoaches, a camel, a giraffe, and an elephant. The cowboys fired rifles, the Indians shot arrows, and the whole ensemble was in a general commotion with clouds of orange dust around the edges.

Wow! I had to see it. I recognized immediately that it was as close to Buffalo Bill's famous show as I was likely ever to see.

William Frederick Cody, also known as Buffalo Bill, had created a traveling show called Buffalo Bill's Wild West and Congress of Rough Riders of the World around the end of the 19th century. Railroads had made travel around the country easy for people and paraphernalia for the first time. Incidentally, since it carried cattle as well as anything, it replaced long cattle drives and ended the golden age of the cowboy. Buffalo Bill realized that the railroad, both by providing transportation and creating romantic nostalgia for the cowboy, dropped a huge opportunity in his lap. He would put on a big traveling and money-making show to display the heroic image of the Wild West.

His show reenacted famous battles of the old west. Custer's Last Stand was the most famous, and Buffalo Bill played the part of General Custer. Chief Sitting Bull, the actual Indian Chief from the battle, played himself for a short time. They also performed a reenactment of a pony express exchange. A rider charged into the main arena, grabbed the mailbags off his horse, threw them on a rested horse, jumped on, and charged off again. Annie Oakley performed her amazing shooting tricks. It was like a circus but with a Wild West theme. The world famous Wild West show even had European tours. I have heard that Buffalo Bill was, at one time, the biggest celebrity on earth. I don't doubt it.

His show ended its run in 1916, long before I was born. I read about it, and my parents told me what they remembered. Daddy told me about seeing the newspaper reports of the last performance. Our Compton's Encyclopedia had an article on Buffalo Bill. It formed an important part of history for me, so the similarity of the name of Cowboy Bob's show to Buffalo Bill's seemed immediately obvious. The poster even looked a lot like one shown in the Compton's Encyclopedia article. Well, Cowboy Bob, whoever he was, wasn't Buffalo Bill, but it was a big deal for Frog Level. I wouldn't miss it for anything.

I couldn't wait until the gates opened to see this extraordinary event. I knew that they would arrive either by trucks or by train during the previous night. All the circuses and carnivals operated that way. They had to fit in as many performances as they could do, so they broke everything down after the evening performance, traveled overnight and set up again the next morning. When they played in a town that was big enough to spend one or more nights, then they got some rest.

Mother and Daddy easily agreed to see the show. Grandmother didn't want to go because of her age. She would be in bed not long after we left. I told Mother I wanted to watch the unloading and setting up, so I would be leaving the house right after breakfast. I got the usual warnings to stay out of the way and be careful.

## Wendell Wiggins

The poster said the show would take place on the large playing field next to the high school. I pedaled there first, but found nothing but undisturbed, dew-covered grass. I decided this meant they were traveling by train. If they were traveling in trucks, they'd already be parked all around the field.

It was maybe a half-mile from the high school to the train depot. I found nothing but a couple of pulpwood cars parked north of the depot and a tank car near the Golden Eagle plant. Sighting down the siding track to the south, I found the red and yellow train cars I was looking for. They were south of Aylette Street.

I leaned my bike against the John Deere tractor store. The workers were beginning to open the train cars and unload some of the support equipment. One of the first things coming off the train was a truck housing an electric generator, several control and electrical distribution panels, and piles of big, black electrical cables. As always, anything electrical fascinated me.

Several boxcars had windows out of which horses stuck their heads, sniffing the fresh air and looking around. I looked up and down these cars for one of the less common animals—a camel or an elephant—but couldn't find them.

The first thing I saw that looked like the Old West was a stagecoach. It was tied down to a flat car. When the generator truck drove off, I walked across the small alley along side the track and began to examine the stagecoach. I always behaved myself in these situations, so I didn't climb up on the flat car or do anything but look at it with intense curiosity. In spite of my good behavior, as soon as one of the workers spotted me, he yelled, "get away." I moved back across the alley and nursed my insulted soul.

I watched until quite a few of the train cars had been unloaded. It surprised me at first that all the people looked, well, ordinary. Nobody had a sixshooter strapped on his belt; nobody wore an Indian headdress. I realized pretty soon that I should have expected it to be ordinary. Even as naive and inexperienced as I was, I knew these people were putting on a show. Still, the ordinariness and the rude "get away" killed a little of the excitement I'd been feeling. I decided to go back to the field where the workers were setting up the show and see how all the pieces fit together.

It surprised me to find the setup so far along when I rode up. Sections of fencing had been placed together to form a large corral. Grandstands with wooden boards for seats were being assembled along both the long sides of the corral, and pens for the animals had appeared and were being filled with horses and racks of saddles and bridles at the ends. Several trailers that I guessed would act as dressing rooms rolled into place behind them. The grandstands, trailers, and other trucks and vans filled in any open spaces around the corral and animal pens so that no one could see the show without paying for admission.

I picked a spot just about where second base would be on the baseball field, where I could hang over the corral fence and watch. I stayed there about ten minutes before another truck arrived and drove me away. I wandered around the outside of the busy enterprise for a while, working my way to where the workers assembled the grand entrance. I watched poles being pulled up, stakes driven in the ground, signs unrolled and hoisted into position.

A few other kids watched, but most of them came, took a quick look, and left. A few adults wandered around, but they seemed to have business to conduct, and they also looked very briefly before going off on some errand. The only other long-term spectator was Edison Wallace, the reporter for The Frog Level Times. In fact, he was not only the one reporter, but also the typesetter, part-time advertising salesman, and delivery boy.

I knew Mr. Wallace from seeing him at several events, but mainly because he regularly attended the Friday night football games to report on them. He always wore an open-necked shirt: no necktie. Except in really hot weather he wore a sport coat. His brown hair was thinning but still there, and he walked and moved like a young person. He seemed middle-aged to me.

Mr. Wallace walked up to me and started a conversation. "Hi, Wendell. Are you going to the show this afternoon?"

Most everybody in Frog Level knew my name. Such familiarity was common in a place as small as Frog Level, and, in any case, they knew me from my father's grocery store.

"Hi, Mr. Wallace. My family's going to the evening performance. Do you think it'll be a good show?"

"Well, I suppose it will be if you care for this sort of thing. I guess most of us like cowboys and horses."

"Yeah, I like cowboys. I go to the picture show every Saturday to see the double feature. I wish one of the famous cowboys was appearing here. Wouldn't it be neat if they had Johnny Mack Brown?"

Mr. Wallace laughed. "Son, I don't think this show can afford Johnny Mack Brown. The promotional materials they sent us don't say anything about performing in any big places. It's a small-time operation."

"Have you seen the camels, or the elephants, or the giraffe?" I asked him.

"No. Where did you get the idea that they have those animals?"

"They're on the posters. The ones plastered all over town."

"Really? Nope, haven't seen them. Well, they're everywhere, but I haven't bothered to look at one carefully." After a pause, "They're on the poster, you say?"

"Yep." I looked around. "There's one over there." I pointed to the corner of the playing field.

"Come on," Mr. Wallace said as he straightened up from leaning on the side of a truck. "Show me."

We walked across the dry, dusty field toward the poster. I kicked the fine red powder to propel little spouts of it in front of my already dirty shoes.

"Yep, a camel, a giraffe, and an elephant," he said.

"Well, it is called an International Livestock Show," I said. "I'd think they'd have even more unusual animals."

"Let's go and see what they've got."

"You mean they'll let you in? They keep shooing me away even though I'm not making any trouble."

"Sure they'll let me in," he said. "I am, after all, the local newspaper reporter. Shows want publicity. You come with me."

"You think they'll let me in too?"

"Sure, if you're with me. Stick close, buddy."

We walked back toward the main entrance. There we stopped and Mr. Wallace looked around, seemingly for someone in particular.

"Come on," he said, and started through the entrance. I stayed as close to his side as I could without bumping into him.

A couple of the workers stared pointedly at us, but said nothing. Just inside the gate, Mr. Wallace stopped again and looked around. "George!" he called out to a man standing in the corral. The man wore khaki slacks and shirt, clearly a uniform. He appeared to be supervising the work all around.

Mr. Wallace opened a gate in the corral fence and we went in. I carefully closed and latched the gate and ran to catch up with him. I caught up just as he reached George.

"Who's the kid?" was the first sentence out of his mouth.

"A friend of mine," Mr. Wallace said; then, with just the shortest pause, "My sister's kid."

I probably showed a strange expression, but said nothing.

George looked at me and screwed up his mouth, then ignored me.

"What's on your mind, Ed?"

I'd never heard anyone call Mr. Wallace, "Ed." Anyone in Frog Level who used his first name called him Edison.

"We'd like to see the unusual animals you have, anything except the horses, cattle, that sort of stuff. Maybe get a picture for the front page of next week's paper."

"Okay, the camel should be here shortly."

"How about the giraffe? Can a person ride on him? Maybe we could put Wendell on his back for a picture."

"We don't have a giraffe," George replied quickly, "Just a camel."

"A camel? One camel? Is that all the International Livestock Exposition you've got?"

"I see you've looked at the poster. We had a camel, an elephant and a giraffe when they made up the poster. The giraffe died and we couldn't afford the elephant; had to sell him to a zoo. Some of our cattle are unusual breeds. Want to see them?"

Mr. Wallace looked down at me. Both of them could probably see a genuine look of disappointment on my face, but "my sister's kid" had inspired me. "Aw, gee, Uncle Ed, no foreign animals?" A quick sniff. "None?" A longer, deeply drawn sniff. "Well, one lousy camel?" I actually managed to make my chin tremble a little.

Mr. Wallace placed his hand on my shoulder, squeezed pretty tightly and said, "Now, calm down, Wendell. It'll be a good show anyway."

I guess I was taking the game too far, or he thought I didn't act very well. Anyway, I left it after one more, "Shucks, Uncle Ed."

"Do you want to see the camel?" George asked. "I'll find you when he gets here."

"Never mind," Mr. Wallace replied. "I'll get a picture during the show."

Back outside the gate, Mr. Wallace began to laugh. "Uncle Ed? Uncle Ed? Boy, you sure do catch on quick. I didn't figure out why you were calling me Uncle for a moment, then I remembered that I said, 'my sister's kid.' I just wanted some reason for him to let you come in. Forget it ever happened."

"Okay, Uncle Ed," I said, struggling not to laugh. He had stopped laughing, so I let it drop.

"You want a press pass to the matinée?" Mr. Wallace asked. "I'd offer you a pair of them, but I have to be here to get a picture of Mr. Thuless leading the opening parade and a few other pictures for the paper."

"Mr. Thuless? The guy who runs the Cotton Mill? Why is he leading it?"

"Apparently the show always picks some local dignitary to lead the opening parade in the first performance. How they chose Mr. Thuless, I don't know. Probably somebody knows somebody. They'll dress him up in a cowboy rig and make a big fuss over him. I have to be sure and get a picture for next week's paper. Looks like it'll be him and a camel, huh?" He seemed to be back in a good mood.

"Yeah, I'd like to have the pass. Thank you. My family's going to the evening performance, but I think I'll enjoy seeing it twice. Will they let a kid in with a press pass? They'll probably think I stole it."

"You go in with me the first time. Then you can go in and out as you please. You have to do a favor for me, okay?"

"Sure. What?"

"Do you know Mr. Thuless?"

"Yeah. I know him when I see him. Nothing else."

"That's all I need. It occurred to me I might not recognize Mr. Thuless in all the cowboy rig. I want you to spot him while he's putting on the outfit. When you've seen what he's wearing, come sit with me until the opening parade is done and point him out. We get front row seats. Not bad, huh?"

"That's great," I replied. "Do you really need me to spot him for you?"

He studied me carefully for a moment. "No, not really. I just thought you'd like an excuse to visit the dressing rooms and rub noses with the performers. Again, I see you catch on pretty quickly."

Actually, Kavanaugh always said I was slow to catch on to what people were up to, but for some reason, Mr. Wallace seemed to be easy to figure out.

I had to run back home for dinner and to tell them that I was going to the matinée on a press pass. Mother made me put on a clean shirt and jeans. She gave me fifty cents to buy popcorn, a drink, or whatever I wanted for refreshments and again, made me listen to all the warnings, dos, and don'ts.

I got back to the show nearly an hour before it was scheduled to start.

## Wendell Wiggins

I didn't see many people around. The crowd hadn't begun to arrive, and the show people were inside the now-closed assembly of vans, trucks, and grandstands. I rode my bike to a row of old elms along the side of the high school lawn, propped my bike against one of them and sat down in its cool shade.

I hadn't been there long when a shiny white Cadillac drove by me and turned in front of the gym. I recognized the driver as Mr. Thuless. I got up and pushed through a row of shrubbery to see where the car went. It stopped in front of the gym and he got out. He certainly wasn't in a cowboy outfit. He was dressed in a business suit, white shirt, and tie. He opened the trunk and took out a suitcase and walked toward the north end of the gym.

Mr. Thuless was well known around Frog Level. Even though I more or less just knew him enough to recognize him, his reputation wasn't very friendly to kids. He never spoke to us on the street; he seemed to actually not realize we were there. I knew a little more than I indicated to Mr. Wallace because I'd been in the back room of our grocery store one day when Mr. Gibson and Mr. Freeman, the two men in charge of keeping the shelves stocked, were taking a break. As they both drank Cokes, and Mr. Freeman ate a Baby Ruth, they discussed the circumstances surrounding the firing of one of the workers at the Cotton Mill. As they described it, the man had simply refused to do some repair work on Mr. Thuless' home, work that was not part of his job at the mill.

"He wanted Sam to clean his gutters and fix one of them that was falling off. He expected Sam to do it on Saturday. No extra pay. It would have taken the whole day, I suspect. Dang, if I would do it," Mr. Gibson explained.

"John Mitchum's wife told Eunice he makes one of them mow his lawn for nothing. Everybody knows he'll fire you if you look at him crosswise," Mr. Freeman added.

So, I knew it wasn't just the kids that didn't like him.

His full name was C. Beauregard Thuless. He wasn't a native of Frog Level or anywhere nearby. Some people thought he came to Frog Level from South Carolina. Nobody seemed to know for sure but one person said the "C" stood for Chester.

A man wearing the same khaki shirt and pants as George had on that morning met Mr. Thuless at the door. He held the door open for him and took the suitcase. I guessed Mr. Thuless was going to dress in the boy's locker room of the gym at the north end where he entered. Now that I knew where he was, I figured I should check to see if Mr. Wallace had shown up yet.

I found him outside the entrance to the corral. He was talking to the early arrivals; asking them what they expected from the show. When he noticed me, he slapped me on the back. "Hey, Wendell. Ready to go find Mr. Thuless?"

"Don't need to," I said. "I already found him. He just went in the north door of the gym. I suspect he's going to dress in the boy's locker room."

"Good work. You might make a good news reporter!"

"Thanks."

"I've talked to enough typical members of the audience. Let's go look up Thuless and see what he has to say."

Mr. Wallace and I walked back to the gym. "I heard you set a tree on fire," he said. "Is the story true?"

"Oh crud," I thought, "Where did he hear about that?" I hoped that people had forgotten it, but occasionally, somebody asked me. My policy was to tell the truth as simply and quickly as possible and get it over with.

"Gee whiz, Mr. Wallace, you're not going to put that in the paper," I said. "It was just a simple accident."

"People love to read about accidents," he replied. It wasn't the answer I wanted to hear.

I stopped walking. Mr. Wallace took a few steps before he realized I'd stopped. "Okay, tell me the story. If it involves you and your family and nobody else, I won't have any reason to write about it."

Well, that didn't help. I still just stood there trying to decide what to do.

"Oh. Somebody else, huh? Did anybody get hurt?"

"No."

"Okay, nobody got hurt. No story. I promise I won't write about it."

I hated this. I wanted to just go home and say nothing, but I didn't want to miss being in on reporting the show, so I began.

"I was making candles in the old chicken house in our back yard. I melted used canning wax and some of my Crayola crayons. Then I dipped a string in the melted wax over and over until it made a candle. I wanted to use it for something, so I decided to use it to look inside an old rotten, hollow oak tree next to the chicken house. I looked only a few seconds and then moved on, but I guess I started some of the rotten wood smoldering. A few hours later, Mrs. Poe, whose house backs up to our yard saw the tree on fire and called Mother. Mother had just dressed to go downtown, and she had to get Mrs. Poe's garden hose and put out the fire, and she got really dirty. I got in big trouble for it. Believe me, my parents have taken it out on me enough. I don't need anything else about it. Please."

Mr. Wallace couldn't help laughing as I told the story. He tried to straighten up when I finished, but he still let out a few snorts.

"Well, it's not news, but it sure is funny. You were melting your crayons? To make candles? Don't you use them like everyone else does?"

"Yes, I do, but they make nice candles."

"Why?" he asked.

"I like to try things. I saw an article about candle making in National Geographic, so I wanted to do it."

"If you saw an article on... on building a rocket, would you try that?"

"You bet," I said. "I've got a couple of books on rockets. I think I might be able to build a solid fuel rocket some day. The liquid-fuel ones have too many parts, and I can't get those things. And, they're too expensive."

"You're dangerous, kid. Come on." He continued to chuckle as we arrived at the gym.

Mr. Wallace showed his press pass to the man in khakis and we went in. We found Mr. Thuless in the locker room. He'd changed into blue jeans, and otherwise had on only an undershirt and socks.

"Glad you came by," he said after Mr. Wallace introduced himself. "I know you. I've seen you around town, and I remember that you tried to sell me advertising in the paper."

"I thought you might not remember," Mr. Wallace said.

"Who's the kid?"

"This is Wendell Wiggins. His dad runs the Jitney Jungle. He's helping me with getting the pictures."

Mr. Thuless didn't seem to care even though he had asked.

"Wallace, a few pointers about taking my picture while I'm leading the parade. I want you on the right side. My right, not yours. Take the picture when I'm about five feet from you. Hunch down a bit. I want to make sure you've got the camera tilted up. Use a flash to make sure that there's plenty of light under the brim of my hat. Got that?"

Mr. Wallace hesitated for a moment before he answered. "I've been doing news photography for nearly twenty years now, Mr. Thuless. I'll get a good picture."

"I'm sure you will," he responded. "I want the picture like I said. Right side, tilted up, five feet ahead of the horse, good lighting. Got it."

"I'll get a good picture," Mr. Wallace said again.

"You're not listening, Wallace. I want the picture to look like I want it to look. They invited me to lead this parade because I have a position of honor in this community, and I don't want a cruddy looking picture in the paper. Got it? If it looks really good, maybe I'll buy a copy from you. Maybe I'll think about some advertising."

Mr. Wallace waited even longer before he answered and looked really unhappy. Finally, he said, "Right side, five feet from the horse, good lighting, tilted up. I can do that."

"Great. And another thing, I want the caption to say—you can put in the usual stuff—besides that, I want it to say, 'Mr. Thuless manages the Cotton Mill, a very profitable enterprise that employs over two hundred Frog Level residents. The Cotton Mill is the lynchpin of the Frog Level economy.' That's all true, Wallace. I want to make sure people know it. Got it? Write it down."

Mr. Wallace stood very still as Thuless dictated. I could tell he didn't like the demands. When Thuless finished, Mr. Wallace started to say something, but stopped. He pursed his lips, seemed to make a change of course, and then began again. "Lynchpin? Is that the word, or two words I guess? Let me get my pad."

"I want it as one word," Mr. Thuless said.

Mr. Wallace pulled a small paper pad out of his rear pocket and took a pencil from his shirt pocket. Mr. Thuless sat down and began to try to put on a brand-new pair of very ornate tan cowboy boots. He dictated the text again, and Mr. Wallace scribbled it down.

"Help me with these, kid," he said to me.

"I don't know how," I answered. I can always figure out how to do things, but I didn't want to help him with anything right now.

Thuless looked sourly at me. "Then go get the guy out there," he said, jerking his head toward the door of the locker room. "Make it snappy, Winston."

"It's Wendell."

"I've got to go," Mr. Wallace interrupted. "C'mon, Wendell, let's get back to the crowd. Turning to Thuless, he said, "We'll tell your guard that you need help with the boots on the way out." We didn't.

Outside the gym, far enough so that the khaki-suit man wouldn't hear, Mr. Wallace launched into a continuous, emotional stream of comments on Mr. Thuless. I won't reproduce what he said. You shouldn't hear it. It was all bad. He characterized Mr. Thuless as several domesticated and wild animals; baboon was one, I remember. He didn't seem inclined to follow Thuless' instructions. He made derogatory comments about Mr. Thuless' family, his upbringing, and his education. I didn't know what a couple of the things meant. Finally he stopped.

"I'm sorry, Wendell. He just really made me mad. He's worse than the stories I've heard about him. I'm okay now. Sorry."

"It's okay," I shrugged. "Are you going to take the picture like he said to do?"

"I'm thinking about that," he said. "Lynchpin, huh?"

As we walked through the dusty field between the gym and the corral, Mr. Wallace stewed and muttered. "Can't even put on his fancy cowboy boots." A few paces, then, "Did you see those brown and white dress shoes he took off? They looked brand new too." A few more, then, "He burns me up. Needs a good lesson."

A few more steps, and Mr. Wallace stopped. "Wendell, did that guy strike you as a pompous idiot?"

"Something like that," I said.

"I've got a job for you. It won't get you in trouble. I'll take care of the risky stuff. You game?"

"What is it?" I asked. Mr. Wallace's assurance I wouldn't get in trouble didn't assure me.

"Go back and hang around the gym door. I'm pretty sure when Thuless is ready, Mr. Khaki will escort him over here. You go in the dressing room and hide his regular shoes. Just put them under the lockers. Push them way back. That's all. Can I count on you?"

That seemed simple enough: hiding his shoes. Even if I got caught, it was just a simple prank. It seemed okay to me.

"Sure," I said. "That's not much of a prank. He'll find them pretty soon."

"I'm sure he will," Mr. Wallace said with a chuckle; "but that won't be the end of it. I'll take it from there."

He chuckled as he headed to the corral. I went back to the gym and sat down on the concrete steps at the rear door of the school. I could see the door to the gym across the roadway. After a couple of minutes, I spotted a paper cup. I sat it on the ground about five feet from the steps, picked up a handful of gravel and began trying to throw the pieces of gravel into the cup. I was sure that my pose as an idle kid made me as completely invisible to Mr. Thuless as if I had been a ghost.

In maybe five minutes more, Mr. Thuless came out. He lit a cigarette and chatted with Mr. Khaki. After the cigarette was done, Mr. Khaki looked at his watch and indicated that they should go.

I waited until I saw them disappear into the ensemble of show vehicles, then hopped off the steps and walked as nonchalantly as I could into the gym. Inside the locker room, I saw the shoes sitting on the bench where Mr. Thuless dressed. His other belongings were in one of the lockers. The clothes that had been in the locker were on the floor behind the bench. I looked around and checked the showers to make sure no one was there, then just sat for a few minutes and listened for an indication that anyone was outside the locker room.

When I had convinced myself that I was alone, I took the shoes, moved down about two lockers and pushed them as far under as I could manage. I took care not to scratch them.

Piece of cake, I thought. I brushed off my knees and walked out of the gym. I showed the press ticket at the gate and went in. In spite of my fear that I might be accused of stealing the ticket, the gate attendants gave me no trouble. I found Mr. Wallace standing inside the corral. He pointed to two front-row seats nearby. I took one.

The show started. An announcer welcomed the crowd, compared Cowboy Bob's show to Buffalo Bill's, and finally announced the Grand Opening Parade featuring the entire cast and led by, "Mr. C. Beauregard Thuless, the Manager of the Cotton Mill. Under Mr. Thuless' leadership, the Cotton Mill is the lynchpin of the Frog Level economy, employing over two hundred Frog Level residents. Mr. Thuless will be riding as Grand Marshall of this performance of Cowboy Bob's Wild West Rodeo and International Livestock Exposition! Please welcome Mr. C. Beauregard Thuless, Frog Level's most famous citizen!"

Mr. Wallace looked at me and pretended to gag. He turned and moved to get in position for his photograph. I didn't know what to expect. I had a strong suspicion that he wasn't going to do it like Mr. Thuless dictated.

He stopped in front of the gate that was being opened to allow the parade to come in. He took the picture, so far as I could tell, exactly as Mr. Thuless ordered. As Mr. Thuless, approached the camera, he raised his arm, tilted his head back, smiled and waved to the crowd. The flashbulb popped. The parade rode around the corral several times. On each pass, Mr. Wallace repeated the picture. After a few passes, Mr. Thuless grinned down and I think he said, "That's enough." Mr. Wallace gave him a thumbs-up.

As the parade exited, Mr. Wallace came to the seat beside me. "Got it," he said.

"I thought you would do something to irritate Mr. Thuless. You did just what he said to do, didn't you?"

"Don't mess with the great and powerful," he said. He had a big grin on his face. "Did you sequester the foot protection?" he asked.

At first, I didn't know what he meant. After a few seconds, I got it: sequester meant hide, foot protection was shoes. "Yep, sequestered with care and attention. Under and down a couple of lockers to the left. Invisible until you put your head on the floor."

"Perfect."

We watched the show. The stagecoach chase and robbery was great. The stagecoach flew around the corral and looked like it would flip onto its side at each corner. Several cowboys wearing red bandannas over their faces chased it and fired their revolvers. A guard on the stagecoach fired a rifle back at them. By the time the chase was over, the corral had filled with smoke and a strong odor of gunpowder. I loved it.

The camel came out with a man on his back, dressed as an Egyptian—at least that's what the announcer said. He made a big deal of the camel's utility and compared it to the horse. He used the phrase "stallion of the desert" several times. The poor old animal looked like it would keel over before they finished.

When the show ended and Mr. Wallace had finished his pictures, I thanked him for the invitation to see the show as a reporter. I said that I thought he had a great job and generally flattered him.

"Wait a minute," he said. "Your job's not done yet. We have to go back and ask Mr. Thuless if he's satisfied."

I looked at Mr. Wallace with a skeptical look.

"Just come on," he said. "Trust me."

"For what?" I asked.

"It's a phrase. Never mind."

We went to the locker room and arrived there as Mr. Thuless pulled on his business pants. He seemed very happy.

"Great work, Wallace. Just perfect. You should have some great pictures. They'll be in next week's paper, right?"

"It's our intention to use the show as the lead article. Top half of the front page. One of your pictures will be there with the lead article. More pictures inside."

"The picture of me leading the parade. That's the front page, right?"

"Yessir," Mr. Wallace replied.

The locker room had lockers on each side and a bench in front of each row of lockers. Mr. Wallace sat down on the bench opposite Mr. Thuless and motioned for me to sit beside him.

Mr. Thuless finally was ready to put on his regular shoes. He looked around for them. He stood, turned around two full circles, and stopped. He looked in the locker. He kicked the pile of clothes that he had taken out of the locker. He stopped and seemed puzzled.

"Can't find your shoes?" Mr. Wallace asked. I began to imagine what he was up to. "I'll do the risky stuff," he had said.

When Mr. Thuless seemed to have exhausted his ideas, Mr. Wallace offered some advice. "Maybe they got kicked up under the lockers. Maybe you should look under the lockers."

"Good idea," Thuless said. He reached down and steadied himself on the bench. He started to kneel and stopped. He grabbed a piece of the clothing he had thrown out of the locker and spread it on the floor. Then he knelt on both knees and put his head down to get a better view.

As soon as Mr. Thuless began to kneel, I saw Mr. Wallace shift the camera on his lap. He rested his finger on the trigger and kept adjusting the camera's position. Just as Mr. Thuless lowered his head all the way down on the floor, the flashbulb went off.

"Oh crud!" Mr. Wallace exclaimed.

Mr. Thuless jerked himself up. "Did you take my picture, Wallace?"

"Nosir," he replied. "I was just checking the flash cable and it went off. No film in the camera."

"No film?" Thuless asked.

"Nosir."

As he bent down again to look for his shoes, Mr. Wallace gave me a very exaggerated, stupid grin. I grinned back.

Mr. Thuless found his shoes. He didn't seem to consider how they had ended up under the lockers.

After we left the locker room, I asked Mr. Wallace what he intended to do with the picture of Mr. Thuless bent over, looking for his shoes.

"Need to know, Wendell. Need to know."

I understood what he meant. During World War II, the military had a policy that people were told only what they needed to do their jobs. It minimized leaks of secret information. The phrase "need to know" had become a common phrase, used when someone wanted an excuse to keep a secret.

Then he added, "Actually, I'm not sure, but I'll work it out over the weekend. Be careful. Don't burn anything down over the weekend. Drop by the paper office on Monday and maybe I can tell you or show you what surprise I've cooked up for Mr. Too-Big-For-His-Britches Thuless."

I got back home in plenty of time to tell my story to Kavanaugh, Mother and Grandmother. I told about the stagecoach chase, the poor old camel, the Indians and everything in the show that I liked. I was still keen to see it a second time, I said. I told it all again at supper. I didn't mention Mr. Thuless' shoes.

The evening performance was exactly the same as that afternoon, except Cowboy Bob rode in place of Mr. Thuless. Several parts of the show that I thought were ad-libbed or at least not carefully planned were done exactly the same as that afternoon. The show wasn't spontaneous at all. I still liked the stagecoach chase.

Daddy remarked on how bad the camel looked. He could judge such things from his experience growing up on a farm. He said that he intended to ask Dr. Daniels, our local veterinarian, if the way they treated the poor camel wasn't maybe illegal.

## Wild West justice

I didn't think much about the show or Mr. Wallace over the weekend. On Monday, I goofed off around the house. It wasn't until the middle of the afternoon that I remembered Mr. Wallace saying I should stop by. I told Mother I was going to town to visit the newspaper office because he promised to show me the printing press. He had promised that. Again, I didn't mention the pictures of Mr. Thuless. Need to know, you know.

At the newspaper office, I asked to see Mr. Wallace. The secretary said he wasn't feeling well and had gone home at around noon. She suggested I come back the next day or call to see if he had returned to work.

I'd parked my bike in the alley that separated the newspaper office from my dad's grocery store. I stopped there to ponder what would happen with the pictures of Mr. Thuless. I guessed that when Mr. Wallace became ill, any plans he had to pull a trick on Mr. Thuless had been given up and that tomorrow's paper would just have the picture of him leading the parade. I went in the back door of the grocery store, said, "Hi," to Mr. Hankins, and forgot about it.

The Frog Level Times was composed on Monday, printed overnight and circulated on Tuesday. Subscribers got their copies through the U.S. Mail. A few places, drugstores and cafes, got bulk deliveries and sold them for ten cents each. One such place was Lufkin's Cafe. It belonged to Colonel Lufkin. I have no idea where the title, "Colonel," came from. So far as I knew, it was his first name.

Five days a week, Mr. Thuless routinely rose and dressed and went to Lufkin's for breakfast. Some mornings he brought a magazine to read while he ate: either Time or U.S. News and World Report. Not many people in Frog Level read those magazines, so appearing with them marked him as a man of the world and distinguished him from most other Frog Level residents. On Tuesdays, however, he always bought a copy of The Frog Level Times. The Times would be special this Tuesday. He would be in the lead picture.

Mr. Thuless parked in front of the Courthouse, opposite Lufkin's. He stopped to look at the stately, domed building made of smooth tan-colored bricks. It is a very fine courthouse. It has entrances at the front and on both sides. The main floor sits about head-high off the ground, so each of the entrances has broad grayish-brown stone steps leading up to them. The front steps end on a grand porch with tall columns made of the same stone. The ceilings inside are very high. Since air conditioning was not common in the '50s, all the offices had ceiling fans that rotated lazily. A gracious dome—gold now, but austere leaden gray then—caps the center of the Courthouse with a decorative spindle at the very top. A statue of a Civil War soldier stands on the front lawn with the admonition, "Lest we forget," engraved on the base.

He walked slowly across Temple Avenue today, uncharacteristically greeting anyone who saw him as if he thought they were important and swung the screen door of the cafe open wide.

Although Colonel Lufkin stood at the cash register, he looked down, apparently absorbed in some issue with the cash drawer. The customers busily gossiped or hungrily tended their plates. Not a single person dared to look up to see Mr. C. Beauregard Thuless make his entrance.

He picked up a copy of the Frog Level Times. It must be last week's edition. No. What was wrong? He couldn't grasp the contents of the picture for a while. Then he realized that the picture was the one Edison Wallace had snapped while he bent down and looked under the locker. The camera had been loaded with film after all. It showed his back end, his dress pants stretched tight over his middle-aged derrière, his feet were visible, covered by his socks, and the suspender on his left leg showed plainly. His head was hidden by... well, the rest of him.

By now, the customers and Colonel Lufkin had looked up; the suspense and the unfolding drama was irresistible. Mr. Thuless swayed from side to side as if he were about to fall over. His face was unimaginably red. His look of distress drew involuntary pity from them all.

Above the picture, the headline contained not his dignified Southern name, C. Beauregard Thuless, but a crass imitation of it referring to his sock-covered feet: "See Beauregard Shoeless," it said.

Under the picture was the caption, "Mr. C. Beauregard Shoeless looks for his shoes under the lockers of the boys' dressing room after he appeared in the opening parade of Cowboy Bob's Wild West Rodeo and International Livestock Exposition."

The accompanying article gave a straightforward account of the show. It mentioned the spectacular stagecoach robbery. It said, "Wendell Wiggins of Frog Level, ten years old, said the stagecoach chase was his favorite part of the show, as it was undoubtedly for many Frog Level youngsters." It mentioned the camel and how the advertising was misleading if not downright illegal misrepresentation. It made no further mention of Mr. Thuless.

After maybe a minute, Mr. Thuless looked up at the faces around him. His expression did not change at all. Then, he turned and walked out with the paper. The screen door slammed, and he took two steps. Then he slowly pivoted back to the cafe, stuffed the paper under his left arm, and opened the door with his right hand. He placed a dime on the glass-top counter by the cash register and left again.

Mr. Joe Brown owned and edited The Frog Level Times. He lived in a few blocks of houses between the high school and Aylette Street known as College Park, a name acquired during the short-lived existence of Frog Level Christian College in the early twentieth century. C. Beauregard Thuless drove directly from Lufkin's Cafe to Mr. Brown's house. It was still not quite seven thirty, and Mr. Brown was reading his copy of the Frog Level Times as he drank a cup of coffee. At least, that's what he normally would have been doing.

This morning, he pushed his coffee cup to the far side of the dinette table and laid out the front page of the paper. Mrs. Brown stood silently at his left shoulder. Mostly, he just shook his head. Every now and then, he muttered something. Mrs. Brown didn't ask what it was.

The Brown's doorbell rang. They guessed who it was, and Mr. Brown volunteered to go to the door. Mrs. Brown went back to the bedroom.

"Good morning, Mr. Thuless, come in," Mr. Brown began. He held the door open. Mr. Thuless hesitated for a moment, wondering if he should go into the home of someone who had just recently injured him so severely. Then, he went in anyway.

"Brown, what are you up to? Do you think I'm going to tolerate an indignity like this? Did you think about who you're dealing with? Whom?"

"Mr. Thuless, calm down. I don't know how it happened, who did it. But, I will find out. I will."

"It's your responsibility!" Thuless yelled in his face.

"Yessir, Mr. Thuless. It is, but I had no idea until about ten minutes ago when I opened up my copy of the paper. I'll find out and take care of it."

"What do you mean, 'Take care of it?' How can you take care of it when it's already done? Already distributed to…" It just dawned on him that the papers sent by mail hadn't been delivered yet. "Get down to the post office and stop them. Don't let them deliver it!"

"I don't know if I can do that," Mr. Brown said as he tried to think of some good options.

"Do it! Just do it! Fix it now!"

Mr. Brown thought the last sentence meant that Thuless wanted him to do something other than stop the mailing, but actually, it was simply Thuless' realization that nothing was going to fix his problem.

"Then, what else do you want me to do?" asked Mr. Brown.

Mr. Thuless stopped and just stared at him. "I'm going to fix you, Brown; you and that pipsqueak, Wallace. Fix you for good! And that kid, Winston, the grocer's son; is he in on this?"

"Who?" Mr. Brown asked.

"Winston, the kid that was following Wallace around Friday."

"I don't know who you mean. A kid with Wallace? He doesn't have any children."

"No, no. Not his kid. The Jitney Jungle kid."

"Mr. Thuless, let me go and see what I can do to stop circulation of the paper. I'll come by the mill as soon as I can tell you what I've been able to do."

It seemed the best he could expect, so Mr. Thuless left and went back home.

Mr. Brown drove straight to the post office and walked directly without hesitation into the Postmaster's office.

"Mr. Kimball, I've got a big problem." He described the situation.

They walked out to the mail-sorting area and Mr. Kimball unfolded a copy of the Times. He surveyed it for about fifteen seconds and began chuckling. "It's about time somebody stuck a pin in that bag of hot air. That's really funny. See Beauregard Shoeless. Did you make that up?"

"No!" Mr. Brown nearly yelled, "I don't know who did it. Just let me have all the papers back."

"We're not supposed to do that," the postmaster said. Then, he looked up at Mr. Brown's face and changed his mind. "Frank, is this the only hamper with Frog Level Times in it?"

One of the mail handlers came over and looked into the hamper. "That's probably about half of them. The others are already bagged and gone."

About half of the newspapers were circulated.

From the post office, he went back to the newspaper office. As soon as the secretary arrived, Mr. Brown had her go around town to the drugstores and cafes and buy the papers. She paid the full ten cents for each one. In the end, not a single person in Frog Level failed to see the picture and read the headline, caption, and story. A few cafes even posted the front page for their customers who missed it. By the end of the day, the going price as a collector's item was twenty-five to fifty cents.

Edison Wallace arrived just after the secretary left.

"I'm in here," Mr. Brown yelled. "Come here! Now!"

As he entered the office, Mr. Brown asked in a calm voice, "Are you feeling better, Edison?"

"Yessir, much better. Twenty-four-hour virus, I guess. It was pretty rough yesterday afternoon."

Exchanging his calm voice for a hoarse yell, Mr. Brown roared, "What in damnation have you done, Wallace?" and threw a copy of the paper down on his desk.

Mr. Wallace looked at the paper for maybe half a minute. A huge smile grew on his face until he broke out laughing.

"What are you laughing at?" Mr. Brown nearly screamed. "What's so stinkin' funny?

"It's great," Wallace started. "Don't you think the old geezer deserves it? Nobody in town likes him. Most can barely tolerate him. Every one of his employees hates him. Anybody who just sees him on the street tries to avoid him. A few people who do business with him have to socialize now and then, but they're not happy about it. What a big-headed jerk!"

"You've ruined me, Edison. He's going to sue me for every thing I've got. Why, Edison, why?"

Mr. Wallace looked up at Mr. Brown. "I didn't do it, he said. "I went home sick yesterday."

Mr. Brown sat completely silent a few seconds. It hadn't for a moment occurred to him that anyone other than Edison could do it. "Then who?" he asked.

"I don't know. I showed you the picture of Thuless on the horse and the copy I'd written when I told you I was leaving. I already had the plates made up. Even though I felt rotten, I couldn't leave until the

plates were ready. Then I gave them to Sandra and went home."
Sandra was the secretary.

"So Sandra did it? Or Chuck?" Mr. Brown referred to the printing press operator who came in late on Monday afternoon.

"They wouldn't do it," Mr. Wallace said. "Neither of them. And if they wanted to, neither of them knows how."

Mr. Brown sat motionless and expressionless. He looked up at Wallace again. "Swear it, Edison; swear you didn't do it."

"I swear it."

"I believe you, and I don't think either Sandra or Chuck would do it. Y'all know that if the paper folds, you don't have jobs?"

"Yessir, and we like working for you. We believe you're a good editor; you're fair, and you're a nice guy."

"Then, who? And why?"

"The 'why' is obvious," Wallace said.

"Yeah, like you said. But why kill the paper to do it?"

"I can't imagine it will kill the paper," Wallace said. He sat down in the chair opposite Mr. Brown.

"What do you think Thuless will do?" he asked.

"I don't know, but he'll put us out of business one way or the other."

"How? He hasn't got a single friend in the whole state. If he sues, there's no way he'll win. Think about it. Everybody, everybody thinks he deserves what he got. Most of them would like to see something much worse than being made fun of to happen to him. We'll just publish an explanation that we don't know how it happened. I say I prepared the article that you saw. You state that you looked at and approved it. Sandra testifies she saw the proper front page, and Chuck states that he just prints what he's given. We end with an apology."

Mr. Brown sat and stared at the wall for a long time. Mr. Wallace just waited. Finally, Mr. Brown allowed a small curl of his lips upward. "He did deserve it, didn't he."

He stared at the wall a while longer. Finally he turned to Mr. Wallace and looked intently at him. "You didn't do it, Sandra didn't do it, and Chuck didn't do it. I'm not going to ask you if you have any idea who pulled it off."

"I'd appreciate that," Edison said. "It would just be idle speculation, anyway. I'm prepared to testify under oath that I don't know who did it."

"Really?" Mr. Brown was impressed; then, he was relieved. "Under oath?"

"Yep," Edison replied, "Under oath."

Mr. Brown showed up at Mr. Thuless' office about two o'clock. Mr. Thuless kept him waiting in his reception room for an hour.

"Mr. Thuless, let me begin by apologizing again. We couldn't stop all the papers. Half of the mailed subscriptions went out before I got there. I recovered the rest. My secretary walked around town and bought all the for-sale copies that were left. That was the best we could do."

"It isn't good enough by a long shot," Thuless replied sarcastically.

"I know," Mr. Brown continued, "We will publish an apology in next week's paper: a full apology. I can't tell you how sorry we are about this. Then, I hope we can consider the matter closed."

"No!" Thuless screamed. "It will not be over! It won't be over until I have your hide, and Wallace's hide hung on that wall!"

"Mr. Thuless, please calm down. Let's be reasonable on this matter. I don't know who composed the article about you. I saw the article that Wallace wrote yesterday at noon. It was not what we published. It showed you leading the parade. It was very flattering. I'm sure you would have liked it."

Mr. Thuless started to ask to see it; then resumed his tantrum. "No. I don't want to see it. I'll see you in court."

Mr. Brown just went on. "I saw what Wallace wrote and composed. My secretary saw it. She placed it in a cupboard in our office until the printer showed up about four o'clock to begin printing the papers.

89

He is strictly instructed to print what we give him. Editing is not allowed. He probably didn't even notice what it was. We are all prepared to swear under oath about those events. I'm offering you an apology. After that, you can sue us if you want to. You won't win!"

Thuless began to speak several times but stopped each time. Brown didn't wait; he went on. "Like I said, you won't win. The jury might have one or two of your social buddies, people who are beholden to you. The rest of them will be working folks from Frog Level, maybe a few of your employees. If not, then family and friends of your employees."

Brown paused again and Thuless said nothing. This time he didn't even begin. He seemed lost in thought.

"Do you want to drag this out? Do you want us covering a trial in the newspaper? We'll have to refer to the picture and tell the story over and over."

Finally Mr. Thuless spoke. "I see your point. I don't want to drag it out. An apology, next week. A full apology!"

"Yessir, we'll publish the correct picture. We'll explain that we printed the wrong one by mistake. We'll explain what the headline meant and how stupid it was." Mr. Brown began to grin as he spoke. "We'll ask people in the community if they have any idea who would want to do it. The story will probably cover the whole front page."

"No, no!" Thuless interrupted. After a pause and a few deep breaths he asked, "A simple apology. May I have a simple, sincere, actually sincere apology? Two sentences: no more. The bottom of the front page."

"Okay," Mr. Brown said, "That's exactly what we'll do."

And that's what he did. The next edition of the Frog Level Times said, "The Frog Level Times sincerely regrets that the wrong picture, headline and caption concerning C. Beauregard Shoeless appeared in last week's edition. Our investigation has determined that no one on the Frog Level Times staff was responsible for this humorous substitution."

Mr. Thuless declined a second offer to apologize for the apology.

About six months later, he resigned and went back to South Carolina.

I was a bit afraid to see Mr. Wallace in the week between the article and the apology. I didn't seem to be involved, and I wanted it to stay that way. On Thursday of the week in which the apology appeared, Mother took a call at home from Mr. Brown. He said that Mr. Wallace and he wanted to make up for the missed opportunity to show me the printing press.

School had started again, so I went to the newspaper office after school on Friday. Sandra welcomed me and called on an intercom to tell Mr. Brown I was there. Mr. Wallace came into Mr. Brown's office just behind me. They were both in a good mood.

"Edison tells me you helped him cover the Cowboy Bob show. I guess you read the article about it?"

"Yessir. It was really funny."

"You know that nobody on our staff wrote that headline or inserted that picture, don't you?"

That statement confused me to say the least. I'd assumed Mr. Wallace was behind the whole thing, so I was left completely puzzled.

"Who did it?" I asked.

"We don't know," Mr. Wallace replied. "We really don't know."

"Gee," I said. "You don't know who did it? I thought…"

Mr. Brown interrupted me. "Don't speculate. It really riled up Mr. Thuless. You wouldn't want to get somebody in trouble by speculating wrongly would you?"

"Nosir."

"It's all settled now. Let's forget about it. Edison tells me that you were a big help at the show. Have you ever wanted to be a newspaper reporter?"

"Nosir. I want to be an engineer or a scientist."

"High aims, son. High and noble aims. I think we can use a few people like you to put the Communists in their place. Good for you.

Want to see the printing press?"

I said goodbye to Mr. Brown. Mr. Wallace showed me the press in the back room of the office. When we were finished, we both stepped out into the alley.

"Bet you didn't think helping me would be so complicated, did you? Has it been fun?"

"Yeah, I've never done anything like that, but I don't think I know what's really been going on. Didn't you write the article that made fun of Mr. Thuless?"

"Nope. I developed the picture of Beauregard's butt. When I was ready to make halftone plates, the plates that go on the printing press, I guess I picked it up by accident, and it got in the envelope with the picture of Thuless on the horse. By the way, I got a really good shot, right side, five feet in front of the horse, good lighting, tilted up— just as any journalist who'd been doing it for twenty years would have done. Anyway, I ended up with halftone plates of both pictures. I used the picture of Thuless on the horse and showed Mr. Brown the final copy. He approved it. I left the halftone plate of Beauregard's butt on my desk. I gave the assembled type and pictures, the printing plates, to Sandra and had to go home; I was sick."

I still had no idea what had happened.

Mr. Wallace continued, "Over the weekend, I told a couple of friends about the picture of Beauregard's butt and what had crossed my mind to do. I told them I was sure it would make me lose my job, so I couldn't do it. We laughed about it for a while, and we all thought it was too good to miss. They said if I happened to be sick on Monday, nobody knew what might happen with me missing."

"So they did it for you? That's great!"

"Whoa, I have no idea what happened, and neither do you. I don't want to know. Need to know, Wendell, need to know."

"You're right, I don't need to know," I admitted. "But, I sure would like to know."

I didn't get involved in the Frog Level Times any more after that, and I didn't hang out with Mr. Wallace again. I did run into him several times as new adventures unrolled and he came to me to find out what was going on. Every time he ran into me, he would ask, "Burnt down anything recently?"

I decided that I would always reply honestly, "Nope." His question didn't cover blowing up things and I figured he didn't have a need to know about that anyway.

# The Piper Cub, 1954

It is possible to fly without motors, but not
without knowledge and skill.

Wilbur Wright


The gods too are fond of a joke.

Aristotle

## Frog Level at war

The Frog Level airport had just one runway. It was paved, but
the asphalt showed cracking and crumbling along the edges.
Given the run-down state of its single hangar, the shortness of
the runway, and the generally low traffic level, it would make
anyone wonder it was paved at all unless that person knew of an
unusual role that the Frog Level airport had served during World
War II.

My father worked six days a week in his grocery store and had only
Sunday to relax and do anything other than work. Actually, the retail
businesses in Frog Level closed at noon on Wednesdays to give the
merchants another half day off, but my father spent it doing chores
around the house. Since he had so little leisure time, he didn't waste
it sleeping. On Sunday, he kept his weekday habit of rising at 5:30
a.m. Bowing to the special occasion of Sunday, instead of eating at
5:45, he would wait until 6:30 to have breakfast with the whole
family. As soon as we finished, he would ask Kavanaugh and me if
we wanted to "go to the woods." We had about three hours to use

before getting dressed for church.

The airport provided a good place to find deer tracks or doves. It sat next to several cultivated fields belonging to the Robertsons. We would either drive down the dirt road through the fields or drive into the airport and down the runway. Either pathway ended on the edge of the swamp. From there we would walk the margin of the cleared ground and make the hunting assessment.

I always hoped an airplane would land while I could see it close-up, but none ever did. Nevertheless, just the proximity to aviation in any form intoxicated me, and I didn't pay as much attention to the hunting business as I might have.

My father almost never left his work while the store was open, but he made an exception to this rule to go hunting either in the early morning or midafternoon about once a week during hunting season. On one of our Sunday morning trips, Daddy described how he had been shooting doves in Robertson's field in 1939 when a plane marked with the US Army Air Corps[8] insignia had landed at the Frog Level airport. The plane left before he could investigate this strange visit, but such landings became commonplace over the next few years.

Before the U.S. entered World War II, the armed forces had begun many preparations anticipating the war. Among those preparations, the Army Air Corps trained pilots to fly warplanes, and not only American men; but under the umbrella of the Lend-Lease program, they trained British and French recruits. One such program was situated in Tuscaloosa, about forty miles from Frog Level. The students received classroom training, flew with an instructor, and finally, flew solo. The planes were P-11Ds, PT-17s and PT-19s. The PT-17 can still be seen today in almost any air show. It is the "Stearman" biplane favored by many stunt fliers.[9]

As you might expect, the Tuscaloosa field had heavy air traffic. The

---

[8]  The Army Air Corps was renamed the Air Force during World War II.

[9]  I learned the details of the training program from the Air Force Office of Historical Research when I began to record this story in 2007.

school needed a second field at which the students could practice landings. The Air Corps paid to pave the runway at Frog Level's extremely rudimentary airport, and it became an extension of the Tuscaloosa training program.

On the Sunday morning when my father told me about the first time he saw an Air Corps plane land, he didn't go into the details of the program. He didn't know them. He just said that pilots were trained there during the war. Another time, he told me about a plane landing in 1943 and how he had been surprised to discover that the pilot spoke French with only a few English words at his command. They shared a cigarette while they tried to exchange a bit of conversation, and then, the pilot had flown off again. I remembered the story on a couple of occasions as I grew older, but I don't think I ever discussed it with anyone until the spring of 1954.

## The secret

Kavanaugh came home from school about a week before the end of the '54 spring semester with an extraordinary story that he told me only after we'd gone into my workshop behind the garage and made sure no one else was around. Some of his friends had noted that his fifteenth birthday would arrive just after school ended, and they'd agreed that some top-secret information should be passed on before school adjourned. Kavanaugh was in the ninth grade. Before classes started that morning, Jeff Taylor told Kavanaugh to meet him in an old wooden building next to the gym at recess. It seemed a bit strange for Jeff to arrange such a meeting since he was in the tenth grade and Kavanaugh typically didn't associate with him. The building was used to store unused school equipment and occasionally for a hideout in which to smoke, so it was a safe place to reveal a secret during morning recess.

There were four boys gathered when Kavanaugh arrived. They nodded acknowledgment of his arrival, and they closed in a circle as he stepped up to the group. Lohman Carlson was the spokesman. He began by covering a little background such as Kavanaugh's impending fifteenth birthday, how they knew he went to the swamp regularly, and how they believed that he had a strong enough character to keep a sacred secret.

Lohman asked, "You would like to know a secret that has been revealed to a select few of the Frog Level Elite, wouldn't you?"

"Of course," Kavanaugh replied.

"Do you know the secret?" asked Lohman.

"What secret?" Kavanaugh said, not sure he understood the question.

"The secret that is revealed to the Frog Level Elite on their fifteenth birthday."

"No, I guess I don't know it," Kavanaugh said as he looked around the circle of faces, hoping for a clue.

"You see," Lohman said with an air of satisfaction. "That's the best part. The Frog Level Elite have kept the secret without fail for eight years now. No failures. No rat fink snitches."

Lohman turned to Billy Chester. "Billy, tell him what happens if he lets the cat out of the bag."

The circle swiveled slightly toward Billy. He leaned in toward Kavanaugh. "If you fail your sacred duty, it becomes our sacred duty to beat the snot out of you. And, we'll do it, gladly, once a week for four weeks. And we'll enjoy it. We really will."

Kavanaugh had no trouble believing Billy, given his reputation and the obvious sincerity in his voice.

Lohman continued. "You have a little brother, don't you? How much younger is he?"

"Three years," Kavanaugh replied.

"So he's twelve now?"

"Yes, he turned twelve last week."

Lohman started to speak and then stopped. He looked uncertain about something, grabbed Jeff Taylor's sleeve and pulled him aside. They whispered back and forth for a while. He appeared to be asking Jeff about some issue, and at one point, Jeff shrugged as if he also was uncertain on whatever they were discussing. Finally, Lohman's stance shifted to indicate he had made a decision.

They both stepped back into the circle and Lohman resumed his leadership role. "An exception to the rule that says the secret is revealed to the Elite at age fifteen is that younger brothers can share the secret if their older brother is willing to take the risk for them. I mean, if you let him know, and then he spills the beans, you get beat up, not him. Understand?"

Kavanaugh nodded.

"So, Sir Kavanaugh, do you wish to join the Frog Level Elite? Do you wish to know the secret?"

This offer seemed strange and possibly a trick, but he was certainly curious. He knew all the boys surrounding him and respected them for their sports ability or other achievements. How could he refuse this offer to join an inner circle? He couldn't.

"Yes, tell me the secret," he said as he swept his eyes around the circle. "I wish to join the Frog Level Elite."

The boys all began to applaud. The two of them closest to him slapped him on the back.

Lohman lifted his arm toward Kavanaugh. "Kneel, Sir Kavanaugh. Kneel and learn the great mystery."

Kavanaugh had, by this time, speculated on several possible secrets: something related to school lore, something promoting a social clique, or maybe a scandalous tidbit about one of the teachers. The secret was indeed fascinating and involved the world beyond Frog Level in ways one would never guess, and much, much grander than anything at school. The secret was…

I have to explain first that I am not "letting the cat out of the bag," "spilling the beans," or otherwise breaking a great oath. I am certainly not a "rat fink snitch." You'll understand why at the end of this story.

In about 1944, an Army Air Corps Piper Cub airplane flew from Tuscaloosa, headed for the Frog Level airport. It either ran out of fuel or otherwise lost power. The pilot lined up for an approach from the east, but the plane could not reach the runway and went down on the east side of the river, the side across from Frog Level, and not accessible from any nearby road. It rested on an island, they said, isolated by an oxbow lake. But the most astonishing part of the story was this: the skeleton of the pilot still sat in the cockpit. No one had found the wreckage until 1946. By then, only the skeleton was left. The person who found the plane and the remains of the pilot had decided to form the Frog Level Elite rather than just throw this information to the public. The pilot died a casualty of the war as surely as any fighter pilot shot down over Germany. He was a Frenchman, judging from some undisclosed clues found on the skeleton. The Piper Cub would become his shrine. The Frog Level Elite would honor him with faithful pilgrimages. He would never be forgotten. Like the American soldiers buried at Normandy, he would find eternal glory in a foreign land.

And so, it was now Kavanaugh's turn to make the pilgrimage, and mine, since he'd chosen to share the secret and risk my ability to live up to the code of the Elite. They told him to draw a line on a map of the swamp to extend the runway to the east, across the river. Where that line intersected the east bank of the river, he would find the Piper Cub. They told him that he must visit the shrine. Upon returning, he must report the text of an inscription he would find on the forehead of the pilot's skull. That way, the Elite would know that he actually had visited the shrine.

Kavanaugh decided to share the secret with me. We usually made trips into the swamp together, and he knew I was nuts about airplanes. He also shared the risk with me. "If you spill the beans, they may beat me up, but I'll beat you up as bad or worse. Trust me," he said.

The rule was, I would get to know the secret, but not be an official member of the Elite until I turned fifteen. After my birthday I would have to make another pilgrimage before I could become a full member. I didn't understand how they would know if I had gone back a second time, but I went along with the rules anyway.

If we had known the details of the training program then, the type of the crashed airplane would have puzzled us. The planes that the cadets flew were P-11Ds, PT-17s and PT-19s—not Piper Cubs. It became a mystery to me only when I got the details from the Air Force Office of Historical Research. I don't know the definite reason why the crashed plane was a Cub, but I have a theory. I believe an instructor flew it. It seems reasonable that an instructor would fly up to Frog Level in the morning to observe and critique the student landings. He would likely fly the most common, economical aircraft of that time, a Piper Cub. In any case, Kavanaugh and I were bothered by none of these issues as we accepted our duty to visit the plane.

Of course, I asked who else was in the Elite. The membership was secret, he said. It seemed that even those in the Elite knew only a limited number of other members. He, of course, knew the boys who had inducted him, but no others. I knew just that Kavanaugh was a member only because of the twelve-year-old-brother rule.

"You'll learn the identity of a few others when you reach fifteen," he said. "I guess that it's like many things in the military. You are given information only if you need to know it. Then, if you're captured by the enemy, there's only so much they can torture out of you."

"But this isn't war," I objected.

"If..." Kavanaugh began, and then paused as he almost let Billy Chester's name out. "If you remember the rules about getting the snot beat out of you if you spill secret information, then it's pretty much like war."

I pondered his analogy for a moment and decided he was right.

**The expedition**

It seemed no wonder that the downed plane hadn't been found. It went down near the river in a marsh at least a couple of miles from any access by road. Even hunters wouldn't likely go there. Nobody lived nearby. Stamps Bridge Road was nearest the crash site, but at that time, only the remains of an old bridge were found there. Still, wouldn't the Air Corps have made an aerial search?

In any case, Kavanaugh and I would need a whole-day hike to get in and back. We also would have to cross the river, and at the moment, we knew of no tree fallen across to provide a footbridge. We decided to take ropes, find some fallen limbs or small trees, and tie them together to make a raft. This was my idea. We had just studied the expedition of the Spanish explorer, Hernando de Soto, through

Alabama. He marched north from Mobile and crossed the Warrior River at Northport with a raft they made on the spot. A few days later, they had used the same raft to cross the Sipsey and come through Frog Level. I wanted to cross the Sipsey like de Soto had done.

We completed the planning, finished off urgent just-out-of-school business, and we were ready to go. We had army-surplus backpacks to carry the rope, and we both always carried a pocketknife. Kavanaugh took a hatchet, and I took a compass and an old but reliable pocket watch that Uncles Miles had given me, and we both carried plenty of food. At Mother's insistence, we took dry socks. We told Mother and Daddy that we were going to see just how far we could go in a day.

We told them that we planned to build a raft to cross the river, go up the east side and cross back by walking on the remains of the old bridge at Stamps Bridge Road. We got Daddy to agree that if we were not back by supper time, he would drive up and fetch us there. We discussed using the bridge remains to go both ways, but building the raft sounded like fun, and it would involve much less walking if we used the raft both ways. We actually had no intention of going as far north as Stamps Bridge Road unless the main plan failed for some reason.

We obtained the considerable length of rope we needed from Mr. Hankins at my father's grocery store. It was really coarse, heavy string that came wrapped around staple goods. Mr. Hankins wrapped it into balls that he kept lying on a stack of flour sacks in the back room of the store. He gave us a ball almost a foot in diameter. We had to rewind it into smaller bundles to get it in the backpacks.

Early on a sunny Tuesday morning in June, as always, we went down Pinion Street, past Barbara Rogers' house, across Aylette Street, and through Grimsley's farm. Finally, we followed the path that we knew well since the first time that Grandmother and Aunt Brazzie took us fishing there. It had taken only about forty-five minutes since we left home.

We dropped our backpacks in the familiar clearing and began to find and gather limbs and small trees to build the raft. We harvested a few pieces about four inches in diameter, a few more around three inches, and the others were smaller. After about an hour of hunting and chopping with the hatchet, we judged that we had enough. We picked out the straightest, largest pieces and laid them out in a fairly clear, level spot, and began to tie them together, each one to its neighbors at the ends and in the middle. They formed a square about six feet on a side but very irregular.

Next, we laid a second layer on top of the first with the limbs running crosswise with respect to the first layer. These were also tied neighbor-to-neighbor and to the first layer. When this was finally finished, we were quite pleased with its appearance and with ourselves. We sat down for a while to admire it and have a snack.

After our snack, we pushed and pulled the raft toward the water. This manhandling loosened our ties and after we reached the bank, we had to retie several spots and add a few extra ties to make the raft fairly rigid again. We pushed it as gently as possible into the water and Kavanaugh stepped aboard. Of course, his step aboard pushed the raft away from the bank and he almost fell in. Much worse, the raft sank below the water level and he got both shoes full of water. Fortunately, he avoided falling, and we had been wise enough to tie a piece of the rope to the raft so that I could pull it back. Clearly, the raft was not big enough to carry out our plan.

Well, it had almost supported Kavanaugh. We would have to add a bit more wood, and we would have to cross one at a time. We discussed this plan for a while, noted that we would need to tie on a rope long enough to allow the raft to cross with one of us aboard, then use the rope to pull it back and carry the other across. Seeing that time was passing quickly, we pulled the raft back up on the shore and began to find some more limbs. We didn't get enough to form a complete third layer, so we tied the new limbs around the edges. When we launched the raft again, it supported Kavanaugh with only a few splashes around his feet. It would definitely support me.

We measured out two pieces of rope that we judged would span the river and tied one on each side of the raft. We had a straight hickory sapling that seemed ideal to push the raft across, so we were ready. Kavanaugh slung his backpack on, picked up the hickory pole, and carefully stepped aboard while I held the raft against the shore with one of the ropes. After all the trouble of construction and testing, it pleased me to see Kavanaugh smoothly poling himself across the lazy river. I spooled out the rope as he went, being careful not to allow the rope to become tangled in the bushes along each shore.

The crossing took only about a minute. When Kavanaugh had stepped ashore, he laid his backpack down a few feet from the riverbank. Then, he tied the second rope to a small tree on his bank, laid the pole across the raft, and I began to pull it back across the river. I experimented with ways to get on the raft without falling and discovered that I could hold on to a tree limb that grew out over the river while I stepped aboard.

I found it pretty difficult to keep my balance. Several times I just pushed the pole into the river bottom and used it to stay upright. Regaining my balance, I would then make a bit of headway. It took me maybe twice as long to cross as it had taken Kavanaugh. Once, I suggested that he pull me across, but he was having too much fun watching me wobble around.

As I neared the bank I saw something that made me forget about how graceful I looked. A fully grown halfigator had grasped Kavanaugh's backpack and was pulling it toward some bushes on the bank.

"A halfigator's got your backpack," I yelled and pointed with one hand.

Kavanaugh spun around and advanced on the beast. It let go of the backpack, opened its mouth and hissed at him. It was too big to be attacked barehanded, so he looked around for a stick, a rock, or anything that might get the halfigator to abandon his backpack. I watched from the raft, completely absorbed by this crisis and motionless except for balancing myself. It didn't occur to me that if I got to the bank, the two of us could be more effective than one. After about a minute of standoff, Kavanaugh spotted a stick that might be big enough to counterattack. He had to run more or less past the halfigator to get the stick. When he passed the half-pint reptile thief, he left its path to the river clear, and it immediately advanced toward the water, slowed down only by dragging the backpack. It would be in the river in a few seconds. I saw that Kavanaugh wouldn't reach the stick and get back in time to cut it off.

Realizing that I was the only possible defense, I gave a hard push on the hickory pole so that the raft lurched toward the riverbank. Pulling it out of the water, I thrust it like a spear at the halfigator just as he dived into the water. He was too far into the water to be deterred by my spear, but the lurch of the raft and my thrust of the pole/spear had left my weight at the front edge of the raft. The edge began to sink. I pushed the end of the pole into the riverbank to stop my tipping forward, but when I pushed on it, rather than righting me, my feet transferred the force of the push to the raft and it slipped backward and out from under me.

I fell into the water with a huge splash just as Kavanaugh got back to the bank. As soon as I surfaced, I realized I was in the water with a halfigator. Grandmother's instructions raced through my mind. Make a big commotion, she had said. Scream and yell. Thrash your arms and legs. Where was the hickory pole? I needed a pole!

"He's headed upstream! Calm down!" Kavanaugh finally yelled to me when he could stop laughing long enough to breathe.

He extended the stick he fetched and pulled me out of the river. When I reached solid ground, we looked maybe twenty feet upriver and saw Kavanaugh's backpack. The halfigator had submerged, so under other circumstances, it would have been humorous to see his evidently self-propelled backpack leaving a small wake as it sailed away. It slowly sank as it filled with water.

Kavanaugh grabbed the rope we had tied to the raft, pulled it back, and tied it to the tree that the other end of the rope was tied to.

We sat down on the shore and exercised our meager vocabulary of curse words. In Kavanaugh's backpack we had lost the hatchet, his "dry" socks, and, most immediately important, his share of our dinner. Mother would be upset over the loss of the backpack; Daddy would be mad about his hatchet. Both of them would give Kavanaugh and me serious grief because of our wet and probably ruined shoes. The damage to my old pocket watch made me saddest. It still ran, but already I could see a small drop of water at the bottom of the face. It was almost exactly noon. I ignored several sympathetic comments from Kavanaugh and dwelt on this tragedy for quite a while until Kavanaugh punched my shoulder pretty hard and yelled at me, "Put the stupid watch back in your pocket and hush your whining!"

"Why did the halfigator go for your backpack?" I asked.

Kavanaugh shrugged his shoulders and offered, "I suppose he smelled my dinner. I made a sardine, mayonnaise, and mustard sandwich. I guess he could smell it pretty easily." I agreed.

I was dripping wet, but, fortunately, the warm weather made it a nuisance rather than a serious concern. I checked my pockets and still had my Johnny Mack Brown pocketknife. Nothing had spilled from the backpack, but it had leaked quite a bit of water and soaked all my food. Kavanaugh salvaged an apple, dried it on his shirt, and we split it.

We ate the apple and discussed our options. First, we considered going back home. We could try again tomorrow or any day later in the summer. This option seemed completely humiliating, and our parents might decide we couldn't go back since I had fallen in the river, so we had to go on. Except for having nothing to eat—a terrible situation for two boys our ages—we could go on. If we hadn't already built the raft, we would be stuck since we'd lost the hatchet. As it was, we just had to hike northwards along the river until we came to the crashed plane. That was what we would do.

After fifteen minutes of hiking, I'd stopped dripping, but I was still very wet and miserable. Kavanaugh kept urging me to go faster, but the heavy wet jeans were sticking to my legs, and I couldn't. Even at our slow pace, judging from the map work we had done, we'd make it to the plane in less than an hour anyway. Well, that would have been a good estimate if we hadn't had to keep detouring around briar patches and fallen trees.

We'd fallen into a steady trek with little talk when I spotted what I thought must be the Piper Cub. Even I knew that a Piper Cub was always painted bright yellow. I saw a small patch of yellow, maybe a hundred yards ahead. I thought I could even see a piece of the Army Air Corps insignia.

"Look," I yelled to Kavanaugh. At first he didn't see it, but when he came to where I stood, he saw it too. We headed off much more quickly now, sometimes just plowing through the briars instead of going around. After a couple of minutes, we could clearly see a bright yellow Piper Cub. While the intact patches of canvas were still bright, the canvas was torn and missing in some places to expose the wooden frame.

Now we slowed down again, impressed by the fact that we might, at any minute, see the remains of the pilot. Neither of us had ever seen a dead person, much less a skeleton. We dreaded it. If it had been anything but a bright sunny day, we might have lacked the courage to continue on. As it was, we wanted to delay it and maybe see only a small piece of the bones at a time. I hoped Kavanaugh would see it first and warn me to harden myself.

When we were about fifty yards from the plane and some bushes still obscured our view of the cockpit, we stopped and knelt down, partially out of a sense of reverence.

"It's really here," Kavanaugh said to himself and to me. "I thought we would find some kind of practical joke. Maybe they had put up a sign with a skull and crossbones on it that said, 'Kilroy was here,' or something like that."

The tail of the plane rested on a rotting tree that had fallen before the plane came down, and it tilted the nose nearly to the ground. The engine and propeller were missing. Forward of the firewall[10] we saw only wires and two metal tubes that were attached to the lower part of the firewall and bent downward in an arc until they touched the ground.

I asked, "Why doesn't it have an engine?"

"I guess it broke off in the crash," Kavanaugh ventured. "Let's go on."

We slowly moved forward until we could begin to see the cockpit.

"Oh, Jeez." Kavanaugh uttered it in a slow moan. "I can see him. There's really nothing left but his skeleton."

---

[10]  The firewall of an airplane is a metal plate that separates the engine from the cockpit. It is intended to stop an engine fire from spreading.

We were now only about twenty yards away, but a lot of bushes and weeds were still between us and the airplane. I had to take only one more step before I could see it too. Just as we had been told, a skeleton sat upright in the front seat of the Piper Cub. The door was folded down so that we could see most of his torso. A few of his ribs seemed to be broken, but otherwise, he was just like the skeletons we knew well from Halloween and the movies.

The reality of the scene made us begin to question the story we'd been given. When it might have been just a prank, we hadn't given much thought to the human tragedy, to why this poor soul had been left to rot in the swamp. Now it seemed so awful. I thought about the inscription that we were supposed to find on his forehead. Who would do a thing like that?

"Why didn't they rescue him?" I said. "Why couldn't they find him? If he was dead, why didn't they take him out and give him a funeral?"

Kavanaugh just shook his head in bewilderment. We glanced at each other and knew we both felt guilty just being there. I could tell that we both were thinking about just turning around and leaving without getting any closer.

"We can't keep this a secret," Kavanaugh said mostly to himself. "It's been nine or ten years since he crashed, but his family would still want to know what happened to him. What are those Elite idiots thinking about? They're the ones who need a good beating!"

The truth of Kavanaugh's scruples was evident to me, and it provided a welcome reason to leave now.

"You're right," I said. For once out of very few times in my entire childhood, I was glad to have an older brother. "Let's go back and tell Daddy. He'll know what to do."

"No," Kavanaugh said. "We have to take his dog tag. His identity won't be clear unless we get the dog tag. We have to go on up to the plane."

"They can get his dog tag when they come to get the body. I mean, when they collect whatever's left of him."

"No," Kavanaugh said firmly. "We used to play Marines and Army and all that stuff in the back yard. We weren't old enough to actually fight in the war, not nearly old enough."

"I wasn't even born for the first part of the war," I objected.

Kavanaugh ignored my protest. "But now that I have even just a small part to play in it, I'm not going to shirk my duty. We have to get his dog tag. Now, are you going to help me or not?"

"Okay, I'll go with you. But, you have to take the dog tag off," I said. "I'm not touching it."

We slowly moved toward the plane. We were about ten yards from the cockpit when I grabbed Kavanaugh's shirt. "What's that in his mouth," I asked. It looked like a stick had been placed in his mouth.

Kavanaugh stared at the skeleton for a moment. "There's a cigar in his mouth," he exclaimed. "What's going on? Why's there a cigar in his mouth!"

We both stared for maybe another 15 seconds and then it hit me. "It's not real! Look at the ribs. They're plywood, and the plies have begun to peel apart. I can see a piece of wire holding his arm on!"

Kavanaugh saw it too. Just from excitement, I hit him on the arm so hard he would have retaliated if we both had not been so relieved to see it was not a real skeleton.

We straightened up from our awed crouch and walked on up to the wreckage.

"Well, at least it's a genuine plane," Kavanaugh murmured as he stroked the wing with his hand. "The arms and legs of the skeleton are just straight pieces of pine and the ribs are plywood. How did it look so good from back there?" He turned his head to look at where we had been standing when we finally realized what we were seeing.

"The head looks pretty real," I said. "It looks like a plaster cast with varnish over it or something like that. Maybe paper mache."

"Bert Logan had one kinda' like that," Kavanaugh said. "He had it hanging over the front door when I went to his Halloween party last year."

An inscription was written on the forehead of the skull. It said,

"C'est la vie; c'est la guerre." That's life; that's war. Kavanaugh knew how to translate it because of some World War II movie he had seen.

We went over the plane and the skeleton thoroughly. I looked carefully at the front of the plane and puzzled over the missing engine. I searched the surrounding bushes and concluded it was nowhere to be found. The two metal tubes that supported it bent down as if the engine had been ripped out, but the wires and other mounting bolts were not torn. Holes in the firewall might have contained other wires, and holes in the pilot's control panel may have enclosed instruments. I didn't know exactly what should be there, so I didn't know what wasn't. The missing engine puzzled me, but I leaned toward the idea that it had been removed after the crash.

"If someone came in and removed the engine, then that means that somebody else knows where it crashed and knows about the Elite," I said.

"Maybe somebody removed it before the Elite was started," Kavanaugh offered.

"Well, whoever it was wouldn't be obliged to keep the secret."

"Yeah, you're right. I'll ask them what happened to the engine when I report on our trip, I mean pilgrimage."

Kavanaugh noted that several notches were cut in the leading edge of the rudder. We both knew that the front edge of the wing and each of the tail parts was called the leading edge. We guessed that the notches had something to do with the Frog Level Elite prank.

The "stick" I'd seen in the skeleton's mouth was, as Kavanaugh had seen, supposed to be a cigar. It wasn't a real tobacco cigar, but one carved from wood and stained with a dark brown wood stain. It looked just like a real one even up close. It had been sanded smooth and stained just the right color. It also had a band carefully carved around it, just like the ones at Freeman's drug store. The band was painted with gold and red paint. Where the brand name of the cigar would be, the letters, JBR, were carved. Most of the band was gold, but an oval to enclose the brand name was in red, and the carved letters were filled with gold.

Neither Kavanaugh nor I knew much about cigars except that we had quite a few cigar boxes in which we kept our marble collections. JBR wasn't a brand that we recognized, but we figured we just didn't know about it.

A dog tag actually hung around the skeleton's neck. I immediately knew it had been produced in one of the vending machines that allowed you to put any three lines of 16 characters or less on an aluminum tag for 25 cents. The dog tag read,

> Pepe LePew
> Lover, 1st Class
> Keese me!

I couldn't help kidding Kavanaugh about this obviously unofficial dog tag. "Boy, Kavanaugh, I'll bet the Air Force is really wondering what happened to this fellow. I think you should take the dog tag and get it to Washington as soon as possible. You'll probably get a medal. I changed my mind, I'll take it off if you'll deliver it."

I got no reply. He just let me babble on about it for a while.

We spent maybe an hour poring over the plane. We discussed each especially noticeable thing we found. Finally, there seemed to be nothing else to look at, and we decided to start back home. After a quick once-over to see if we missed something, we started walking back south along the riverbank. As we had been told, the airplane rested on an island of sorts. An old, nearly-filled-in oxbow lake separated it from the rest of the east bank of the river: one more reason it hadn't been found by anyone other than the Elite. Since our shoes were already soaked, it made no difference that we had to wade through it.

It was only 3 o'clock in the afternoon, so we had plenty of time to get home. We walked slowly and avoided any bush with stickers as best we could. As we went, we discussed what we had found. First, we traded our thoughts about how clever and funny the whole prank was. We both thought it was remarkable that the secret of the plane and its dummy pilot had been kept even a few years. Then, we wondered who had started the whole deal. Kavanaugh could hardly wait to ask the Elite for a whole list of details.

We talked about the wooden skeleton and how it was beginning to fall apart. I offered, "If you want to, you can tell the Elite that I'll make some new ribs to replace those that are falling apart. We'd have to come back to measure how big to make them and also come back to put in the new ones."

"I'm not sure we want to be coming up here all the time," Kavanaugh replied. "Somebody will find out where we're going."

"Oh shoot. We're down here to go fishing or some other tom fool business all the time," I said. "Nobody ever checks up on us."

"You're right," Kavanaugh admitted. "Wait till I find out if the Elite already have any plans to fix it and if they have other things for me to do."

"Can't you tell me who else is in the elite?" I asked.

"We've already gone over that," he answered emphatically.

After a while, I began again. "Anyway, if they want to do repairs on it, I'd be glad to help." Not being totally altruistic, I realized that if I got in on some Elite activities, I would learn whom a few of the members were anyway.

Our thoughts and discussions lasted until we came back to where we tied our raft. As we prepared to cross back, Kavanaugh spied his backpack snagged on bushes about ten yards up the river on the other side. We decided to retrieve it after we crossed.

Kavanaugh went first again. Having the experience of the morning under our belts and not being in any hurry, the recrossing went smoothly. We had lost the hickory pole, but we discovered that pulling on the rope worked better anyway. We hauled the raft out of the river, pulled it about twenty feet back from the riverbank and tied it to a large gum tree. We both thought that we probably would use it again.

"I wonder if it will hold up for three years until I'm fifteen," I thought out loud.

"Maybe," Kavanaugh replied. "Probably some snot-face fisherman will find it and tear it up."

"Yeah," I agreed. "Maybe we can hide it somewhere." The thought of having to build another raft in three years wasn't appealing, but hiding it didn't seem practical. I decided I would just climb across the bridge remains at Stamps Bridge Road if the raft weren't still there.

When we found Kavanaugh's backpack, it was torn open and the hatchet was gone. We left the remains snagged on the bush.

We got back home around five o'clock and remembered too late that we'd forgotten to discuss the story we would tell everyone about our plan to "just see how far we can go." Of course, Mother asked where we'd gone as soon as we came in the house. Kavanaugh answered before I could think what to say. He outlined how we crossed the river on a raft and passed over the troublesome details except to note that we both got our shoes wet. As Mother examined our shoes and started working up to really being angry with us, he said we had hiked up the east side to Stamps Bridge Road and we just got bored and tired of having wet feet, so we turned around and came back.

We spent quite a while apologizing for the shoes. Finally, Mother consoled herself that we wouldn't need new shoes until school started, and that by then we probably would need a bigger size anyway. Picking this moment when Mother's sympathies were going our way, we also told how Kavanaugh lost his backpack, emphasizing that a halfigator took it, and we couldn't help it. We repeated the whole scene with Daddy at supper time. As usual, he was angrier than Mother, but he focused, as we expected, on the lost hatchet. Fortunately for us, he also wanted to hear about building the raft and the halfigator standoff, and he took some delight in hearing about my dive into the river.

Lying in bed that night, I thought back over the events of the day. It had been a great day: a really great day. What a wonderful secret! I really wanted to know who was in the Elite. I really wanted to be fifteen and become a full member. I really wanted to know who started the Elite. I really hoped that after Kavanaugh reported back about our expedition that at least some of this information would come out. And then, being really tired, I went to sleep.

**Living with the secret**

Lohman Carlson lived a long way out in the country, so Kavanaugh could not just ride his bike over there. Kavanaugh called him on the phone, but Lohman immediately warned him not to discuss the expedition over the phone. This irked Kavanaugh, but he accepted it as an Elite rule. Lohman said he would be in town on Friday night. Kavanaugh arranged to meet him at Scottie's.

In one of the booths with its shiny green plastic-cushioned benches and Formica table, Kavanaugh joined Lohman Carlson and Jeff Taylor. They ordered drinks and some French fries. As soon as the waiter left, Kavanaugh began to tell the story. Jeff and Lohman listened without much interest in most of the story. They laughed pretty hard when he told about the halfigator and how I fell in the river. As he told how we approached the plane and that we thought the skeleton was real, they hooted and punched each other in the ribs. They simply didn't believe Kavanaugh felt obligated to get the dog tag. He skipped over our reluctance to see a real skeleton.

"So what did the inscription on his head say?" Lohman asked.

" 'C'est la vie; c'est la guerre.' It means 'That's life. That's war.'"

"Jeez, how did you know what it means," Jeff exclaimed. Apparently they hadn't known until Jeff had asked Mr. Webster, the school librarian, under the pretense that he'd read it in some book.

"Very well done, Sir Kavanaugh," Lohman Carlson said quietly so no one outside the booth could hear. He grinned broadly and reached across the table to shake Kavanaugh's hand. "What else did you observe?"

Kavanaugh told them about the dog tag. They all laughed about it for a while. Jeff Taylor started a pretty good imitation of Pepe LePew, and his efforts drew quite a bit of attention. After Jeff had attracted a lot of laughs, Lohman tried to respond with a rendition of one of Pepe's cat girlfriends, but it fell flat, and, before long, everyone went back to their own conversations. Kavanaugh asked about the notches in the leading edge of the rudder.

"Very observant, Sir Kavanaugh." Lohman seemed impressed with the thoroughness of our examination, but more impressed by his own importance in the Elite.

"Yeah, they're pretty easy to spot." Kavanaugh was still nearly in awe of the detailed Elite prank, but he was already beginning to tire of Lohman's pompous ways.

He leaned over toward Kavanaugh and used an almost whisper. "That's how we'll know if your brother makes a second trip to the Piper Cub. Each younger brother has to go back when he turns fifteen, count the notches, and add a notch. Since he won't know how many other little brothers have made the pilgrimage by then, he has to make the trip to get the right count. Pretty clever, eh?"

"Okay, I'll tell him," Kavanaugh replied.

"No, no." Lohman leaned over again. "He can't know until he's inducted when he's fifteen. He doesn't get any of what we're telling you now. He has to wait."

"Okay." Then, thinking about how unhappy I would be when he told me nothing, he asked, "Nothing?"

"Nothing!" Lohman glanced sideways at Jeff. His face showed a bit of sympathy for Kavanaugh's situation, but after a few seconds he nodded in agreement.

Having gotten through the report on our pilgrimage, Kavanaugh moved on to a question that he'd been very anxious to ask. "Can you tell me now who the other members of the elite are?"

"No, absolutely not. You already know the four of us who were at your induction. You'll get to know a few more later. Kavanaugh took that to mean that he would meet some other Elite on future business occasions.

They went over a few more details. Kavanaugh asked about the missing engine. Neither of the other boys knew what had happened to it and didn't really seem to care. He mentioned the skeleton's deteriorating ribs and asked if they had any plans to repair them. They didn't.

They all sipped their drinks for a while; then Kavanaugh remembered what he really wanted to learn most of all. "Who started the Elite? Who made the skeleton, the dog tag, the cigar?"

Lohman sort of shrugged his shoulders and seemed at a loss for words. Jeff answered. "We don't know. So far as we can tell, nobody does. Most of the Elite I've met think the founders wanted it a secret.

I've discovered one member who made the pilgrimage in 1950, but he didn't know either."

"What do you mean, 'We don't know.' " Kavanaugh smelled a rat. "How did you meet the 1950 member? Who was he? You said you couldn't tell me who the members are, but now you've met at least some of the older ones."

Lohman held up his hands to calm Kavanaugh down. He indicated that they should all go out together and discuss a couple of more items of business outside. They doled out some very small tips, paid their tabs, and went outside.

It was a nice early summer night. Lohman pulled a pack of cigarettes from his pants pocket, tapped the pack to shift a couple of cigarettes out and offered them to Jeff and Kavanaugh. They declined, but he lit up and indicated that they should cross Temple Avenue to the side of the post office where his car was parked. Once there, Lohman turned off the sidewalk on a concrete walkway that led to the post office basement. It had a sign indicating that the local Selective Service Board had offices there. Lohman hooked a foot over the lower rail of the steel railing protecting the stairwell and perched on the top rail. Seeming satisfied that the locale was private enough, he began the remaining business.

They would invite Kavanaugh to participate with the boys who had inducted him to choose the next member of the Elite. Lohman, the senior member, would drop out of the group. Following this rule, the inducting party was always kept at four. He would pass the leader's role and the official records to Jeff Taylor, the next most senior member. The records were very limited to recent business such as the current count of notches on the rudder. An essential rule was that no historical record could be kept. Kavanaugh would attend four inductions, inherit the leader's role, and then also retire from the induction committee. After each member retired from the induction committee, he never participated in Elite official business again. There was no other official business.

Kavanaugh pondered this strange arrangement and was about to comment on how they were missing a great opportunity to be members of a progressively growing brotherhood and to register his dislike of this setup.

Before he could protest, Lohman turned to Jeff and said, "Having almost finished the business of inducting Sir Kavanaugh, I pass the leadership of the Frog Level Elite to you, Sir Jeff. He pulled a folded, wrinkled piece of notebook paper from the same pocket as held his cigarettes and placed it firmly in Jeff's hand.

"Sir Jeff, you may now reveal to Sir Kavanaugh the secret identification token of the Elite. Give him the secret handshake."

It was just too good. The Elite had a secret handshake that he could use to recognize the members of the Frog Level Elite. Kavanaugh laughed out loud. "Really, a secret handshake," he blurted out. Both Lohman and Jeff shushed him. Much quieter, he said, "Show me. This is great."

Jeff extended his hand, and Kavanaugh grasped it in the ordinary way. They both held firmly and moved their hands up and down as usual. Jeff held on a while longer, then pumped his fist tighter in a couple of friendly squeezes, and let go of Kavanaugh's hand. There seemed to be nothing Kavanaugh could notice out of the ordinary.

"Did you get it," he asked.

"No, I guess I didn't. What's the secret?"

Jeff extended his hand again and they shook. Again, He held Kavanaugh's hand a bit longer than usual, then pumped his fist tighter in two quick squeezes. Immediately, Kavanaugh blurted out, "That's it, isn't it? The two squeezes."

"Yep," Jeff replied. He explained that the handshake began in a completely ordinary way. When it had been held long enough for any incidental or accidental squeezes to take place, the Elite gave two quick squeezes and held on just long enough to see if the other person responded. If the other person were also an Elite, then he responded with three quick squeezes. If the shake were given to a nonElite, it would be considered just a very friendly greeting.

"So, that's how you found the 1950 member?"

Jeff grinned and nodded. "Yep. Use the handshake only when you think someone might be a member. No point in using it when you shake a girl's hand or some young kid. not even with most older people. Certainly, anybody old enough to turn fifteen before the plane crashed wouldn't be a member. You can probably think of a few guys in your class that we would never invite to join. It's really very selective. Nobody knows, but I guess maybe fifteen to twenty people in all have been inducted. We wouldn't have asked you if we didn't know you spend a lot of time down in the swamp. We figured that you might stumble on it anyway."

Kavanaugh thought he had just been insulted, but he couldn't dwell on it because he was so busy digesting the whole handshake business.

"You mean that in.... what is it, around ten years since the crash, that nobody but the Elite have found the wreckage?"

"So far as we know nobody else has seen it. Most people who go down to the river just go to fish. You can't see it from the river, so anybody in a boat would miss it. There's no reason for anybody to go where the plane is. No houses anywhere near."

Finally, they were finished with the Elite business. Lohman gave Kavanaugh a ride home. I was in our bedroom when he came in, and I asked for the whole story.

"I can't tell you," he said. "Most of the stuff is secret until you become a full member at fifteen."

"You're kidding! You are kidding, aren't you?"

"No, I'm not kidding. They didn't tell me much. In fact, there's some rule about not keeping any long-term records. Most of the members only know a few other members."

"They don't have regular meetings?" I asked.

"Nope."

"Who started the prank?"

"I don't know. They don't either."

"You're kidding."

"No. I'm not kidding. I didn't set up the Elite; I don't like the way they do everything; but I can't tell you what I learned. I'm sorry."

"But I won't get to be a full member for three years. That's a quarter of my whole life, so far." I liked to use this fractional-life measure to keep lengths of time in perspective. It made three years seem like a very long time.

Kavanaugh looked at the bedroom door and waved at me to hush. Both Mother and Daddy were just outside the bedroom listening to the radio.

"Well, don't give me grief for the next three years. Don't make me sorry I included you."

The whole thing made me really mad. The idea that Kavanaugh might have gone on the expedition without me made me madder. Build the raft by himself? Never. The raft was my idea. The idea to get the huge ball of rope from Mr. Hankins had been mine.

I just sat there and stewed for a while. Finally, I asked pathetically, "Isn't there anything else you can tell me?"

Kavanaugh contemplated for a while. "They didn't know what 'C'est la vie; c'est la guerre' meant. They had to ask Mr. Webster." He thought again and finally said, "They don't know what happened to the engine and they aren't interested in repairing anything. That's all I can tell you."

And that was it. I wheedled Kavanaugh every now and then hoping to get something out of him, but it didn't work. As you might expect, life went on, and slowly I spent less and less time thinking about it. Every now and then I would compute how long it was until my fifteenth birthday.

**The real secret of the Elite**

As I waited to turn fifteen, I thought about going back to the Piper Cub sometime by myself just to look it over, but I never found time to do it. I was busy studying electronic circuits, and building one circuit or another to see if I could make it work. The County Library had one book on electronics, but it was twenty years out of date. I had little money, so I usually took apart what I already built to use the components in the next project.

The first issue of Popular Electronics magazine came out in October of 1954. I bought it each month to study the circuits in it. The first generally available transistor had just appeared on the market, the Raytheon CK722, and each month's issue of Popular Electronics contained an advertisement for it. I just had to get a couple of them and build a radio.

My grandmother died in the summer of 1955. Her health declined steeply over the previous year, and it made us sad to see her lose her strong spirit and the whatever-needs-to-be-done fearlessness that had characterized her whole life. We all missed her, and I think everyone in the family often wondered, "What would Lizzie do here?" when confronted with a problem.

Taken together, the electronic projects, my grandmother's illness and death, and another big adventure—a hunt for a fabled marble collection—completely occupied me through 1955; and so, I came to the summer of 1956 with the Frog Level Elite not occupying my thoughts very often.

My older first cousin, Burr, who had just become a First Lieutenant in the Air Force, came home for a short visit, and Burr's mother invited my whole family to dinner to see him and hear about his military career.

Burr's real name was James Bradford Randolph. When he was about six years old, he became fascinated with the small things that lived in the fields and woods behind his home. He would sometimes spend the entire day back there watching and chasing them. Before long, aided by a book his father gave him, he began to build traps and became very good at trapping birds, mice, moles, frogs, and all manner of small critters. He would keep them long enough to show them proudly to his older sisters, then release them.

In one unusual and very deadly phase of this career at about age eight, he decided he would provide his own meat to relieve the burden on his father of providing it. The idea was sort of like my desire to provide fish for the family though I hadn't copied the idea from Burr. When he announced this plan to his mother, she protested mildly, then said okay, figuring that he would never produce much game.

When he arrived in her kitchen late that afternoon with six robins, defeathered and actually cleaned as well any chicken ever bought from our grocery store, she cooked them for his supper, but also decreed that henceforth, she would select the meat for supper.

More typically, Burr would treat the critters kindly. For about two years, he tamed, fed, and played with a squirrel. He named him Nuts. My mother made a small red vest for Nuts and he could be seen all day romping in the trees in his unusual outfit. Most sadly, it also led to his demise when a crazy gunsman shot him to see what bright red article a squirrel would be carrying around the treetops.

Burr almost always came in from the day's adventures covered with cockleburrs. The Frog Level locals call them cuckleburrs. They are the oblong seed pods of the weed, Xanthium strumarium, and they grow everywhere around the southern U.S. The pods have curled spikes on them exactly like Velcro. Some people nowadays call the weeds "Velcro weeds." They stick to clothing at the slightest touch. Either Burr's mother or one of his sisters would have to spend several minutes picking the cuckleburrs off James Bradford, so they began to call him Cuckleburr. It was soon shortened to Burr. Till even this day, his friends call him Burr.

Burr outgrew his critter phase and became obsessed with airplanes. He built model airplanes. He collected aircraft magazines and books. Thus, it wasn't at all unexpected when he went to the University of Alabama, graduated as a Mechanical Engineer, and joined the Air Force.

Kavanaugh and I knew that our cousin was a real go-getter, and his military status awed us thoroughly. We hadn't seen him since he left for the Air Force. We wanted to tell him all about the marble hunt since that was the most exciting news we had to offer. So, when Burr's mother invited our whole family to dinner, we couldn't wait to see him and hear all about his exciting military career.

Aunt Rose met us at the door and ushered us into the living room. Burr's sisters, Ann and Lily were also there for the occasion. Everybody was exchanging greetings when Burr came in. I was closest to the hall door where Burr entered. Kavanaugh was over by the door to the side porch petting the family bulldog, Jiggs. Burr grabbed my hand and shook it vigorously while grabbing my shoulder with his other hand.

"Hey, Wendell! How old are you now?" He held on to me awaiting my answer.

"I'm 14 now," I answered, looking up to his smiling face atop his 6 foot, 3 inch frame. He bent over a bit, wrapped his arm around my neck, and gave me a couple of friendly punches to my stomach.

"You look like you're going to be quite a big man. Going to play football? Are you going to be the next Johnny Mack Brown?"

I didn't get to answer. Lily came up and pulled him away to greet my mother. Burr worked his way through the crowd and eventually got to Kavanaugh. He grabbed Kavanaugh's right hand and grabbed him around the shoulders with his left arm in a combination wrestling hold and friendly greeting just as he had done to me.

"Kavanaugh, you look like you've been trying out the Charles Atlas[11] techniques," he said, referring to some of his body building materials he had given to Kavanaugh years earlier when he went away to college.

Kavanaugh didn't answer. The wrestling hold broke for just a moment, and Burr and he looked intently at each other. Burr broke out laughing and grabbed him again, lifted him off his feet and carried him across the living room and the hallway, through the dining room and into his bedroom: a room that had probably been a study before the family grew to the point that they needed another bedroom.

I had no idea what was going on. The much bigger greeting Burr gave Kavanaugh made me jealous, but it wasn't uncommon for my older brother to get attention that I didn't get. I just sat down beside Anne on the sofa and waited for a break in her conversation with Mother so I could tell her about the marble hunt. I didn't tell her

---

[11] The Charles Atlas Body-Building Course was advertised in almost every comic book. It featured a short cartoon strip in which a "ninety-pound weakling" took the course and turned into a muscle-bound he-man. Every boy wanted to buy it, but few had the money.

because Aunt Rose called us all to supper before I got a chance. Being the youngest one around was definitely a disadvantage in this group.

We all wedged into chairs around the dining room table and Burr and Kavanaugh responded to a second call from Aunt Rose. Both Burr and Kavanaugh grinned happily. They took the two empty chairs that remained side by side. I looked back and forth from one of them to the other, trying to figure out what was going on. I went over the things we had in common with Burr. I couldn't think of anything that explained the secret powwow in Burr's room and the smug grins. It finally hit me that it must be something about the Elite. Burr must be a member of the Elite! But how did he and Kavanaugh discover their common bond?

I couldn't stand it any more. I had to know what was going on. I couldn't maneuver around the packed dining room and ask Burr quietly,so I had to do it across the table. How could I ask without revealing the existence of the Elite? I got Burr's attention and whispered across the table, "Burr, are you a member of the secret club? You know, the pilgrims?"

I thought that was pretty harmless, but Kavanaugh's face turned angry and worried. Burr raised his finger to his lips to shush me. "After supper," he said. "I've got a lot to tell you after supper."

Burr's still happy demeanor calmed down Kavanaugh. The dishes began to circulate and everyone filled their plates with Aunt Rose's delicious food. I looked across the table at Burr, and he was engaged in at least two simultaneous conversations with the adults. I looked at Kavanaugh. A couple of times he was busy with eating or listening to some conversation. When I finally caught his eye, he tightened up his lips in a very self satisfied grin and said without using words, "Don't you wish you knew what I know?"

Clearly it had to be the Elite. That explained the secrecy. I pondered what Burr had to say and thought over everything I knew about the Elite and what rules I should be sure to remember in the presence of an older Elite member. I remembered clearly that Kavanaugh refused to tell me anything of consequence after he returned from reporting on our expedition. Nobody could blame me for not following the rules if I didn't know them.

I realized with some pleasure that I could ask about what happened to the Piper Cub engine. This led me to try to remember all the questions I wanted to ask. As I followed this line of thought, I stopped to calculate when Burr turned fifteen. I wasn't completely sure of Burr's age, but I thought he was about twenty-eight. Working backward, I figured that he would have been fifteen in 1943. That must be wrong, that was during the war, maybe before the plane crashed. Wait a minute, Burr had to be too old to....

James Bradford Randolph. Burr's full real name was James Bradford Randolph: JBR: the initials on the cigar band!

Again, I couldn't contain myself. In a whisper aimed at Kavanaugh and Burr, but loud enough to interrupt all the conversation at the table, I yelled, "JBR. Burr's JBR!"

Burr's grin returned again, but Kavanaugh looked puzzled. I realized immediately that Burr hadn't told him about being JBR. Burr put his finger up to his lips again. Now I had a secret that Kavanaugh didn't have, so I could keep quiet contentedly for a while. I replied to Burr's motion by drawing my finger across my lips to indicate that they were zipped closed.

My father spoke for the adults, "What's going on with you, Wendell? We all know that Burr's initials are JBR. You're disturbing the whole table." He wanted me to be quiet, but he couldn't be too angry with me since Burr clearly was in on whatever was going on. I didn't say anything.

"The boys and I have a secret that we have to discuss after supper," Burr offered in explanation. Then eying both of us, he ordered, "Okay, sailors, zip it up. Loose lips sink ships!"

Kavanaugh and I kept quiet after that. I could see that Kavanaugh was thinking hard. After about a minute, his face lit up and he grinned and nodded to indicate he had figured out what I discovered.

Our family had a rule that you couldn't leave food on your plate. My parents weathered the Great Depression and wouldn't tolerate waste. I watched everyone's plate. I was hungry and the food was good. On the other hand, I didn't want to end up with a pile of food when the others had cleaned up, so I planned to have an empty plate just as the adults finished.

We moved on to dessert. My strategy here was simply to ask for a really big piece of the cake. I would have no trouble downing it before the adults finished.

Finally, the meal ended, and Kavanaugh and I were excused. We waited to see if Burr would also get up. After just another minute or so of conversation, he slid his chair back and said that he had business to take care of with us. He waved us to his bedroom, and I made my way around the table as fast as I could. As I came through the door to Burr's bedroom, he motioned for me to close it.

"Well, Wendell, I didn't think you'd make it through supper. Kavanaugh tells me that you're kind of in the Elite, but not quite."

"Yeah, I got in by the twelve-year-old-brother rule. I'm fourteen now, and next May, I'll be a full member."

Burr chuckled. "I already told Kavanaugh that Jack and I didn't make any such rule. You have to tell me if you find out who made it up."

I tried to digest everything implied by his statement. Who was Jack? Why was Burr making up or not making up rules? Who got to make up new rules? I had to start asking all this somewhere, so I asked, "How did you and Kavanaugh know that the other one was a member of the Elite?"

Kavanaugh grabbed the only chair in the room, and Burr sprawled on the bed. Burr motioned for me to sit on the floor. I leaned up against a cedar chest that sat along the wall.

"From the handshake," Burr said.

"He doesn't know about it," Kavanaugh injected.

"Oh, part of the twelve-year-old business, I guess." Burr looked at Kavanaugh.

"Yeah. They said I couldn't tell him."

"There's a secret handshake?" I asked. "Oh boy, that's terrific. How does it work?"

Kavanaugh gave a quick explanation. Burr leaned off the edge of the bed and extended his hand. "You do it," he said.

I took his hand, shook and squeezed.

"No. Wait three or four seconds before you do the squeezes. Try again."

I got it right the second time.

"Okay, okay. let me start from the beginning." Burr did, indeed, start from the beginning. When I'd first heard the story about a pilot crashing and dying in the swamp, I thought it was the most unusual, mysterious, adventure ever to happen around Frog Level. Then, the part about the pilot turned out to be a prank, but it was still pretty good. Now the story Burr told gave it new levels of adventure and unlikeliness.

The story started with the crash. Burr told it just as we already heard, except that the pilot climbed out of the wreckage with only minor scratches, swam across the Sipsey, and walked up to the Frog Level airport. There he phoned back to the base in Tuscaloosa, and a training plane came to fetch him.

Since the wreckage was inaccessible by road and had relatively little value, the Air Corps just left it where it crashed. So far, no romance and not much adventure. Then Burr jumped to the spring of 1946 when the war was over; but, he reminded us, he didn't know about the crash yet.

Burr and his best friend, Jack Hunter, were in love with aviation. Like most everyone at the time, they noticed the huge variety of stuff that was available as war surplus. In particular, Jack hit on the idea of assembling a working Piper Cub from parts obtained through surplus auctions and sales. They both agreed to work equally on assembling the plane, but since Jack would supply the money, the airplane would belong to him. He and Burr accumulated many of the parts in the early months of 1946. They got a wing from an auction sale in Tuscaloosa. They got a fuselage that had been abandoned at the Frog Level airport just for asking. Nobody else wanted it. A few odds and ends were still missing as well as one main part: the engine.

Jack's father had served in the Air Corps and knew a little about the training program. He told them about the crashed plane across the river from the Frog Level airport. They believed that no one had scavenged it, so if they could get to the wreckage some way, they could salvage the engine. But would it be stealing from the government?

When Burr and Jack were at the auction where they bought the wing, they spotted a sergeant observing the proceedings. They approached him and began to ask about the crashed Piper Cub. The sergeant appeared to know nothing about it.

"So you boys want to salvage the engine?" He looked at them skeptically for a moment, and then, without a word he turned and walked behind the makeshift stage on which the auctioneer hawked the surplus. At first, they thought he was just going to ignore them. Then they saw him begin speaking to another sergeant. He turned halfway toward the boys and pointed to them. Both men came back to where Burr and Jack waited.

"You boys say there's a Piper Cub in the Sipsey Swamp, eh?"

"Yessir. It's across the river from the Frog Level airport. It crashed during the war while it was coming in for a landing."

"Have you boys seen it?"

"Nosir, but my dad who was in the Army Air Corps during the war told me about it," Jack answered.

"Ain't no such thing." The sergeant shook his head emphatically and frowned. "The Air Force has no record of a plane going down there. You boys are crazy. If the Air Force knew about such a crash, they would have recovered the plane long ago. Now get gone and don't waste our time any more. If you can find your make-believe engine, you can have it."

Burr and Jack were disappointed with this turn of events. Judging from the sergeant's remarks, there actually wasn't a plane to be salvaged. They hadn't been able to find an engine at any of the sales, and just buying either a new or refurbished one was too expensive. If Jack hadn't already successfully bid for the wing, they might have just given up the plan right there and then; but disgusted and demoralized, they strapped the wing to the pickup truck that they were driving and headed home.

When they got home and told the story to Jack's father, he laughed at the sergeant's response. "The sergeant just told you that the Air Force has no interest in the crashed plane. If he acknowledged that he knew of government property in the swamp at a known location, then somebody would be responsible for dealing with it. By pretending it doesn't exist and that you boys are nuts, he doesn't incur any responsibility, and he told you, you're welcome to it."

Jack's father had already bought a surplus jeep at an auction near Montgomery. They asked to use the jeep, and Jack's father agreed. They would have to cross the river on the Tuscaloosa highway and turn into the woods along the east bank of the river. Then, they would have to make their way through about two and a half miles of woods and underbrush.

I had a really hard time listening with patience. I wanted to jump ahead. I figured I already knew what had happened to the engine. As Kavanaugh and I explored the wreckage, as I knelt in the weeds and studied the bent tubes and dangling wires, I would never have guessed that my cousin had taken the engine. The story just got better at every turn.

Burr and Jack envisioned the trip as a leisurely drive through a lovely forest on a bed of pine needles and didn't get under way until about noon. The trip was not so pleasant. They were foiled by underbrush so thick they couldn't push through with the jeep. When they tried to go along the riverbank, they got buried in mud. They ended up traveling much slower than Kavanaugh and I had done on foot when we went on our pilgrimage. Finally, about four in the afternoon, they made it to the crash site.

As we had discovered, an oxbow lake almost surrounded the plane, and they couldn't cross the muddy end of the lake with the Jeep, so they had to leave it about fifty yards from the plane. They grabbed all the tools they brought, hiked the remaining distance, and got to work.

The propeller was almost completely gone. Only a spray of wood fibers radiated from the hub. Otherwise, the engine appeared to be in very good shape. The cowling had remained more or less intact and sheltered it from the weather. Burr removed the cowling and began to disconnect wires and hoses while Jack climbed into the cockpit to salvage a few of the instruments. He didn't stay long. Yellow jackets had built a nest under the pilot's seat, so the minute Jack sat down, they began to swarm all over him. He bolted from the cockpit and ran away from the plane as fast as he could. He tripped on blackberry vines once, got up and ran again. Burr began to laugh at this cartoon-like show until the yellow jackets identified him as part of their problem and sent him off as fast as Jack, but in the opposite direction.

After a while, Jack and Burr carefully returned to the plane. Each one had several stings, and the yellow jackets were still swarming around the cockpit. They could do nothing but wait until the yellow jackets calmed down. After about forty-five minutes, they could approach the plane without redisturbing the wasps. Jack didn't try to get into the cockpit again, but went to work with Burr on removing the engine.

They disconnected everything joining the engine and the fuselage except the main mounting bolts. Expecting the engine to rest securely on the metal tubes that angled down to the bottom of the firewall, Burr removed the upper bolts and stuck them in his pocket. A couple of seconds after he stepped back and readied himself to attack the lower bolts, it broke loose from the firewall and nose dived into the ground. The tubes hadn't been strong enough to hold the weight by themselves, and they had each curled down in an arc until the engine hit the ground.

"That's what I figured out!" I exclaimed. "Since the firewall and the mounting bolts weren't bent up, I figured somebody had removed the engine. I just couldn't figure out why the support tubes were bent."

"Pretty good detective work," Burr said.

Then, as he started to go on with the rest of the salvaging operation, the key to the whole thing hit me. "You and Jack started the Elite! You guys started the whole thing! You made the skeleton! You made the cigar!"

Burr began to laugh at my excitement. Kavanaugh rolled his eyes and shrugged. "Boy, it took you a long time to figure that out."

"Okay, okay," Burr laughed. "You're right, but let me tell the whole story. Be patient." Burr began again.

The sun set and twilight settled in as they worked on the airplane. The jolt of the plane when the engine fell had stirred up the yellow jackets again. Fortunately, the darkening sky and cooling air calmed them, and after about fifteen minutes, the salvaging resumed again.

Jack got a couple of the instruments out by leaning in through the door and working carefully. When they were finished, Burr and Jack had to make several trips back to the Jeep to carry everything. The engine was quite heavy, but they finally loaded it into the back of the Jeep.

During the first part of the return trip they could see the broken bushes and tracks that marked their incoming path. Eventually, it got dark enough that they missed the path. The last half of the trip had to be made with Burr walking ahead of the jeep with a flashlight so he could see the markings of the path.

"Well, that's how we got the engine. Jack and I worked through the summer of '46 putting it together. By August, we cranked it up in Jack's back yard. The engine ran beautifully. The wing wasn't attached completely since we had to get it to the airport before we attached it. We'd have flown it, but Jack's dad wouldn't let us take it up until an airplane mechanic that he trusted had inspected it. We couldn't get it done before both of us had to go off to school.

"Jack's dad hired someone to take it to the airport and got a mechanic to attach the wing and inspect the whole thing. Jack flew it once at Christmas that year, but I was home only for two days and the weather was too bad to fly. I knew I'd never have the time to fly it, and Jack decided he wouldn't either. He donated it to the Frog Level Civil Air Patrol. I think Wyman Lister and Leonard Dobbs flew it every now and then, although I don't think either one of them had a valid pilot's license."

Burr had lost eye contact with Kavanaugh and me as he finished. He seemed to be remembering it for himself as much as for us.

"Tell us about how the Elite got started," Kavanaugh said. "You only just got started before we had to go to supper."

Burr came back from his thoughts and laughed again. "I can't imagine that it's still going on now. I thought it might last two or three years at most."

A few days after they had come back from the salvage expedition, Burr had the idea to send some of his younger friends on a "wild goose chase," as he put it. But just telling them that they would see a crashed airplane wasn't enough to lure many of them into the swamp, he thought. He told Jack that he wanted to send some kids to find the airplane and together they hit on the idea of a skeleton. That would do it. "Hey kid, want to see a skeleton down in the swamp?" After a bit more discussion, they came up with the "Frog Level Elite" and the idea that the members participated in a ritual, made a pilgrimage.

Burr built the skeleton in the remainder of the summer when he and Jack were not working on the plane. Knowing that he would not be back often, he and Jack selected two fifteen-year-old boys that they thought were sufficiently idealistic and displayed the characteristics of military leaders and made them the first inductees into the Frog Level Elite.

"So, what's this about twelve year olds?" he asked.

"You mean you don't know?" Kavanaugh replied tentatively.

"Nope. That wasn't part of what we cooked up. How does it work?"

Kavanaugh explained that a younger brother could be partially inducted. He explained how a second trip had to be made when the boy turned fifteen and how he must count the notches. It was the first time I'd heard what the notches meant and what I was supposed to do. Burr knew nothing about the notches. We all eventually decided that somebody had invented a new rule just because he had a younger brother.

"Are Kavanaugh and I going to be in trouble because I found out this stuff. I guess I'm not supposed to hear it until I'm fifteen. I don't want to get beaten up."

"Nobody has to know you know. As founder of the Elite, I hereby grant you an exception to all aren't-supposed-to-know rules." Burr raised his arms and swung them around as if in some important ritual. "Benon ebenu, by fotry mezon," he said. "I think I got that right. Now, what's the part about being beaten up?"

I looked at Kavanaugh. "You tell him," he said.

"Well, when Kavanaugh was inducted into the Elite, they said they'd beat him up if he or I told any of the Elite's secrets."

"Well, Whaddya know. More new rules. Jack and I didn't make that one either; didn't need to. Has anyone ever turned Quisling?"

"What does that mean?" Kavanaugh and I said almost together.

"Quisling was an infamous Norwegian traitor during World War II. Now a Quisling is anybody who acts as a traitor."

"No, not as far as I know," Kavanaugh answered.

"Good. Jack and I picked boys who were patriotic. We appealed to their pride and trustworthiness. No threats needed."

I wanted to make sure I got the part about the notches in the plane's rudder. "You said I am supposed to add a notch to the rudder when I go back next year?"

"Yep. But don't tell them you already know that. Let them tell you when they formally induct you."

"Tell us about the cigar and the dog tag," Kavanaugh asked.

"That wasn't part of the setup when I first put the skeleton in the plane. I put the French phrase on the skull so we'd know if the boys actually went to see the plane. I carved the cigar during my first semester at Alabama. I painted the band with some leftover model airplane dope I had, and Jack and I took the jeep in again during Christmas vacation and put it in his mouth. The dog tag came from a student hangout in Tuscaloosa. You've seen the machines where you put in a quarter and print whatever you want on the tag, haven't you?"

Kavanaugh and I both answered yes.

"See, I told you it was from one of those machines," I reminded Kavanaugh.

## Odds and ends

Burr, Kavanaugh, and I talked and laughed for quite a while until the adults clamored for Burr to come out and talk to them. Burr seemed very pleased that his prank had lasted so long.

Neither Kavanaugh nor I saw much of Burr after that. He came to visit his parents every now and then, but his visits were short, and Kavanaugh and I were becoming busier too.

Later that year before my formal induction, someone spilled the beans. That's why I can tell this story without violating a trust. It had to happen eventually. When the news got out, a lot of people wanted to visit the plane and see the skeleton. The gawkers quickly wore a path through the woods that must have been very close to the one that Burr and Jack used originally. And, as you may expect, the plane and the skeleton were soon vandalized. Kavanaugh and I walked in on the newly worn path just a few weeks after the news got out. The skeleton was gone, as was the cigar and the dog tag. People climbing on it and punching holes in the canvas had damaged the plane. It made us sad.

I never became an official member of the Frog Level Elite. It bothered me for a couple of years, but eventually I stopped being sad about it. I decided that I was a member of the true Elite: the boys who were fortunate enough to grow up in the Sipsey swamp.

# The Marble Hunt, 1955

## Marbles

From about the age of eight until thirteen or fourteen, like many kids, we played marbles. The game is a bit dull after a while without something at stake, so we played "keepsies." In keepsies, you keep the marbles you win instead of returning them to the original owner. It's good training for poker and various other adult activities.

Every player has to have a stock of ordinary marbles and at least one taw. The ordinary marbles are about five-eighths of an inch in diameter. A taw is usually larger, ranging from about three-quarters of an inch to over one inch. It is used for shooting. The extra weight gives it an advantage over smaller spheres, and thus the optimal size is limited by what the user can properly grasp and propel.

By referring to marbles of uniform size as ordinary, I do not mean to imply that they were completely interchangeable. At the top of the pecking order reigned true agates: marbles made by rounding and polishing lumps of the translucent mineral called agate or the equally uninformative, formal name, chalcedony quartz. This

135

mineral forms underground in cavities of other rocks as the minerals that make it are carried into the cavity by underground water currents and deposited. Variations in the dissolved minerals over millennia produce colored bands that follow the shape of the cavity. When a piece of agate is rounded and polished, the colored bands swirl across the spherical surface and produce either an especially highly valued or more prosaic marble.

Following agates in value are "cat's-eye" marbles. A strip of molten colored glass is folded into a larger strip of clear glass; the resulting ribbon is chopped into uniform pieces; and they fall onto spinning rollers that form them into spheres as they cool. After the rolling, the colored inclusion often looks like the elongated pupil of a cat's eye; thus, the name.

At the bottom of the order are opaque, colored glass marbles. Down at the dime store, these might be labeled falsely as agates, but a savvy Frog Level player will know the difference.

At the beginning of a game, each player contributes an agreed-on number of marbles to form the playing stock. If a player offers high-quality, true agates or cat's eyes, he might be allowed to contribute less than the agreed number. Someone draws a circle and a "lag line" on the ground. Everyone drops their marbles into the circle, and the players stand back a designated distance and throw their taws at the lag line. The closest one shoots first, the next closest second, and so forth. In turn, each player cradles his taw in his forefinger with the thumb behind it. He "knuckles down" to the ground and flips his thumb forward to fire his taw at the playing marbles. Any marble knocked out of the circle now belongs to the shooter. If he captured at least one, the same shooter shoots again, if not, the next shooter takes his turn. Play continues until no playing marbles remain in the circle.

You can readily imagine that some of us played consistently better than the others. I should just say that most of them played better than I did. My brother, Kavanaugh, definitely won more than I did. As I recall, only Jamie Wilson scored in my bracket. Thus the superior players accumulated marbles while the rest of us periodically had to visit either Elmore's or Anhalt's dime store to replenish our supplies. A package usually cost twenty-five cents.

They came in a bag made of coarse fiber, dyed bright red, with mesh openings large enough to see the contents clearly. If they were run-of-the-mill opaque glass, there might be twenty-five of them. Cat's eye marbles cost more: maybe fifteen for a quarter.

During my marbles career, the reigning champion was Jack Stonecipher. Nobody could beat him on a regular basis. To encourage us to play him, he might offer to be last in the shooting order or to put in more than the agreed number. Since he had a large collection, his primary ploy was to offer lots of cheap marbles, maybe twice what the rest of us contributed. If one of us had a marble he really wanted, he might offer to put in for us if we would put in just that particular one. He was good enough to pick off his chosen target in the first or second turn, and he would get back at least as many others as he had given.

In addition to being the stuff of the game itself, the marbles were collector's items: gems to be hoarded, polished, and shown off. We arranged especially nicely figured agates and cat's eyes to show. While a player only needed one taw to play, several large taws made the best display. Large marbles stolen (with permission) from household decorations might be quite beautiful, though they were rarely agate. Taws that were too large for actual play made exceptional display items. A strict rule stated that playable taws could not be metal. Nonetheless, ball bearings and other machine parts yielded metal balls of varying sizes and materials. Any collection was poor without a few shiny stainless steel ball bearings. Plain, rusting steel was no good. Best of all were the copper alloy balls we scavenged from electrical equipment and that acquired a wonderful patina with the proper fondling and polishing.

We kept our marbles in cigar boxes. Cigars were sold in drugstores then. Given their current-day reputation for ruining one's health, it seems strange indeed that they would be sold in a store devoted to improving one's health, but such it was and still is in some places. Kavanaugh and I would regularly visit Freeman's drugstore to ask for empty boxes. Bill Freeman was a business partner with my father, so we got special treatment and often got a prime-quality box. The boxes were fascinating and beautiful in their own right. Still fragrant with the cigar aroma, they were decorated with pictures of strange women or tropical beaches. The lids closed snugly and precisely, and if you cared for it properly, the small nail that originally sealed the box could be used over and over to secure it. Even though only two layers of paper usually attached the lid, you could open and close the box perhaps thousands of times before it began to give way.

Before Jack began playing, his older brother, Eli, reigned as king. They both had varied talents. In addition to marbles, both Eli and Jack were top-notch trumpet players in the high school band. They were overall pretty good athletes though neither played on any of the ball teams. Both studied engineering and math quite successfully, and Jack went on to get a Master's degree. Our story grows out of the Stonecipher brothers and their hobbies.

**A most unusual idea**

In the fall of 1955, the school year began on a Monday in late August just like it did in so many American communities. It hadn't been like that in years before. Perhaps since the Alabama public school system was formed or maybe since the end of the Civil War, the term started in late summer and then recessed when the cotton crop ripened so that farm children could help with picking for a few weeks. The recess was known simply as "cotton picking" and was bittersweet since we had to start school early, and then just about the time we settled into a routine—vacation again! But with the advent of mechanical harvesters, the need for cotton-picking vacation vanished, the schools abolished it, and we moved a notch closer to urban America with a typical school year.

Our classes were not grouped in the common four-year Junior High School and four-year High School. We were in "Grammar School" during grades one through six, "Junior High School" during seven and eight, and in "High School" during nine through twelve. Grammar School occupied one building, and Junior High and Senior High shared a second building. Thus, all the kids in grades seven through twelve could interact at recess if they were so inclined.

Eli Stonecipher graduated the previous spring and went off to college at Auburn. Jack Stonecipher, Eli's brother, was in the ninth grade, I was in the eighth grade, and Kavanaugh was in the eleventh grade.

On the first day of school at morning recess, Jack started at the Junior High end of the building and went down the hall handing out a mimeographed[12] leaflet. I can't reproduce the true appearance of a mimeographed page, but here is more or less what it looked like and what it said.

---

[12] A mimeograph is a machine that prints multiple copies of a page using a master copy of waxed mulberry paper. One side of the page is covered with ink, but the ink cannot penetrate the wax. If the waxed sheet is struck by a typewriter key or marked with a pointed tool, the metal cuts through the wax and ink can flow onto the printed copy only where it was marked. A freshly printed page brought with it not only the information printed on it, but also a pungent smell from the ink solvent that was considered by some as very pleasant and by others as abominable. The people with the page held over their faces and inhaling deeply were the ones who liked it.

# A Treasure Hunt for
# All Frog Level Adventurers!

All the best of Eli Stonecipher's marble collection has been hidden somewhere in the Sipsey Swamp. Clues to the location of the marble collection will be issued once per week on Friday. The clues will be sold for $1.00 each to those who wish to hunt for the collection. The marble collection will belong to the finder.

Included in the collection is Old Bessie, over 20 display-quality taws, and Eli's finest agate, cat's eye, and special playing marbles.

Sale of clues is final. No refunds will be given

The usual chatter and shuffling died out as he passed, and a murmur punctuated by "Wow," "Cool," and other exclamations replaced it. Soon the whole school focused on this unprecedented coming event, and even teachers joined the discussion clusters forming in the halls and classrooms.

Perhaps you might think I'm exaggerating the unanimous dramatic reaction of the whole school. If so, you don't understand that nearly everyone in Frog Level played marbles at some time in their childhood, or you fail to appreciate how fondly most of us held onto our collections long after we no longer knelt in the dirt and shot for keepsies. Maybe you don't understand how famous Eli's marbles career had been and how renowned his collection had become. Eli was so much older than I, and our childhood society so stratified, that I wouldn't dare ask him to show me his collection; instead, I begged Jack to show it to me even before I'd begun to compete.

I especially wanted to see Old Bessie. She was a copper-nickel alloy marble about one-and-a-half inches in diameter. One of Eli's kinfolk had worked on construction of the Tennessee Valley Authority electrical network. He salvaged Bessie from some discarded electrical equipment and gave the treasure to Eli. Jack made me wash my hands before I could touch her. She was as beautiful as I had heard she was. I could hardly see the copper color at all. It was overlaid with translucent layers of black, green and silver. The layers seemed to vary in thickness and the resulting overall color swirled around the surface. I can think of no better thing to compare her to than a pearl: a huge, perfectly round, multicolored pearl.

I have not exaggerated.

Coming up with a dollar to buy each clue was a problem. Now, over fifty years later, young people will certainly require some education to understand how expensive a dollar a week would be. The Consumer Price Index compiled by the Bureau of Labor Statistics indicates that the goods bought by a dollar in 1955 would cost over seven dollars in 2004. This seems a poor indicator to me. The price of many items seems to have inflated much more. Housing and cars have certainly gone up much more. Nonetheless, many of today's kids would have trouble raising seven dollars a week, just as we had trouble coming up with a dollar a week then.

# Wendell Wiggins

Kavanaugh had begun to work at my Dad's grocery store. A full day's work from six a.m. until ten p.m. profited him five dollars minus the social security deductions, or, as we called them, the ducs. A dollar a week would be possible for him if he hadn't also begun to accumulate the expenses of teenhood: cologne, hanging out at Scottie's, magazines, and maybe a date. Both of us needed emergency rations to fuel our growing bodies, and thus, might need a quart of milk or a Baby Ruth at any moment. I got an allowance from my parents. I can't remember the amount for sure, but it was under a dollar a week.

Thus, teams began to form to share the cost of a clue and to provide troops to hunt. Kavanaugh and I decided that fifty cents each was still too much to comfortably bear, so we asked Jimmy Petersen who lived a few houses down from us to join us. Billy Wayne Fuller approached Kavanaugh about joining our team, but since we were sure that we would find the marbles, we couldn't bear the thought of splitting the hoard more than three ways.

By Friday, six teams had formed. They were:

Team One:
Kavanaugh Wiggins
Wendell Wiggins
Jimmy Petersen

Team Two:
Paul Carpenter
Miles Starett

Team Three:
Danny Workman
Montgomery (Monty) Baucus
Jim Bakkus

Team Four:
Bob Sargent
Walter (Wally) Service
Jamie Franklin

Team Five:
Donis Gray
Billy Wayne Fuller
Alastair Cutler

# The Sipsey Swamp Stories

Team Six:
Barbara Jane Custer
Penny Smithson
Connie Jackson

Yes! A girl's team had formed. We found out that most girls played marbles at least a few times, and some of them were pretty good. This surprised us. Few girls lived in our neighborhood, and boys and girls segregated themselves rather thoroughly by the games they chose to play. No girl wanted to play endless games of tackle football, and we considered touch football beneath our manly dignity. Shooting our BB guns also had little appeal to most girls. Thus, we went our separate ways, and it never occurred to us to invite the one girl in our neighborhood, Barbara Rogers, to play marbles. Probably our loss.

Kavanaugh and I didn't think Jimmy Petersen added much to our team beyond his 33 cents per week. He almost never went into the swamp with us, so he probably wouldn't understand the clues.

We worried that Team Two might have an edge in figuring out the clues because it was made up of a couple of the smartest boys in school. Miles played trumpet in the band, and I think he played basketball for a year or two in high school. He participated in several of the social clubs, but I can't think of much else to say about him. Paul's father was a doctor; and that fact, along with his mother's college education and two very talented and pretty older sisters, put him in an upper social level. He liked science and music, played clarinet in the band, and although he was tall, he played no sports..

Three boys we never even knew to play marbles made up Team Three. Like me, they were not particularly athletic except for Jim Bakkus who tried football for a while but never made the first string. Monty Baucus' family was very wealthy though they rarely showed it. Monty and I played games a lot. I particularly remember that he always won at Monopoly. Now, I consider Monopoly to be at least three-quarters luck, and James Reilly beat me when he was only five years old and I a wise sixty-one: hardly an even match of skill and experience. Nevertheless, Monty always beat me at Monopoly, and I never figured out how he did it. Given the degree of luck involved, I should have won at least a quarter of the time. Whatever made his success, it carried over into adulthood and made Monty the wealthiest person I'll ever know. Danny Workman was a nice guy, good playmate, and moderately smart. Team Three had to be watched, but probably was not a serious threat.

A really eclectic bunch formed Team Four when none of the members found obvious partners. Wally Service was smart, but quiet, and I never ran into him except in school. Jamie Franklin was also a homeboy, not very smart and not at all adventurous, so far as I knew. Bob Sargent gave us the most concern because he always rambled out and about, knew many people, carried a reputation for foolhardiness, and was simply unpredictable. He might stumble onto something.

Team Five seemed a motley bunch like Team Four. Donis Gray and Alastair Cutler were unlikely to get out and hustle for the marbles, but Billy Wayne Fuller coupled a moderate degree of intellect, curiosity, and social ability with an inclination to always try something new without too much forethought. We would have liked to have him on our team except he lived far away, and we just didn't think of him until after we'd already invited Jimmy Petersen to join us.

None of the male teams took Team Six seriously. I never saw any of these girls outside her home except at school or maybe out shopping with her mother. They certainly knew nothing about the Sipsey Swamp, never went fishing, were probably deathly afraid of halfigators and cottonmouth moccasins, and wouldn't have a clue about how Jack and Eli would think while planning the hiding place. Penny and Connie were best friends. Connie had the reddest hair and the most freckles ever seen on one human, radiated intelligence, but remained very quiet, and played flute in the band. Penny was quite definitely not the smartest in school and so naive and trusting that anyone found it easy to pull jokes on her, and we did it often. She always took the jokes well, laughed at herself, and was pretty and personable enough to be very well liked by everyone. She and Connie made a great "Mutt and Jeff" couple. Barbara Jane Custer always wore a pony tail, dressed neatly and fashionably, and answered to BJ. She was smart and I liked her, but again, I can't remember much else to say about her except that her father was the

County Game Warden.

I did worry a little about Penny and BJ in one respect. They were certain to mine the "intelligence" better than any of us boys were. As everyone knew, girls communicated often and well. If anybody— adult or kid—knew anything of value, they would find it out. In any case, maybe we could pull some jokes on the girls before this was over.

By Wednesday we heard that some adults would purchase the clues. We worried about this, as we considered it, "unfair competition," but it soon became clear that the adults were participating just to see the clues and understand what the kids were up to. Most of the adult "teams" had only a single person, but as they signed up, we didn't know what to expect, so we called them teams anyway.

Adult Team One:
Peter Church

Adult Team Two:
Mr. Winston
Coach John Roper

Adult Team Three:
Maggie Tetley
Elizabeth White

Adult Team Four:
Roy Popper

Adult Team Five:
Roy Williams

Adult Team Six:
Bill Arquette

Adult Team Seven:
Buster Grimes

Peter Church taught math and geometry. Since Jack liked math and, in fact, seemed to have a personality much like Mr. Church, they were good friends. Mr. Church signed up out of this friendship.

Mr. Winston taught shop and agriculture. His stiffly upright personality makes it impossible for anyone to remember his first name. So far as we knew, it was Mister. John Roper was the coach.

They chipped in just out of a sense of duty to support any extracurricular activity.

Maggie Tetley was the band director, and Mrs. White taught High School English. Both liked Jack and Eli, and both were charmed by the unusual, clever idea of the hunt.

Roy Popper, Roy Williams and Bill Arquette all went to the same church as Jack and I did. They chipped in based on the church friendship and their long acquaintance with the Stonecinphers. Mr. Arquette was the county highway engineer, and he had given Eli a summer job to earn some spending money for college, so that formed another connection.

I'm not sure of Buster Grimes' interest in the hunt. I guess he had some business relation to Jack's father.

In the end, most of the adults didn't participate other than to pay for their clues. One adult, however, had already played a crucial role in the hunt even though he didn't know it.

## The game begins

Most of us arrived at school unusually early on Friday. A crowd gathered in the study hall, and I could pick out the teams by the clustering and whispered exchanges. Jack showed up only about ten minutes before the first bell and established a place of business at the end of a study table. We queued up with a little bumping and vying for position and purchased our first clue. It was on letter-size heavy paper and folded horizontally twice, just as one would fold it before placing it in a business-size envelope. After determining that only our team could see it, we broke an old-fashioned wax seal and unfolded the paper. Here is what we saw.

unset and evening star, and
one clear call for me

September 2, 1955  Clue 1

The text filled the center third of the paper between the first and second fold. I reproduce the text here very easily using a word processor on a PC and having a choice of almost limitless fonts and sizes. In 1955, it was nearly impossible to produce such a document without professional printing equipment. Like the original announcement, the clue had been produced on a mimeograph machine. The text was printed in large Roman typeface except for the initial letter that employed some very ornate, old-fashioned style. Since Jack didn't have a typewriter that could produce such large letters nor the fancy first letter, he carefully engraved the entire text on the mimeograph stencil by hand.

What did it mean?

I recognized the text immediately as the first line of a hymn from our church hymnal. The first line of the clue also served as the title of the hymn; Kavanaugh knew its source as a poem by Alfred Lord Tennyson called *Crossing the Bar*. Now Kavanaugh was not a great expert on dead English poets, but he fervently read Classics comic books. These wonderful comic books presented classic works of literature. Thus, we learned stories from Alexandre Dumas, Edgar Allen Poe, Herman Melville, and other authors of whom, otherwise, we would have known nothing until college literature classes. Tennyson had come to Kavanaugh's attention as he savored an illustrated version of the bloody poem, Charge of the Light Brigade. Impressed enough by the vision of military glory, he followed up with the Compton's Encyclopedia that rested on the bottom shelf of a lawyer's bookcase in our living room just below the complete works of Alexandre Dumas and other leather-bound classics which we never read since they had no pictures.

Of course, the hymnal gave credit to Tennyson with a small-type, "words by A. Tennyson" at the top of the page, but we would never have read the credit if it were not for the intense boredom that an hour-long sermon can produce. The text of the beautiful poem is as follows.

> Sunset and evening star,
> And one clear call for me!
> And may there be no moaning of the bar,
> When I put out to sea,
> But such a tide as moving seems asleep,

# The Sipsey Swamp Stories

Too full for sound and foam,
When that which drew from out the boundless deep
Turns again home.

Twilight and evening bell,
And after that the dark!
And may there be no sadness of farewell,
When I embark;
For tho' from out our bourne of Time and Place
The flood may bear me far,
I hope to see my Pilot face to face
When I have crossed the bar.

We could make out some of the meaning and by asking around, consulting Compton's Encyclopedia, and for a much fuller explanation, the Encyclopedia Britannica in the High School library, we learned the details.

The author is embarking on a sea journey in the age of sailing ships. His ship is leaving in the evening, and the call for boarding comes at sundown with a "clear call" for the passengers to board. Sailing ships had to choose their departure time carefully. If they attempted to leave as the tide came in, the flow of the river would be against them and make it very difficult. The periodic flooding of the river deposits a sand bar where the river widens into the ocean and makes unusually shallow water there. If the ship attempts to depart at low tide, the bottom of the wooden ship will scrape against the sand bar, and create "the moaning of the bar," a sound said to be extremely mournful. The sound makes the passengers apprehensive, and they thought it was a very bad omen for the beginning of a rather dangerous trip.

Tennyson then describes the fullness and quiet power of the outgoing tide in beautiful phrases. He senses the appropriateness of traveling with the tide as it goes back to its home in the depths of the ocean.

The word bourne puzzled us. The Britannica informed us that it was an archaic form of boundary.

He wishes his friends and family will not miss him or be sad for his departure. He eagerly wants to meet the expert guide who has navigated the ship safely over the bar. But why does he refer to the guide as "pilot" rather than the customary term, "captain"? It happened that my cousin, Fred Duncan, visited us the following Sunday to drop off Aunt Elsa for a visit. Fred had served in the navy during World War II. He explained that while a captain knows how to direct the ship in open water, he can't know every harbor well enough. Instead, when a ship approaches a harbor, a pilot is brought out in a small boat and takes command of the ship while it enters and leaves the harbor. Maybe this rather obscure detail will be important in deciphering the clue.

The encyclopedias mentioned some philosophical meanings, but we decided that wasn't important.

In fact, we rather quickly and nearsightedly focused on the opening phrase and its near repetition in the second verse. The clue actually contained only the opening phrase. Something makes a noise at sundown, a "clear call." We thought of the Cotton Mill. It was the only factory that had a whistle to signal the beginning and end of work, and it sat on the edge of the swamp. The train ran through the swamp and used a whistle to signal its approach to crossings. Thus, the whistle sounded reliably as it followed a daily schedule: another "clear call." Could it be a bird call that is heard only at sunset? How would that be tied to a location? The clues had to point to a location.

As soon as one team's theory about a clue came out, we all tended to latch on to it. All the teams lacked the confidence to ignore an idea that might not be so clever but was just first and trust their own wits. We were afraid that while we worked it out, the other guys might find the marbles and make us look silly and incompetent, so we missed many good interpretations. Since reaching adulthood and working in both academia and industry, I've found this mental cowardice to be very widespread and responsible for many poorly developed ideas and products that come out of our large corporations.

Given the quick identification of the Cotton Mill as a potential reference in the clue, we and most of the other teams searched around it. There were many potential hiding places around the old mill and the abandoned loading docks from days when cotton was transported on the river. Most of the marble hunters thought that we might not simply find the marbles as we followed the purchased clues, but we might find new clues instead. We all appreciated Jack's love of intricacy. No one, however, found the marbles at the Cotton Mill, nor did they find any further clue.

Ayres' blacksmith shop circulated as another possible reference. The hammer rang very sharply and clearly on the anvil. Maybe if you stood at the shop and sighted to the evening star it would give you a bearing to the prize.

Unfortunately, the sighting led away from the swamp. The evening star lies in the western sky and Frog Level lies on the western side of the swamp. The same problem occurred if one sighted the sunset. This sighting would only work if one were already into or across the swamp rather than on the western edge.

A swell of complaint arose before the next Friday came. Just what did it mean that the marbles were hidden "somewhere in the Sipsey Swamp"? Jack had a firm rule that he wouldn't discuss the marble hunt except at the Friday clue sale. He wouldn't answer questions, and he wouldn't discuss the already-distributed clues. If other people started a discussion of the hunt, Jack would sit silently until the topic changed. A few of the kids tried to irritate him enough to make him say something, but he was consistently and totally silent. We put the complaint to Jack on Friday, and he promised to clarify the bounds by the next Friday. Mr. Shoemaker, the principal, also appeared at the clue offering and said that the distribution of the clues disrupted classes due to the commotion just before the first bell and due to the recipients whispering in class all day. Henceforth, he ordered, clues would be issued after school on Friday outside the southernmost front door of the school building. This business out of the way, we purchased the second clue.

Rock of ages cleft for me,
let me hide myself in thee

September 9, 1955  Clue 2

It's hidden in or under a rock. The rock is split or cleft. This was the most popular interpretation. The first clue had been both the first line of a hymn, and it contained the title of the hymn. This one was also the first line and contained the title. Was this structure important? The two hymns so far were universally popular. Might it turn out that all the clues used hymns in the Church of Christ hymnal? If they did, did it mean Jack and Eli had written something in one of our hymnals?

Kavanaugh and I asked our parents if we could ask the congregation to look through the hymnals and alert us to anything that might be a clue. They didn't like the idea. They said church services shouldn't be interrupted by such foolishness. We suggested the request be put in the bulletin that was handed out before church services on Sunday morning. They didn't like that either, but they eventually said we could ask the minister, Brother Flowers. At first, he thought it was funny. Then, the thought of somebody writing in a hymnal or "defacing" it, as he called it, occurred to him. He said we should be ashamed to suggest that one of the Stoneciphers would do such a thing. We gave up on getting the congregation to help, but we spent the services each week looking through all the hymnals in our pew. We would swap them from some other pew to the one we were going to sit in before the services started to get books we hadn't already searched. We found a few examples of "defacing"; we learned that "S.P. loves P.A."; but nothing seemed to relate to the marble hunt.

New searches of the Cotton Mill and Ayres' shop were done specifically looking for large rocks with no success. We began to wonder if we should look at the overall religious theme rather than the specifics of the texts. Maybe it directed us to a church. There weren't many churches in the swamp, but at the supper table my father pointed out two that might be considered to be in the swamp. We didn't have time to search them, but we found out later that Team Three had searched both of them to no avail.

The next Friday after school, as Mr. Shoemaker had decreed, Kavanaugh, Jimmy and I gathered outside the door on the sidewalk. Jack announced a very specific definition for "somewhere in the Sipsey swamp."

"If you stand and place your hand on the marbles, it is possible to get to the edge of the river without crossing a public road."

To numerous requests for more information, he simply repeated the same statement. We paid for clue three and received:

On Jordan's stormy banks I stand

September 16, 1955 Clue 3

It was again the title and first line of a hymn, but we couldn't see what this recurring structure of the clues might mean. We figured that the reference to the Jordan River actually meant the Sipsey. Where was there a rock on the bank of the river? My mother reminded us of a spot where we had picnicked when Kavanaugh and I were young. After a bit of begging and whining, she and my father agreed to take us there on Sunday afternoon. Large rocks are very scarce around Frog Level. Sitting as it does some miles below the last foothills of the Appalachian Mountains, the soil is composed of sand, gravel, and clay that washed down from the mountains over eons. The large boulders stayed up on steeper hillsides to the north. Nevertheless, when we arrived at the picnic spot, there sat one enormous boulder. It was partially buried in the sand and clay of the riverbank so that one had to guess its true size as if it were an iceberg. The top of it was over six feet off the surrounding ground and broad enough to spread out a picnic cloth and provide seating for several diners. Rising so far off the ground, it would take ants quite a while to join the feast. It wasn't hard to see why it had become a favorite picnic spot.

We searched around it for cracks in which the treasure might be hidden. It was too early in the afternoon to see the evening star, but we sighted in the direction we believed it might be at sunset. Along any likely line of sight, we saw only dense forest and a wall of brambles.

As we guessed at the direction in which to make our sighting, my father had mused, "If you want to sight the sunset, the time of year will make a big difference in which way you look." I suppose we had already learned this in school, but it hadn't occurred to us in connection with the marble hunt. That night we laid on the floor of the living room and confirmed from Compton's that, indeed, the direction of either the sunset or the evening star would vary widely with the time of year. To make matters worse, the evening star, actually the planet Venus, became the morning star at other times. Not wanting to abandon one of our favorite clue theories, we decided that Jack assumed the marbles would be found within a few weeks of the start of the hunt, and thus the current direction of the sun and star were the right ones.

The first clue still bothered us. Maybe we'd concentrated too much on the first line. Maybe we should consider the whole poem. Kavanaugh had just started English class with Mrs. White who attended our church. We cornered her after church on Sunday and asked about the poem. What were the "clear call" and the "evening bell"? Were they the same? Did the clear call mean specifically a bell?

"I'm not sure," she replied. "I think it's likely that they used a bell to call the passengers. I know that ships carried a bell to use for various signaling purposes. But let me ask you, why do you think the poem is the text of one of our hymns?"

We looked at each other. We hadn't thought about our approach to Mrs. White turning into a class session. Neither of us wanted to venture a wrong guess. We probably stood there for twenty or thirty seconds while we searched for a way out of this. Finally the very obvious reason worked its way to the surface of Kavanaugh's brain.

"It's used in a hymn because of its religious meaning."

"Very good," she said exactly as if in class. "And what is the religious meaning?"

"It's about dying and going to heaven." I beat Kavanaugh to the answer, motivated by defending my intellectual honor. I hadn't just figured it out; I remembered it from the encyclopedia.

"Very good," she repeated; this time directed to me. "The whole poem is a metaphor about the poet's death. The audience for whom Tennyson wrote the poem knew the mechanics of embarking on a voyage very well. They wouldn't consider the poem a mechanical puzzle. They would have gone directly to the metaphorical meaning."

Neither Kavanaugh nor I could think of any other question, or we were afraid that it would just result in more questions for us.

Sensing we were finished, Mrs. White smiled and said, "You know I'm an adult marble hunter. Since I've shared my understanding of Crossing the Bar with you, let me in on what you've found out."

"Well, we haven't made much progress," Kavanaugh offered. "Lot's of people thought the Cotton Mill's whistle might be the 'clear call.' Nobody seems to have any really good ideas."

"Okay," she said with a broadening smile and a wink. "Let me know if you get a hot lead."

She excused herself, called to her daughter, and they walked to her automobile. Kavanaugh and I just stared at each other.

"What exactly is a metaphor," I finally said. "I know it's saying one thing when you mean something else, but I don't know the details."

"It's when you use one situation to explain another one," he said. After thinking a moment, he continued, "If I said that Frog Level is heaven, I wouldn't mean it is up in the clouds somewhere. I'd mean it was a wonderful place to live." Another pause, "Actually I'd say it's hell."

"Make up your mind!" I got the idea, but I didn't think his example was very clear.

Keeping our conversation with Mrs. White in mind, we turned back to the marble hunt, looking at the metaphorical meaning of the clues. After thinking about this for a while, we realized we had been constructing metaphors all along without knowing it. We had translated "one clear call" to the Cotton Mill whistle without realizing we were making a metaphor. Maybe Jack is constructing a metaphorical system of clues. We have to look at the metaphors in the clues, or maybe Jack is forming his own metaphors. We were rather confused.

We looked at the poem again to understand Tennyson's metaphor. We went back to the encyclopedias to read the stuff we skipped.

The clear call comes at sunset because the day represents the poet's whole life. The voyage represents his transition into the afterlife. No wonder it takes him "from out our bourne of time and place!" Instead of carefully watching the tides, he simply wishes his life will end when it has run its proper course, and he and his family can accept it as the right time: no "moaning of the bar."

Now that we were aware that we made metaphors, we began to make them more far-fetched. We decided that Tennyson's "clear call" is not a bell or a hammer hitting the anvil. It's not anything you can see. It's the radio station! What clearer call than the signal from the tall tower ringing forth from all the radios in town? How could we have missed it? The radio station and tower sat right in the middle of the swamp on the Tuscaloosa highway!

We listened carefully to the chatter about the hunt at school on Monday. We were afraid, of course, somebody else would figure it out or had figured it out and beat us to the radio station. Even though I mentioned it in several casual ways in my conversations with other marble hunters thinking I might elicit some response, no one else seemed to have thought anything about the radio station. We went home after school on Monday and got our oldest beat-up shoes. Mine were way too small and hurt my feet, but we knew that they would be covered in mud when we came home. With a little fib about whether we were actually going into the swamp, we rode our bikes to the radio station. We had to more or less wade out to the tower since it sat in a low, flat marsh from which all the trees had been cleared. The announcer, Buford Sumter, came out and asked what we were doing. The simple explanation, "We're looking for the marbles," elicited a sigh, and he went back in after giving a warning not to touch the tower. Most adults in town had already become accustomed to "hunting for the marbles" being an excuse for seriously bizarre behavior.

On Sunday, when we focused on the radio station, I realized we wouldn't be able to sight the evening star the next day because it would be too early in the afternoon. I sighted the star just as it went down Sunday evening and noted its direction on a small pocket compass. We decided that the most likely first ploy to investigate was to stand at the base of the tower, sight the direction of the evening star, and follow the path out while searching. As soon as we sighted, we knew we had it. The sighting went exactly to a large concrete block to which one of the cables that held up the tower attached. There sat the "rock of ages." In fact, we saw two concrete blocks along the same path, one closer for wires attached to the tower about halfway up, and another one farther out for the wires that held the top of the tower. We ran and fell over briars and each other, splashed mud, and didn't mind any of the trouble. We had found the marbles!

We stopped at the first concrete block. We spontaneously laughed out loud on finding a deep crevice molded into the concrete, a "cleft" as predicted by the "rock of ages" clue. We pulled the weeds and briars out of the way and jerked them loose where they coiled around the guy wires. Okay, it wasn't the first one; it had to be the farther one.

We didn't find the marbles in the cleft of the second anchor block either. We sat on it and discussed what minor miscalculation we had made. We searched both blocks again. We searched the anchor block at the end of each guy wire. The station cabin that contained the transmitter and studios sat up on pilings to keep it above floodwaters. We searched the underside of the station cabin. Then, sad and demoralized, we went home.

With some considerable minimizing of the hazards involved in wading through the snake-infested mush around the tower, we laid out our lament at the supper table that night. It had seemed a sure thing. My father asked about "On Jordan's stormy banks." Had we considered that the sighting might point to a spot on the riverbank? The river was, after all, visible from the radio station. Had we gone that far, he asked. Our spirits buoyed by another tack to take, we planned the next afternoon's adventure. We were so sure of our plan on that first trip that we hadn't invited Jimmy to join us. We wanted the glory for ourselves. We decided to invite him the next day lest he bolt the team and we loose the 33 cents per week.

The three of us arrived at the radio station the next afternoon. Mr. Sumter stuck his head out the door and looked at us. Seeing who it was, he just rolled his eyes, shook his head, and went back in without saying anything. At the tower we sighted along the same direction we had determined for our first search. We identified a large pine tree that marked the intersection of our sight line with the river. More importantly, as we soon found out, the sighting was downstream from the "honey hole."

At that time, the population of the United States was smaller than it is today, and we didn't get in each other's way so easily. We were also blissfully ignorant of what we now call environmental issues. Thus, it was considered sensible to pipe the municipal sewage down the side of the Tuscaloosa highway and dump it into the river. The spot where the sewer pipe entered the river had a distinctive aroma that had earned it the humorous euphemism, "honey hole." The drinking water for Frog Level was drawn about two hundred yards upstream, and no one made use of the river that required sanitary conditions for many miles downstream.

Frog Level fishermen held sharply divided opinions about fishing the honey hole. On the one hand, no other place could compare for the population density and size of the catfish that could be caught. On the other hand, if a person had any qualms about the purity of his food or even a lingering thought of where it came from, it just wasn't an acceptable place to fish. Each fisherman had to come down on one side or the other of this issue.

To avoid the mud, we biked back up the highway to the east side of the river. We parked the bikes and walked along or near the riverbank until we found our target pine tree. It stood about equal distances downstream from the honey hole and upstream from the railroad trestle. We hunted for as long as we could stand the stench. Nothing.

We went back another afternoon by walking along the railroad to the trestle. Using it as a bridge we searched both sides of the river and especially the concrete abutments of the trestle, thinking that they might be considered the "rock of ages." Nothing.

On Friday we got clue number four.

Far and near the fields are teeming
with the waves of ripened grain

September 23, 1955  Clue 4

Well, we no longer had any doubt about the theme: every clue was the first line—not the title—of a hymn. Why? We revived the idea that the marbles were hidden at a church. We ruled out the Hopewell Church and Bethlehem Church, both up the Winfield highway, because they were on the wrong side of a road separating them from the river; and so, they didn't meet Jack's definition of "in the swamp." My father knew of Rehobeth Church, just north of the Townley road that qualified. The old Shirley Cemetery was near there, and it seemed to qualify. Thus, we had two cemeteries to search. We could ride our bikes to both of them, but they were a long ride away. We coaxed our parents into another Sunday afternoon trip that ended with no marbles and a serious inquiry by our parents as to whether we didn't have anything better to do.

We puzzled over the content of the clue, but other than the suggestion that the marbles were hidden in a cultivated field, we could see nothing. You might correctly surmise we had no shortage of cultivated fields. The next Friday brought clue number five.

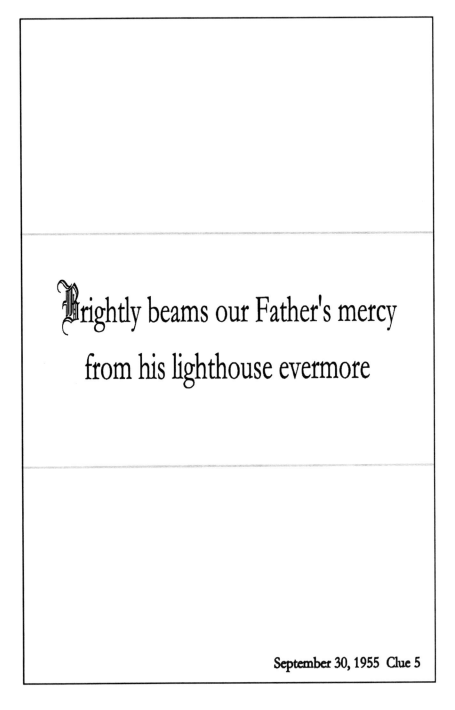

Brightly beams our Father's mercy
from his lighthouse evermore

September 30, 1955 Clue 5

The beams from our metaphorical lighthouse—the radio station—immediately came to mind. The few teams that had not searched the radio station by now did so. We searched again. We looked for a cultivated field. It was one of the few places that, because of its location in the depths of the swamp, had no cultivated fields.

## We've found it!

Even though it was getting late in the fall, the weather hadn't turned uniformly cold yet. We commonly went trick or treating on Halloween in our shirtsleeves or whatever flimsy costume we assembled. As I rode to school the next Friday morning, the sun radiated the yellow tinge that announces summer is over, but it was still good to be outdoors.

I moped through school doodling clue excerpts on my papers and, when that got dull, tried drawing radio receiver circuits from memory. I would try writing down mathematical relationships of the circuit components based on my education from the Amateur Radio Relay League Handbook. If some class activity seemed about to require my attention, I would pause until it blew over and then go back to doodling. Thus, I whiled the day away until the end of seventh period and time for a new clue. Maybe there would be some exciting exploring tomorrow. Kavanaugh worked at the grocery store on Saturday, but I could reconnoiter, and he could join me in the hunt on Sunday afternoon after church.

I gathered the books I needed from my locker, walked past the library with a nod and "bye" to Mr. Webster, and out the south front door. Most of the purchasers were already there, and Miles Starett was handing Jack his dollar bill. I put down my books and fished in my pocket for the four quarters I had collected from our "clue fund" that we kept in one of Kavanaugh's cigar boxes.

The clue for this week was:

Down in the valley with my savior I would go, where the flowers are blooming and the sweet waters flow

October 7, 1955  Clue 6

I just finished the purchase and read through the clue maybe twice when someone said, "honey hole." I think it had been said already a few times before I noticed it because as I looked up, everyone else was looking around, and the phrase "honey hole" echoed from one person to another.

"It's the honey hole," yelled Bob Sargent just as I got it. The "sweet waters" in the clue referred to the honey hole. I felt excitement swell up in my chest and a flood of thoughts clamored in my head.

The honey hole was just fifty yards upstream from where we began our search when we sighted from the radio-station tower to the evening star. Did we sight the star badly enough to be off by fifty yards? Maybe. In any case, when we started from the railroad, we hadn't gone as far upstream as the honey hole because of the smell. I remembered looking upriver and seeing the large concrete block that anchored the end of the sewage pipe. When we walked down from the Tuscaloosa highway, we had walked in the part cleared for the radio station tower rather than right on the riverbank, and we were on the opposite side of the river. We missed the actual honey hole.

"Oh crud, it's going to be too late to find it before these clowns," I thought. "If I go for Kavanaugh and Jimmy, the others may already have found it before we get there."

"Where the flowers are blooming? What does that mean?"

Miles Starett bolted as soon as most of the group had fixed on the idea of the honey hole. He had gone into the school to call his teammate, Paul, and now reappeared around the north corner on his bike, headed south toward the Tuscaloosa highway. This visible threat galvanized the rest of us into action. I grabbed my books and ran for the bike shed between the main school building and the vocational agriculture building. Realizing that the books would slow me down, I dumped them behind a dense shrub bush, grabbed my bike, threw a leg over, and headed down the sidewalk in front of the school looking to see if Miles was still in sight. He wasn't.

It occurred to me then that no one from Team Three had been in the group. Had they already collected their clue, or were they just going to miss out on the hunt? Oh boy, Monty would be really mad!

Alastair breezed past me on his Cushman motor scooter. We might call it a moped today but it lacked any of the curved metal on modern bikes. It had a welded frame of metal tubes but no covering except crude fenders to catch the mud splashed by the wheels. The tires were small and fat, and a flat padded wooden board on top of the engine served as a seat. The Briggs and Stratton engine was indistinguishable from the one on the school lawnmower. It didn't go very fast, but much faster than our heavy, bulky Schwinn bicycles. I remembered with a wince that Paul Carpenter also had a motor scooter.

To get to the honey hole, we had to ride down the road that passed in front of the National Guard armory until it ran into the Tuscaloosa highway, turn left on the highway, and ride about a mile to the river. Just before the bridge, a dirt road turned off. Maybe it's better described as a path, since it was nothing more than two bare ruts where the maintenance truck came down to the sewer outlet for inspections. The dirt path went about a hundred yards along the river and ended in a clearing where the truck could turn around. Somebody apparently mowed the grass pretty regularly. The sewer pipe laid buried another maybe twenty yards farther south at the end of the clearing until the ground began to slope down to the river, and then it was encased in a concrete shell. A corrugated steel pipe emerged from the concrete and made a forty-five degree dive into the water.

Alastair arrived first, then Miles, Paul, and Bob Sargent, and then I arrived. Everyone combed the bushes around the outlet pipe and climbed over the concrete. Alastair ran off toward the bridge and across it to the other side. Seeing him go, the rest of us realized we had simply assumed that the marbles were hidden on the side of the river where the pipe was. Jimmy, Kavanaugh, and I had already searched the other side farther down, so I decided to stick near the pipe.

Connie Jackson arrived on her bike and immediately began pestering me about what had happened so far. I tried to simply walk away, but she followed me. I told her to search somewhere else but she moved off only a short distance and continued to talk. I just began to ignore her.

I'm sure you all have experienced the loudness of silence. After a loud noise has persisted for a long time, the absence of that noise attracts our attention more than if the volume were doubled. Thus, when Connie's continuous commentary ended abruptly, I lifted my head from the bushes and turned to find Connie and see why she had fallen so conspicuously silent. She stood about ten feet away, staring out across the river.

There it was. A red leather bag hung nearly in the middle of the river on a limb of a giant oak tree. It hung about three feet above the water.

The others noticed us staring, and soon the whole group was transfixed. BJ arrived on her bike. Alastair came back from the other side of the river. Finally, the spell broke, and huddles formed for each team to make plans. It was clear that none of us could get the bag without some plan and paraphernalia to accomplish it.

BJ and Connie whispered; Paul and Miles huddled. Bob suggested that he, Alastair, and I combine since we were each the lone members of our teams. After a short moment of contemplation, we both emphatically declined.

Bob stared out at the bag for about another minute, then jumped on his bike and furiously pedaled away. BJ and Connie left on their bikes. Fearing that I was losing valuable time, I hopped on my bike and headed home while I tried to come up with a plan. Paul, Miles, and Alastair were the only ones left at the river, not in any hurry because they had motor scooters.

I formed a plan—a pretty good one, I thought—and worried about it until I had turned onto Ayres Street and headed North past the National Guard armory. Since I couldn't think of any better ideas, my mind relaxed and began to prematurely enjoy the glories of winning. I judged that with all the publicity and gossip surrounding the hunt, we could expect a front-page picture in the Frog Level Times. My friend, Edison Wallace, would certainly come to me for an account of the climax of the great marble hunt. Jimmy, Kavanaugh, and I would be lined up, and I would be holding the marble bag. I'd let Kavanaugh have most of the quotes. "According to Kavanaugh Wiggins, the competition has been stiff since the beginning of the contest. 'We've been pretty close since we figured out the radio station connection,' he said." No, not that phrase because the hiding place really didn't have anything to do with the radio station, it just happened to be close. Or did it? Were we right all along but just sighted the evening star sloppily? I turned the corner at the Grammar School onto Temple Avenue.

"Wendell Wiggins applied his considerable knowledge of physics to fabricate the elaborate plan knowing his older brother's strength and athletic ability would pull it off." I liked that one. We had to give Jimmy some of the credit. I pondered it past the church and the cotton field. "Jimmy Petersen contributed one-third of the Wiggins' team finances." We'd have to do better than that, but now I swung into the driveway and hopped off the bike while still moving.

I found Kavanaugh in the house getting his homework minimally out of the way so he could do something more interesting.

"We've found it. It's in a red bag hanging on an oak-tree limb over the river. Everybody's trying to reach it. We've got to hurry, now. I've got a plan. I'll get what we need; you get Jimmy."

"Where is it?" Kavanaugh asked.

"On a limb out over the river; just upstream from the honey hole. Hurry!"

"In a red bag?" he asked, directed as much to himself as to me.

"If you don't move now, it'll be too late. You can admire the bag tomorrow."

"What's your plan?" Kavanaugh yelled at me as I ran out of the bedroom headed to the garage.

"What's going on?" Mother greeted me as I came through the family room. "Marble business, I suppose?"

"We were right! It's down by the radio station. Toward the river. Several teams are after it. We have to hurry."

I used the got-to-hurry excuse to avoid going into more detail. I didn't care to paint a clearer picture of the bag hanging out over a halfigator-infested river surrounded by water moccasins hiding in the bushes just a few feet from the honey hole.

In the garage, I found the ball of nylon cord and two meat hooks needed to execute my plan. I had made the plan by scanning a mental image of our garage as I rode home and selecting from the items at hand. The hooks were left over from some renovation of the meat department at my father's store, and he brought them home with the idea of using them in dressing a deer carcass. The origin of the nylon cord was still more odd.

Mother had designed an addition to our house, adding on two bedrooms and a bathroom, and turning what had been a bedroom into the new have-to-have for modern American families—a family room. We would no longer sit in a central hallway next to the woodstove, listening to the radio; we would sit in our spacious, centrally heated family room, watching TV. Yes, television. Not long after the new family room was ready, we got our first television.

Mother needed curtains for her new bedroom. What better place to find them than the World War II surplus I've already mentioned. But, bedroom curtains? Why would the army have surplus bedroom curtains? They didn't, but Mother found something else that she knew would do the job.

She found an ad in some magazine for surplus parachutes. She thought the fine, strong, nylon fabric would be ideal for curtains, and such fabric was hard to find in normal outlets.

Two parachutes arrived via parcel post. Mother carefully dissected their seams to yield smooth, translucent, cream-colored panels. The cords, of which there were maybe twenty per parachute, and each about ten feet long, she tied together and wound into a ball. A few lengths had been used to tie up pole beans, but they seemed too fine for that purpose, so they sat in the garage waiting for this glorious moment when they would enable us to win the marble hunt!

While I gathered the materials, Jimmy and Kavanaugh left for the honey hole. As I loaded the cord and hooks into my bike basket, Mother came out the back door and looked skeptically at the preparations. I was afraid she was going to slow me down by asking a lot of questions, but after eyeing me for a moment, she said, "I'll finish my chores and come down to see what you're doing."

When I arrived back at the river, Donis, Billy Wayne, and Alastair had shown up with a logging rope and a ball of string. After overhearing their plans that involved Alastair going across the river, Jimmy and Kavanaugh were guarding the path back to the road so he couldn't go up to the bridge and cross to the opposite side.

Bob Sargent soon arrived with a handsaw. We didn't pay much attention to him since he was still the only member of his team present. Donis asked, "What's the saw for?" He gave no answer, and we all moved on to our business.

I gathered with Jimmy and Kavanaugh and began to lay out our plan. While we were huddling, Alastair made a dash by us and escaped. He headed up to the bridge and across to the opposite side carrying the ball of string his team had brought.

BJ, Penny, and Connie arrived next with BJ's father in a pickup truck and a flat-bottom bass boat in tow. They were greeted with calls of, "No fair! Adults can't hunt! What'd you expect from girls?"

BJ's father leaned over and exchanged a few words with her, apparently about the reception they were getting. After that, he seemed determined to ignore us and helped the girls get their stuff out of the truck. Connie carried a paddle, Penny had some towels, and BJ carried a pair of rubber boots. Then BJ's father began to look for a place to put the boat in the river.

Miles and Paul came back on Paul's motor scooter with some loops of rope, a roughly twelve-foot-long two-by-four board, and a stick about three feet long that appeared to be a two-by-four cut lengthwise. Paul wore swim trunks. I was amazed they had been able to ride the scooter with the long board. I would've loved to see them come through town.

We were seriously distracted by the commotion made by the other teams, and we tried to guess their plans so we could thwart them. We continuously urged each other to get back to work, but none of us could resist watching the others. Kavanaugh headed up to the bridge on foot just as Alastair had done a few minutes earlier to cross over carrying the parachute cord.

Bob Sargent began to pick a fight with Miles and Paul. He called them several insulting or obscene names. He slapped at Miles and grabbed the rear of Paul's swim trunks to pull them down. This dastardly move earned him a serious kick aimed at his belly but he deflected it off to one side and it only knocked a bit of air out of him. While they were arguing and fighting, Jimmy grabbed their rope unobserved and threw it into a clump of bushes.

"Atta boy, Jimmy," I yelled to him. "That ought to keep 'em busy a while."

BJ's father had found the spot he wanted and began to back the truck up toward the bridge. The chosen spot was ideal for launching a boat and doubtless had been used periodically for that purpose. It suited me too, since it would take a few minutes for the girls to get back downstream after it was in the water.

Across the river, Kavanaugh taunted Alastair and managed to trip him once. Then he turned to our plan and left him to his. Alastair found an oblong rock about the size of his fist and began to tie the string around it. Once he secured a knot, he attempted to throw the rock across the river. He had, however, failed to unwind enough string, and the momentum of the rock lifted the entire ball of string and carried it into the edge of the river. He had to wade into the river and took quite a while retrieving it and untangling it from some weeds. Meanwhile, Kavanaugh found a stick about an inch in diameter and about two feet in length. He tied the parachute cord around the center of the stick, picked just the right spot and began to form neatly stacked loops of cord at his feet. Alastair climbed back up from the riverbank just as Kavanaugh finished his arrangements.

"I don't mind if you watch, Alastair. I'll show you an old trick I learned in the Philippines," Kavanaugh crooned to him, softly, and with the most obvious condescension he could muster. "Maybe you'll get it right next time."

Kavanaugh and I used the "trick I learned in the Philippines" as a general introduction to any episode of showing off. We picked it up from my cousin Leonard who had flown cargo planes in the Pacific during World War II and used it for the same purpose.

Kavanaugh laid the cord over his extended left arm to keep it clear of his legs. Then he arched his right arm back as if holding a football and slung the stick across the river. The stick crossed the river easily, pulling the parachute cord behind it and went maybe ten feet over my head. After it hit the ground, the nylon floated down gently into my open hand.

Keenly aware that most everyone was watching, I turned around to the audience upstream and bowed. "Thank you, thank you. Let's hear a big round of applause for Kavanaugh the Great." No applause.

We finally noticed Bob up in the large oak tree from which the red bag hung with his handsaw, and he began to inch out the limb that held the red bag. The likely outcome of his now-clear plan alarmed us. Jimmy began to talk him down. He argued to Bob that if he cut off the limb, then either someone else would beat him to the bag, a halfigator would grab it, it would float off down the river, or it would sink.

Alastair required two more tries before he got his string across the river. When Donis finally retrieved it from the briars on our side, he tied it to the logging rope, and Alastair began to pull the rope back to his side of the river.

The boat was in the water by then, and the girls loaded up. They put the towels and paddle in the boat, BJ's father pushed the boat in as far as he could while leaving a portion of the bow on shore for the girls to step in. BJ went first, then Penny, and finally Connie. This arrangement put BJ in the rear, Penny in the middle and Connie in the front. BJ's father pushed the boat off the riverbank and it slowly pivoted around and began to move downstream.

As soon as Alastair had pulled one end of the logging rope to his bank, he located a pine tree and tied the rope around it. On our side Donis located a sweet gum tree about twenty feet back from the river and roughly ten feet downstream from the large oak. It had suffered from living in the shade of the oak and was gnarled with signs that a deer had chosen it for a scratching post, and it forked only about two feet off the ground. I still wasn't sure what Donis and his team were up to, but I wondered if the small sweet gum would withstand a strong pull on the logging rope. Donis chose it so that the rope passed almost exactly under the red bag. I'd already spotted the gum tree as just the spot I wanted to occupy. I thought about fighting

Donis for the spot but decided against it, since his rope didn't interfere with our plan, and the other teams were making progress too fast to allow any wasted time.

Finally, Miles and Paul found their rope in the thicket where Jimmy had thrown it. They moved upstream about ten yards with their paraphernalia and looked for a clear opening into the river. After a lot of discussion, Paul took a long piece of the rope and began trying to throw it over a limb of another oak tree on the upstream side. He got it over about ten feet from the bank. They tried to catch the dangling end with the long two-by-four they brought, but the lumber was too heavy for them to hold it up from just the end. Miles found a long, skinny limb, and using it, they pulled the dangling end of the rope back to them.

Miles tied it around Paul's waist, and he tried several positions for cinching the split two-by-four under the rope. He finally seemed happy with an arrangement that looped the rope twice around the stick and secured it across his body well below his arms. Paul waded into the river.

The plan that Miles and Paul had hatched was clearly the most complicated of all. I didn't figure it out until the competition was nearly done.

They planned that Miles would hold one end of the rope. It went from his hand out over the limb and down to Paul's waist. This arrangement allowed Miles to pull almost directly upriver on Paul, who would swim downstream while Miles spooled out rope. When he was directly under the bag, Miles would pull on the rope just enough to keep him from floating on downstream while he used the short stick he carried to dislodge the bag from where it hung. It was complicated, but it just might work.

The girls were drifting along now, but the Sipsey favored the rest of us with its slow, lazy pace. It appeared they hadn't worked out the details of paddling, so they experimented and heatedly discussed the results of each attempt with vigorous arm waving and lots of "Give it to me" or "Let me try it."

I took up a position just to the river side of the gum tree and on the upstream side of the logging rope that was now pulled tightly across the river. I pulled a length of nylon cord that I judged to be well over half the distance to Kavanaugh and let it pile at my feet. Kavanaugh held the other end of the cord on his side, and the unused ball lay at his feet. I tied the meat hooks onto the parachute cord and motioned to Kavanaugh to pull it back across until the hooks were lined up with the red bag. We would move the hooks until one of them snagged the bag strap, and then I would haul it in. Having now seen something of each of the other plans, I felt quite sure that success for us waited only minutes away. Really, we just had to get the bag before the girls got to it.

Bob continued to inch out the limb with the handsaw. Jimmy helped me keep the cord untangled but spent the remainder of his time trying to convince Bob to stop his advance out the limb. It wasn't working. I decided to try.

"You idiot, the bag is full of marbles. It's heavy. It'll sink and none of us will get them!" I yelled as loud as I could, not entirely to get his attention but also in the hope that some of the others would begin to pressure or at least distract Bob. He paused for maybe ten seconds and then continued along the limb. It shook more and more with each lift and stretch of his body.

Billy Wayne began to take off his clothes. Everyone stopped and stared. All the action halted at this unexpected indecency. Throwing his shirt over a bush, he unzipped to take off his pants.

Jimmy: "There's girls here you dope."

Billy Wayne: "I don't care."

Miles: "Jeez, be decent."

Donis: "My God, you're crazy."

Billy Wayne: "I don't care."

Finally with nothing on but his undershorts, and with everybody, including the three girls, staring at him, he waded into the river and grabbed the logging rope.

Penny still tried to figure out the paddle. She kept turning the boat sideways, backwards, perfectly aligned down the river, but no position lasted for more than a few seconds. Finally getting a lucky stroke, she pulled even with Paul to cut him off from the red bag. She pushed the end of the paddle into Paul's ribs and pushed him farther toward the bank. "Lay off, Penny," he sputtered as he turned to the boat and pushed the paddle away.

"Can't take it, huh?"

"Lay off, I said!"

Connie piped up in the standard taunting tune, "Prissy, sissy, missy. Paul is pitchin' a hissy!"

Penny and BJ joined in the chant. Bob had just joined in as well when Paul grabbed the end of the paddle and pulled it out of Penny's hand. He tucked it under his arms along side the split two-by-four and began to swim again. The boat fell behind Paul's steady advance, and he would soon find clearance to cut in front of it. With no paddle and no idea how to cope with this turn of events, Penny began to cry.

Billy Wayne waded out until his feet left the bottom. He grabbed the rope and it sank into the water. As he pulled himself out toward the middle of the river, the current pulled him farther downstream. It soon became clear that he would be well away from the bag by the time he got out to it, and the rope was too far down in the water, so Donis urged him back to the riverbank so they could raise it, move it upstream, make it tighter, and try again.

Bob had been slowed down considerably by watching the fight between Paul and Penny and the failure of Billy Wayne's first attempt, but now he began to inch out the limb again. The limb sagged noticeably so that the bag, rather than its original three feet above the water, now hung only two feet above it.

Kavanaugh steadily pulled the cord back to bring a meat hook to the bag strap. I kept a steady tension on the cord to keep the hooks up. We had only about twenty feet to go, but we were still learning to coordinate with each other. Nobody else was close. We'd pretty much written off Bob as a nuisance, Donis' team busily moved their rope, and Paul and the girls remained about ten feet upstream. I almost began to relax. I yelled across to Kavanaugh, "Lash LaRue couldn't do it better. Reel it in, Red Ryder!" I have no idea what I meant by that, but it just came out because I was so excited.

Donis had untied their rope from the gum tree and found another one about five feet upstream but almost twenty feet farther back. After he tied it, he decided it was not far enough upstream, and he untied it again and headed to the trunk of the oak tree.

The girls had figured out how to paddle with their hands and were all leaning over the sides of the boat and beginning to make headway. Penny had dried up to a sniffle when she spied Billy Wayne pulling on the logging rope in his shorts. She broke out anew into a bawl. BJ slapped her on the side of her head. "Shut up and paddle," she ordered.

Paul had pulled considerably ahead of the boat and tried to get around the front of it and lined up with the bag. A serious problem became apparent when he made little headway: the rope looped around the bank side of the boat and wouldn't slide under it. In fact, as he tried to swim to the center of the river, he was carrying the boat with him. As I watched, it reminded me of when I stood on the log and the fish pulled me away from shore, and I laughed to myself. Paul stopped swimming, and he and Miles shouted ideas to each other. They agreed that Miles would let the rope go slack. Paul would dive and pull hard on the rope to slide it free.

It worked. The rope slipped partway under the boat. Back on the surface they both pulled hard at the same time to get it out from under the boat. Of course the tension also pulled Paul back up the river. To stop himself, he put his hand up and pushed on the front of the boat. His push propelled the boat backwards and stopped him, and it also freed the rope. It made the girls very unhappy because they lost a good five feet of progress, were spinning around, and believed they had almost been tipped over.

Billy Wayne was making headway again pulling hand over hand along the logging rope.

With all three girls paddling, they passed Paul again, although he was just a few feet short of the bag. Connie stood up in the front of the boat as they neared the logging rope, and BJ passed her a hunting knife that we hadn't seen before. She grabbed the rope and, with a broad smile on her face, unceremoniously cut it. Since he was unprepared for the instant slack, Billy Wayne went under. He came up sputtering words I won't record, and the rest of us launched a loud cheer. Even better for us, he was right in Paul's path.

Kavanaugh and I made a first attempt to snare the straps of the bag, but we missed, and we realized that judging the alignment of the hooks would be difficult. Another problem also appeared; I had put the hooks on the cord backward so that instead of the point facing upstream toward the bag, it faced away. We needed to lower the parachute cord, pass it under the bag, and come up on the upstream side.

Bob now had climbed out on the limb until the bag hung only about one foot above the water. This made it more difficult to move the hooks under it but we managed and began to move in for another try at snagging it.

No sooner had we begun to close in than we realized that Connie now intended to cut our cord just as she had cut the logging rope. As she reached for the rope I jumped up on the fork of the gum tree and lifted the cord as high as I could reach. Kavanaugh lifted his side as well, and Connie couldn't reach our cord. I held onto the gum tree while the front of the boat passed under our cord.

If I waited until the boat had passed completely under it, Connie would get the bag before we could get it. She would already have it except that they were too close to my side of the river. They needed to move toward the center of the river by about three feet. I jumped down from the gum tree and prepared for another try, but as Connie prepared to grab the bag, she passed the knife to BJ in the rear of the boat, who stood up and grabbed our cord. She turned to me and grinned from ear to ear.

"No, please!" I pleaded. "I'll do your homework. I'll buy a raffle ticket from you!" "Please BJ, you're too nice to do it."

"Am I? Nah!" and she raised the knife.

At the same moment, in an attempt to pull the boat backwards, away from the marbles, Paul grabbed the rear of the boat and pulled down hard. BJ vaulted backward in an Olympic-quality back-flip—a perfect ten—and into the water behind Paul.

The knife went into the river with her, so our cord appeared to be safe now. BJ's backflip pushed the boat downstream of the bag, but it spun around so that Connie had to come back upstream only a few feet to get the bag.

Kavanaugh and I had one last chance to get it. With no time to spare, I moved a few steps downstream bringing the cord into contact with the red hand straps. Kavanaugh pulled the cord until the nearest meat hook pressed against the strap and pulled it about a foot farther from Connie and possibly out of reach. We held the position in hope she would drift out of reach and we could make the final snag.

The sound of Bob sawing on the limb had been missed in all the commotion and it was actually hard to hear with BJ screaming and her father yelling back, "Swim Baby, swim for Daddy!"

Crack!!! The limb broke and fell into the water. Paul and the boat had just drifted downstream enough to be missed by the falling limb except for the outer twigs and leaves. The red bag landed about three feet to the left side of the boat. Penny stared at it but didn't make the slightest move. She seemed to be simply frozen by the deluge of events around her. Connie leaned over and reached for it, but on her first attempt, she splashed her hand in about a foot short of the bag. Preparing for a second try, she raised up and braced one hand on the edge of the boat.

Paul had been holding on to the rear of the boat and watching to see if BJ really needed help. Deciding that she was making no headway towards the riverbank, he kicked off the boat to help her. This second lurch occurred just as Connie extended herself out for her second try at the bag, and it sent her center of gravity over the edge, rapidly followed by the rest of her. Connie was a good swimmer. We all knew that, so no one worried about her. Paul's push off the boat and Connie's fall made it spin around and nudge the red bag. The boat, the bag, the limb, and Penny continued to float down the river. The flotilla carried the parachute cord with it, unnoticed by us in all the commotion.

"Hey, Connie," Bob called from up on the limb. "Do you see the halfigator behind you?"

Connie screamed and flailed in the water. Paul grabbed BJ and began to push her toward shore and her father, who had waded into the water by now.

"Where is it? Where is it?" Connie yelled.

"Behind you! It's going around your left side! Pull in your arm! Swim! Swim! Go right! Go right! Oh, jeez, did he get you? Did he get you? Swim! Swim!"

The rest of us had stopped whatever we were doing, and we were staring at the Connie-Bob-halfigator emergency. We all soon figured out that Bob made up the halfigator, so one by one we broke out laughing. I think the sound of laughter eventually gave away his joke to Connie. She made no sound, no protest; she simply began to paddle normally.

Then we turned our attention back down the river in time to see Penny go around the bend holding the red bag in her lap with a strange look on her face.

**Enjoying the prize**

Mother arrived just about the time that Connie, BJ, and Paul were climbing out of the river. Billy Wayne had his pants back on, but the water from his undershorts soaked visibly through them. I don't think she realized that Penny had disappeared down the river. Seeing me dry on the shore, and following my waving to see Kavanaugh on the opposite shore, she displayed no great alarm at the situation. She did, however, seem to have a clear skepticism about the lack of good sense being displayed by all.

We explained briefly about the red bag and what happened to it. Mr. Custer clearly didn't like the outcome of events. We could see in his face that he would not have supplied the county-owned boat if he had known what was going to happen. He announced to us all that it would be no problem picking up Penny at the railroad trestle and excused himself to get on with the rescue. He hurried Connie and BJ into the truck and headed out to get Penny.

Mother wanted an explanation about why Billy Wayne's pants were wet and why Paul was in swim trunks and BJ and Connie were soaked. Where was her parachute cord? We explained as briefly as we could get away with. She almost laughed a couple of times, but at least pretended to be mad about losing the parachute cord.

"So the girls got the marbles, eh?" she asked rhetorically. She didn't seem to share our disgust about losing them.

Kavanaugh, Jimmy, and I rode home slowly on our bikes discussing the afternoon's events and cursing our luck. We had come so close. If only I had put the hooks on the cord correctly. If only we had done this or done that. If only... if only.

We went over it in detail at supper. We began to see the humor in the events a little more clearly. We told about Bob Sargent with a bit of exaggeration and mocking. We let slip that Billy Wayne had stripped down to his undershorts. We wondered out loud about how many marbles were in the bag.

Later, as I lay awake in bed going over the events, I pictured the limb cracking and falling into the river. I smiled to myself as I pictured Paul, BJ, and Connie splashing around and all the shouting that went on. It had really been a moment of bedlam. While I tried to remember just why I hadn't seen Penny pick up the bag, I finally focused on what seemed to be a serious mystery. "Kavanaugh, it didn't sink. The bag didn't sink!" But he was already asleep.

Kavanaugh had to work at the grocery store the next day. I went over to Jimmy's house to rehash everything. I pointed out that the bag didn't sink. I made the guess that Jack sealed it somehow to keep the water out. We were dying to know about the contents, but I didn't know any of the girls well enough to just show up at her house. Any boy in school, no problem; but a girl? That was a much more formal issue. In the afternoon, Jimmy went by Connie's anyway and brought back the news.

"The bag was empty. No marbles. Not a one. Nothing."

The bag had turned out to be a red ladies' purse. It was completely empty except for a single water-stained, mildewed letter. It said:

> My dear Sister Olive,
>
> We could no more go to Birmingham
> together unaccompanied than we could go to
> Venice. All the work that was set before us

has been accomplished.

Rev. Hollingsworth is a good and strong
Christian man.

Your brother in Christ,
Cliff


We had, of course, no Internet then. We did, however, have a
telephone system, and it worked, or I should say, was worked by the
local ladies with an efficiency that would have shamed the FBI. In
less than forty-eight hours they determined that the purse had
belonged to Mrs. Vera Olive. Her daughter, Melba Newton,
confirmed it was her bag from the description she was given.

Mrs. Olive had died about two years earlier. She lived with her
daughter, Melba, near Hubbertville on the family farm. After she
died, Melba moved many of her mother's belongings into a storage
shed that earlier had been a chicken house. It sat behind the main
house on the edge of a field usually planted in corn. A flood the
previous year rose higher than any seen in several decades, and the
water came over two feet into the chicken house and carried away
many of the deceased Mrs.Olive's belongings.

Cliff, it seems, was the Reverend Clifton Roberts. Rev. Roberts had
been minister of a Baptist church on the Covin road for many years
before his retirement two years ago. Mrs. Olive and her husband
were members of Rev. Roberts' congregation before they bought the
farm near Hubbertville and moved there.

What did the letter mean? Some of the phrases were obvious enough.
"We could no more go to Birmingham together unaccompanied,"
pretty clearly referred to the custom that no unrelated man and
woman less than around thirty years different in age could ride
together unless accompanied by another woman, preferably the
man's wife. This seems strange today, but it was rigidly enforced in
Frog Level then.

I remember particularly that Christine Terney, a young divorced or
widowed woman who moved in across the street from us with two
young children and no automobile, could not ride to work with my

father even though her only other option was to walk. They left the house at the same time, and Mrs. Terney worked only a block away from the grocery store at the hospital. This awkward and cruel state of affairs resolved only after Aunt Brazzie mentioned it in the Ladies' Bible Class one Monday afternoon and a special dispensation was voted by the charitable ladies.

But what would have been the reason for Rev. Roberts and Mrs. Olive to go to Birmingham in the first place? No one knew.

The most popular analysis of the letter centered on the Mission to Cuba. Several decades ago, when Teddy Roosevelt had rescued the island from Spanish tyranny, relations between the U.S. and Cuba were cordial. It was not uncommon for a church or a few churches to sponsor a mission to Cuba. A group of the church people would go there in the spring or fall, either just after school let out or just before it started, to help the Cuban people in some way and to hold gospel meetings. They thought it worthwhile to convert the mostly Catholic Cubans to Baptist theology.

Rev. Roberts and Mrs. Olive had gone in a group sponsored by the Covin church, the First Baptist Church of Frog Level, and Baptist churches from Sulligent and Vernon. Some missioners apparently commented that, at the time, the minister and ministree were unusually close companions during the trip.

Had Mrs. Olive suggested another mission to Birmingham at some time? It disappointed many of the mystery followers that the letter carried no date.

What was "the work set before us"?

Why did it mention Rev. Hollingsworth, the minister at the Hubbertville Baptist church?

The kids didn't spend much time worrying about the letter, but the speculation provided entertainment for a large segment of the Frog Level adult population for several weeks. It was widely, even generally concluded that Rev. Roberts and Mrs. Olive had allowed their Cuban romance to linger many years.

Rev. Roberts, though retired, still lived near Covin and was seen in Frog Level shopping or on some other business about once a week.

A few people ventured to ask him why he wrote the letter and what it meant. He professed to have no memory of writing it, no idea what letter from Mrs. Olive might have preceded it, nor any idea what the text concerned. He reiterated his commendation of Rev. Hollingsworth and said only and precisely that, "Mrs. Olive was the most charitable, loving, Christian woman I ever met. No further comment."

"But Rev. Roberts, what sort of matters prompted you to write to Mrs. Olive at all?"

"Mrs. Olive was the most charitable, loving, Christian woman I ever met. No further comment."

Edison Wallace, the Frog Level Times reporter, showed up at the honey hole just after all the marble hunters left. Over the weekend, he visited Billy Wayne's home and, based on very sketchy information from him, paid a visit to Mr. Custer. Having decided it was a bad idea to use the County's boat for private purposes and wishing to minimize his role in the whole affair, he took the position, "It's the kid's adventure; I think you should get the story from them."

A few more inquiries similarly yielded little information. It seemed that everyone he talked to wished just to forget the whole affair, each for his own reason. Billy Wayne belatedly decided he did not wish to have people thinking of him floundering around in the river in his undershorts. Bob Sargent decided that his approach, though projecting an image of resourcefulness and devil-may-care attitude, was actually a poor way to get the marbles and might be ridiculed. Paul decided that snatching the paddle from Penny and flipping BJ and Connie into the river was at the very least ungentlemanly. So, Mr. Wallace decided to trade on our acquaintance, and asked me to come by the newspaper office.

The secretary, Sandra, remembered me, and greeted me with a wide smile. "Are we going to have another humorous article next week?" she asked.

"No ma'am. At least not a humiliating one like last time, I hope."

"Oh, I don't know," Sandra said. "From what I hear about that letter, it might be a little scandalous."

I laughed. "I really can't comment on that," I said.

She called Mr. Wallace from the printing-press room, and we sat down in his office.

"How are you, Wendell? Haven't seen you in a while. Bring your matches?"

I knew he'd get some reference to fire into the conversation, so I was prepared. "No matches, just a dozen candles," I said matter-of-factly.

He laughed and moved on. "I've heard about the big adventure down at the honey hole, but nobody will give me the details. Seems like they all have something to hide, except maybe you. I hear from Billy Wayne that you and your team made a good effort. He also told me Mr. Custer was there with a boat belonging to the County. Tell me about it."

I really wanted to tell about the idea I came up with for getting the marbles, but I also had an uneasy sense that if I told the whole story, it would get me in trouble with the other people who had been there. Well, apparently Billy Wayne already blabbed a little.

"The clue we got last Friday made everyone immediately head for the honey hole. We found a red leather bag hanging out over the river from a tree limb. The girl's team ended up getting it, but it was empty." I thought that was a pretty good synopsis.

"I know all that. Tell me about the commotion in the river."

"What commotion?" I asked.

Mr. Wallace looked unhappy. He twisted his face around through several expressions until he came to a small smile. "A brotherhood of marble hunters, huh. The code of silence."

"Need to know, Mr. Wallace. Need to know," I said with a big grin.

I probably would have told him some or most of it, but his words crystallized the concept in my head. The marble hunters were a brotherhood; well, maybe a sisterhood too, no, a kidhood. We had mutual respect, a code of silence. I smiled to myself, thinking about the Frog Level Elite.

"Do you understand how we figured it out from the clue?" I asked.

He was only mildly interested in the clue, but I explained it: how "sweet waters" was translated into "honey hole."

"So, you're not going to tell me, are you? Then tell me about catching the high school chemistry lab on fire."

I hesitated a while, and Mr. Wallace leaned back in his chair to wait.

"It's one or the other isn't it?" I sighed. "Either I rat out everybody down at the honey hole or you'll write about the fire. Is that the deal?"

"Well, pretty much, that's it. Come on, Wendell, I'm a newspaper reporter. I need news. Setting the high school on fire is definitely news. Tell me what Mr. Custer was doing there, and I'll leave it at that."

"Why do you want to know about him?"

"The boat. I hear he had a boat there that belonged to the County. Misuse of public property; that sort of thing."

"Jeez, I don't want to get him in trouble. He didn't wreck the boat or anything like that, did he?"

"No. I'll tell you what. Give me the exact story. I'll write a short article about what happened at the honey hole. I'll make it humorous. You know that lots of adults are interested in what you kids are doing. Lord knows they've seen you hunting for the marbles all over the place. Buford Sumter told me you and Kavanaugh were searching around the radio tower. I hear lots of things, but never quite enough to make the newspaper.

"I'll run it at the bottom of page one and include a short statement about Mr. Custer and the boat over on page two or three. I won't suggest anything was improper. If some of his superiors want to make trouble for him, that's not your fault or mine. In fact, since I already know about the boat, I could write just that, and it would stand out as an exposé of his actions. It'll be less a problem for him if it's buried in a bigger story."

I succumbed to his blackmail, but tried to gloss over some of the embarrassing details. Mr. Wallace backed me into a corner each time, and I had to give the whole thing. He made notes and laughed quite a bit. I found it easy to believe he would write a humorous article.

"Man, that's quite a tale," he said. "Tell you what. I'm going to write the story but not use the names of the kids. I'll just say up front that I don't want to embarrass anybody. You know, when we report some kid breaking the law, we don't give his name unless we have to give it to tell the story."

"That sounds like a good idea. Thanks, Mr. Wallace. And please don't mention where you heard it."

"Okay, that's that. Now tell me how you set the chemistry lab on fire."

"But you said it was one or the other. You said if I told you the honey hole story, you wouldn't write about the fire."

"I won't put it in the paper, but I want to know what happened. Just personal curiosity. I'll bet it's better than burning the tree down."

"Okay. My group was doing the first experiment of the chemistry class. The exercise had us mix saltpeter, powdered charcoal, and sulfur to demonstrate the difference between a mixture and a chemical compound; to show that it was just a mixture. The workbook told us to dissolve the saltpeter out of the mixture with hot water. Next, it said to dissolve the sulfur with carbon disulfide. Carbon disulfide is very flammable; man, is it flammable! The lab book cautioned us to be sure we extinguished the Bunsen burner before we got it anywhere near our workbench. We turned off the gas and set it over to one side. It didn't warn us that a hot burner can ignite the carbon disulfide even after you turn off the flame.

"I brought the flask over to the workbench. Fortunately, it had just a few spoonfuls in it. The burner was still hot and it caught the carbon disulfide on fire. I dropped the flask and it spilled on the floor. I stamped out the flames before it burned anything else. That's all there is to tell."

"It didn't burn anything else? Nothing?"

"You've already heard this story, haven't you?"

"Yeah, I just wanted to hear it from you. Lost your eyebrows, didn't you?"

"Yessir. Singed them off. That's all."

I didn't tell him that I'd already burned off my eyebrows once before in my shop. I'd save that for another time.

The next edition of the Frog Level Times carried an article about the incident at the honey hole. It used fictitious names for the kids: Little Boy Blue, Bo Peep, Jack Sprat, Jack Horner, and so forth. It gave the full story, swimmers, girls overboard, sawing off the tree limb, the ropes strung across the river, and Mr. Custer and the county's boat. Several adults told me that it was really funny and asked if I had been there. I admitted it, but refused to identify the characters other than Jimmy, Kavanaugh and myself.

## We gotta figure this out

Though worn out by the excitement of the battle for the red bag and then completely disheartened by discovering it was empty, we slowly focused on the fact that the hunt was still on, and our energy returned by the next Friday.

The next clue, however, quickly extinguished our regained enthusiasm for the hunt.

Rescue the perishing,
care for the dying

October 14, 1955  Clue 7

Nobody could come up with any reasonably compelling theory from this new clue. A few lame jokes about how it referred to BJ or Connie floundering in the river were circulated. Otherwise, we were depressed by the lack of direction, and we showed up the next Friday with less than great enthusiasm.

Guide me, Oh thou great
Jehovah

October 21, 1955  Clue 8

Again we tried out a lot of lame jokes about needing divine guidance. We went back to the overall religious theme. We looked for churches or church connections again. Paul approached me one day at the morning recess and questioned me about the Church of Christ. He had the idea that since Jack Stonecipher attended the Church of Christ, maybe some aspect of our particular theology had to be known to understand the clues. I answered all his questions like, "Why don't you have a piano or organ? Is your baptism different from the Baptists?" and several others.

There were lots of peculiarities that he didn't know about. He hadn't ever heard of an anti church, and I didn't bring up any of that stuff. I kept the conversation to myself and pondered it most of the rest of the school day. Nothing much occurred to me, and after mentioning the conversation to Kavanaugh, I dropped it.

Friday again brought a new clue.

𝕴 am thinking today of a beautiful land I shall reach when the sun goeth down

October 28, 1955  Clue 9

Well. It mentioned sundown again. Okay, but sighted from where? We had pretty much worn out the sundown angle.

Maybe the key event or place materialized after sundown. What would one do at night in the swamp? Few people went there at night. Mother mentioned that when she was young, they would go down to the gas seep and picnic, using the natural grille it provided. The gas seep was a place where natural gas just flowed out of the ground under its own pressure. She said they usually stayed until after dark. We rode our bikes and then hiked to the gas seep the next Sunday afternoon but came up empty handed. At least I knew where it was now. Maybe I'd come back and picnic.

We received clue number ten, still with little enthusiasm.

Do not wait until some deed of

greatness you may do

November 4, 1955 Clue 10

A complete blank. Everyone drew a complete blank.

The next Monday, a small whisper of discontent about the hunt began. I don't think anyone complained to Jack at first, but the high enthusiasm and adventurous spirit we had at the beginning of the hunt had vanished. Jimmy and I talked to Donis about whether we might make some specific complaint. We didn't. We just complained to each other until Friday rolled around again.

Clue number eleven came on Friday.

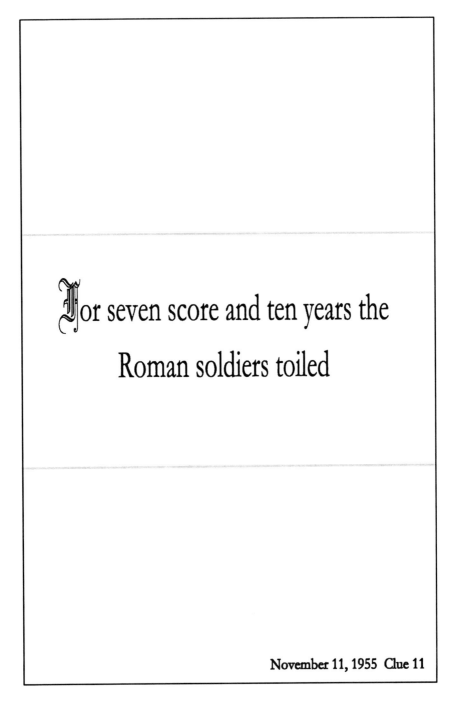

For seven score and ten years the Roman soldiers toiled

November 11, 1955  Clue 11

This was not the first line of a hymn! It certainly was not from our hymnal. We all cross-checked with the other teams, who checked the hymnals at their churches, and no one had ever heard of a hymn that began this way. A search of the hymnals in the county library found nothing. Finally, at last, we had something new to think about.

We all quickly converted seven score and ten to one hundred and fifty. We converted one hundred and fifty to the Roman CL.

Roman soldiers? What did Roman soldiers mean? Who were our metaphorical Roman soldiers? The National Guard? Did they drill and practice in the swamp? The Armory sat on the east side of town but not in the swamp. Football players were sometimes referred to as gladiators. Gladiators were Roman. So what?

Were we the Roman soldiers? Would we have to toil a metaphorical 150 years? Maybe 150 days? It had so far been seventy days since the beginning of the hunt. When all the clues had been produced, we would have passed eleven weeks or seventy seven days. Still not 150. Equating other time periods with a year gave either too short or too long a period.

What about CL? Was it someone's initials? L could be Lufkin. There were Storey, Prentiss, and their father, Colonel Lufkin. Colonel Lufkin? He went to our church, so I asked him if he knew of any connection. I think I discovered the only person in Frog Level who hadn't heard of the marble hunt.

We thought of a few other L names; Lollar, Lindsey, but the ideas went nowhere. Oh well, this next clue was the last one. Maybe it would be the whole ball of wax.

We got the final clue.

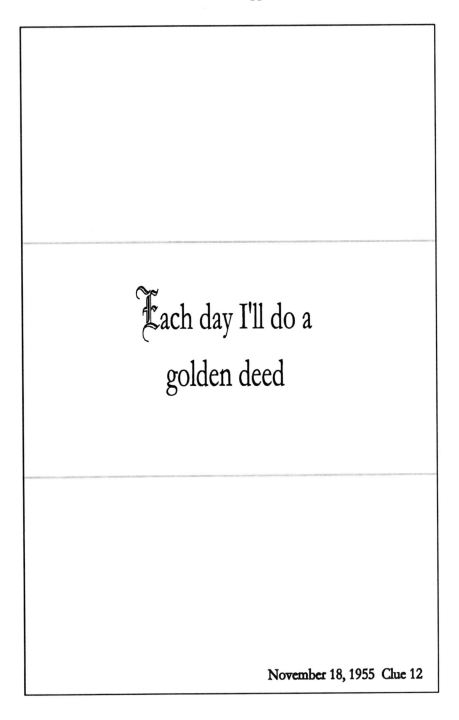

Each day I'll do a
golden deed

November 18, 1955  Clue 12

Everybody was simply disgusted. Nothing happened for a while.

We came to the Thanksgiving holiday. The sense of disgust grew steadily, and some of the hunters complained directly to Jack. The rest of us just began to put our mental energies elsewhere.

On Wednesday morning before Thanksgiving, Mr. Shoemaker made a few usual announcements, and then addressed the marble hunters. "I am pleased to announce that Jack and Eli Stonecipher have donated the entire proceeds from the Marble Hunt to the band. The $156 will be exactly enough to buy two new uniforms for the band. Miss Tetley and I commend these fine young men for their generosity and school spirit."

The announcement dampened the complaints to just an occasional mutter. How could we complain if the money went to a good cause?

Over the holiday we read over the clues and discussed a few new ideas but conducted no searches.

**Stonecipher deciphered**

When I returned to school after Thanksgiving, the hallways were buzzing. Paul and Miles had figured it out. They were mum, but before lunch it came out. Miles had told it to Sylvia Bromley and she blabbed it to BJ, Penny and Connie. Penny spread it everywhere: the first letters of the clues spell something. Up and down the hallways echoed the news headline, "Stonecipher's been deciphered!"

I spent the rest of the morning trying to remember the clues and arrange the first letters. We had a test in Math, so I couldn't work on it during Math period. Finally lunchtime arrived and the team huddled in the hallway.

What words could we make? How many words were there? Kavanaugh had a different lunch period than Jimmy and I, so he made a few comments and hurried off to class. He didn't have anything very promising. Jimmy had written the letters down on little squares of paper and we shuffled them around on the lunch table. He came up with "Big Red Soffrd" just as Danny Workman came by and looked.

"I think you've got it! Now if you can just figure out what a soffrd

201

is!" he exclaimed for all around to hear. We didn't join in the general laughter. As he walked off, he turned halfway and said, "By the way, it's two words."

We were stunned. Danny's team had figured it out already. We assumed that Miles and Paul hunted over the weekend, and now maybe another team was ahead of us. We nearly panicked and gave up, but by the time school ended, Jimmy, Kavanaugh, and I all independently came up with "Ford's Bridge."

After we spelled Ford's Bridge, an F remained unused. We soon decided that it was the F from "For seven score and ten years, the Roman soldiers toiled." Okay, it wasn't the first line of a hymn, so that gave us an excuse to not use it. Again, we had no idea why this clue didn't fit the pattern, it just didn't.

Ford's bridge made the first crossing of the Sipsey north of Frog Level, not counting the impassable Stamps Bridge. You go up the Winfield highway and turn right toward Townley. Ford's Bridge sits in the middle of a long, straight stretch of road through the swamp. It provided a most excellent place for drag racing, and we all knew the quarter-mile of road centered on the bridge served as the official local drag strip. The racers even painted lines across the highway to mark the start and finish lines. They entered the bridge occupying both lanes with no place to go should a car appear coming the opposite way. Maybe some of them considered this a special feature to warn off the chicken-hearted or, for that matter, anyone with more than half a brain.

A bridge had been there for a very long time. As one of many public-works projects during the Great Depression, the original wooden bridge had been replaced with a steel and concrete one. Bids were requested and a contractor from near Florence had won the bidding. Around the time of this story, the road to Townley was being widened and straightened to cut about an hour off the trip from Frog Level to Birmingham. The 1930s Ford's Bridge received maintenance as part of that project. Sometime since the events of this story, it has been replaced again. The new one sits just to the north of where the one I describe sat.

The bridge was 880 feet long, composed of ten sections, each 88 ft long. The end of each section sat on a concrete beam running across the top of a row of posts. There were nine rows of posts plus the end supports. The fourth and sixth set of posts were placed near the riverbank and the fifth sat directly in the center of the river. Rubber marks from drag racing almost covered the cement surface. Deep slopes dropped down from the dirt-fill roadbed toward the river on both sides.

Scrub brush and a few saplings covered the ground on the north side of the bridge for over a hundred yards upstream. I never knew why it didn't have big trees like the rest of the surroundings. On the south side, the highway crews kept trees cut back for maybe twenty or thirty feet, and beyond that, the typical Sipsey Swamp forest began.

Jimmy, Kavanaugh and I showed up at my father's office, and, with much pleading and explanations that it was now or never, he agreed to take us to the bridge. Of course, some of the other teams were there by the time we arrived. Danny, Monty, and Jim Bakkus searched the bushes but appeared to have no serious lead on us. Miles and Paul were noticeably missing.

When they arrived in Paul's dad's station wagon with a long extension ladder, we learned that they had searched the surroundings for several hours before deciding that the marbles were hidden up on the bridge, and they'd given up for the night.

They carried the ladder down the south side of the bridge and extended it up to lean on the concrete beam at the top of the second set of posts from the west. Miles climbed up and looked. He leaned side to side and stared lengthwise down the underside of the bridge. He pivoted on the ladder and looked back at the embankment on the near end. He stepped down a couple of steps and looked again. Finally he came down and reported that he could see only between two of the steel beams running the length of the bridge. They would have to move the ladder over between each pair of beams and look again. They did this systematically. The rest of us converted the sloping dirt embankment under the end of the bridge into an amphitheater. With his usual perfect timing, Edison Wallace arrived just as Miles had descended from examining the tunnel between the last pair of beams. Miles then proceeded to hold what we now know as a "press conference."

"We have searched the terrain around the bridge very thoroughly. We have paid attention to the most widely held theories, such as the idea that the treasure is hidden in the 'rock of ages,' and looked for sighting opportunities for the sunset or evening star. The search yielded nothing. Convinced the treasure is hidden on the bridge structure, we surveyed it from a variety of angles using a Nikon 10x50 binocular. Again, we found nothing."

Miles seemed to be warming up to his spokesman role. "Today we returned with a thirty-two foot extension ladder that enabled us to climb up and survey the space under the bridge. We were particularly keen to look on top of the concrete crossbeams. We considered them to afford an ideal hiding place, protected from the weather and, especially noteworthy, protected from casual viewing.

"We have surveyed the space between each pair of lengthwise steel beams. The concrete cross beams on which the lengthwise beams rest, are rectangular in cross-section and flat and smooth on top. They have no indentations. Therefore, by sighting down the bridge between each pair of lengthwise beams, we can see the top of every crossbeam clearly. I saw nothing more than a few birds' nests. We conclude that the marbles are not, repeat not, hidden on the bridge structure."

### The end of the road

No marbles. With the deciphering of "Ford's Bridge," I had thought it was finally over for better or worse. Now it seemed that we had to go through more of the same: more thinking, more hunting. I was just getting tired of the whole thing. It almost made me just cry.

I think every one of the teams searched around Ford's Bridge several more times. Christmas came and went.

I'd written out the clues and found several ways of arranging them into a treasure map or directions to the treasure. Perhaps Ford's Bridge was only part of the answer. Kavanaugh and I tried out most of my theories. One Sunday at church, Bill Arquette, one of the adult team members, asked to hear my theories and asked if anything new had come up since the searches at the bridge. My charts happened to be in the back of the car, so I got them to show him. As I went through them, I pointed out the seven score and ten, 150, CL. He apparently hadn't heard of or thought of the derivation of CL from the clue. The adult team members didn't follow the kids ideas very carefully. He admitted he just read his copy of the clue each week and laid it aside. The moment I mentioned CL and pointed to the CL inscribed in one of my diagrams, he broke out laughing.

"What?" I asked.

At first he just said, "Oh, nothing."

After we got home from church and were eating dinner, Daddy recalled Eli had worked for the highway department the previous summer, his last summer before college. Bill Arquette supervised him, and Eli must have confided something. Bill Arquette knows something that we don't. Why did he realize it when he saw the CL?

He wouldn't say so, but when I told people how he had reacted to the CL, everyone realized he knew where the marbles were. After weeks of badgering, he admitted he knew. At least, he was 99% sure he knew, but hadn't actually seen them. However, out of respect for Eli and Jack, he wouldn't give the secret away.

More than ever, some people suggested that the hunt was a scam; that Eli and Jack hadn't really hidden the marbles. Bill Arquette's reaction to the CL and confession seemed to confirm that the clues really pointed to something. Most importantly, we simply lacked any new ideas, and the interest in hunting died out. Kavanaugh and Jimmy said I could have the clues. They didn't care any more.

Years passed. Not many from my present-day perspective but a good chunk of a lifetime, it seemed then. We had other adventures.

Then one Saturday in the fall of 1957, Duff Hawkins showed up at the grocery store, where I now worked every Saturday, and he wanted to know if I would sell my set of clues. Duff had been too young to participate in the hunt; but now, as each kid grew up and developed an interest in marbles, someone would tell him the story of the big marble hunt. Some versions concluded that there really wasn't a treasure to be found. It was all a ruse, a scam to get money for the band. Duff, however, was a true believer. I could see in his eyes that he wanted to hunt. He wanted to hatch theories. He wanted the legendary marbles. I agreed to sell the clues to Duff for fifteen dollars. Each team member got five dollars: a small profit instead of a total loss.

Again time passed, and the memory of the marble hunt came up less frequently.

The same year I went to graduate school in Baltimore, Duff Hawkins entered the University of Alabama as a freshman. He was most definitely not the brightest kid from Frog Level. His dad was obviously very sharp—a dentist that graduated from a school in Illinois and a better one than anyone had any right to expect in Frog Level. Duff just didn't get it—whatever it happened to be. If someone told a joke, Duff didn't get the punch line. If most people could sense a shared emotion in a group of friends, Duff didn't feel it. Even in sports, he had no sense of where the play was going.

Duff found a girlfriend at the University, Melinda Stover from Montgomery. They took a liking to each other, dated regularly, and, by the Spring break in the second semester, he invited her to come home with him and offered a canoe trip down the Sipsey as one of the high points of the weekend.

His mother took them and the canoe up a newly cut road along the side of Ford's Mountain in the family Ford, wood-panel station wagon. The road skirted the mountain and then dived down to run along side the river at a bend. It was possible to carry the canoe a short distance through the woods and into the river.

They loaded a picnic lunch, paddles, towels, suntan oil, mosquito repellent, and cushions into the canoe and slipped off down the river. Melinda had decided it was a great adventure when she spotted a raccoon on one bank. Such exotic wildlife! She found a position in the bow that gave her an unobstructed view of whatever denizen of the Sipsey might show itself next, and, she judged, gave Duff an elegant view of her hair streaming in the soft breeze. Given the lazy current of the Sipsey, it had been maybe twenty minutes before they reached the last, roughly ninety-degree turn in the river before going under Ford's Bridge.

They had just begun to negotiate the turn when Melinda turned halfway around and asked, "What does CL mean?"

Duff didn't get it right away. "What?"

"What does that symbol on the side of the bridge mean? It looks like a C and an L printed on top of one another."

Duff looked up and stopped paddling. The canoe went about twenty feet before Melinda was pushed into a cluster of blackberry bushes on the left bank. Duff was oblivious to her squeals and protests. Only after she grabbed a second paddle and used it to push away from the bush did the canoe begin to drift downstream again.

Duff's head rotated counter to the canoe, his eyes locked on the CL cast into the concrete of the bridge. The letters stood around fifteen inches high. Vee-shaped grooves in the concrete formed the letters in neat Roman typeface, with smooth, perfect serifs directly over the center cross beam of the bridge, but not written out in the normal position. I reproduce them here:

The encounter with the bush and Duff's failure to rescue her dulled any tender concern that Melinda might have over his apparent disorientation, but she was becoming worried for her own safety.

"What's the matter, Duff? What's wrong?"

"Nothing. Nothing. I can't believe it! Why didn't anyone else see it?"

"What, Duff? What are you talking about?"

Getting a bit of his composure back, he began to explain the marble hunt. He certainly hadn't forgotten it. He had carefully planned, had eagerly anticipated, that he would begin the story as they glided under Ford's Bridge. Melinda listened attentively. Duff just got as far as Jack's announcement of the hunt when he started to stand up in the canoe, almost overturning it and yelled, "That's why!"

He turned sideways with one hand on each side of the canoe. "They didn't see it because you have to be back…" His head swiveled left and right twice. "You have to be back almost fifty yards to see it. They never went far enough upriver! It's already hidden."

With a bit of urging, Duff calmed down again and continued the tale of the hunt but in more detail than Melinda cared for. Finally, she pressed him to get to the end, then asked, "What are you going to do now?"

She didn't like the answer. Duff had realized that if they continued down-river to the Tuscaloosa highway bridge where his father had agreed to meet them at five o'clock, there wouldn't be time to look for the marbles until tomorrow. It couldn't wait. Melinda dropped a few hints about how nice the day was, how much she enjoyed watching the butterflies hover around the canoe, and about the way the fish splashed, but she couldn't break his obsession with the new discovery.

When they came to Stamps Bridge road, Duff beached the canoe by the remains of the old bridge. He announced to Melinda that it was only just a mile to the Howton's where they could call for his mom or dad to pick them up.

Melinda had long since decided the day gave her a valuable peek into the soul of Duff Hawkins; that she had seen as much as was needed; and it remained simply a matter of disentangling herself from the labyrinth she had found. "Oh, just a mile," echoed her lilting purr.

That evening, she made several comments to Duff's mother, comments that offered his mother an opportunity to share some insights on her son's social graces or lack thereof, but Melinda got only a sweet smile in return. When school resumed after the weekend, Melinda appeared to have gotten much more interested in her studies and simply couldn't find time for Duff. Duff wondered why she had become so studious all of a sudden.

Back at the house, they unloaded the canoe and, after a couple of phone calls by Dr. Hawkins, they went to Mack Riser's house, borrowed his forty-foot extension ladder and drove out to Ford's bridge. But before they left, Duff made one more call to a number he'd written on the back of one of the clues—to Edison Wallace.

When they arrived, just as Paul and Miles had done years ago, they carried the ladder down the south side of the bridge. It took over thirty minutes through the briars that were no longer regularly trampled by marble hunters. Unlike the previous ladder bearers, they didn't stop at the first or second pillars but continued on to the riverbank. They positioned the ladder on the riverbank, extended it fully, and laid it against the center bridge support. They chose to place it on the north side, as close to the CL inscription as they could. Duff climbed up the shaky ladder. He paused a couple of times while Dr. Hawkins experimented with ways to stabilize the ladder. Finally Dr. Hawkins was satisfied, and Duff climbed up until he could see the top of the crossbeam.

And there it was: all the best of Eli Stonecipher's marble collection. Unlike all the other cross beams, the center beam had a trench of rectangular cross-section along its length, about a foot across and a foot deep. Laid out in the trench were six sections of rubber inner tubes, apparently from rather large truck tires. Each section had been cut about eighteen inches in length, a cigar box of marbles placed inside the inner-tube section, and the ends sealed with rubber cement. They were all in perfect condition: no leaks. Duff carefully carried each section down the ladder and handed it to his father as Edison Wallace snapped pictures of the great occasion. They opened one of the rubber casings, a heavy one, with a pocketknife and found a Muriel Cigar box, and inside the box were 500 or more true agate marbles.

The Frog Level Times carried a picture at the top of the front page showing Duff holding the open box out toward the camera. My parents called me and relayed the news. It made me feel sad to know that the marbles were always there, sometimes just feet away from me, and I hadn't found them. After the disappointment faded, I was pleased to realize that it had been a real hunt: no scam, no farce; well, plenty of farce provided by us hunters; and we had lot's of fun in the hunt. I wrote a note to Jack congratulating him on staging such a clever stunt.

The cache consisted of six cigar boxes of marbles. One had only cat's eyes, another only taws, and another the special display-only marbles including Old Bessie. Besides the six boxes on the bridge, Jack presented Duff with six more boxes of assorted marbles, explaining that there were just too many to wrap and hide.

## Odds and ends

On my first trip back to Frog Level after Duff found the treasure, as always, we went to Sunday morning church. As happened on each visit back home when the service was over, all the old folks that watched me grow up greeted and hugged me. They seemed pleased and comforted somehow just to see I had survived all the trips into the swamp and the various exploding rocket motors that I built. I made a special effort to say hello to most of them before I came around to Bill Arquette. I had to know how he knew.

"I think you heard that Eli worked for me the last summer before college," he began. "We were patching a few places on the roadbed of Ford's Bridge.

"Eli's job was to get samples of each batch of concrete so we could test them for strength. He had a stock of cardboard tubes, and each time the workers began using a new batch, he would fill one with concrete, label it and set it aside. I showed up in the morning to check on the work and take the samples for testing. Eli didn't have any other responsibility, but he had to stay on the job site all day."

Bill Arquette grinned from ear to ear and giggled randomly as he related the story. Keeping the secret had been very hard on him.

"When they removed the crumbled roadbed over the center cross beam, Eli was able to see the channel in the beam. I think it was the first one poured when they replaced the old wooden bridge with the concrete one in the '30s. They made a channel in the form to save a little bit of concrete. I'm just guessing here. After the first one, they must have decided that it took more time making the channel than they saved in concrete, so they did away with it on the rest of the cross beams. All the others have no channel. After they poured the roadbed, there was no way to see the channel in the center beam unless you climbed up on it under the roadway. When Miles climbed up near the end of the bridge and saw flat-topped beams, he thought he could see anything sitting on any of them. He didn't know the center one was different."

"Wow, if it hadn't been for the CL, no one would ever have thought to climb up there." In my opinion, Eli and Jack chose the hiding spot perfectly. It really couldn't have been better if they engineered it and built it. Finally, I understood why the clue about the Roman soldiers was included: to guide us to the CL on the center beam. I asked Mr. Arquette, "Why did they label it with CL?"

Mr. Arquette leaned in toward me. He seemed very glad I asked. "Most of the building crew were not professional road builders or even regular construction workers—just guys who needed work during the Great Depression. And, it turns out, none of them lived around here. They lived mostly around Florence and Muscle Shoals, so none of them was around here to understand the clue like I did. When a draftsman draws a view of a structure that has a center of symmetry, as the bridge does, he draws a dashed line along the symmetry axis and places the CL mark on it. Traditionally, the C and L are both placed right on the centerline, one on top of the other. CL for center line.

"The novice workers saw the CL on the side-view drawing of the bridge and just thought it was some sort of decoration to be built into the bridge. They carefully fashioned the letters—I guess out of wood—and placed them inside the concrete form so that when they filled the form and then removed it, the letters were cast in place. Eli saw it while the roadbed was torn up. Like the channel, once they put on the roadway, you couldn't see the CL. At least, no one who was interested in the marbles saw it until Duff came down the river in his canoe."

So that explained it all. I suppose it would have been better if my team had found the marbles, but Jimmy, Kavanaugh, and I would just have fought over how to divide them up. In retrospect, I'm sure the hunt itself was the best part. I certainly won't forget that afternoon at the honey hole.

The unexpected fallout from the hunt was remarkable as well. The letter in Mrs. Olive's bag is still being discussed and debated in quilting circles and at covered-dish dinners. Melinda saved a lot of time in getting to know Duff, Duff got the marbles, and I got a story to recall all these years later.

# Theawatoosa, 1957

Act 1, Scene 5

There are more things in heaven and earth, Horatio,
Than are dreamt of in your philosophy.

Act 3, Scene 2

Hamlet: Do you see yonder cloud that's almost in shape of a camel?
Polonius: By th' mass, and 'tis like a camel indeed.
Hamlet: Methinks it is like a weasel.
Polonius: It is backed like a weasel.
Hamlet: Or like a whale.
Polonius: Very like a whale.
...
...
'Tis now the very witching time of night,
When churchyards yawn and hell itself breathes out
Contagion to this world.

Excerpts from *Hamlet* by William Shakespeare

## What you don't know can't hurt you

I don't know when I first heard of John Tubalcaine. I just always knew who he was. At least, I knew some of it. He was one of a few eccentrics who lived around Frog Level and were obviously different, even to a kid.

In my eyes, John Tubalcaine's strangeness came from the fact that he lived alone in a huge unfinished black building on top of Mount Nebo. My story starts when Kenny Livingston and I paid a visit to him; but, I need to give you a little background and explain how, although I didn't know it at the time, my family bore a small responsibility for his hermit's existence.

As you've learned already, the Church of Christ formed one of the focal points of my childhood because my family on my mother's side devoted themselves to the institutional Church of Christ. They varied in the care with which they followed the teachings, but almost all worked to build up the institution and its offspring, the Christian colleges, the orphan homes, and so forth.

In the early 1900s, some of my Grandmother Lizzie's brothers, with other faithful members of the Church of Christ, decided to found a Christian College in Frog Level. They envisioned it growing into a large, well-known center of teaching the gospel along with the arts and sciences that would equip young people for productive, moral lives. They built a sturdy brick building and faculty members were recruited.

Of course, choosing the leader of this college was given careful consideration. Wanting to get the very best person for the job, my Great Uncle Horace sent an inquiry to his brothers who had migrated to Texas, asking if they could find a candidate among the Christian scholars of Texas. They found John Tubalcaine.

Mr. Tubalcaine seemed to be ideally suited for the job. He knew Latin and a little bit about Greek literature. He knew a lot about English literature and had mastered an amazing range of practical skills such as typing, bookkeeping, blacksmithing, woodworking, and several others. Of course, he was a fervent Christian: a member of the Church of Christ. In addition to these skills and qualifications, he had a vision. He believed that one lived a good life only by practicing three disciplines: to be a strong Christian, to become well educated, and to make the things needed for living a comfortable, secure life. Many visionaries saw the importance of religion and learning, but John Tubalcaine added the need for each person to know some specialized skills and to apply them to produce the practical items that he and his community needed.

Mr. Tubalcaine moved to Frog Level with his young wife and took up the duties as head of the new Frog Level Christian College. Lacking enough wealthy supporters, the school went out of existence after only a few years. This left Tubalcaine out of work. He was, however, an enthusiastic and energetic visionary who would not accept defeat so easily. Many of his friends urged him to take the generous severance pay and build a home for his young wife. When he had settled in Frog Level or even Tuscaloosa, he would certainly find employment and build a happy life.

But he was a visionary. He took the money and bought around a thousand acres of land including what we now know as Mount Nebo. The mountain was really just a hill a couple of hundred feet high. It rose up on the east side of the Sipsey River not too far off the Townley highway, and it had no name when he bought it and named it. It provided a beautiful view of the Sipsey River and the flat terrain on both sides: a view that reminded him how Moses climbed the biblical Mount Nebo to look across the Jordan River and see the Promised Land. When he died without entering the Promised Land, the Israelites buried him there. Mr. Tubalcaine thought of the Sipsey as his Jordan, and he wanted to build his Promised Land on his Mount Nebo.

What a bargain he saw. In his vision, Mount Nebo had everything one needed to support a utopian community. It was covered with trees for lumber to build houses, a school, and community workshops. It sat on top of coal, oil, and gas to supply energy, and soil, rock, and gravel for roads and monuments. Being on the banks of the Sipsey River, it offered transportation, fish, mussels, and clams, and clean water for recreation. Thus, John Tubalcaine and his wife had a thousand-acre home but no house to shelter them.

Tubalcaine built a one-room house at the foot of Mount Nebo, close to the road, to keep his wife warm and dry. Next to it he built an open shed to serve as a kitchen and his bedroom. So pressing was his plan to build his utopia that he could spare neither more time nor money to build a finer house. It didn't matter. Within a short time—a year, maybe a couple of years—they would live with a band of friends and fellow visionaries in a mansion on top of the mountain.

It may seem that Tubalcaine wasn't concerned for his wife, or worse, he didn't love her. Nothing could be farther from the truth. She loved and married him for his grand visions. He married her because he worshiped her. She was his ideal. His visions had been with him since youth, but he had never acted on them. When he found her, he found his incentive to work for their realization.

He went to work with a few followers. They felled trees and sawed them into lumber. They drew sap from the tall yellow pines to make paint and pitch to protect the large two-story building that began to rise on the mountain. Tubalcaine began to publicize the imminent opening of his new Mount Nebo Christian College in the fine building and to make plans for the furnishing of a Community Workshop in one wing.

Though he seemed to have boundless energy, his helpers grew tired of the long hours of back-breaking work. One by one they lost sight of the vision that had seemed so bright when he first described it: the vision that seemed to recede into the future no matter how hard they labored.

Because John Tubalcaine worshiped his wife, because he thought of her as more angel than human, he failed to notice her most human needs. His neglect of her was an unconscious sin growing out of his obsession with achieving the great plan now under way. Too delicate for the rough labor of constructing the large building, she sat alone in her bedroom for hours each day. Even on Sunday, instead of traveling into Frog Level to worship with the large Church of Christ there, Tubalcaine held services with his workers on top of the mountain. In time, it became harder for her to fend off the winds and rains and bear the lack of companionship. Her bright vision of the future gave way to foreboding, and she died in early spring two years into the project after a short illness.

In his mind, her death was inseparable from the collapse of his dream. In any case, Tubalcaine could no longer carry on alone with no money and no helpers. He rented out a space over Dorcas Hubbert's women's clothing store and began to teach trade school. He didn't have the facilities to teach the practical arts he loved most—blacksmithing, machining, leatherworking and woodworking. Instead, he taught the skills most in demand. My mother and father learned bookkeeping from him, and Mother also learned to type.

As at least partial realization of his failures overtook him, and age blurred his utopian visions, and World War II stole the trade-school students, he retreated to his mountain and rarely was seen in Frog Level. Blind to the consequences, he had imposed a near hermit's existence on his wife, and now, freely and willingly, he imposed it on himself.

If his utopian inclinations, his vision, his hermit's way of living, unusual education and wide-ranging skills were not enough to make the citizens of Frog Level uneasy with him, he had yet one more distinction: the meaning of his name. A few people didn't know the meaning of his name, but, like most people who grew up there, I learned it from school gossip. Mr. Tubalcaine was a Devil worshipper they said. He kidnapped livestock, took them up the mountain and sacrificed them to Satan, the whispered stories went. Once, he had stolen a baby from its crib and ate it, they said.

I learned a more realistic version from my grandmother before she died.

Kavanaugh and I had a routine to follow in preparing for Sunday School. The church provided each regular attendee with a copy of The Gospel Quarterly containing a lesson for each Sunday. The lesson began with a Bible verse to memorize and a thematic portion of scripture, followed by a discussion, and ending with a list of questions for the student. We were expected to memorize the verse, read the Biblical text and discussion, and then take our Quarterly to Grandmother. She asked us the questions and critiqued our answers. We had finished studying only when she said we had.

In one week's lesson, the Bible text included Genesis, Chapter 4, Verse 22, "And Zillah, she also bare Tubal-Cain, an instructer of every artificer in brass and iron: and the sister of Tubal-Cain was Naamah." When we took the lesson to Grandmother to answer the questions, I had a question to ask first.

"You know Mr. Tubalcaine, the old man who lives on Mount Nebo? Is he named for Tubal-Cain in our Bible text?"

"I suppose he is," she answered. "Has anybody ever told you what his name means?"

"Yes ma'am. Some of the kids at school say he worships the Devil; that he sacrifices animals to Satan." I left out the eating-the-baby part.

"Well, the Bible doesn't have anything to say about him except what's in your lesson text. Other ancient books have a lot more to say about him. Josephus says he was wicked, a murderer, and made war on his neighbors. During the Middle Ages, some theologians came up with the idea that Satan was his father. All sorts of hogwash like that. That's what it is, just hogwash. The scripture is telling you he is the person who invented metalworking. That's all."

"Wow," I said, "Who would want to be named for him? Do you think Mr. Tubalcaine worships the Devil?"

"No. Like I said, it's an old myth. The Bible just gives Tubal-Cain credit for inventing how to make things from metal. That's a good thing. Mr. Tubalcaine believes very strongly that we all ought to know how to make the things we use every day—pots, tools, pocketbooks, chairs, plows. He actually has a very appropriate name, considering his beliefs. There's nothing in it to do with the devil. Don't you listen to anybody who says he works for the devil, and don't you ever say anything like that. He's a good man."

So I knew the meaning of his name and knew my grandmother's opinion on it, but his name still added to his oddness and mystery.

In 1957, when the remainder of this episode takes place, he had become the eccentric old character I remember. Most people in Frog Level knew he held court on Sunday afternoon for the curious who drove up the nearly impassable driveway to his unfinished home, school, and community workshop on the mountain. At this point, I didn't yet know how involved my family had been in his fate. I just thought he was an interesting old hermit, and I wanted to see the Sunday afternoon show for myself.

Kavanaugh would go off to school at Auburn soon. He still lived at home for the summer, but no longer showed much interest in hanging out with a young kid brother. He also wasn't interested in an old hermit. I needed to find a new companion for my adventures.

## The end of innocence

Kenny Livingston and I had formed a partnership to build rockets. The United States was just beginning "the Space Race" with the Soviet Union. It was a couple of months before the Soviet Union would launch Sputnik, the first artificial satellite. NASA didn't exist and wouldn't for another year. But the German V2 rocket had attracted the attention of the U.S. government and every science-oriented kid in the country.

What kid wouldn't be head-over-heels mad about rockets? They were in the news constantly. Walter Cronkite told us how important they were for the defense of the nation. The newsreels at the picture show featured the blastoffs, and sometimes, the spectacular explosion that happened when the rocket failed and fell back onto the launch pad or made a neat fireball in the sky.

Kenny and I shared the cost of a hundred-pound keg of powdered zinc with some other Frog Level rocketeers. Mixed with powdered sulfur, it made a wonderful rocket propellant. We could get the sulfur at any drugstore. It burned to produce clouds of white smoke and lots of hot gas to push the rocket. Our rockets didn't carry any payload. The idea was just to see how far up we could get it to go. We judged the highest altitude it achieved from how long the rocket took to fall back to earth. One of our first attempts had gone up about a half mile.

As Kenny and I got to be good friends, we took time off from building rockets and went fishing a couple of times. I told him about some of the adventures that Kavanaugh and I had in the swamp. Kenny hadn't participated in the marble hunt because he was living with an aunt in Birmingham that year. In spite of his limited knowledge of the swamp, he wanted to try almost any new adventure.

So, on one late-summer Sunday afternoon, Kenny Livingston and I hopped on bikes and headed up the Winfield highway to Mount Nebo. About an hour later, we came to Mr. Tubalcaine's driveway. The driveway was so steep and rough that we couldn't ride up it, so we leaned the bikes against a couple of trees and walked the rest of the way.

As we walked up, I wondered if Mr. Tubalcaine would remember me. Kavanaugh and I met him when we went to Mount Nebo on our bikes and Kavanaugh got caught in the briar patch, and I had seen him in the grocery store a few times and bagged groceries for him.

My thoughts were interrupted by the sound of an automobile engine coming up behind us. We stood to one side of the driveway and allowed the car to pass. Two boy-girl couples were inside, and we traded waves with them.

"Now that's the way you do it, Wendell," Kenny said as he jabbed his finger out at the car chugging ahead of us.

"Way you do what?" I asked.

"I'll bet they're dating," Kenny replied. "It doesn't cost them anything to come up here. Anything else will cost the guys something. I've got to remember this."

"Brilliant," I replied sarcastically. "Wait till you see if they ever get another date after this before you try it!" But, as I considered it more carefully, I thought it might be worth a try.

We reached the top of the driveway and joined the couples who had come to see the crazy old man for the tour and lecture. Mr. Tubalcaine had one foot propped up on a weathered-hickory, cane-bottom chair that he apparently left out in front of his building where he could sit while waiting for guests.

He was welcoming the couples as we walked up. He welcomed us as well, but made no indication he recognized me even after I gave my name. Apparently deciding that the six of us guests made a quorum, he turned to the building and began to describe it and its functions. He spoke of it as if it were an operating institution.

"That part of the second floor is the community workshop. The school occupies the first floor here."

His building stood taller and much larger than we imagined: two stories high plus a tower, with three wings, and a wood-shingle roof. The exterior remained unfinished. It had no panes in the windows and the walls were covered with a thick, rough, black coating. We learned later in the lecture that he made the black coating by mixing pine rosin and sawdust from pine heartwood. It had begun to peel in a few places. We could see through the second floor windows that the interior structure there was still bare lumber, as was the state of affairs on the first floor except for a few rooms where Mr. Tubalcaine lived. While these rooms had unfinished board walls and canvas coverings over the windows to keep out the weather, only one room appeared to have any contents. Even it had no floor. Only the foundations of the walls rose from the ground.

Then he guided us inside and indicated that we should sit in four school desks arranged before a lectern with two sheets of plywood for a makeshift floor. Kenny and I deferred to the older people— maybe less than five years older—but we were polite Southern boys. We stood behind the desks.

A large hot-air furnace sat on a mat of bricks in the center of the occupied room. It was the kind of furnace in which a cast-iron firebox is surrounded by a much larger metal shell. It was so large that we guessed it had been intended to heat the whole building. Only a few ducts were attached to the furnace, so most of the heat vented from the top of the shell into his living space. Since a prediction of fall was in the air, the door of the furnace stood open, and a small fire glowed inside.

What appeared to be Mr. Tubalcaine's entire wardrobe hung over one end or the other of a metal-frame bed. A desk with books piled high on it sat near the furnace with a single facing chair. Two bookcases held his reference books, the books left over from the trade school, three to six copies of each, about a dozen church hymnals, and other assorted textbooks.

Standing at the lectern, Mr. Tubalcaine began with a formal welcome and recounted his plan for the utopian community: a plan that he still hoped to achieve. Then he passed out copies of his textbook on typing. It reminded me of the hymnal at church; and, sure enough, when I looked at the title page, I discovered that Francis Poole, Frog Level's only printer, publisher, and songwriter had produced it. He gave us typewriter keyboards hand-drawn on cardboard and instructed us on how to place our hands. Since Kenny and I were standing, we placed our pretend keyboards on a low bookcase.

Next we received a short lesson on woodworking. Mr. Tubalcaine stood beside a chart that showed several different methods for joining furniture parts and had us memorize the names of the joint parts. A few comments on religion, the value of learning, and the importance of producing for ourselves the items of everyday life concluded the class.

The two couples thanked Mr. Tubalcaine for the lecture and told him how it impressed them that he knew so much about so many different topics. Then they wandered back to their cars and headed down the driveway. Kenny and I hung around looking at the building and marveling how only a few people built such a huge structure. We spotted the sawmill not far away and were examining it when Mr. Tubalcaine came up.

"You're the Wiggins boy who builds rockets," he said.

"Yessir. This is Kenny Livingston who builds them with me."

"Hello, Kenny. Did you boys finish looking at the building?"

"I guess so," I said. Kenny seemed to agree.

"Let me show you one more thing," Mr. Tubalcaine said as he turned and started slowly back to the entrance to his living area.

"Do you know that Noah used pitch to seal the ark? I suspect that he used pitch made from petroleum since it's available there, but it might have been made from tree rosin just like I used here. Either one works very well. I use it for lots of things."

We had gone inside his living area and continued to follow him around the bed and into an adjoining room. There, on sawhorses, sat a traditional wooden casket. I could see in the interior that it was made of very rich yellow-pine heartwood, and it was covered with the same pitch and sawdust as covered the outside of the building. The lid to the casket leaned against a wall nearby.

"I like to plan ahead. My work here isn't done yet, but I'm prepared. The Lord works in mysterious ways, his wonders to perform."

This unexpected presentation of a casket and the reference to God's mysterious ways gave both Kenny and me the creeps. It reminded us of the stories about Mr. Tubalcaine that the kids told at school. We admired the casket very briefly, said we needed to get home, and headed back toward the driveway.

Mr. Tubalcaine followed us out. By the time we were rounding the corner where we could see the driveway, a few self-deprecating, humorous remarks from Mr. Tubalcaine and the bright sunshine dispelled our creeps, and we stopped to say goodbye.

We rather foolishly complemented him on the fine building and gave wishes for the school's success. While he could speak of his project as if it were on the path to completion, he recognized the hollowness of the same outlook in us. Even we could see it in his face. We fell silent.

"Where do you boys fire your rockets?" he asked after a while.

"Kenny lives just this side—the east side—of the Sipsey on the Tuscaloosa highway. We have a launch site on the back side of a hill from his house. They fly out over the swamp so they won't hit anything they shouldn't."

Mr. Tubalcaine pondered this for a moment and then, for the first time since we arrived, a broad smile spread across his face. It lasted for just a few seconds, and then, in a flash, his eyebrows tilted and his eyes opened wide. He asked us very seriously, "Have you boys ever run into Theawatoosa down there in the swamp?"

Kenny and I just looked at each other. Before we could think of any kind of answer, we all heard the sound of a car coming up the driveway. I turned to see the car and then decided to ask for more information.

When I turned back to Mr. Tubalcaine to ask, "Who?" the strange wide-eyed look had vanished from his face, and he was unmistakably very angry. What had we done?

I had no time to wonder about it or to begin an apology for who-knows-what. Mr. Tubalcaine was off to intercept the car. Before the two men inside could even open the door, he slapped his hand on top of the car and began loud demands that they turn around and motioned the same message with his arms. The men began to get out anyway. Kenny and I decided it was time to leave. We were relieved to conclude that these men made Mr. Tubalcaine angry instead of us.

As we walked down the driveway, we exchanged theories about who the new arrivals were and why Mr. Tubalcaine seemed so unhappy to see them. The reception he gave them was so different than the warm reception he had given the young couples and us.

"The mention of Theawatoosa made him mad," Kenny said.

"Really? Why do you think that?"

"Well, he couldn't have even seen who was in the car when he got mad."

I realized Kenny was right. The sun had reflected from the windows so that I couldn't even see how many people were inside. "But he's the one who mentioned it," I said.

"Yeah, I know. Can you think of anything else that might have made him mad?"

"Maybe something we said about the casket," I offered.

"Who knows?" was Kenny's last observation.

As we got back on the bikes, I asked, "Kenny, do you have any idea who or what is Theawatoosa?"

"Nope," he replied without a pause, "And I'm sure not going back up there to ask him."

Now that Grandmother had died and Kavanaugh worked at the grocery store, I ate breakfast alone. Mother usually had a second cup of coffee with me. It seemed like a good time to ask, "What is Theawatoosa?"

"What did you say?"

"What or who is Theawatoosa?"

"Who told you about him?" she asked sharply. I could see and hear that she was angry. Why did the mention of Theawatoosa make everyone angry?

Since I had no idea why she got angry and didn't want to say anything that might make her more upset and already wished I hadn't asked, I weaseled an answer, "I heard people discussing it."

Mother assumed she knew the real answer: Aunt Brazzie.

"Did Aunt Brazzie tell you about Theawatoosa?"

I answered truthfully, "No," but mother already assumed I was fibbing.

"Theawatoosa is a make-believe goblin that some parents made up to scare their children into behaving. I never scared you with him. Some people have got nothing better to do than talk about old stuff like...."

She seemed not able to find the right word and just let the sentence drop. Then she went on.

"I'd suspect Herman or James but you haven't seen Herman in six months and James is in Colorado in the veteran's home. Well, I assume you're old enough to know better."

She went back into the kitchen, and I let it drop. In fact, I finished my breakfast as quickly as I could and carried my last biscuit back into my bedroom to be sure the conversation didn't go off in a bad direction.

**The inquisition**

Since Mother mentioned Aunt Brazzie as my likely source, I figured she was my best bet to get the real lowdown on Theawatoosa. Both Kenny and I felt sure that we weren't going back to Mount Nebo to ask Mr. Tubalcaine. I was pretty certain my mother wouldn't get angry if Theawatoosa were, in fact, make-believe as she said, so I'd visit Aunt Brazzie as soon as I could. I wished I could ask my grandmother. She would know and give me a straight answer. Thinking of Grandmother reminded me of what she said about Tubal-Cain and how some people thought his father was Satan. Make-believe goblins, children of Satan, evil names from the Bible, black caskets in the living room: everything about my trip to see Mr. Tubalcaine was giving me the creeps.

Wizzie would go across to Brazzie's almost every day up to the last year before she died. They usually had some project in the works. Some times they cut strips from woolen clothes to weave into braided rugs. Sometimes they'd make up a batch of one of Aunt

Brazzie's medicinal compounds.

When Grandmother was alive, I would often end up at Aunt Brazzie's to help her cross the street, to fetch her back for supper, to carry something to her, or any number of other reasons. A couple of years ago, one of Aunt Brazzie's daughters moved back to Frog Level with her two daughters, Zoe Ann and Jeannie. I'd visit to fix a broken doll or play checkers with one of my cousins. Thus, it seemed not at all unusual for me to pay a visit to Aunt Brazzie, and Mother needn't know I was inquiring about Theawatoosa.

I went over the next afternoon. The weather was warm, so I was pretty sure that Aunt Brazzie would be sitting on the front porch with some sewing project. She sat there in warm weather and in her bedroom in a rocker by the fireplace when it turned cold. I can't recall ever seeing her sit anywhere else in her house.

I went up the two sagging wooden steps and sat down on the metal glider swing that rested against the front wall of the house. Aunt Brazzie sat in a wicker chair against the front railing of the porch opposite the glider swing. Behind her was a solid wall of wisteria that twined through every opening of the wooden railings.

"Hi, Aunt Brazzie. What'cha working on?"

She didn't answer the question since she knew I wasn't really interested. "I've got a box full of canning jars in the kitchen. Would you carry them out to the barn for me? Put them in that old corn crib."

Yes, ma'am," I replied, then got up and went inside. At the back of the house I encountered the distinct smell of Aunt Brazzie's kitchen. She made coffee by filling an aluminum pan with water, throwing in some grounds and boiling it. After breakfast, the pan would sit on the stove until Aunt Brazzie cleaned up at the end of the day. I don't know why it smelled so strongly or so unlike percolated coffee, but I've never encountered the smell anywhere since. And, of course, Uncle Doc's pipe smoke and the whiff of Aunt Brazzie's snuff and maybe the smell of warm laundry water in the big washing sink added to the aroma. You probably think it smelled awful, but it didn't to me. It embodied the spirit of my great aunt's house that I had known since birth. I savored it.

Brazzie's husband's name was Hester Pinion, but every one called him Doc for some reason unknown to me. He was old, maybe a few years younger than Aunt Brazzie, but at least pushing eighty. Lean and sprightly, he moved as easily as a man ten years or more younger. He smoked cigarettes or a pipe, had a thick mustache, and always smiled and laughed easily.

After dumping the jars in the barn, I came back and flopped on the glider. Aunt Brazzie made no sign of speaking and continued her sewing.

"Aunt Brazzie, who or what is Theawatoosa?"

She put her sewing down in her lap and just peered at me for a while. At first, I thought she was going to be angry too, but her expression softened as she stared at me, and I could tell she was just pondering a very unexpected question.

"Where did you hear about that?"

I'd already decided to be very straight with her concerning how I'd heard the name and tell her truthfully that I knew absolutely nothing else about it.

"Kenny Livingston and I rode up to Mount Nebo last Sunday afternoon to see Mr. Tubalcaine's big house. He gave us a lecture on typing and woodworking."

I filled in several other details including the casket.

"As we were leaving, he asked us if we had ever seen Theawatoosa while we were setting off rockets in the swamp."

Aunt Brazzie alternately smiled and looked sad as I described what I had seen at Mr. Tubalcaine's. She clearly knew the whole story.

"So John Tubalcaine told you," she said more or less to herself.

"What is it?" I urged her again.

"Did you ask your mother about him?"

Okay, a small nugget of information. It's a him.

"Yes, I asked her and she told me it's a make-believe booger[13] man. She thinks you told me about him."

"And where did she get that idea?"

Uh oh, this was threatening to go badly due to my previous lack of candor with Mother. I realized I had a truth I could use to deflect her questioning.

"I told her it wasn't you."

It worked; she went on. "I can't talk to you about it. Your mother would whip me if I did."

Well, that was clearly an exaggeration.

"Aunt Brazzie, my mother isn't going to whip you and you know it. Tell me."

"I can't and I won't talk to you about it. She would at least never speak to me again. Now go on!"

I just sat there for a while. Aunt Brazzie picked up her sewing again to show that the conversation was over.

I made one last try.

"When did you learn about him?"

She picked up a fly swatter and swung it at me. It didn't reach across the porch but I got the message and gave up.

"Anything else I can do for you before I go?" I said.

"No. Tell your mother to come over later."

"Okay," I muttered. I wasn't going to deliver the message, have Mother come right over, and learn the reason for my visit.

One more long-forgotten question popped out from my memory as I started to get up, and I sank back down on the squeaky glider. "Aunt

---

[13] Booger was a catch-all word for a demon, monster, ghost, etc. It was pronounced like the word for a piece of dried mucus. Yeah, I know, it's gross, but like all kids, we liked gross.

Brazzie, do you remember the first time that you and Grandmother took Kavanaugh and me fishing?"

She looked at me blankly for a moment, and then a real smile came over her face for the first time since I arrived. "Oh lord, yes! What a day. What a mess!"

"When Grandmother was warning us about halfigators, you mentioned Mr. Hollingshead jumping in the river on top of a halfigator. You started to say something, I think something about Grandmother, but you never finished the sentence.

Aunt Brazzie pursed her lips in thought and slowly relaxed as nothing came to mind. She looked up at me apologetically.

"Oh, it was something like 'if you hadn't.... done something'."

Her face lit up and the same laugh that had been stifled for six years since that day in the swamp made it to the surface. "Josh Hollingshead jumped on top of the halfigator because your Grandmother dared him to. Riding him to Mobile was her foolishness; she's the one who said that. Poor old Josh just didn't have the sense to resist her devilment. I guess we know where Herman and James learned their wicked ways. The apple doesn't fall far....."

She stopped in midsentence. I had no clue why she stopped, but it was just like when Grandmother whacked her with her walking stick. I knew how the sentence ended, so I just waited.

"Is this your round-about way of getting me to talk about Theawatoosa?"

"No ma'am. What does Mr. Hollingshead have to do with Theawatoosa?"

"Absolutely nothing," she said.

And then she bent intently to her sewing, and I could see that all conversations were definitely over for now.

As I walked back across Temple Avenue, I pondered the conversation with Aunt Brazzie, and rather than shedding any light on the Theawatoosa question, the whole thing puzzled me more. I visualized the image of Mother whipping Aunt Brazzie, and it made me smile and triggered the memory of how Grandmother had whacked Brazzie's shin with her walking stick. The scene around me faded into all sorts of imaginations and rememberings, and I began a fantasy in which no one ever finished a sentence till six years after it began. I imagined talking to Aunt Brazzie six years later, and she came out with, ".... from the tree."

I yelled out loud or to myself; I don't know which, "Watch out, don't step off...." and after a long pause, "four years, five years, six years... the edge or you'll fall off the cliff. Oops, too late." I suppose I giggled, but I don't know. I was lost in the fantasy until I awakened in my shop, staring blankly at an electric motor I had dismembered the previous week.

I got Daddy to drop me off at Kenny's the next day to work on our latest rocket. We were working on a one-and-a-half-inch steel electrical pipe with an improvised nozzle made from a pipe fitting welded on the rear. We spent a lot of work getting the fins attached accurately.

As we prepared to load the powdered zinc and sulfur fuel, I gave Kenny an account of my inquiries. As I recounted the conversations, our inclination to believe that something was being hidden grew stronger. The unexplained anger that the question provoked from Mother and Aunt Brazzie's absolute refusal to discuss it whetted both our curiosities. There had to be something here more than a fairy-tale goblin. Kenny had made a single inquiry to his father and got a "I don't know." But Kenny's father was a man of few words and often seemed to be angry because of something Kenny didn't even know about. At the time, Kenny thought better of pushing the topic and accepted the answer at face value. He assumed Theawatoosa was not widely known; but now, considering the results of my inquiries as well as his, he began to suspect the "I don't know" meant "I don't want to talk about it."

I told Kenny the origin of Mr. Tubalcaine's name and what it meant.

"Gee, that's really weird," Kenny said. "Your grandmother says he's a good Christian man, but he's named for a son of Satan? Brother Pritchard says there are people who just pretend to be Christians so they can influence real Christians. Maybe he's one of those. Maybe the story about him making sacrifices to the Devil are true."

Kenny and his family attended a Pentecostal church like the one that Dwight and Jessie had attended. They were believers in miracles, speaking in tongues, healings, and other very literal interpretations of the Bible, so he was not as surprised by the idea, "Son of Satan," as I was. The preacher at their church was Brother Pritchard.

By the way, the title Brother or Sister applied to any religious person in Frog Level. A few preachers and pastors claimed a specific title such as Reverend, but you could safely use Brother or Sister to refer to anyone in a religious context. On Sunday morning everyone at church was Brother Jones or Sister Smith, but people who served as preachers or elders kept the titles all week.

Kenny thought his preacher should know about esoteric beings, goblins and demons, and he might be more inclined to discuss things our parents were not comfortable with. Given my one experience with Pentecostals at the river baptism, he didn't seem to be the unbiased authority I wanted, but I agreed anyway. We'd ask Brother Pritchard.

Brother Pritchard wasn't a full-time minister. Even if they had been wealthy enough, the Pentecostal churches didn't pay their preachers. They felt that one should not be paid to do God's work. The preacher simply took whatever the congregation dropped into the collection plate as a "goodwill offering." Brother Pritchard worked, Monday through Saturday, as a sheet-metal mechanic. He made heating ducts and other items from galvanized steel or aluminum sheets. His shop occupied what had earlier been some sort of retail store just beyond Five Points, an intersection only a block from my home.

The next day, Kenny hitched a ride into Frog Level with one of his older brothers and walked the mile from downtown to our house. He showed up not long after breakfast, and Mother told him I would be found in the back room of the garage—my workshop. Kenny came in the shop, and after a few minutes showing him the electronic circuit that puzzled me at the moment, we walked up Temple Avenue and angled left at Mr. Garrison's store on the road to the county prison. We reached Brother Pritchard's shop halfway up the hill.

When we entered, he was at the sheet metal brake, a device that bends a sharp corner in sheet metal. He had a stack of sheets he had cut and was making two bends in each sheet before stacking them to his right to await the next operation.

He recognized Kenny immediately, they exchanged friendly comments about church happenings, and Kenny introduced me. Brother Pritchard recognized me from the grocery store as soon as he heard my name.

Then Kenny asked, "Brother Pritchard, who is Theawatoosa?"

We should have expected it by then, but were nonetheless uneasy when a dark scowl came over his face.

"Oh Lord, spare these young men from the demons of this earth. Kenny, have you encountered this demonic spirit?" He grabbed Kenny by both his shoulders.

"Nosir, Wendell and I just heard his name, and we're wondering who he is."

"Thank you, Lord!" Brother Pritchard addressed his comment to the ceiling. He still held Kenny with both hands. He took one hand off long enough to pull me about two feet closer.

He took a deep breath and leaned toward us. "Theawatoosa is a spawn of the devil, a spawn of the devil! Do you know what that means?"

"Nosir." We weren't even sure what spawn meant, but we looked it up later and found it meant offspring, children, especially a whole brood of them.

"When God created the heavens and the earth and saw that it was good, Satan looked down at the Lord's beautiful creation, and he was jealous and decided to create something of his own. He hadn't no idea how to make a whole universe, so he made creatures that slouch about in God's creation. They're misshaped and horrible in all kind of ways. Nothing right or good comes from Satan. You know that. They've lived on since the creation of the world, some 6000 years now, and they hide from God's good creatures. Theawatoosa is one of them, and some people say he hides down there."

He swept his left arm out and pointed toward Grimsley's farm and the swamp.

"Don't you boys never go down there alone. Shun the very appearance of evil. Clothe yourselves in righteousness and gird yourselves with the sword of the Spirit. Ephesians, Chapter 6."

"Have you ever seen him?" we asked almost in unison.

"No, I haven't. He mayn't live down there, but then, he just might. I don't doubt that his kind are all around us. We tend to run into evil when we least expect it."

We got several more admonitions to avoid evil and attend church regularly. We attended church very regularly since our parents gave us no choice, and we usually steered away from evil except when it looked too nice. We certainly weren't going to hang out with a deformed child of the Devil. No need to worry, Brother Pritchard.

As we began to move toward the door, Brother Pritchard asked, "Why are you boys asking about that demon?"

I answered, "We went to see Mr. Tubalcaine's Sunday-afternoon show this last weekend, and he mentioned him."

My answer actually made Brother Pritchard shudder like he had just gotten a high fever.

"Oh Lord in Heaven!" he yelled. "Not him again! Stay away from that… that false prophet, that devil worshipper! Let's pray, boys."

He grabbed Kenny again, fell on his knees, and pulled Kenny down with him. He looked up at me and motioned with his head for me to kneel. I just stood there.

Brother Pritchard began to pray in language I had learned to associate with gospel-meeting preaching. He implored God to save Kenny and me from the evil spirits we'd attracted. He told God what a good boy Kenny was. He pretty much demanded that God drop some awful punishment on Mr. Tubalcaine. He finished up by begging God to build some sort of spiritual fortress around Frog Level.

I felt very uneasy—actually, I guess, embarrassed—by Brother

Pritchard's outburst and prayer. I wanted to get out of his shop as soon as I could, but I remembered what Grandmother said about people thinking Mr. Tubalcaine was evil because of his name, and I felt obliged to defend him.

"Brother Pritchard, Mr. Tubalcaine isn't evil just because of his name. The bible doesn't say Tubal Cain was evil."

He seemed very surprised and maybe a little offended that a kid would take exception to his theology. "You're wrong there, Wendell. Satan was his father."

"Nosir, that's not in the Bible. My grandmother told me Josephus or some medieval professor said that."

Now Brother Pritchard got really worked up. He pulled his eyebrows together and wrinkled his lips as if they had a drawstring around them. "So your grandmother is an expert on Josephus, is she? I'm not going to argue with you. You're Church of Christ, aren't you? The Bible says by their fruits ye shall know them, and I know the fruits of that old hermit, Tubalcaine. Now you boys go on. You go home and study what the Bible says about demons and evil spirits. And you better pray that none of them gets in your heart! Now shoo!"

I started for the door, not even looking to see whether Kenny came along. He quickly excused himself, thanked Brother Pritchard, and assured him we would stay way from Mr. Tubalcaine and the swamp.

The story we got from Brother Pritchard sounded certainly more interesting and a lot scarier than the fairy-tale explanation from my mother and the no-comment I got from Aunt Brazzie. If Brother Pritchard was right, that sort of explained why everyone became agitated when we mentioned Theawatoosa. It wouldn't be the first topic on which my parents felt I wasn't old enough to know about it.

Kenny was mad at me because I didn't kneel down for the prayer and I argued with Brother Pritchard. "I know your church believes a lot of things differently, but you should show some respect for any minister."

"I'm sorry, Kenny," I said. "It's just that I don't believe Mr. Tubalcaine is evil. Did he do anything to make you think he's evil?"

"No, nothing other than bring up Theawatoosa. Why did he do that? And another thing, Tubalcaine means Son of Satan and Brother Pritchard says Theawatoosa was created by the Devil, sort of a child of Satan. Maybe they're connected somehow."

As we walked back to the house, Kenny and I admitted to each other that Brother Pritchard's explanation was not what either of us expected. A demon living about a mile away from my bedroom gave me fearful thoughts even though I didn't actually believe in demons. Well, I thought they didn't exist, but I couldn't be completely sure. Some people thought they were real, and what if they were right? Brother Pritchard seemed to believe for sure. If they weren't real, why wouldn't Mother and Aunt Brazzie just laugh about it? I began to wish really badly that Mr. Tubalcaine hadn't brought it up. I sort of wished we hadn't gone to visit him. If I had lived in Frog Level for fifteen years without Theawatoosa bothering me, why would he bother me now? Well, maybe just knowing he existed and thinking about him attracted him. He was, I guess, a spirit, and he might know what I thought. Even the bright sunshine wasn't enough to keep the creeps away.

The more I thought about it, the worse I felt. My grandmother, my parents, and everybody at church seemed to really believe in Satan and Hell. They said God would really hear a prayer I said silently in my head. If it was true, then why couldn't there be other invisible, spirit things I didn't know about. Jesus cast out demons, whatever that meant. There must be demons somewhere.

I suppose because he trusted Brother Pritchard more than I did, Kenny accepted the explanation even more uneasily.

Back in my shop, we decided we had to ask someone else about Theawatoosa. But who? Since we asked the preacher of Kenny's church, I suggested we ask Brother Flowers, my preacher. I supposed him to be trustworthy and forthcoming. Furthermore, the doctrine of the Church of Christ held that miraculous, supernatural events no longer occurred. The Age of Miracles ended with the death of the last Christian Apostle, they said. When God answered a prayer, he did it in some invisible, undetectable way, they said. We wouldn't likely hear a confirmation of the "spawn of the devil" theory. That made me feel better—a little.

Kenny came to the house on Thursday morning. He took Kavanaugh's bike, and we rode down to the church building, arriving just as Brother Flowers would be finishing his daily radio broadcast. We waited outside his office until we heard him give the usual ending to the daily sermon, then we knocked and went in. He greeted us warmly, saying how our visit was very unexpected. It was. I'd never visited him during the week and Kenny certainly hadn't. Church services on Sunday morning, Sunday night, and Wednesday night were quite enough religion for a week.

After I introduced Kenny, Brother Flowers launched into small talk that he thought young people would like, punctuated by guffaws to which we responded politely.

Finally his patter subsided enough that we could get down to business. I asked the main question. "Kenny and I went up to hear Mr. Tubalcaine's lecture last Sunday. He mentioned Theawatoosa. Who is Theawatoosa?"

Very predictably by now, his expression turned somber, and he leaned forward.

"Theawatoosa is a personification of evil. He lives in the hearts of people who don't have God in their hearts. He tempts them to do bad things. He convinces them that evil will bring happiness, but it never does."

I jumped in with a question, not only because I wanted its answer, but also, because I sensed Brother Flowers warming up to a small sermon just for us.

"But is he real?"

"Of course, he's real. Evil is just as real as the goodness of Jesus."

"No, I know evil is real, but could I see him if I ran into him?"

"Can you see love? It's real. Can you see the evil thoughts in a murderer's heart? They're real."

I tried again. "Is Theawatoosa just a spirit or does he have a manifestation I could see with my eyes?"

I thought "manifestation" was just the right word, broad enough to make Brother Flowers deal with my intended meaning. I'd taken the word from a vampire comic book that showed spirits and ghouls appearing and making things fly through the air. It referred to these real physical events that usually resulted in somebody being very unpleasantly exterminated as "manifestations."

Brother Flowers seemed to like the question. He raised a finger for emphasis.

"Can you see a bank robber shoot a policeman? Can you see the children of some drunk going to bed cold and hungry at night? We can see the manifestation of evil all around us every day."

I gave up. I wasn't going to get the distinction I wanted, much less be able to dig for details.

I had one more question before we left. "Brother Flowers, we asked the preacher at Kenny's church, Brother Pritchard, about Theawatoosa yesterday."

His face fell. I realized he had thought he was the first person we asked.

I went on. "He said Theawatoosa is a spawn of the devil. I guess that's sort of what you're saying." I chose my words carefully to try to tell Brother Flowers what had happened without having him make dismissive comments about Brother Pritchard and hurt Kenny's feelings."

"That sounds like what he would say," Brother Flowers said with a grin. I hoped Kenny wasn't looking at him.

I went on quickly. "He really doesn't like Mr. Tubalcaine. Do you think Mr. Tubalcaine is evil?"

Brother Flowers looked puzzled at first, then seemed to be trying to remember something. Finally, he smiled. "I'll bet he thinks Tubalcaine's the Devil Incarnate." He chuckled and shook his head. "Would you know what I meant if I referred to the Wallace-Ketcherside debate?"

"Nosir. No idea."

"Well, I'm sure you know that preachers like to talk. Oh, do they!

All of us. Well, some preachers who disagree with each other set up debates about whatever they disagree on. This is usually one Church of Christ preacher against another. The debates are advertised. They publish the affirmations—that's the points they're going to argue—and sometimes, if the preachers are well known, they get really big audiences. It doesn't happen in churches where some central authority sets the dogma. Since the Church of Christ congregations each get to decide their own beliefs, it happens all the time. I mentioned the Wallace-Ketcherside debate because it's the most recent really big one.

"Anyway, a few years ago, no maybe twenty or twenty five years ago, Mr. Tubalcaine wanted a debate. He couldn't find a Church of Christ preacher to oppose him. He tried hard to get Brother Kitchens to oppose him on the orphan homes, but Kitchens wouldn't do it. Finally, he got Brother Pritchard to agree to do it. The issue he got Pritchard to agree to was whether we still have miracles and gifts of the Spirit today. Of course, he said yes, and Mr. Tubalcaine said no. Most people agreed that Mr. Tubalcaine won. He knew some of the original Greek text of the Bible and could quote a lot of learned opinion. Pritchard couldn't do anything but quote Bible verses.

"So, Brother Pritchard has held a grudge against Mr. Tubalcaine ever since. I'm not surprised that Pritchard would say he's evil. He is a fervent pentecostal, so he would naturally think of Tubalcaine as evil. His name certainly doesn't help."

"Do you think Tubal Cain in the Bible is evil?" I asked.

"I don't know," Brother Flowers said. "It doesn't matter. I guess if I was named Tubalcain, I might change my name."

Kenny and I thanked him for the information. He followed us out of the office and invited Kenny to come to church services with me. The way Brother Flowers spoke about Brother Pritchard insulted Kenny, and he didn't want any more church anyway, so he deflected the invitation by commenting on a football he had seen on the bookshelf in the office, and we got away with no further religious discussions.

Brother Flowers' explanation of Theawatoosa was not the same as Brother Pritchard's, but it was too close for my taste. Were we learning about a supernatural being that roamed just a mile from my house? Maybe he had manifestations or maybe not. That would explain why everyone became so unhappy when we mentioned him. If Theawatoosa were a spirit, some people might think they would attract him just by thinking or saying his name. Even if he were only a spirit, with no physical manifestation, I still didn't want him messing around in my mind. But why hadn't we been warned to avoid him before John Tubalcaine mentioned him? Maybe he was real but didn't actually live down in the swamp. Maybe he was just a make-believe goblin as Mother had said, but why didn't everyone know that? We were really confused. We had to have a firm answer that at least most adults agreed on. One thing confirmed we weren't just being the butt of a joke made up on the spot by Mr. Tubalcaine: everybody knew about Theawatoosa, and everybody took him very seriously.

At least now, I knew why Brother Pritchard disliked Mr. Tubalcaine so much.

Our next choice in trying to sort out this deepening mystery, maybe, was Colonel Lufkin, the man who ran Lufkin's Cafe. He had two sons, Storey and Prentiss, who were our local experts in electrical technology and electronics. Storey installed electrical wiring and appliances, and Prentiss repaired TVs and radios. Colonel Lufkin seemed to me to have always been ninety years old. I didn't actually know how old he was, but in my youth-distorted estimate, I guessed ninety. So we picked him primarily for his age and supposedly associated wisdom, and because we figured anyone who turned out such smart sons must be smart.

Again, Kenny hitched a ride into town the next day. We were working through our expert consultants one a day. I rode my bike down to meet him in front of the Courthouse. It was a good meeting place from my point of view. I guess I liked it in much the same way that C. Beauregard Thuless liked it. A large granite drinking and ornamental fountain stood where the walkway to the Courthouse joined the sidewalk, but it had been dry as long as I could remember. A couple of times my mother had described the scene there when the last public hanging occurred not long after she moved to Frog Level. I always thought of that when I passed by.

Kenny perched on the fence by the old fountain. The ornamental cast-iron posts and two round steel rails that ran horizontally between the posts were perfectly sized so that you could sit on the top rail and hook your heels on the lower rail. It also provided the perfect perch from which to survey what went on in downtown Frog Level. You could see Temple Avenue from the Curb Market and Nichols Hardware on the north end to the railroad tracks on the south end. It also served as the perfect place to be seen. Thus, on Saturday afternoon, young men lined the fence. Kavanaugh and I always wanted to go sit on the courthouse fence when Mother made us go to town with her on a shopping trip. She wouldn't allow us to do it, saying that, "You don't want to be the kind of person who sits on the courthouse fence." She never explained what that meant.

I leaned my bike against a post, hooked one foot on the lower rail and perched beside Kenny. It was too nice a morning to be in a hurry, so we sat and allowed the summer heat to make one of its last irresistible appearances.

After scanning the morning traffic and noting Hal Bankston talking to Buster Grimes in front of the First National Bank, I began, "Miles Starett told me that he and Paul are interested in splitting another keg of zinc dust. Can you come up with fifteen dollars for a quarter keg?

Kenny groaned. "I know we need it, but I can't come up with it. Can you?"

"Not really. I'm trying to save my money to buy a Heathkit vacuum-tube voltmeter kit."

"Yeah," Kenny nodded. "I think we better use potassium nitrate for now. It's easier to pack in anyway. I think we've got enough zinc dust to fill one more after the inch-and-a-halfer," referring to the rocket we were currently building.

Eventually I suggested we get on over to Lufkin's Cafe. We walked across Temple Avenue, opened the screen door and took two stools at the counter.

I could see back into the kitchen and didn't see Colonel Lufkin. I started to say that he might not be there when Kenny spotted him sitting in one of the booths talking to Cecil Hubbert. We both ordered milkshakes even though we'd eaten breakfast only about an hour earlier, and we waited for Mr. Hubbert to leave. He crushed out his cigarette and got up just as we were about finished. We both slurped the remains of our milkshakes through the straws and headed to the booth before an adult could preempt us or Colonel Lufkin could get up.

"Good Morning, Colonel Lufkin. This is Kenny Livingston."

"I know Kenny. He used to ride his bike up and down the road in front of our house."

I hadn't thought about how close Kenny lived to the Lufkins.

"Colonel Lufkin, we'd like to ask you a question."

"Sure, sit down boys."

I slid into the booth opposite Colonel Lufkin, and Kenny slid in beside me."

"Do you boys want anything to eat?"

Kenny let out a fake burp and said we had just finished milkshakes.

I got down to business. "Colonel Lufkin, we've recently heard of something called Theawatoosa, but the people we've asked don't agree on who or what he is. Can you explain it to us?"

He didn't get mad. About the time I finished, he smiled. Yes, he smiled, and it slowly turned into a big grin and a chuckle.

"My, my," he said. "I haven't heard that name in years. It must be twenty years or more now."

We were pleased with this pleasant reply and relaxed a little, but I was impatient. "But who is he?"

"I imagine you boys have studied the civil war, haven't you?"

We just nodded yes to encourage him to go on.

"After the civil war was over and we lost, there were lots of Union troops still passing through, and after they stopped coming, there were the carpetbaggers. A lot of Confederate troops brought home more than just a hunting rifle and weren't inclined to part with their guns. Some people built a shed down in the swamp and stored the bigger guns there. Some people say they had a cannon or two.

"Of course, they didn't want any passers-through to go meddling around in the swamp, so they made up a story to scare them off. If any Yankees showed their face here, they probably heard pretty quickly about Theawatoosa, a demon who lived in the swamp and prowled around at night. I heard that if somebody had a cow or pig that got sick and died, they'd dump it by the old gas seep. Then, if any visitor was a skeptic about the demon story, he'd be taken down to the gas seep and shown the bone pile where Theawatoosa ate his supper."

Well, now we had yet another new explanation. No two the same yet. Colonel Lufkin's explanation contained the make-believe aspect of Theawatoosa and yet explained why everyone around Frog Level knew about him. This one sounded pretty reasonable if we could find several people who agreed on the story, but I wanted a few more details.

"Colonel Lufkin, how did you hear about Theawatoosa? I guess you learned it when you were a little kid."

He didn't seem to have ever questioned the origin or reliability of the legend, and he just pondered the question for a moment.

"No, I don't think I heard about it until I was grown up. I think my boys heard it somewhere and told me."

Oh, crud. He wasn't the ancient authority we hoped for. He just heard it from his kids.

"Colonel Lufkin, do you believe it?"

"Of course, most everybody knows the story of Theawatoosa."

"But Colonel Lufkin, everybody we've asked gives us a different answer!"

"I wouldn't know about that, boys."

He stared at the wall for a few seconds and then said, "Why don't you ask your school principal, Mr. Shoemaker. He's got about as much education as anybody around here."

We walked back across Temple Avenue to where I had parked my bike, and we perched on the courthouse fence rails again.

"Kenny, I don't think we're getting anywhere with asking people. We still haven't got the same answer from any two people."

"Yeah, but as you pointed out a few days ago, everybody has heard of him. We've just got to get to the source of all these different ideas about him. Why don't we ask Mr. Shoemaker? Seems like a good idea to me."

"Oh, okay, but he's just going to give us another different answer," I said with a sigh of resignation.

"Look, Wendell. Everybody gives us different details but they all agree that Theawatoosa is a monster of some kind. He's real, he's a fairy tale, he's a civil-war legend, he's a spirit, or whatever. I think we're dealing with some sort of evil or at least a really good story here. Don't you want to get to the bottom of it?"

"Okay, we'll ask Mr. Shoemaker," I agreed. "I think he's over at the high school in the afternoons after Summer School finishes. Monday?"

We agreed on Monday.

I wondered why Mother hadn't brought up Theawatoosa again. Our conversation ended very much unfinished, and I expected her to finish it, though it worried me that I somehow would be in trouble when it was all over. Why hadn't Daddy had anything to say? If Mother felt as unhappy about it as she seemed, she surely discussed it with him. I hadn't mentioned Theawatoosa to Kavanaugh because he would make fun of me or give some made-up-on-the-spot preposterous answer. Besides, if he knew anything about a monster in the swamp, I'd have heard it from him long ago. And, we wouldn't have been wandering around the swamp for several years now with a monster on the loose.

I spent the weekend expecting to hear about it any minute, but no one mentioned Theawatoosa.

Monday afternoon, I met Kenny at the High School. Mr. Shoemaker was as surprised to see us as all our other interviewees had been. He called us into his office, and we sat opposite him at his desk.

"What brings you boys here? Can't wait for school to start?"

Yessir, we can wait. We just have a question that we can't get a good answer to."

"Okay," he said as he adjusted a couple of pens on his desk and leaned back in his chair. "What's on your minds?"

I had asked the last couple of times, so I looked at Kenny to indicate that he should ask.

"Mr. Shoemaker, we went up to Mount Nebo Sunday, a week ago, to see John Tubalcaine. He asked us if we had run into Theawatoosa down in the Sipsey Swamp. We've been asking around to try to find out who or what is Theawatoosa. Can you tell us?"

Like Colonel Lufkin and much to our relief, he smiled as he heard the question. He shook his head to indicate something about the question amused or puzzled him.

"How many people have you asked?"

I had to count in my head: Mother, Aunt Brazzie, Brother Pritchard, Brother Flowers, and Colonel Lufkin.

"Five," I said.

"I'll bet you got a different answer from every one of them," he said. "Am I right?"

Kenny and I answered in unison, "Yessir."

Mr. Shoemaker picked up a pen and twirled it around a finger as he arranged his answer.

"There seems to be general confusion about the origin of Theawatoosa. On the other hand, I don't think I've ever run into anyone who grew up in Frog Level who hasn't heard of him. I'm surprised that you boys haven't heard of him before now. I have my own theory to explain how all these tales got started. You boys know about the gas seep, don't you?"

We both nodded yes.

He went on, "When you look at the flame from the gas seep in really damp weather it has a lot more color than in dry weather. Some people think they can see a ghost or demon dancing in the flame."

A glimmer of hope that we'd finally found the answer began to fill me, although I'd felt the same thing at the beginning of Colonel Lufkin's explanation. Now, both Kenny and I were fully attentive.

"I think the idea of a demon living down in the swamp and dancing in the flame goes back to the Indians who lived here. The little bit I know about Indian mythology has lots of characters like Theawatoosa, and it's an Indian name. Did you know that?"

"No sir. Is it related to Tuscaloosa? It sounds kinda the same."

"I don't know of any connection in meaning but it's probably from the same dialect," Mr. Shoemaker said.

"Why does every one have a different version of the story," Kenny asked.

Mr. Shoemaker smiled and said, "Kenny, have you ever played Pass the Secret?"

"Yessir," he replied. "You mean it just got changed as one person told it to another? Why didn't they discuss it and get the story straight?"

Mr. Shoemaker shrugged. "Why don't people pay attention to lots of things? Why do they forget almost everything we teach them within about a year after finishing high school? Why do we have vicious gossip and rumors going around all the time? I don't know."

"Have you ever seen the figure in the gas flame?" I asked.

"Well, I've seen the gas flame when it was really colorful. The dampness must dissolve some minerals, and they come up with the gas and make the colors. But did I see Theawatoosa? Actually, I don't think it would be too hard to imagine that I saw something. If I were predisposed to believe it, I could say I saw an eight-foot tall monster dancing in the flame."

"Colonel Lufkin said that people made up the story after the civil war to keep Union troops from going into the swamp and finding hidden weapons. Did the people just adapt the Indian's story after the war?"

"I hadn't heard that version," mused Mr. Shoemaker. "I suppose they certainly might have. It would be more believable than something made up on the spot since the Union troops would realize that everyone in town knew about it. If Colonel Lufkin mentioned the gas seep, there must be a connection."

I thought I could see the pieces of our mystery falling into place. One last question. "Most of the people we've asked about Theawatoosa get mad or very serious when we ask them. Why is that?"

"Well, some people take these things very seriously. Some really believe in evil spirits and think you shouldn't even talk about them."

"But even my mother got angry when I asked her," I told him. "She doesn't believe in evil spirits. At least I don't think so."

"No. I suspect she doesn't believe in such things. Your mother's too smart for that; she might be just exasperated to think you believed in the stories."

"I suppose so," I said. His story didn't seem to explain the conversation with Mother as I remembered it, but we'd certainly gotten a better explanation from Mr. Shoemaker than any of the others.

"Thank you, Mr. Shoemaker. I hope we understand now, but it's hard to believe people in Frog Level would be so confused about a legend that's been around so long. I'm going to ask my mother about why she got upset when I asked. I don't want her to think I would believe that stuff."

I looked at Kenny as I finished my denial of belief. It offended him a little since he still had a lot of faith in Brother Pritchard.

Kenny and I sat on the front steps of the high school for a while and mulled over what seemed to be the final explanation. While I was less scared of a real demon, Kenny wasn't ready to let go of that idea yet. Lots of loose ends didn't fit exactly, but it seemed likely they would come together if we asked around a bit more. I wondered how many more different explanations of Theawatoosa we could get if we continued to ask. Neither of us had the appetite to keep it up though,

246

and we were ready to move on to something else. We had devoted over a week now to almost nothing else.

Before I headed back home, I intended to visit the library and get a book on Nikola Tesla that I already read, but wanted to go through it again to see if I could understand the Tesla coil better. I really wanted to build one.

I was also very determined to talk to Mother and find out why she had been so unhappy when I mentioned Theawatoosa, why Aunt Brazzie wouldn't discuss it, and get an absolutely honest story about what was going on.

I reached Temple Avenue at the library, went in and checked out the Tesla book. As I came out and threw the book in my bike basket, I saw Mother go past in our car headed to town. I decided to follow her and finish our conversation about Theawatoosa right away. I stood up on the pedals and turned down Temple Avenue as fast as I could go. I couldn't keep up, but I could keep her in view until she turned right at the flagpole.

By the time I turned at the flagpole, the car was nowhere in sight and I thought I'd lost her, but I went on another block and found the car parked in front of Robertson's General Store.

Robertson's General Store was one of the landmarks in town. It had been there so long it seemed as natural and permanent as the hills, a large wooden building that hadn't been freshly painted in a few decades. Ancient advertisements painted on its sides in the early 20th century were barely readable now. It sat on a crumbling concrete retaining wall rising about waist high above the street to make it easier to load a wagon, and it had a porch over part of the front. Enameled steel signs for RC Cola and Nehi fruit-flavored drinks, tobacco, and agricultural products decorated the wall under the porch roof. The entrance on the right entered the clothing, fabric and housewares section, and the entrance on the left opened into the grocery, hardware and farm section. In the hardware section I could buy calcium carbide, another easily available material from which to fabricate pyrotechnic and exploding goodies.

I leaned my bike against the right side of the building, climbed the concrete stairs and went in the right entrance where I was sure to find

Mother browsing the thread or fabric selections for some sewing project. She wasn't there. I scanned across the store and spotted her at the far back of the hardware section. She was in intense conversation with John Tubalcaine.

I stepped behind the Coates & Clark thread cabinet so she wouldn't see me. The conversation went on for another several minutes. Both of them seemed relaxed; they smiled and even laughed together at times. Then they would bend closer together and become serious.

What were they talking about? I considered walking up nonchalantly and joining in, but I was sure they wouldn't continue the present conversation. I also wanted the opportunity to ask Mr. Tubalcaine the big question, "Who is Theawatoosa?" But that wouldn't work now. I figured I'd get the sort of made-up-on-the-spot answer adults always gave kids. It was probably the perfect opportunity to extract the answers that I had just resolved to get, but unexpectedly finding my mother and Mr. Tubalcaine in what appeared to be a conspiratorial conversation killed my courage.

Finally, Mother reached in her pocketbook, took out some folded papers and handed them to Mr. Tubalcaine. She turned and started back to where I was.

I turned and ducked out the entrance before she could see me. I had no idea what was going on, but I suspected it had to do with Theawatoosa, and I wanted some time to think it through before I confronted Mother or was confronted by her.

I rode up the loop road rather slowly, past Norris Bankhead's house, past one elegant house after another, and turned right to go past the water tank and work my way back to Temple Avenue. The road sloped pretty much downhill back to the house, and I could relax and consider how to approach Mother.

The conversation between Mother and Mr. Tubalcaine suggested they were plotting something. Maybe I was in some kind of trouble that I didn't even know about. Maybe the grownups had a scheme to insure we didn't find out the truth. I imagined a multitude of conspiracies.

I couldn't reach a firm decision, so I stopped at Vern Garrison's store and bought a Butterfinger to gain more time before arriving home. I sat down on the front steps of the store, munched, and thought some more. It occurred to me that Mother probably just told Mr. Tubalcaine that I asked her about Theawatoosa, and they were laughing about things done years ago. Maybe the papers she handed him had nothing to do with me, probably some church business. Finally, I realized it was supper time and gave up. I decided on the original plan: direct, insistent inquiry. After all, what had I done wrong? I could argue with a clean conscience that in any wrongdoing I committed, I meant no harm. I got back on my bike with confident innocence and righteous fervor.

Daddy was already home and ready for supper when I got there. Kavanaugh was out tonight on an end-of-summer celebration with some old high-school buddies. Thus, only Daddy, Mother and I sat down at the supper table.

We began to pass around the serving dishes and fill our plates.

While I was still occupied with this important task, and waiting until we'd all served our plates before launching my conversation, Daddy spoke up. "Have you boys found out who Theawatoosa is?" He got us right to the heart of the matter.

"Nosir, we haven't?" But before I could lay out the motivation for our inquiry and the confusion we had discovered, he continued.

"I hear that you've asked just about everybody in Frog Level, 'Who is Theawatoosa?' and you're not satisfied with any of the answers. And furthermore, you don't even believe your mother."

Well, we hadn't asked "everybody" I said with a bit of protest in my tone. But with a little exaggeration aside, they had laid out their case before I could give mine. And, as I should have expected, they probably knew everything Kenny and I had done in the past week.

I began anyway. "Everybody we ask gives us a different answer. I didn't necessarily not believe Mother, but she got mad at me as soon as I asked the question, and Aunt Brazzie is so afraid of Theawatoosa, she won't even talk to me."

Mother got into the conversation. "I didn't get mad at you, and what makes you think Aunt Brazzie's afraid of Theawatoosa? She might have any number of reasons not to talk about him."

"Yeah. You're right," I conceded. "But you were upset by my question and, for whatever reason, Aunt Brazzie got upset when I asked her. No, I remember; she was afraid of you! She said you would whip her. She did!"

## Out of the frying pan

Mother put down her fork and looked at Daddy. "Don't you think it's time Wendell and Kenny go down in the swamp and see for themselves?"

He replied, "I think that would be better than going around town asking more people for information that they won't believe anyway. Before long, somebody's going to come in the store all upset—not about Theawatoosa, but about these boys."

This completely unexpected turn of the conversation stunned me. I had expected, at least hoped, to finally get a firm answer, but instead, they were suggesting that Kenny and I go looking in the swamp for a thing, something still undefined, a spirit or a legend.

"What is it?" It was as much a plea as it was a question.

"It's all the things people have told you over the last week. Believe them or go see for yourself." Daddy said this with a tone of finality and went back to eating.

I looked at Mother. She shrugged and her expression told me she absolutely agreed that we should go see for ourselves.

Daddy finished off his mouthful and quoted, "Jesus said unto them, an evil and adulterous generation seeketh after a sign; and there shall no sign be given to it, but the sign of the prophet Jonas. Matthew 16, verse 4."

I looked at him, not understanding this sudden, very unusual quoting of scripture. A lot of church people quoted scripture, but not my father.

"It's what Brother Flowers preached about last Sunday," he said. "Maybe he was preaching to you. You obviously didn't listen. What kind of sign are you looking for? How about the real thing?"

He turned to Mother with a grin and said, "That was nice. I can't remember when I've been able to use the weekly scripture for some practical problem."

It surprised me to find out he had listened to the sermon!

Mother got back on topic. "We think you and Kenny should just go down and see for yourselves. You'll need to go to the old gas seep. That's where he's always seen. They say it's going to rain tonight so it'll be just right tomorrow night. Call Kenny right after supper and tell him to come tomorrow night. I'll fix y'all some snacks to take, and you can get down there before dark and wait for him. I can go pick up Kenny if he doesn't have a ride."

I wasn't at all sure I wanted to do this, but how could I get out of it now? I ate a little and pondered the unexpected challenge. I'd been down in the swamp many times and never was afraid of anything but halfigators and cottonmouths, and I knew how to handle them now. I absolutely was sure that my parents wouldn't suggest the trip if a monster were going to attack me. I started to think it might be fun. Probably nothing would happen except we'd see interesting colors and patterns in the burning gas and then, maybe, my parents would explain the whole business.

"Great," I said. "I'll finally get to see Theawatoosa. Are you sure I'll recognize the old booger?"

"I think you'll recognize him. You don't believe the swamp is full of boogers, do you?"

I recognized that they were making fun of me, and I fell quiet. After supper, I called Kenny. He was as surprised as I'd been about this new direction in our inquiry. While he proclaimed himself ready to go, I clearly detected hesitation in his many questions about just what we were going to do. Finally, he agreed to show up the next evening for supper and I hung up. I went to my bedroom and started studying the information on Tesla coils in the book I picked up that afternoon.

Kavanaugh came in after I had gone to bed. I thought this was the time to bring it up to him. I felt confused and totally disgusted to find out he seemed to know everything that had gone on. Someone, probably Mother, filled him in on the whole affair.

"When did you hear about Theawatoosa," I began.

"Why, I saw him when you were just a baby. He came in our room one night. I guess you were too young to know what was going on."

"C'mon, Kavanaugh. Please tell me what's going on. I've gotten the run-around long enough. I don't need more made-up junk."

"Then I guess you'll have to go see for yourself, just like Mother and Daddy said. Your parents always know best."

"Okay," I said, changing my tone to put a challenge to him. "You come along with Kenny and me tomorrow night."

"I'd love to," he said, trying to sound sincere. "I can't, though. I have to work at the store the next day, so I need to sleep. It's my last chance to get a little more money before I leave for Auburn."

I saw that he would play me for as much humor as he could. I rolled over and tried to go to sleep.

I intended to study the Tesla book the next day, but the Theawatoosa business kept filling my mind. I went through the stream of events several times and struggled to make sense of it. Giving up on the electronic work, I began to gather supplies for the expedition.

Kenny arrived about 5 o'clock. Mother helped us pack two backpacks with snacks.

Daddy welcomed Kenny to the supper table. He engaged Kenny in conversation about his Dad's work, his older brothers, and generally talked so much it became clear he was steering the conversation away from Theawatoosa. When supper was almost over, Daddy turned to the important business at hand. "I went to the swamp this afternoon to see if you can cross the river at Grimsley's. Adams Creek had the usual boards over it. There's a tree fallen across the river about a quarter-mile down from the first clearing. You can climb across it."

"But, I thought you were going to drive us down the Tuscaloosa highway and take us in from there. It's much closer." I seemed to lack control over any aspect of this operation.

"Nope, you boys say you know the way. It's not going to be very dark when you walk in, and I hear you're planning to spend the night. It'll just be a nice hike."

Kenny and I didn't mind walking, we just wished that we knew what was going on. A few last minute preparations after supper, and then we piled into the car and drove down to the swamp.

Daddy drove us to the very end of the familiar dirt road through Grimsley's farm. He turned off in the small rutted clearing worn out by many other turnings-around. Kenny and I got out and everyone said their so-longs. Daddy reminded us especially to use our flashlights as we walked along by the river to see any cottonmouths or halfgators that might be in the path. With tongue in cheek, Mother reminded us to conserve the batteries in case we needed them to see Theawatoosa or to get back home if we needed to return before dawn. Daddy started to go over the directions to the gas seep again, but I politely cut him off with assurance I knew how to get there.

Kenny and I started along the footpath to the river. As Daddy said, boards lay across Adams creek. We got to our usual fishing spot; then, we followed the trail until we found the tree lying across the river just as Daddy said we would.

When we left the car, the sun had already gone down, but the sky still glowed enough to illuminate the path. By the time we crossed the river, a few stars began to show, and we were under full tree cover. The moon hadn't come up yet; so we had only the light from our flashlights. Puddles from the previous night's rain covered the path, and we had to detour through the bushes fairly often. Nevertheless, we arrived at the gas seep after about an hour of hiking.

The discarded picnic paraphernalia identified the gas seep plainly. We found a steel drum that had been cut and welded to make a grill. It sat near the gas seep, and we could see ruts in the dirt where people dragged it over the fire or off to the side. A couple of five-gallon cans lay to one side. We guessed they were used to fetch water from the river to put out the fire.

Even though we couldn't see an opening in the ground, a sandy depression about a foot deep ran more or less in a straight line for roughly fifty feet. The ground was bare in the depression. We guessed it was because the fire killed anything that tried to grow there.

We looked around and chose a spot about fifty feet back from one end of the seep toward the river. This spot had three advantages: any closer to the seep would leave us exposed in the clearing; it put the river to our back to minimize the chances of someone coming up on us from behind; and it was relatively dry.

Then we realized that we had no matches. In all our preparations, we hadn't thought of having to light the gas. I felt irritated for not thinking of it, but not too surprised. I tended to get caught up in the anticipation of an adventure such as this. Trying to figure out Theawatoosa preoccupied me as well, and while Kavanaugh and I had spent the night in the swamp before, I never completely lost the fear of a dark, lonely, isolated night. I had plenty on my mind.

I might easily forget the matches, but Mother always remembered everything. Why hadn't she remembered to put them in? I emptied my bag on the ground as Kenny held the light. Then we emptied his bag. No matches. We searched our pockets. No matches.

In the spot we'd selected, we spread out a plastic tablecloth that Mother had provided to keep us dry. We laid down on it and spread out our supplies, especially the snacks. We left the flashlights at hand but turned off. It wasn't to conserve the batteries as Mother warned us, but we began to realize just how alone we were, and we didn't want to reveal our location to whomever or whatever might come along.

We discussed walking back. Why stay here all night if there was no fire to watch? And to be frank with you, we both were just plain scared at this point. Both of us mentally reviewed the worst of the explanations we had heard. Mr. Shoemaker's most reasonable explanation was forgotten in our instinctive tendency to anticipate the worst possibility. So we had two good reasons to leave: no fire, and we wanted to leave.

In the end, the deciding factor was our reputations.

"I thought you wanted to see Theawatoosa," Mother would say. "I thought you were looking for the truth. I guess you'll just have to take somebody's word for it."

"I don't want to hear that you're pestering people about this any more," Daddy would say. "And don't tell me you're an outdoorsman. Was it only Kavanaugh that had the gumption to spend the night in the swamp?"

Kenny's own voices played in his head. Heaven only knew what our friends would make out of it when the story got around.

So we just had to wait out the night.

The planned event that we'd come for wasn't going to happen. We would not see the flame and imagine a demon dancing in it. But the other possibilities remained: real demons, demons invading our minds, or some horrible event we hadn't even thought of.

We took some comfort from our hiding place. It was in a cluster of dense bushes. The leaves were beginning to turn yellow but hadn't begun to fall off, and we imagined ourselves to be well concealed as long as we kept quiet and left our flashlights off. We whispered to each other as quietly as we could. Even the whispers seemed too loud sometimes, and we fell silent. We spoke only to relieve the mounting tension in our chests and to gain support from knowing we were both still there.

I'm not sure how long this lasted. It may have been ten minutes or two hours. The waiting ended with a new sound we hadn't heard while we lay there. I'm not sure what it was. It might have been a twig breaking. It might have been a foot scuffing on the ground. One thing was clear: it was a new sound. We both stopped breathing. Then the same sound repeated or another new one. We finally had to breathe. I reached out and grabbed Kenny's arm to make sure he hadn't moved.

How do you sense someone's presence? I suppose it's sounds too faint to be recognized. Maybe visual cues too peripheral or dim to be fully recognized. All of us have experienced the realization of a person's presence even though we can't say how we realized it. And now, Kenny and I both knew someone was there. Out by the gas seep or beyond it. The fact that they were some distance away made us freeze in the hope they wouldn't know we were there.

But in spite of our best efforts, we gasped when the gas seep burst into fire in a dull explosion: a poof, not a bang. After the initial explosion of the accumulated gas, the flames settled into a wispy blue light with streaks of orange near the edges. It made no further sound.

The light from the flames glowed very dimly but illuminated the trees and bushes nearest our end of the clearing. The burning gas obscured the opposite end of the open expanse, but we searched it for any indication of the presence we sensed. We saw nothing, but were still sure it was there, and it probably lit the flames.

Kenny and I waited barely breathing. Again, I had no idea how long the flame just danced. It was long enough that I began to search the patterns in the dancing light for something that might look like a demon. The waiting ended when a small, bright-yellow flame appeared near the ground at the far end of the seep. It grew, appearing to climb up what, at first, seemed like a tree trunk. I gained enough presence of mind to remember there were no trees near the middle of the clearing just as it became obvious that the climbing yellow flame had moved. As the yellow fire grew to about a foot in height, it radiated enough light to outline a human figure: a human whose leg was on fire.

I call it human in the sense that it had two legs, a torso, two arms, and a head, but it exceeded human size, being maybe eight feet tall. I remembered Principal Shoemaker's comment about seeing an eight-foot figure in the flame, but this was no simple colored flame. No clothes covered it. Its body shone a pale brown color and appeared as if it was composed of raw muscles, uncovered by skin.

I recognized the bundles of muscle from the illustration of the human body in our Compton's Encyclopedia. It showed the body on several clear plastic pages. The first page depicted a nude human figure. When you turned the page, you peeled away the skin and saw exposed muscle arranged in bundles, stretched from bone to bone. And that is what I saw: bundles of muscle fibers without the benefit of skin to cover them.

The second leg burst into flame, and fire began to envelop the torso.

The light grew to show the facial features: a prominent nose, a wide mouth, and black holes where the eyes should be. No eyes, just black holes. The head seemed to be covered in a black hood.

It was now clear that the figure walked along the length of the seep in the flames toward the end where we hid. Both of us had begun to tremble with fear. I wanted to run but couldn't because I clung to the idea it didn't know I was there. If it continued in the direction it was headed, it would pass us.

It got worse. Now fire covered the entire body of the demon. The light coming from its body illuminated the clearing brightly. At each side of the demon, made visible not by reflected light, but from the absence of it, walked another figure. These were about the size of a normal human, but they were totally black. Each one seemed to be a hole in space where light shone and was simply swallowed up.

It got worse. The demon's accomplices carried spears. They held the spears upright, tilted toward his head and crossed behind him.

It got worse. As it came to the end of the gas seep, it paused. It turned slightly away and then turned to face us and began to walk directly toward us. It knew where we were!

It got worse. The demon's head tilted down until he looked directly at us and the black holes that were his eyes burst into brilliant red flames that shot out of the eye sockets.

I don't know how it happened, but I found myself on my feet. I yelled, "Kenny, come on, run!" as loud as I could and leaped out of the thicket of bushes. Sometime after the demon appeared, I'd grabbed my flashlight and it was now locked in my fist. I was vaguely aware that Kenny had emerged from the thicket just behind me, and we both ran faster than ever in our lives away from the clearing and back alongside the river.

We probably did our once-and-only four-minute mile back to the oak tree across the river. Kenny had been ahead of me since shortly after we began to run. He'd left his flashlight at the clearing so he stayed just far enough in front of me that I could illuminate the pathway ahead of him.

Kenny leaped from the riverbank over several of the tree limbs, but ducking under and climbing over other limbs slowed him down. He'd cleared the branches and was running down the trunk of the tree by the time I got there. I tried to make the same jump that Kenny had done, but I missed and plunged one foot into the river. I caught myself before my right foot hit the water; but, to keep from falling in completely, I had to let go of the flashlight. It, of course, went straight into the river. I righted myself on the tree by holding two branches and ran across the trunk.

We would have been completely blind at this point if the moon had not just begun to rise. Kenny calmed down enough to wait for me on the west bank. We began to run together, but at a somewhat slower pace since we had no light and started to tire. We were much too winded to talk.

We ran until we reached the driveway to the Grimsley's mansion. We looked back for a while and saw nothing following us. Feeling safer back in town with a streetlight only about fifty yards away, we began to walk and get our breath.

After a while, Kenny spoke first. "What was it?"

"I don't know," I replied. "I don't know."

I replayed the scene in my head. It was just a collection of terrible images. I couldn't dwell on any one for long. More or less involuntarily, I said, "Did you see his exposed muscles? Oh jeez, he didn't have any skin!"

Kenny didn't understand what I meant, so I described the muscle bundles running up the legs and told him about the Compton's Encyclopedia drawings.

"I did see them but I couldn't figure what they were," Kenny replied. He shivered and let out a low moan. "You think it was a real... a real demon?"

"I don't know. I can't imagine what it was, Kenny. It walked right through the flames, and it was burning but didn't care!"

"I thought it was a trick until the flames shot out of his eyes. A person in a costume couldn't do that," Kenny said.

"Well, it couldn't walk through fire and be on fire either," I said.

By now we had crossed Aylette Street diagonally and turned onto Pinion Street. I could see my house ahead.

"What were those two things, whatever-they-were in black?" Kenny asked.

"I don't know. It was like there was no one there: just something that absorbed all the light. Like a hole in space." Just forming the idea, "a hole in space," that described so well what we had seen, brought back all the fear. I didn't let Kenny see, but the thought made chills run up me, and tears formed in my eyes.

As we came up to Temple Avenue, I realized I had no idea what kind of scene would take place inside. I quickly devised a plan to avoid it.

"Kenny, my parents will be asleep. I don't want to wake them up. Let's go spend the rest of the night in my shop."

Not knowing my parents well and imagining that events might mean he had to get back to his home in the middle of the night, he readily agreed.

We walked around to the back of the garage. I found a couple of braided rugs my grandmother had made, one blanket, an old sofa pillow, a bag of fabric scraps, and an oddly shaped piece of rubber foam. We arranged these on the concrete floor and lay down. Only then did I realize just how tired I was. We left the light on in the storeroom.

"Would your mother or father rig that up to scare us?" Kenny asked.

I hadn't really considered the possibility, so I was silent for a while as I pondered it.

"I don't think so. I'm pretty sure my mother wouldn't come down in the swamp at night. My father wouldn't take time off from the store in the middle of the week to rig up something like that, and I don't think he'd know how. I couldn't do it."

I thought a bit more; then shook my head and said, "My brother, Kavanaugh, would do it for sure, but I don't think he'd have any idea how to do it either. They'd have to find someone who could rig up a pretty realistic demon. It looked real, Kenny"

It comforted me to consider that the whole thing was a trick, but I couldn't begin to figure out how it had been done. I was at a complete loss to think of anyone I knew who could rig up such a scary scene.

"Do you think it could be someone from your family?" I asked Kenny.

"No. They're all too busy, and they've never done anything like that. I mean, my sisters play little tricks on people, but just simple things."

We finally fell asleep from extreme fatigue and didn't wake up until my mother came in with hot chocolate and biscuits. It was almost nine in the morning.

### Be sure your sins will find you out

"Wake up, boys. Breakfast time." She put the breakfast tray on my workbench and pulled in an old rocking chair from the storeroom.

"Well?" she said.

We knew what she meant, but neither of us wanted to answer just yet. I reached for the cups of hot chocolate to buy time. I handed one to Kenny and sipped the other.

"How did you know we were here?" I asked.

She smiled and chuckled as she answered, "I was looking out the dining-room window when you came up Pinion Street. I got back to the bedroom in time to see you go in here."

After allowing us to realize once again how closely watched we were, she asked again more directly, "Did you see Theawatoosa?"

I answered. "We sure did! Why didn't you tell us what to expect?"

"I didn't know what you were going to see."

It wasn't a direct answer, but it carried a significant message that she had not been the architect of the scene last night. "Is that true?" I asked. "You didn't know Theawatoosa looks like a giant human, his body burns, and red flames shoot out of his eyes?"

Her eyes got big. "Red flames shoot out of his eyes?"

She seemed genuinely surprised. She was either unaware of what we saw or she was putting on a great act.

Kenny and I filled in more details as we munched the biscuits. We pretty faithfully described the scene until we came to the part where we bolted. In that part, we emphasized how close the demon had come and said we had to run to keep from being set on fire. Of course, it wasn't true, but we were not just going to come out and say we ran because we were so scared we'd have died if we stayed there a moment longer.

Mother wanted a few more details. Then she asked, "How would you like to go back again tonight? Daddy and I will go with you, Kavanaugh too, I think. I'm sure your daddy will want to see this demon, and I certainly do."

Kenny and I looked at each other. "Are you kidding?" I asked.

"No. I think we should all see for ourselves. Maybe we should invite Brother Flowers, Brother Pritchard, Colonel Lufkin and all your authorities on Theawatoosa. Since they can't agree on what it is, they'd be interested to see him, I'm sure."

It became clearer in my mind that somebody used the the flaming demon to pull joke on us, but I still wasn't sure who was behind it. Mother's offer to go back seemed a sure sign that she was in on it somehow. I decided to join in the fun.

"Mother, you don't understand how awful it was. Theawatoosa is probably eight feet tall and he has no skin over his muscles. Red flames shoot out of his eye sockets. Kenny and I would have been burned to death if we hadn't run at the last minute! How will you be able to get out of the way fast enough? Kenny and I are willing to go back, but I'm not sure you better come along."

"So now in the light of day, you've got your courage back," she teased with a big smile on her face. "Don't worry about me. I can take care of myself."

"If you, Daddy, and Kavanaugh are there as observers, who's going to propel the demon?" I asked. I still didn't think they were directly involved, but I thought the challenge might elicit some more clues.

"Don't worry, Theawatoosa can also take care of himself," she said as she got up. "Now I've got a full day's work to do, and I have to go by the store to check some invoices, so you boys do whatever you've got to do and be here for dinner at noon sharp. I'll fix us a picnic supper, and we'll eat down at the gas seep like I used to do.

Kenny and I lounged around for a while more and then killed the day discussing how we thought the demon operated. We both felt pretty silly over the whole affair by now and worried out loud to each other about who was in on the prank.

Did all the people we had asked about Theawatoosa know that we were being kidded? Had their answers been purposely outlandish to keep us probing? We went back over the people we'd consulted and stories we'd gotten. For the most part, no one other than Kenny and I knew whom we were consulting until we arrived to ask our questions. They couldn't have been forewarned. Only Principal Shoemaker had been suggested by someone else, Colonel Lufkin.

"Oh no!" I exclaimed, "You did it! You arranged...."

Kenny just shook his head calmly. After considering it again, I rejected the idea. Kenny didn't pretend or lie very well.

My thoughts returned to how it was done. It had to be a puppet, but it was a good one. Did it hang from a wire? We'd walked around the clearing before we settled down and hadn't seen anything that seemed out of place. And how would anyone know where we would settle down, and thus, where to position the wire? We didn't know until we looked around and picked the spot. If not on a wire, it had to be supported and propelled from the ground. The ground had ruts and holes, and a few bushes and lots of weeds lined the edges of the seep, so it would be hard to roll a carriage. We guessed someone held it up.

"The black things at Theawatoosa's sides!" Kenny exclaimed. I got the idea at the same time. The two black figures we saw in silhouette must have been carrying Theawatoosa. This meant that at least two more people were in on the plot. I guessed Kavanaugh was one of them. I'd know for sure if he found an excuse to disappear tonight.

We made guesses at several other aspects of the demon appearance throughout the day. We couldn't, however, make any reasonable stab at whom the second black figure might be, nor could we come up with who designed and built it.

At dinner, we were quizzed about what we had seen the night before. Kavanaugh seemed very interested in our account of the previous night. He made some comments that suggested he had at least a general idea what had happened already. We maintained the humorous attitude we developed with Mother earlier. We were tight-lipped in our guesses as to how the trick was pulled off because we didn't want to be wrong. Neither Mother nor Daddy offered any explanations and kept up the pretense that Theawatoosa was one or the other of the demon types our consultants had proposed. It became even clearer than ever that they knew exactly what we had been told.

After dinner Kenny again said he thought our consultants were coached on their stories. I convinced him it didn't necessarily follow. I explained how just about everybody in the county came into our grocery store and often paused to talk with my father. I was sure they filled him in after our visits.

Kavanaugh quizzed us again before he went back to work at the grocery store. Were we scared? Did we think it was a real monster? He asked us to describe Theawatoosa's walk through the flames three times. He still wouldn't tell us what he had to do with it or how much he knew.

The afternoon seemed to drag along. Finally, Daddy's car turned in the driveway, and before long, we were ready to go back to the gas seep. I wondered what new surprises might be planned for us. I wondered if Principal Shoemaker or Brother Flowers might show up. I hoped no one else would be there.

We went though town, down the Tuscaloosa highway, turned off just after crossing the river, and arrived at the end of the dirt path to the gas seep. We got out, and Kenny and I carried the picnic fixings the remaining quarter-mile or so. We had a pleasant dinner of cold fried chicken, potato salad, and stuffed eggs. Kenny and I were quiet. Daddy studied the woods around us with his usual interest in wildlife and hunting. Mother seemed the most interested in our main purpose for being there. Kenny and I offered to carry the picnic paraphernalia back to the car but Mother said we should put it all on a big stump on the side of the clearing away from the river. It was getting dark and she wanted another blow-by-blow description of what we had done and seen the previous night.

As we gathered the picnic supplies and moved down the clearing, we began to notice burn marks on the weeds and bushes along the gas seep.

As we studied them, Daddy said, "I guess it wasn't just your imagination."

"It certainly wasn't imagined," I said emphatically.

"It looks like it always does after the gas seep has been lighted," observed Mother.

It hit me for the first time that the gas seep was unlit now. Someone or something extinguished it since last night.

Kenny and I pointed out the place where we'd hidden. Daddy took out his pocketknife and cut away some of the bushes to make it easier for us all to sit where Kenny and I had lain last night. Our equipment lay scattered, just as we left it. I recounted how we had settled in, and again went through the sequence up to the point we bolted and ran.

After a few more questions, we fell quiet and waited.

This time I guessed it was a little earlier than it had been the previous evening when we heard soft rustling that indicated something was coming. The initial noises seemed louder than the night before. Whoever was coming didn't care as much about being heard as last night.

We all witnessed a faithful replay of the spectacle. The seep burst into flame; the flames ignited the monster's legs. What I had believed before to be raw bundles of muscle appeared to my calmer eyes as bunches of cornstalks tied into leg-sized bundles. As the flames climbed up the figure of Theawatoosa, I made out the black figures at his sides much sooner than before. What had appeared to be spears carried by the black figures and crossed behind the demon's head were now pretty obviously the sticks that held up the cornstalk mannequin.

At the end of the gas seep, the demon paused, turned away from us and then toward us and came right at us. Whoever was in the black robes performed an exact replay of the previous night.

Then the climactic event happened: his eyes burst into flame, and the bright red glare was just the familiar glow of roadside flares.

The black figures shook the sticks that held the demon, and he trembled violently and shed flaming corn leaves almost as if he were going to explode. As the shower of flames subsided, they tilted their sticks forward and Theawatoosa lunged at us and fell on the ground.

Daddy was first to stand up, and he lit his flashlight and shined it on the black figures.

"You fellows put on a great show. It would have scared the devil out of me," Daddy said with a laugh.

The black figures reached up at the same time and pulled hoods from their heads. There stood John Tubalcaine and Uncle Doc, Aunt Brazzie's husband.

Kenny and I were both speechless. Finally, I got out, "Would somebody please explain all this now? I still don't know what's going on."

Mother promised to explain as soon as we put out the fires. Kavanaugh, Kenny and I hauled buckets of water from the river to put out the smoldering corn stalks and then got two more buckets to quench the gas seep later, when we were ready to go. We got the picnic supplies, and we all sat on logs that had been arranged by other picnickers along one side of the gas fire. The heat of the flames felt good as an early fall chill began to creep up from the river.

Mother began. "When I was young, my brothers, James and Herman, were real devils. They always had some mischief in the works. I was on the receiving end of it sometimes, or Rose, or my mother, or one of the neighbors, or some unlucky neighborhood dog. Since my daddy worked at the bakery for long hours each day or worked day and night on the farm before that, Mother would usually end up trying to discipline them. They had been at it since they were barely old enough to walk. One of Mother's first methods was to threaten them.

" 'Theawatoosa is going to get you if you don't stop that!' she'd say.

"Or she might use a longer version. 'Theawatoosa lives down there in the swamp. He's made out of the very fire of Hell. He's going to come up here some night and carry you off. He's attracted by evil. Just the kind of devilment you two are always committing. He knows you're here, and he's goin' to get you if you don't straighten up.' Of course, at that time she meant the Warrior River swamp instead of the Sipsey.

"They got too old to be scared of a monster, but then she used it on me. And, of course, Herman and James didn't tell me it was just a made-up story. They backed her up. 'Oh Gene, he's gonna get you for sure,' James would say. 'I'd try to save you but he can knock out a person without even touching him. It wouldn't be any use.' Sometimes it scared me so bad I couldn't sleep until dawn.

"When you and Kavanaugh were born and your grandmother came to live with us, I told her that if she ever mentioned Theawatoosa to you, I would kick her out of the house, and she'd have to go live with Brazzie. I was not going to have you boys scared like I was. She never did, and I'd almost forgotten it till you asked me about it at breakfast. I remembered it instantly, and it didn't occur to me you were much too old to be afraid of a make-believe monster. I wasn't mad at you; I was mad at whoever mentioned him. I would've just let it go if I hadn't heard from Brazzie that you asked her.

"I expected you to ask me about it again, but you didn't. I got busy with other things, and then your Daddy told me you and Kenny were asking everybody in town. That's when I decided to have a little fun myself."

I interrupted. "But how did everybody know the story? If Grandmother made it up, how did they get all those crazy ideas about Theawatoosa?"

Mother smiled and laughed her silent laugh. Usually, the only indication that she was laughing was a smile and her stomach bouncing up and down.

"You know that your grandmother was an authority on religion. People used to consult her and Brazzie on all sorts of things. They asked her for advice on controlling their children, and she replied with Theawatoosa. She told them to use it to keep their kids in line. Sometimes, if their kids were misbehaving some way around our house, she might tell the kids directly that Theawatoosa would haul them off. I learned in the third grade that every kid in my class had been threatened at least once with Theawatoosa; maybe by his parents, an aunt or uncle, or maybe directly by my mother.

"I was really surprised when I moved to Frog Level and found out that even here people knew the story. I suppose that with your great-aunt and great uncle living here a long time, I should have expected it. Of course, the story had been retold who-knows-how-many times from person to person, and the details were different. In just a generation or two, people came to believe it had been around forever, and it was true in some way. The explanations Brother Pritchard and Brother Flowers gave you are the common ones; at least among religious folks. I'd never heard the civil-war version nor Principal Shoemaker's explanation that people saw him in the gas flame.

"It really surprised me when I heard about you asking around. While I knew that lots of people knew the story twenty years ago or more, I figured it was long forgotten by now. I was amazed when everybody you asked still knew it. Of course, you just asked grown-ups. Well, they all had some different version of the story, but the name, Theawatoosa, survived. I wonder how many generations this is going to go on. People seem naturally inclined to believe in demons."

Mr. Tubalcaine spoke up. "I heard a version of the story not long after I moved to Frog Level to lead the Christian College. Then, a couple of months later, your grandmother invited me to supper, and I mentioned it in the conversation. She started laughing and several others at the table started laughing too. Before long the whole table was roaring. When they finally stopped laughing, your grandmother told me the whole story; how she made it up some twenty five years earlier at that time. It just came back to me on the Sunday afternoon when you boys were up at my home, and I figured you knew about it. Those thieves from Birmingham came up before we could talk about it. They want to buy my mountain for next-to-nothing. Thieves!"

"But how did you end up involved in Mother's plan to scare us?" I asked.

Mr. Tubalcaine smiled a rare smile. "I ran into her in your Daddy's grocery store one day, and she asked me if I remembered mentioning it to you. I did. She said she needed some help to teach you a lesson, so I volunteered. Your mother had a vague idea of what she wanted to do, but I knew how to make torches out of corn stalks and a few other tricks that we needed. She met me in Robertson's store one afternoon a few days ago and gave the money to get the materials."

I looked at him for a minute after he fell silent. "You sure did a good job! It scared us worse than anything I've ever seen. I'll bet you know a lot of things. You knew how to build your big building."

He smiled again but said nothing more.

I turned to Uncle Doc. "Uncle Doc, how did you get involved in this?"

He spat tobacco juice into the gas flame and chuckled. "Oh, they just needed somebody to carry the devil. I guess when they think of old Beelzebub, they think of me." This turned the chuckle into a good laugh, and the other adults joined him.

Mr. Tubalcaine spoke up, "Well, Hester, I've been accused of being the devil quite a few times because of my name, so I guess we were the perfect pair to do it."

I turned back to Mother. "Why did you arrange this complicated stunt? Why scare us like that? It was worse than what your mother did."

"No it wasn't," she said. "How many night's sleep have you missed? Just one, last night, and anyway, you were asleep when I came in this morning! Like I said, I wanted to have some fun. I also wanted to teach you a lesson about trusting your own head. Before Mr. Tubalcaine mentioned Theawatoosa, did you believe in demons?"

"No. I hadn't had any reason to believe in them. You taught me that ghosts and all supernatural boogers are fairy tales."

"Did you ever run into any demons or ghosts, or see anything like that?" she asked.

"No, ma'am."

"Then you should have stuck by your guns. We didn't teach you to believe in them, and you for sure never saw one. If you had grown up differently, then I'd be sympathetic. I wasn't and I'm not now, in your case."

I remembered another question to ask. "Mr. Tubalcaine, Uncle Doc, how did you know where we were? You aimed Theawatoosa right at us, so you knew where we hid."

Uncle Doc slapped one knee and laughed so hard he couldn't answer, so Mr. Tubalcaine replied, "We were sitting on a log down at the other end of the clearing when you boys came up. A few bushes covered us, but mainly it was just dark back under the trees. You made no attempt to hide, so we saw you spread out your blanket and settle down. You kept your flashlights on for quite a while."

"Yeah, I should have known the answer. It never occurred to us somebody was watching. We were really stupid, Kenny."

Pretty much the whole story had been told now. Kenny asked a couple of questions about how they lit the road flares that made Theawatoosa's eyes. Then we picked up and headed for the cars.

Mr. Tubalcaine had come in an old pickup truck that looked like it would fall apart before it went another mile. I asked Daddy to wait just a minute so I could ask him another question. I went over to his truck as he arranged some tools in the back.

"Mr. Tubalcaine, Thank you for mentioning Theawatoosa. If you hadn't, I never would have known about some of my family history, I don't really know much about the things you've done, but I think it's good that you've tried to accomplish big projects like building a school and a community workshop. I hope I can do something like that someday."

He didn't react for a moment. I didn't know whether or not I had said something I shouldn't have said. Before he spoke, he put his hand on my shoulder and held it. I could feel a slight tremor in his hand.

"Thank you, Wendell. You don't want to do what I've done. The world is changing and you need to change with it. I know you will."

"It seems like I never remember to ask questions at the right time," I said. "There's all this stuff I want to know, but I can't remember it when I have a chance to ask."

"What do you want to know," he asked.

"Lot's of things. First of all, I understand that lots of people think you're evil because of your name. My grandmother told me a little about it and said you weren't evil; that Tubal Cain in the Bible wasn't evil either. I wondered if you knew how your family got the name and if you ever thought about changing it."

"My name. Everybody thinks a name makes the person."

He started to go on, but Daddy called for me to get in our car. "Just a minute," I yelled.

"No, go on," Mr. Tubalcaine said. "Why don't you come back up to my mountain some Sunday, and we'll have more time to talk."

School started, the weather turned cold, and I got busy with other things. I didn't get back up to Mount Nebo. I kept meaning to go, but I just never got around to it.

# The Oil Well, 1958

There's various kind of oil afloat, Cod-liver, Castor, Sweet;
Which tend to make a sick man well, and set him on his feet,
But ours a curious feat performs: We just a well obtain,
And set the people crazy with "Oil on the brain."

A verse from *Oil on the Brain*, by Joseph E. Winner, 1865

## Floating on oil

F rog Level was very ethnically diverse. We had people who traced their ancestors back many generations to origins among the English, Irish, Scots, and Welsh. Okay, we had all variations that the British Isles could offer. Some of the people claimed ancestors from other European countries, but they identified mostly with their English-speaking heritage. They mainly thought of themselves as just plain Americans. Of course, we had about a twenty-five percent population of African Americans, but they weren't called that in the 1950s. The politically correct, respectful term then was Negro. Frog Level, along with much of the United States, was racially segregated, and the education, the housing, and the range of jobs available to Negroes was very limited.

Almost everyone in Frog Level was nominally a Christian. Though many of them hadn't been inside a church in many years, they would call themselves Christian if asked. Only a couple of Roman Catholics lived in Frog Level, and the nearest Catholic Church was in Birmingham, about eighty miles away. I never saw a Catholic priest in person until I was about seventeen years old. We had two families of Jews, but no synagogue.

In this remarkably homogeneous, ordered, or you might say limited, little town, we had one very small but notable minority: one family that proudly preserved its French identity: the Alberts. They sometimes inserted French phrases in their speech even if nobody else would understand them. Everyone in their family over sixteen years old had traveled to France at least once—an unusual accomplishment for Frog Level people. They would speak at length about the wonders of French food and art with the tiniest prompting or none at all. The patriarch of the Albert family was Leon Albert.

Leon had two sons: Alphonse and Ambrose. Father and sons ran a pulpwood-buying operation. Pulpwood is a generic term for wood not big enough to make decent lumber but just fine for making paper. The Alberts would buy wood by the truckload from anyone who showed up at the railroad yard with it. That business was not, however, Leon Albert's passion, oil was. I've no idea how Leon got the oil bug, but he had it. He knew without doubt that Frog Level sat on a huge lake of oil just waiting to be tapped. I've always thought it strange that the one other person who most fervently shared this conviction was John Tubalcaine.

When the pulpwood business had taken in enough money to finance a drilling effort, Leon would try again. He had drilled three wells already. No oil, only lots of worthless natural gas. Few people used natural gas for lighting, heating, or cooking then. It had been used in Frog Level for a few years after 1910 when some wells were brought in locally and before electricity became widely available. After electricity came to town, people considered gas as old fashioned, messy, and dangerous. Now the local pipeline had been abandoned, and no long-distance pipeline to carry it out of Frog Level passed within many miles. Gas was completely worthless.

As Leon got older, Alphonse and Ambrose took over more of the pulpwood-buying operation and eventually inherited the drilling itch as well. It was time for another oil well, the first one that would be managed by Leon's sons. Maybe the boys would enable him to see the realization of his dream before he died.

The state regulated oil and gas drilling in Alabama very casually then; permit applications were almost always issued. A few regulations specified how to clean up after the well was abandoned. No public hearings were held, and the Frog Level Times didn't carry any news that might have alerted people that the Alberts were on the move again. The first most people knew about the new well was when the trucks began to arrive with pieces of the drilling rig.

The drilling site was down the Tuscaloosa highway on the town side of the river. The first trucks to arrive carried what seemed to be railroad ties, but bigger than normal. Next came parts of a crane. The workers assembled the largest crane I'd ever seen from the parts, and it began to lift the wooden timbers off the flatbed trucks and lay them side by side, beginning right along the edge of the highway. The timbers soon began to form a wood-paved road into the swamp. As each timber was laid, steel hoops that looked like over-sized horseshoes were driven into holes near the ends of the timber to hold them together. The workers called the horseshoes "staples." They indeed functioned just like small, everyday staples, but they were so big, it would never have occurred to me to call them that.

When the road had reached roughly fifty yards off the highway, a bulldozer rumbled down it and began to clear a spot half the size of a football field at the end. The bulldozer removed every trace of vegetation it came to and left a smooth red-dirt clearing. About two days after the clearing was prepared, a rough, hand-lettered, wooden sign appeared where the road met the Tuscaloosa highway. It said, "Leon Albert Avenue." No one seemed to know where the sign came from, but everyone, including the Alberts, thought this was completely appropriate, and the sign became a fixture of the well site.

Then the parts of the rig began to arrive. The truck brought large steel beams, angles, rods, and all sorts of steel shapes. I couldn't begin to guess what they would make, but as they were bolted together and latched with steel pins about two inches in diameter, they formed the base of the drilling rig. Then the other parts arrived just as needed to continue the assembly operation.

The superintendent of a rig is called the "tool pusher." This title didn't seem sufficiently respectful to me, raised as a good Southern boy, so I called him the superintendent. The man who runs the machinery is called the driller. The men who handle the drill pipes are roughnecks, and the lowest, odd-job workers are called roustabouts. The small rig down in the Sipsey swamp used a toolpusher, a driller, two roughnecks, and a single roustabout.

The tool pusher was Max Dobbs from Abilene, Texas. He was no relation to the Dobbs side of my family. I wondered if he knew any real cowboys. Even though I no longer played cowboy or sat through a Western double feature on Saturday morning at the Richards Theater, I still thought cowboys were adventurous stuff. In any case, Abilene, Texas seemed far off and romantic.

The driller was Rufus LeBlanc from Bayou LaFourche, Louisiana. He seemed strangest to me. First of all, he was the skinniest strong man I ever saw. His bones stuck out at his shoulders. His arms and legs were bony. My first impression of this guy was the ninety-pound weakling in the Charles Atlas advertisements, before he took the bodybuilding course. Then I saw him lift a fifty-five gallon steel drum marked on the side as 300 pounds. Still stranger, he had a strong Cajun accent I'd never heard. Not strange to me, but distinctive, he chewed tobacco. As we boys got to know him, he told us a few really funny jokes. But strangest and most entertaining was to watch him work on the rig.

He would dance at the controls. Dance is the most accurate word I can find. The driller has several controls to manage. He has a motor-speed lever that comes up through the floor of the rig from the diesel engine, and a longer lever sticking up almost six feet from the floor that controls the weight on the drill bit. He has two clutches—one a hand lever and one a foot pedal with a latching device. He has to step on the pedal with one foot and kick the latch in place with the other. He clearly enjoyed doing this work. We feared his strangeness, loved his almost cartoonish character, and respected his talents.

But there was one more member of the crew that we learned did not usually work on a drilling job. Just a look at him and you could see he didn't seem to fit in. His name was John Ferguson. He seemed cleaner than the others were, wore neater clothes, and he worked in a small trailer that sat about forty feet to the left of the rig when viewed from the highway. An article in the Frog Level Times said that he would conduct experiments on how to get better oil flows from the well using "acoustic stimulation." It didn't elaborate except to say it would produce more oil.

The very specialized oil drilling didn't provide much work for the local laborers or income for the local economy. The roustabout came into our grocery store and bought snacks and drinks. He would show up at 6:30 each morning with a case of empty Coke, RC and NeHi bottles and leave with full ones. Colonel Lufkin had agreed to deliver lunch plates from his café each day, whatever the special happened to be, for the crew.

As the crew set up the drilling rig, they were introduced on several occasions to the native cottonmouth moccasins. They decided they needed a snake wrangler. This opening provided a job for some local worker. Of course, they didn't want to pay much, so the job was right for one of the Frog Level Negroes, they decided. J.C. Wilson, the son of our housekeeper was lucky enough to get the job. It paid five dollars a day.

Not long after the rig was set up, before the actual drilling had begun, the roughnecks were loading up a rack with forty-foot sections of pipe. One of them stood on a very small platform up near the top of the rig, and the other stood by a stack of pipe on the ground. The man on the ground attached a steel cable to a section of pipe, the cable pulled it up into the rig, and then was lowered for another section. As the roughneck reached down to attach the next piece, a cottonmouth struck him midway up his arm. Cottonmouth bites are seldom fatal, but they hurt, they have to be treated, and they require quite a while to heal. The roughneck had to go back home to Texas and was replaced by another one.

Mr. Dobbs fired J.C. for letting the roughneck get bitten. It didn't matter that he killed several cottonmouths—about one a day—and he'd even found and killed two halfigators that crawled under the rig. He had to go.

### Electricity on the brain

School had just ended for the year. During the term I biked down to see what was going on almost every day after classes. Now I had even more time to watch. I found Bob Sargent there on several occasions. Bob hadn't changed at all since he hatched the idea of cutting off the limb to get the red bag during the marble hunt. He was still a do-first-and-think-later person. Everybody who knew him kidded him about the honey hole incident and a few of his other ill-conceived schemes. He often hung around with Kenny Livingston and me when we were ready to fire a rocket.

We both were fascinated by watching the machinery and explaining to each other, whether we understood or not, the function of every piece and why the drillers did any minute maneuver. John Ferguson clearly had more time to kill than the others did. He worked with his machinery in and around his trailer as he waited for the well to reach paydirt. He had lots of electronic stuff that particularly attracted our attention. Bob and I and any other gawkers were not allowed on the cleared work area. We were clearly instructed to stay in the vegetation or we would be run off completely. Occasionally Mr. Ferguson would come over and talk with us while he smoked a cigarette. He didn't ask our names and volunteered very little information, but he verified that his trailer was full of electronics. The diesel generator beside the trailer supplied his electronics only, he said.

"What does it put out?" I asked.

"Twenty kilowatts. More for short periods."

"Jeez," Bob exclaimed. " Twenty kilowatts. That would run a huge radio station."

Mr. Ferguson had already headed back to the trailer. No more questions today.

I learned more about "acoustic stimulation" from our occasional conversations with him over the next week or so. His electronics drove a device sort of like a high-powered loudspeaker he would lower into the well. It was supposed to shake the rock and open cracks to allow the oil to flow out. Clayburn Engineering had a patent on it, but had never proven it to work. They approached the drilling company and offered to pay for the right to try it out on a well somewhere. The drilling company offered Leon Albert and sons a small discount if they could use their well. It would slow down the drilling only a little, they said, and might result in significantly more oil. Leon was in no hurry, and he liked more oil. The discount would have been unnecessary, but it was a done deal.

One day as Bob Sargent and I were sitting in the lower limbs of an oak tree, Mr. Dobbs, the superintendent, came over and chatted with us. Bob asked if they had found another snake wrangler. They hadn't. Bob said he could keep the place free of cottonmouths and halfigators. No problem. After a little negotiation, Mr. Dobbs hired him for two dollars a day plus one dollar for each cottonmouth he killed. This arrangement pleased Mr. Dobbs when he figured two dollars a day plus the one cottonmouth per day that J.C. had killed for a total of three dollars per day. The arrangement also pleased Bob when he calculated how many cottonmouths he could produce. He began his new job the next day.

Even though Bob now had a real job at the drilling rig, he would still hang out with me in the oak tree a good bit of the time. I was jealous of his new position and income because I had no idea that I would soon also be part of the drilling operation. An unlikely combination of my fascination with electronics and a newfound friend provided an opportunity. Here's how it came about.

The electronic devices of the 1950s, such as filled Mr. Ferguson's trailer, were not at all like what we have today. The devices used vacuum tubes. Tiny transistors were just beginning to be used in portable radios and some cheap record players. Vacuum tubes are big, get very hot, and require high electrical voltages to operate. A television set had about a dozen vacuum tubes in it, and it consumed as much electricity and generated as much heat as an electric heater.

About four months before the drilling rig arrived, my cousin, Leonard Dobbs, had offered me an obsolete and defunct television set to play with and tear apart. It had been a demonstration TV in his family's farm supply store. I suppose the idea was to drum up business for the furniture and hardware store that Leonard's uncle, Miles, operated. A lot of people came through the farm supply store every day and would see the TV. It served as a community meeting place of sorts. The TV set was a 1950 model; and, like all TVs of that vintage, it had a round picture tube. When television picture tubes were first made, the round shape was the only way the manufacturers knew to make them strong enough to safely withstand the pressure of the outside air.

The image was, as now, rectangular, so it didn't fit the round front face of the tube. Each television either showed only the central part of the picture tube or left dark areas around the edges of the image. Beginning in late 1950 and 1951, more nearly rectangular picture tubes became available, and no one wanted the old ones. Clearly, it wouldn't help the furniture store to display an out-of-date TV.

*My 1950-model Zenith round-screen television*

Mother said that I could have it if Leonard would remove the picture tube. The heavy tube was made of fragile glass and contained poisonous chemicals. She was unaware that the remaining circuits would generate twenty-five thousand volts—enough to make a spark an inch long and easily sufficient to electrocute me and half the neighborhood.

Without the picture tube, the TV wasn't useful for anything but salvage, but that's what I wanted. I removed the power supply—a big one on a separate chassis and large enough to drive a decent amateur radio transmitter or a really nice hi-fi amplifier. I disassembled the remaining stuff for the individual parts, and I dissected some of these to see what was inside.

Over the last year or so, I'd made a new friend, Terry Sayers, who worked as one of the announcers on the local radio station, WWFL. I knew him and his family from church and knew him as a star trumpeter in the high school band. He was about ten years older than I.

Earlier that year, the radio station studio had moved from the small transmitter building in the swamp to what had previously been a funeral home on Temple Avenue. After getting over the creeps about the previous occupants and their activities, I began to stop on the way to or from downtown to home. I would enter the large studio that was separated from the control room by a soundproof wall and window. Terry would see me and wave me to come in the control room and keep him company. I sat quietly as he read the advertisements, the news, and announced the records. While they played, we could talk.

He showed me how to produce and deliver the hourly news. A United Press International Teletype machine sat in a closet in one corner of the control room. A Teletype was a mechanical device that replaced Morse code transmissions for telegrams and news transmissions. It had a spool of yellow paper in it and a typewriter mechanism. It connected to a telegraph wire that carried electrical codes to trigger the keys of the typewriter. It sat idle about half the time; then, it came to life with a machine-gun-like rat-a-tat-tat when some news item was being sent.

Terry would tear off the paper where it came out of the Teletype. Then he would pick up the pile that had collected on the floor in front of the machine since the last time, and carry it back to his chair at the control console. He scanned backward until he found the most recent "hourly summary." He laid the paper across the edge of the console and tore it at the top of the hourly summary. Then he judged two feet of paper against his arm and tore it at the bottom of that length.

"Two feet of good ole UPI news equals exactly five minutes, the length of our news segment," Terry instructed.

"What if two feet comes in the middle of a story?" I asked.

"Just finish with a repeat of whatever you said about that story the previous hour."

Still not sure that this was foolproof, I asked, "What if the story wasn't in the summary from the last hour?"

"That's easy, you say, 'More on this important news story next hour. Stay tuned to WWFL for the latest news.' Then go on to the commercial."

The training came in handy two summers later when I ran the radio station on Sundays.

Terry always asked what I was up to. Few adults showed an interest in my oddball projects and fewer encouraged me, but Terry always did. It mattered a lot. I described my model airplanes, the rockets, my electronic projects, and the TV disassembly. He knew just enough electronics to listen sensibly, and he asked about the details of the radio transmitter I wanted to build.

Terry also introduced me to most of what I know about jazz music. He lived in New Orleans for a few years. He said he played with Jack Teagarden while Teagarden worked in New Orleans in between tours. He'd enjoyed the chance to play in a well-known band and to live a bohemian life style, but he found it hard to make a living that way and decided to come back to Frog Level.

"Do you like Louis Jordan?" he asked. Of course, since it was a spoken question, I couldn't know the spelling of Jordan.

"Oh, I guess so." I had seen the suave French actor, Louis Jourdan, in the movie, *Three Coins in the Fountain*, a couple of years earlier.

"Let's put on *Saturday Night Fish Fry*. It isn't what we usually play, but it won't hurt to jive up a few Frog Level housewives now and then." He fetched an old seventy-eight rpm record from the racks lining the back of the control room.

As the record got into the body of the song, I said, "That sure doesn't sound like he did in *Three Coins in the Fountain.*"

"What?" Terry said it in a way to indicate that while he heard my words, he didn't understand why I would say them.

"He sounded much more... well, sophisticated."

Terry's eyes got big for an instant; then he burst out laughing so hard he slipped out of his chair and fell to coughing in between the laughs. He was still choking and laughing when the record stopped, but managed to get another one started without too much dead air in between.

When he got his breath back, he explained. "Louis Jourdan is a suave movie star, presumably French. Louis Jordan is one of the greatest jazz artists ever. He started playing about 1930 and plays in Harlem now. He's been in the movies too, but I doubt that many people confuse the two of them. One of the all-time great sax players. Clarinet too. He wrote *Is You Is or Is You Ain't My Baby.* You know that, don't you?" Terry had begun to stare at the ceiling, and I think he forgot I was there for a moment. He started humming to himself.

I called him back to the present by apologizing. "Ohhh... I never heard of Louis Jordan before. Oops!"

So it happened that Terry Sayers and John Ferguson sat down next to each other at the counter in Lufkin's Cafe one morning and exchanged greetings. They soon discovered that they both knew New Orleans, and began to share anecdotes about the music spots and cafes they both liked. After reminiscing a while, the conversation changed to Ferguson's work in Frog Level. Just as Terry took an interest in my electronic fiddling around, he showed an interest in the acoustic stimulation. Ferguson ran through his usual layman's explanation. As he came to the end, he shook his head sadly. "I may not get to try it at all. I lost the transformer in the power supply for the controls and the first-stage amplifier. It's custom made, and it's not easy to get a replacement. Wait a minute, you guys don't happen to have any spare power supplies lying around the radio station, do you?"

"No. But what sort do you need?"

"Three hundred to four hundred volts. At least five hundred

milliamps; no, at least six hundred. And of course we need several amps of filament current, six and twelve volts."

Terry smiled while he drained his coffee cup. "I think I may know where you can get one. There's this kinda smart kid who salvaged the power supply out of an old Zenith television; you know, the old round-tube kind of television that served double duty as a space heater. I'll bet it meets your requirements."

Terry told him how to find me in the phone book. I was at the grocery store doing my Sunshine Cracker stocking job when he called. Mother took the message. As soon as I got home and we finished dinner, I called Mr. Ferguson. I told him it put out three hundred and fifty volts, and I had tested it at a current of seven hundred milliamps. I wasn't sure how much filament current it could supply, but I recited the list of tubes in the television and we both quickly estimated the current it must have supplied. I could tell over the phone that he was excited.

"How much do you want for it?" he asked.

"Well, I've been planning to use it with an amateur radio transmitter."

"I'll pay you well for it. Say thirty dollars?"

Thirty dollars was six weeks work at the grocery store on Saturdays. It really tempted me, but I had other compensation in mind.

"I could lend it to you. I'd especially like to see your equipment and maybe help you hook it up. I'm pretty good at wiring things."

He was quiet for a moment. "I don't know." Another pause. "Okay. When can I get it?"

I told him I could be down at the drilling site in about thirty minutes.

He told me later that he really didn't want a kid in his trailer, but he remembered that Terry Sayers characterized me as "kinda smart" and he decided to take a chance.

Mother agreed I could go after she issued the usual cautions and warnings.

The power supply originally had only a cable to connect it to the rest of the television, but no on/off switch and no regular power cord, since they were built into the main part of the television. I added a cord, an on/off switch, a nice green light to indicate that the main power was on, a second switch to turn on the three hundred and fifty volts and a red pilot light to indicate it was on. I liked how professional it looked.

It took some serious fiddling around to get it in my bicycle basket and to stabilize the bike with all that weight up front, but I managed to rig it. When I finally arrived at the well site, Mr. Ferguson met me halfway down the wooden road. He laughed and slapped his leg when he realized I was the kid who hung around all the time. He had never asked my name. He helped me steady the bike the rest of the way and then lifted the power supply out and carried it up the three steps into his trailer.

"I told Mr. Dobbs you would be helping me and that he had to let you come on-site. He isn't happy, but he said you could be at the trailer when I'm here. You are definitely not allowed to go near the drilling rig. Understand?"

"Yessir. I'll be careful."

Ferguson smiled for the first time I had seen him do it. "I remember that you and our snake wrangler are buddies. He's doing pretty well for us."

"Yeah, Bob's a good guy, but kind of crazy sometimes."

"What kind of crazy?" Mr. Ferguson asked.

"Oh, nothing too bad." I thought about telling the story of Bob up in the oak tree at the honey hole, but it was too long and complicated. I'd wait for another time, so I just said, "I mean, what sort of guy does it take to be a snake wrangler?"

"I guess I see what you mean," Mr. Ferguson replied.

I scanned the racks of electronics and spotted a chassis on the table at the far end of the trailer that had melted wax all over one end and knew it was the defunct power supply. "Boy, that transformer really melted!" I hoped he would be impressed by my knowing observation.

He looked at me and then followed my gaze to the wax mess. "Yep, it sure did! Smelled really great."

"I'll bet," I agreed.

"No. I mean it. I love the smell of hot electronics." He grinned as he stared at the wax.

"Me too." I figured he would think I was just being agreeable, but I knew I had found a kindred spirit.

Ferguson's rig had a 6SN7 tube generating the signal for his acoustic stimulator. It was connected to a pair of 6V6 tubes for reasons I didn't understand. The signal from these fed into a pair of 12AX7 tubes; and they.... oh, never mind, I'll spare you most of the details.

My power supply ran the low voltage stuff. He also used an eight-hundred volt supply, and four exotic ceramic tubes used two thousand volts. This high-voltage stuff really impressed me. I kept my hands in my pockets as Mr. Ferguson explained it all. I wanted him to know that I was not about to stick my fingers into his equipment.

The test on the Frog Level well couldn't be done until it reached the oil-producing zone. To test his equipment in the meanwhile, he had a "test transducer" set up outside the trailer. It was made up of the cores from four of the biggest public-address speakers he could find. The horn had been removed from each speaker leaving a strong permanent magnet and a metal housing. Four of them were mounted on top of a steel frame. Mr. Ferguson said he would give me a demonstration as soon as we got the new power supply hooked up and checked out.

Mr. Ferguson kept his word and let me help with the wiring. I was pleased he seemed to like my workmanship. We didn't finish wiring it that afternoon before I had to head home for supper. Before I left, he introduced me to Mr. Dobbs, who reinforced the warnings Mr. Ferguson had given me. There would be no second chances, he said. If I got in the way, I would be kicked off the premises instantly.

I came back at eight o'clock the next morning. Mr. Ferguson had finished assembling the equipment and was running checks on it. He placed a step ladder next to the test speakers, or, as he called them, the "test transducers." I stood on the ladder and Mr. Ferguson stood on the steps of the trailer. He pointed out the parts of the speaker cores and how they were connected to the electronics.

"Okay, you stay right there," he said.

"Why?" I asked.

"I want you to see just how this works," he answered. "Never take somebody else's word for the important stuff."

I placed one hand on top of the ladder and leaned toward the speakers.

"No. Grab the ladder with both hands," he ordered.

I did as he said. When he saw my hands firmly on the ladder, he went inside the trailer. I saw him turn a knob and then push a red button. A deafening blast of sound about a second long came out of the speakers. I suppose the sound was so loud that I might have flinched and fell off the ladder, but that was not why I'd been instructed to hold on. At the same time the sound burst out, a blast of air hit me in the face and nearly knocked me off the ladder in spite of my grip on it. I think the front legs of the ladder might have lifted up.

"Gee whiz, that was loud! Where did the air come from?"

Mr. Ferguson came back out of the trailer with a big smile on his face. He stood on the steps of the trailer and began to explain. "The four speakers are arranged in what's called a quadrupole. See how they're evenly spaced around in a circle? Two of the speakers push air out at the same time that the other two are pulling in. You heard only a small part of the sound that occurs in the center of the four speakers because they more or less cancel each other outside the small space at the center. The sound there is over a hundred times stronger than what you heard. And, by the way, I had it turned way down.

"The blast is generated by the humidity in the air. The sound waves probably condense and evaporate the water and expand it. Notice the steel plate behind the speakers from you? You don't get the air blast if I remove the plate. I'm not completely sure how it happens, but it's always much stronger on humid days like today. I figured it would be pretty good. You okay?"

"Yeah," I said. "I'm fine. That was really neat. Can we do it again?"

"No. You've seen that trick. Now let's do the executive demonstration."

Mr. Ferguson told me to wait there, and he walked over to where the empty soft drink bottles waited to go back to the grocery store the next morning. He came back with an empty Coke bottle; the old six-ounce kind made of really thick glass. He placed it in the center of the four speakers. He moved the ladder away from the test rig and said we should both go inside the trailer.

"Stand here," he said, indicating that I should position myself behind the right side of the door. He stood at the left side of the door where he could see outside and reach the controls. He again touched the same knob he had used before the last demonstration and turned it about three quarters of the way to the right. One of the roughnecks passed by the trailer and saw what we were doing.

"Jeez, Ferguson, you're like a twelve-year-old kid," he said.

"At least I'm not a beer-swilling roughneck," he replied. The roughneck just smiled and went on.

When the area was clear, Ferguson leaned out the door and yelled, "Fire in the hole!"

He pushed the red button. An even louder burst of sound came out, but the main event was that the Coke bottle simply disappeared in a fog of white smoke. The air blast that I had experienced propelled the fog out about ten feet from the test rig. Then it settled to the ground.

"See how the sound is stronger in the center of the speakers?" Ferguson couldn't help laughing at his serious understatement.

"Yeah, I noticed. What happened to the coke bottle? Where are the pieces."

"It's out there on the ground."

I looked hard for fragments of the bottle. "No, I don't see anything."

"The fog?" Ferguson said. "You saw the fog?"

"Yes."

"That was the coke bottle. The sound is so strong it breaks the glass into little pieces about the size of plain old dust."

Mr. Ferguson went on to explain that he had discovered his dramatic demonstration by accident. He said he used it any time he wanted to impress his managers or various visitors. It never failed to impress, he said. It certainly impressed me.

Since the real test inside the well wouldn't happen for a while, I didn't have much to see, so I began to go by the well only about every other day and chat with Mr. Ferguson about electronics. He gave me a nice book on electronic circuit design and a copy of a slightly out-of-date Sylvania vacuum tube reference book. I spent hours poring over it to learn the characteristics of different vacuum tubes.

**Snakes and baboons**

Each time I visited the well site, I checked on Bob Sargent to see how he was doing. Very well, it turned out. He produced, on average, slightly over three cottonmouths per day, and recently, he had produced five a few days. Mr. Dobbs passed by and commented that Bob's productivity was unbelievable. Both he and I caught that the word, "unbelievable," seemed to carry a heavy meaning.

When Mr. Dobbs had walked out of earshot, Bob whispered, "I guess I better ease up. Would you like to see how I get them?"

"Sure. Do you have some scheme to search the clearing and not miss any?"

"Oh, better than that," he said. "Come on."

We walked around the edge of the drilling operation, being sure to stay away from the rig so I wouldn't get in trouble with Mr. Dobbs. As we went, Bob pointed out several piles of limbs, weeds, and leaves around the edge of the open ground. We left the clearing and walked about fifty yards to the riverbank along a path that Bob had made. At the river, the path got smaller and turned north. Brush piles just like the ones along the back of the clearing were spaced along the path. When we were safely out of sight of the rig, Bob went over to one of the piles and lifted some of the limbs off the top. Under the brush was a snake trap.

The trap consisted of a cage made of hardware cloth, the square-grid, galvanized wire mesh that you see in any hardware store. It was closed on the bottom and sides and the wire mesh bent over the top to form a border that turned down and ended with the pointed wires pointing into the cage. Several very decayed chicken necks were lying in the trap. Needless to say, the chicken necks were surrounded by a swarm of flies. The flies had attracted lots of frogs. They hopped into the brush pile, and some of them had fallen into the cage. Attracted by the unhappy sounds they made, cottonmouths would crawl in to dine on the frogs. They slid easily over the wire mesh but found themselves confronted with the overhanging edge and the sharp wires if they tried to leave. There was a big cottonmouth coiled up in the cage now.

"See, that's my problem," Bob exclaimed. "I emptied this cage just this morning and it's full again. I could get seven, eight, maybe ten a day; but Mr. Dobbs is already getting suspicious that not all the snakes I present to him were found on the well site. I throw over half of them back in the river. How can I convince him he has a really big snake problem?"

"How many would you catch each day if you didn't have the traps?" I asked.

"Not even one a day if I just patrolled the clearing. I do patrol the clearing carefully each morning and evening. I don't want to make J.C.'s mistake. I suspect that J.C. had some scheme to insure that his work was appreciated, but I don't know what he did. Obviously he didn't have a network like I've got."

Mr. Dobbs had, indeed, become suspicious of Bob's amazing productivity. One day not long after Bob had shown me his system, Mr. Dobbs climbed up the rig near the end of the workday and stayed there when it shut down and the crew left. They had all been warned not to notice that Mr. Dobbs sat on a girder at the top of the rig and leaned back against an upright beam. He rode to work that day with

Rufus LeBlanc, so his vehicle wasn't there to tip off Bob. Mr. Dobbs had a pair of binoculars and followed Bob as he visited the traps, pulled out the cottonmouths with a hooked stick, efficiently beheaded some of them and threw the others into the river.

Mr. Dobbs was sitting in a folding chair on the rig platform when he came back up his path with the snake heads. He congratulated Bob on his industriousness, his clever scheme for catching so many cottonmouths, and his restraint in throwing some of them back to avoid seeming greedy. Then he fired Bob and ordered him off the site.

Cephus Daniels, another Negro, was hired at five dollars a day. He was a farmer, known for his very well kept farm, and for being well-spoken and reliable. He could guard the drilling site during the day and still do chores before and after. His wife and kids took care of the other farm work. He remained the snake wrangler during the rest of the time the rig worked in Frog Level.

Bob and I continued to visit every day or two, but Bob had to stay out of the clearing now. It seemed that one thing or another kept life interesting at the drilling rig; so just as Bob's scheme ended, my cousin, Leonard, took up the slack.

Leonard came of age just in time to go off to World War II. His nature compelled him to choose the most glamorous way to fight the war; he joined the Army Air Corps. He was too big and too slow-reflexed to make a fighter pilot. I don't know how he rated as a bomber pilot, but I'll guess that he lacked some leadership skill or had too much of some other quality, so he ended up assigned to ferry cargo and soldiers from one Pacific island to another in a C-47. Though it was not as glamorous as he had wished, it was not a job for a cowardly or shy person by any means. He flew out to the Solomon Islands long before they were secured, through the Philippines before they fell to Japan, up through the Aleutians, and around the Pacific several times.

His job required him to sit around waiting for the cargo to be loaded or a detail of soldiers to be rounded up for transport. I understand that as the U.S. occupied an island, one of the first nonofficial establishments to be set up was a bar. Leonard usually waited patiently in the bar. Given the chaotic, or desperate, or hurried conditions of war, no one had the time to carefully examine the pilots before a mission to see if they were sober and rested. In most cases, only one pilot, copilot, and mechanic flew with each plane. You either flew or you didn't, and not flying was often not an option.

As is the case for almost everyone in wartime, Leonard's career-defining moment came swiftly and unexpectedly. He emerged from a bar on Espiritu Santo and took off on a short hop to another of the New Hebrides islands. Taking off was no problem—push the throttle full forward and manage to stay on the runway until the plane lifts itself. The copilot was a good navigator, and there are not too many trees or mountains to hit in the middle of the Pacific Ocean, but landing always requires some finesse. Leonard made such a decisive landing that he left the entire tail section of the airplane sitting at the end of the runway. He taxied on up to the cargo area and apparently was still unaware of the missing part of his plane when the emergency brigade arrived.

Leonard's father practiced small-time politics. If you could tolerate his always-lit cigar, he provided great conversations. He always had a story about some scheme that he pulled off or some conniving he did with a well-known politician.

In any case, his political influence usually got Leonard out of various troubles that he seemed to accumulate regularly. He managed an honorable discharge for his son, and Leonard came back to Frog Level as a war hero. I only learned the story of his final landing after I was in college.

I liked Leonard, especially his tall tales about the war. They were even better than the ones his daddy told. Most of his performances would begin with, "Let me show you a little trick I learned in the Philippines," followed by some bar trick or a joke. They were always cleaned up just enough for family, or nearly so.

Leonard heard about how I supplied the TV power supply to Mr. Ferguson's research project, as had most everyone in town. Since Leonard had the idea of giving me the television, he decided he incurred some obligation to investigate and make sure everyone knew the whole story about the origin of the electronics. The gossip chain exaggerated my contribution much more than I ever could have done. This, in turn, exaggerated Leonard's natural inclination to think himself the center of attention in any circumstance, and he showed up at the drilling rig one afternoon.

I happened to be there because Mr. Ferguson's scheme soon would be put to the test. He had me watching a voltmeter as he tuned the circuits so I could tell him if a change made the voltage go up or down. Leonard walked right up the steps of the trailer and said his name, but nothing more. He assumed Mr. Ferguson knew who he was and why he had appeared.

The look on Mr. Ferguson's face clearly indicated that he had no idea who Leonard was, so I took up the introduction of my cousin, including his war hero status, which was valid so far as I knew at the time. On this basis as a cousin of mine, Mr. Ferguson began to show Leonard around and answer his questions. Leonard found it all very familiar, he said.

"Oh yeah, that looks just like the BC-458 transmitter on a C-47," he said.

As he warmed up to telling how he knew everything, his hands poked deeper and deeper into the equipment. Everything was turned on for the tests that we were doing when Leonard came in. Finally, though I noticed he had restrained himself considerably, Mr. Ferguson had to grab Leonard's hand to keep him from touching a copper bus bar that carried the eight hundred volts. Leonard resented being grabbed and jerked his hand back.

"You were about to touch the eight-hundred volt bus," Ferguson explained half apologetically.

"I know that, you dummy," replied Leonard.

He turned to the main control panel. "Where do you turn it off?" he asked as he reached up and began to turn knobs.

Ferguson moved to place himself between Leonard and his equipment. He had to shove Leonard backward toward the door to get in front of the panel. Leonard didn't fall back gracefully, but stuck out his arms to push Ferguson back. Leonard was off balance, however, and the push simply propelled him back through the door and left him teetering on the top step. Leonard's push threw Ferguson partially off balance, and he reached for a chrome-plated handle on one of the equipment racks to steady himself. Leonard stopped his fall by grabbing a ten-gallon can of diesel oil used to fuel the generator that sat beside Ferguson's trailer. It stopped him, but knocked the oil can over and the oil began to pour all over the four public-address loudspeakers in the test rig.

Mr. Ferguson held on to the rack handle. The weight of his body pivoted him around until his forearm struck the red button that activated the system.

The deafening noise began and did not stop until Mr. Ferguson could get his feet under him, realize what had triggered the stimulator, and move his arm away from the red button. It ran at full power for at least ten seconds. While it ran, the diesel oil vaporized just as the coke bottle had done, and it sprayed out and up to form a gray cloud that spread until it began to engulf the drilling rig.

The Tuscaloosa highway is fairly busy during the daytime, and it happened that Wyman Lister was passing at the moment the cloud of diesel oil sprayed out. He pulled over to the side of the road to see what was going on. He leaned over and rolled down the passenger-side window to get a better look. He couldn't see much except the gray cloud, but the wind carried the smell of diesel oil right into his face. He could reach only one conclusion: they had struck oil and it was spraying out of the well to form a large gray cloud.

He leaned back into the driver's seat and spun the wheels of his truck to head for town and be the first to announce, "They've struck oil!!"

His destination was Hubbert's auto parts store. He walked, almost ran, inside, and without waiting for anyone to acknowledge him, he shouted, "They've struck oil! It's spraying all over the place." Bill Wallace, a mechanic for the Chevrolet dealership across the street was there. He exited quickly to get back to the shop and spread the word. Herbert Mullen left for the fabric store to tell his wife and the other six people who were there. Mr. Hubbert yelled back to his machinist in the back room, then went out the front door and across to Monroe's Cafe to alert everyone there. In a couple of minutes word spread to the meat processing plant, the jail, the veterinary clinic, and an ever widening circle of businesses. The phone switchboard lit up faster than the operator, Patty Jones, could answer. In less than ten minutes, probably not a single person downtown had not heard the news.

The drive from town to the well site was five minutes or less, so cars and trucks began to arrive while Leonard and Mr. Ferguson were still calming down after being separated by the roustabout. Leonard still shouted at Mr. Ferguson, "You stupid baboon!" every minute or so.

The roughnecks and driller had stopped drilling when the oil fog blocked their vision. They were wiping oil off the gauges and levers. Mr. Dobbs had emerged from his office and received an explanation from Ferguson. The vehicles lined both sides of the road, leaving just enough room for other cars to carefully pass in between them.

At first, I didn't understand why a growing crowd of people milled around at the highway. I headed down the wooden road to see what was going on. The first arrivals informed me they heard that the well had struck oil. They asked me why no cloud of oil was spraying up from the well as Wyman Lister described. The reference to the cloud of oil made me understand what happened, and I began to announce over and over that it was a mistake: no oil strike. I became the defacto press secretary.

Not wanting to embarrass Leonard and maybe myself by kinship association, I reported simply, "We had an accident that spilled some oil into Mr. Ferguson's test transducer, and whatever falls into the test setup is vaporized by the high-energy acoustic waves. As soon as Mr. Ferguson shut off the test setup, everything went back to normal."

I thought the "high-energy acoustic waves" and "transducer" marked me as an expert in most eyes.

The disappointment spread faster than had the good news. Some of the people headed back to their cars, but some decided to stay and swap notes with their neighbors and, maybe, offer a few opinions about the wisdom of the whole drilling enterprise.

Thus, the wooden road was lined with a few clusters of conversing spectators when the Alberts, Leon, Alphonse, and Ambrose, arrived in their Cadillac. They rolled down the windows as they turned off the highway and waved to the crowd with broad smiles on their faces. They were at the drilling rig before it struck them that very few people waved back, and no one was smiling like they were.

Mr. Dobbs saw the familiar Cadillac turn off the highway, and he met them at the end of the road.

The spectators stood back a respectful distance just as they usually did at the scene of an automobile accident, so they couldn't understand what was being said. The gestures, however, were quite clear. Alphonse threw both arms up at full length and let out a moan. Ambrose took a step backward and turned first one way and the other as if he wanted to leave but couldn't decide which way to go. Leon, their father, at first stood motionless, and then, stiff as a board, he fell backwards on the ground.

The bare dirt of the rig clearing had been regularly massaged by the comings and goings of big trucks and tractors, so it was soft enough that he was undamaged by the fall. Alphonse knelt down to see what had happened to his father. Mr. Dobbs also knelt down with real concern on his face, and he immediately ordered a roughneck to call for an ambulance.

The Verlaine funeral home ran the only ambulance service in Frog Level. Their two hearses doubled as ambulances. Everyone heard the siren approaching and stepped back off the wooden road. Leon Albert had regained consciousness again and seemed very agitated. He kept mumbling just loud enough to be heard by the closest part of the crowd. "Not again. Not again. Lord, not again."

After the hearse departed, Superintendent Dobbs broke the news about the diagnosis rendered by the hearse driver, "Mr. Leon Albert has suffered a heart attack." Alphonse got in the Cadillac and followed the hearse, but Ambrose stayed behind and was in deep conversation with Mr. Dobbs.

Mr. Leon Albert got out of the hospital the next day. The common gossip held that it was his fourth heart attack in the last two years, and he seemed no worse for the episodes. It led most people to question the convenient timeliness of his attacks.

The next day I apologized to Mr. Ferguson for Leonard's behavior. He took it all in a good mood and didn't seem to hold it against me, but he said that I should warn Leonard to stay away. He explained, "I thought he was about to throw the load switch off. If he had, it would have ruined the ceramic vacuum tubes. I don't have a budget to buy new ones, and they would take several weeks to get here anyway. I hope he doesn't hold a grudge against me."

I assured him, "I think Leonard will probably forget about the whole thing pretty soon. He won't want to remind anyone that he was part of the big mess. He always moves from one project to another pretty fast. Usually doesn't finish most of them. Don't worry about him."

We decided it had a funny side and got back to preparing for the real test of the acoustic stimulation system.

Leonard didn't forget. He wasn't inclined to let the affair pass and decided that Mr. Ferguson and the whole drilling crew had insulted him. At the very least, he saw Ferguson's pushing him away from the controls as an insult. He was, after all, a retired Army Air Corps pilot, and Ferguson was a stupid baboon.

He definitely didn't forget. I didn't see or hear about the warning signs at the time, so I assumed the whole thing was over with.

For example, Leonard decided to take a joy ride in the Civil Air Patrol Piper Cub, the one Jack Hunter donated to them. He had been seen making sharp turns over Frog Level with the door open and one leg hanging out. I don't think he had a valid pilot's license.

In another incident, he got a speeding ticket on the Winfield highway. The officer knew him and his father's connections and decided to ignore the empty whiskey bottle on the front seat.

I gather that still other warning signs went unnoticed.

Bob Sargent approached me at the grocery store a little over a week after the altercation and false alarm at the oil well. I was stacking heads of lettuce on the display rack.

"What kind of guy is your cousin, Leonard?" he asked.

"He's okay. Why do you ask?"

"I hear he got into a fight with Mr. Ferguson at the oil well."

"It wasn't a fight. They had a misunderstanding over the acoustic simulator controls, and Ferguson told him to leave them alone." I left out the shoving.

"What do you think Leonard will do to retaliate?"

"Nothing. Why do you think he's going to do something?"

Bob shrugged. "I don't know. I saw him in front of the farm store, and he still seemed worked up about it. He didn't seem to like me bringing it up. What would he do if he was gonna do something?"

"Leonard is just a lot of hot air. He talks big but never follows through. A politician, just like his daddy."

That seemed to satisfy Bob. "Okay, I just thought I'd ask."

The next Monday revealed the real reason for Bob's questions. The drilling crew arrived at 6:30 as usual and went to work to start the coffeepot and have the machinery running by 7:00 sharp. But on this day, the drilling rig didn't start up, and our Police Chief, Buford McClatchy, had Leonard in the city jail by 7:30.

As the crew arrived and fanned out to their tasks, the first yell came from the shed where they kept the coffeepot. The roughneck found a cottonmouth in the large galvanized sink there. At first, this seemed like trouble for Cephus Daniels. It seemed strange that a loop of duct tape hung around the cottonmouth as if he had been tied to the faucet, but had wriggled loose. Then they found one in a paper bag tied to the driller's main control lever. A third one was taped to the stack of drill pipe. Finally, two more were duct taped to John Ferguson's chair in his trailer. And that explained it. Mr. Dobbs called Chief McClatchy. He got Leonard out of bed, handcuffed him, and threw him in jail.

The school year had just started, and classes began before the drama became the daily gossip. I heard it all after I got home. I cornered Bob Sargent the next day. "Okay, Bob, you knew this was going to happen, didn't you?"

"Yeah, I knew something was up, but you said Leonard was just a lot of hot air."

I jabbed my forefinger into his shoulder. "I know what Leonard did. What did you have to do with it?"

"I guess Leonard heard about my job as snake wrangler and how they fired me. I didn't really mind. I guess they caught me fair and square, but Leonard figured I'd have a score to settle. I didn't, but when he offered me five dollars apiece for six big cottonmouths, I wasn't about to turn it down. Thirty dollars! You'd do it!"

It had taken only two hours to get the six cottonmouths. He just revisited some of his old traps behind the oil well.

"That comes out to fifteen dollars an hour! Fifteen an hour!" Bob clearly didn't think himself at fault for what Leonard did with them in any way.

I didn't squeal on him. I shared his opinion that Leonard was responsible for what he did with the snakes, not Bob. I was also sure being thrown in jail would do him some good, and eventually, I would hear a funny version of it straight from the horse's mouth.

Mr. Dobbs didn't file charges, and Leonard's daddy got him out after one night.

## Odds and ends

They drilled to five thousand, three hundred feet before abandoning and filling the well. They found nothing but a huge flow of worthless gas. It was a little over three years later that a gas pipeline finally came through Frog Level and gas wells became valuable properties.

John Ferguson's experiments were inconclusive, mainly because they found no oil. The gas flow actually increased by about fifty percent during the one hour they operated the well after his test, but no one cared.

About thirty years later when I managed R&D for Western Geophysical, the world's largest oil and gas exploration contractor at the time, a delegation of Russian geophysicists looking for research support approached us. The Soviet Union was crumbling, and they were allowed to come to the West in hope of taking some capitalist dollars back home. They had the idea to vibrate oil formations in hope of increasing the oil production just like Mr. Ferguson had done, but using a hydraulically driven shaker rather than an electronically driven one. I spent most of the conference reminiscing to myself, and after their presentation was finished, I asked them if they knew of any previous tests of the idea. They said it was conceived and tested only in Russia.

I insisted that I thought it had been tried in the US many years ago. "Nyet," they said, "Only in Russia." But I knew better.

# College, 1959

You have to do your own growing no matter
how tall your grandfather was.

Abraham Lincoln

One's mind, once stretched by a new idea,
never regains its original dimensions.

Oliver Wendell Holmes

## The world is changing

In the spring of 1959, a very unexpected opportunity dropped in my lap. About a month before school ended, I came home one afternoon, and Mother greeted me with a question.

"How would you like to go to college this fall rather than a year later?"

She explained that Mr. Shoemaker, the High School Principal, called. He asked her to come by his office when it was convenient. No, I wasn't having any problem, he just wanted to discuss my future with her. She went to the school first thing that afternoon.

Mr. Shoemaker pointed out to her I had taken just about all the courses the Frog Level High School had to offer. The only elective courses I hadn't taken were typing, agriculture, and home economics. He surmised that I wouldn't care for agriculture and home economics. Since computers were still pretty much science fiction, nobody imagined I would ever really need typing.

Moreover, Mr. Shoemaker had been observing me and realized I spent more time scribbling rocket designs and electronic circuits than I did on school work. All my teachers agreed I was bored. Only twelfth-grade English and History remained before I satisfied the requirements for a High School diploma. Both those classes were offered in Summer School, mainly for students who flunked one of them in the regular session and needed to make them up to get a diploma. If I took those two courses this summer, I could enter the University of Alabama in the fall.

Of course, I was stunned. I had no idea such a thing was possible. I would never have the nerve to suggest it. But when I saw the possibility, I leaped at it. Yes, yes, yes, I want to go!

The decision made for a busy summer. I had to work at the grocery store to get money for incidental expenses. I had to attend Summer School each morning. As if someone were running an experiment to see just how busy they could make me, Mr. Jeff Dunn, the manager of our local radio station, WWFL, stopped in the store while I was working and asked if I would like to run WWFL all day each Saturday for the summer.

Well, this was just about as unexpected as the offer to graduate early. He explained that he had only one announcer at the moment, Buford Sumter. Terry Sayers had resigned and moved back to New Orleans a few weeks ago. Mr. Sumter needed at least one day a week off until they could find another announcer.

I thought it would be just great. Not only would I enjoy cranking up the transmitter each Saturday morning—it was electronics, after all—but the job had all sorts of other grown-up duties to perform. I'd have to check the weather instruments each morning and record them in an official U.S. Weather Service logbook. I'd get to edit and read the news just as Terry Sayers had shown me, read the advertisements, and introduce the songs. I'd be about as close as anyone in Frog Level got to being a celebrity. Well, that wasn't true. The good players on the football and basketball teams were much bigger celebrities.

My father put a stop to the fun immediately. He pointed out that Saturday was the busiest day of the week at the grocery store, and he counted on me to work through the summer.

I told Mr. Dunn that I had to work at the store. Thanks anyway, I said. But it wasn't a missed opportunity yet.

Mr. Dunn asked Buford Sumter if he would agree to have Sunday off instead of Saturday, and he said okay. On top of everything else, I had a Sunday job too.

The job at the radio station provided several other stories I could tell, but that's for another time.

The point of all this for now is, I had no more time to spend in the swamp. No time for adventures in that hectic summer of 1959. No matter how busy, there was one more trip I just had to make before I left the swamp for good. I didn't make it until I was home on a weekend after the semester began at The University of Alabama.

**Let the dead bury the dead**

The leaves were falling like rain as I walked up the gullied road to Mount Nebo. I'd waited until about four o'clock to go there because I wanted all the curious gawkers to be gone. The sun hung low, and clouds blew past it to change the scene from yellow gold to gray within seconds. The cool October air felt good to breathe.

The ground leveled off, and I saw the huge black building ahead. I expected to see Mr. Tubalcaine sitting out in front to welcome his visitors, but the old hickory chair that I remembered sat empty. Maybe it was too cold or too late for the old man to sit out here. I paused and looked around for maybe a minute, then walked around the corner where I would find the door to his room. I froze halfway through a stride when I saw the black-tarred casket sitting on two stacks of red bricks in front of the door.

I stared at it, not knowing what to think. I'd started up the dirt road smiling to myself and enjoying the feeling that I knew this place and its strange occupant. Now, a knot formed in my stomach, and I felt out of place. After only a few seconds, I noticed that the lid wasn't on the casket. I would have to go on and look inside.

I slowly shuffled toward the dull black box. It couldn't possibly have looked more ominous. About ten feet from the casket I stopped again. I'd come close enough to see just a few inches into the inside where a rim about an inch deep around the edge reflected the deep orange color of the heart-pine wood. Everything else inside was black.

The knot in my stomach tightened. The interior of the casket looked exactly like the black holes in space Kenny and I had seen walking beside the flaming Theawatoosa. I stared hard trying to see something in that black space: anything to fill that black void, anything.

I stood there completely confused, my eyes locked on the black inside of the casket, trying to understand the image that I couldn't take my eyes off. I made no sense of it. Finally, my reason overcame the fear and lack of understanding. "It's not a hole in space," I told myself. "Remember what the whole Theawatoosa business was about. Use your head. Use your head!"

Of course, the next thought, that it was Mr. Tubalcaine's black-shrouded body, didn't make me much happier. Just then, a voice came from the direction of the casket. It said, "I figured it was time to make use of my handiwork. I couldn't stand the thought that it might go to waste."

I jumped involuntarily and maybe let out a small squeak. It would have been a full scream if I hadn't wrestled it down. At that moment, just over the casket, I saw a small movement inside the door and looked up at it. Mr. Tubalcaine emerged with a smile on his face.

"Oh, hi," I said. "It really surprised me to see your casket sitting out here."

"Yes, I guess it did give you strange ideas. You must have thought I'd just climbed in and turned out the lights." He still smiled and chuckled a little.

"I realized a while back that it was unlikely that I'd ever use it for its natural purpose. Some day I'm going to pass away sitting by the fire or wandering through the woods up here. Nobody is likely to find me until it's long past suitable to use the casket. I put it out here on those bricks and filled it with some good, black dirt from the woods. I plan to put flowers in it next spring."

Just as when I saw Theawatoosa the second time without the overwhelming fear, the hole in space became very obviously dirt.

Mr. Tubalcaine's casual attitude restored my better mood. He suggested that we go inside where it was warmer. Inside, he pulled up a rocking chair to the open door of the old furnace and indicated I should get a straight chair from across the room. I sat down on the other side of the furnace door. Neither of us said anything for a while.

"You asked about my name the last time I saw you, just after we'd killed off Theawatoosa."

"Yessir. It seems strange you're named after a Biblical character that everybody thinks is evil. Most popular Biblical names are the good guys: Joseph, Paul, Moses, Joshua. How'd your family get Tubalcaine? Brother Flowers said if he was called Tubalcaine, he'd change it."

"He did, did he?" he chuckled. "I guess that just shows again what an odd bird I am. I chose it. I named myself Tubalcaine."

I just stared at him for a moment, mentally checking to see if I heard correctly. "You chose the name? Your parents weren't named Tubalcaine?"

"It's a complicated story, Wendell. I haven't told anybody about it since.... He paused a long time, searching for the memory. When he spoke again, his voice came out hoarse and soft.

"I haven't told anyone since I explained it to my wife." Again he paused maybe a whole minute. I could see he was waiting for the emotion to pass.

"I was born out in West Texas; south of Winters, it's called now. My parents' name was Wright. That's what they used, but, of course, Mother wasn't born with that name and my father had changed his name. He had to. That's why we lived out in the middle of nowhere in Texas.

"My parents met and married in Georgia. Somewhere near Marietta.

My father worked in the Phoenix Foundry and Machine Works. An accident happened one day that killed one of his work crew. I don't know why, but they accused my father of killing him, murdering him. He believed he would be arrested and hanged, so he and my mother left and moved to Texas where nobody would find them. My father changed his name to Wright."

Mr. Tubalcaine fell silent again. I didn't say anything; just intently tried to picture the events. After a while he went on, his voice remained very soft.

"I don't even know what his real name was, and I don't know my mother's maiden name. I lost both of them when I was nine years old: too young to ask the obvious questions. I lost them in a big storm, a tornado I guess. My father had dug a small storm shelter. They put me in it when they saw the storm coming and went back to try to save some of the animals. When it was over, they were just gone. Just gone."

"Mr. Tubalcaine, I don't know what... I don't know...." I was obviously at a loss for words, as happens to me much too often.

Mr. Tubalcaine looked up and smiled a half smile. "It's okay. You don't need to say anything. It's good to have a reason to tell the story after so long.

"I stayed there three days, looking for them. I had to do something, so I decided to go to Abilene. It was about forty miles away, but I didn't know which way or how far. I walked to the big road and started hitching a ride.

"I got to Abilene in about a day and a half. People were very kind to me. In Abilene, I thought maybe I could find some kind of work. People hired very young kids back then. No laws against it like now. They didn't pay much, but they might give you a place to stay and something to eat.

"My father had told me about working on machinery, and he did his own blacksmithing; at least, when he could get some steel. I knew how to work the bellows for a forge, so I started around the blacksmith shops in Abilene asking to be a helper. Mr. MacDonald took me on and allowed me to stay with his family. They didn't formally adopt me, but they treated me like one of their children. They asked me what my name was. I didn't want to say Wright because it wasn't really my family name. Riding in the wagon on the way to Abilene I had begun to think about it. I decided that I would be John Tubalcaine."

"You chose Tubalcaine? Did you know what it meant?"

Now he smiled a big smile. "Of course, I knew what it meant. That'd be a really strange name to just pull out of your hat. It was the only name for me. I'll explain, but first let me get a cup of tea. Let me fix you one."

"Okay," I said. I didn't usually drink hot tea, but it seemed important to like it now. He talked about his new flower box and chuckled as he heated a kettle.

"I thought about manufacturing pine caskets after I closed my trade school in Frog Level. By then, people were using the fancy metal ones. I had failed at enough businesses by then. Didn't want another one."

"The trade school wasn't a failure," I said. "My parents studied there. They both learned bookkeeping, and Mother learned typing. I'll bet you graduated lots of students."

"You're right. It was World War II that killed it. It would have ended soon any way. Times change, Wendell. When the boys came back from the war, they wanted to go to college. You haven't lived long enough to see it yet, but things change. Everything changes, for better or worse. It's up to us to make it better. Worse happens all by itself; entropy, they call it."

He handed me a cup of tea and settled back into his rocker. After a few sips of the tea, he went back to his amazing story.

"I suppose this all sounds like a sad picture show, but it's true. 'Truth is stranger than fiction.' I'm sure you've heard that, but do you know who said it?"

"Nosir, I don't."

"Mark Twain. Wendell, where will you be fifty years from today? What will you be doing?"

"I don't know." I thought a while. "Maybe I'll be an engineer in Huntsville?"

"Too likely. Life is not made of the likely," he said and shook his head. "From what I hear about you, you won't have any trouble becoming an engineer. The famous quotation from Mark Twain is just the first part of what he said. The whole quotation is, 'Truth is stranger than Fiction, but it is because Fiction is obliged to stick to probabilities. Truth isn't.' Do you understand that?"

He let me ponder it for a while. Finally, I replied, "If I were to write a story about you; how you built this big building way up here on Mount Nebo, your vision for a home, school, church, and community workshop, about the Theawatoosa stuff, nobody would believe it."

"That's exactly right," he said. "Anyway, to get back to my story and why I chose Tubalcaine.

"We had three books in my home. I mean my parents' home before the storm. My mother had wanted to bring more, but she could carry only three when they left Georgia. As you might guess, one of them was a Bible. Secondly, she chose a collection of ancient Greek literature; English translations, of course. The last one became my favorite after Mother taught me to read: *A Thousand and One Gems of English Poetry*. It was a collection of poems from Chaucer to Longfellow. Mother used those books to teach me to read.

"My father, as I said, did some blacksmithing when he could. He farmed so we could eat, but his pleasure was in making things. It didn't matter too much what it was: a chair, a horseshoe, a new plow handle, a toy. He made several puppets for me out of mesquite wood. Mother and I would use them to put on plays for Daddy."

Mr. Tubalcaine's voice became hoarse and thin again as he told about his father. He paused and we both sipped the tea. He started again.

"Because my father got such pleasure from making useful things out of wood, metal, whatever he could get his hands on, one poem in the collection was my favorite. I guess it was the family favorite."

He put his cup on a small stool beside his chair and stood up. "I want to show you something. Let me get it. While I'm up, how about you throw two of those logs in the furnace." He pointed to a stack of firewood near our feet.

He walked between our chairs and across the room to the bookcase that I had examined on my first visit and took a package wrapped in heavy paper from the top shelf, wiped and blew the dust off it and came back to his rocking chair.

He carefully unfolded the paper and laid it on the firewood. Inside the paper was a copy of *A Thousand and One Gems of English Poetry*.

"I couldn't find much of our belongings after the tornado, but I did find this. I suppose if I could have only one thing, it was this book I wanted."

He let the book fall open. It opened exactly where he wanted it.

"Here's a poem written by Charles MacKay. He edited this book and included a couple of his own poems."

Mr. Tubalcaine held the book open and began to recite the poem, but I noticed that he didn't really need to read it.[14]

> Old Tubal Cain was a man of might
>> In the days when the Earth was young;
> By the fierce red light of his furnace bright
>> The strokes of his hammer rung;
> And he lifted high his brawny hand
>> On the iron glowing clear,
> Till the sparks rushed out in scarlet showers,
>> And he fashioned the sword and spear.
> And he sang—"Hurra for my handiwork!
>> Hurra for the spear and sword!
> Hurra for the hand that shall wield them well,
>> For he shall be king and lord!"
>
> To Tubal Cain came many a one,
>> As he wrought by his roaring fire,
> And each one prayed for a strong steel blade
>> As the crown of his desire:
> And he made them weapons sharp and strong,

---

[14] The poem, the spelling, and the format are copied from *A Thousand and One Gems of English Poetry*, Selected and Arranged by Charles MacKay, LL.D. Published by George Routledge and Sons, London, 1896. Mr. Tubalcaine's copy was an even older edition.

# Wendell Wiggins

Till they shouted loud with glee,
And gave him gifts of pearl and gold,
And spoils of the forest free.
And they sang—"Hurra for Tubal Cain,
Who hath given us strength anew!
Hurra for the smith, hurra for the fire,
And hurra for the metal true!"

But a sudden change came o'er his heart
Ere the setting of the sun,
And Tubal Cain was filled with pain
For the evil he had done;
He saw that men, with rage and hate,
Made war upon their kind,
That the land was red with the blood they shed
In their lust for carnage blind.
And he said—"Alas, that I ever made,
Or that skill of mine should plan,
The spear and the sword for men whose joy
Is to slay their fellow man."

And for many a day old Tubal Cain
Sat brooding o'er his woe;
And his hand forbore to smite the ore
And his furnace smouldered low.
But he rose at last with a cheerful face,
And a bright courageous eye,
And bared his strong right arm for work,
While the quick flames mounted high.
And he sang—"Hurra for my handicraft!"
And the red sparks lit the air;
"Not alone for the blade was the bright steel made;"
And he fashioned the first ploughshare.

And men, taught wisdom from the past,
In friendship joined their hands,
Hung the sword in the hall, the spear on the wall,
And ploughed the willing lands;
And sang—"Hurra for Tubal Cain!
Our staunch good friend is he;
And for the ploughshare and the plow
To him our praise shall be.
But while oppression lifts its head,
Or a tyrant would be lord,
Though we may thank him for the plough,
We'll not forget the sword!"

He closed the book and brushed the cover with his hand.

"That's why I chose Tubalcaine as my name. Much better than Wright, it honors my father. I think it expresses the way he felt about making things. It also honors my mother since it reminds me how she taught me to read and to love learning; learning anything."

"You're right about life being unexpected," I said. "I would never have guessed how you came to be named Tubalcaine."

He let me look at his treasured book for a while, then he wrapped it in the paper and put it back on the top shelf of the bookcase.

I stood up to go. "I guess I'd better be going. I have to be back for Sunday night church services."

"Your mother said she arranged our Theawatoosa show to teach you to rely on your intellect and learning, didn't she?"

"Yessir. I feel really stupid about the whole thing now."

"Don't worry about it. You'll see some humor in it in a few years. Just learn the lesson. Sit down again for a minute."

I sat in the cane-bottom chair and waited. Mr. Tubalcaine had been leaning forward through our whole conversation. He'd seemed intent on telling his story. He leaned back in his rocking chair now and appeared relaxed for the first time since we began to talk. He just sat for maybe half a minute.

"As I said, Wendell, times change. We've seen a lot of change lately and it looks like it's just getting started. The invention and building of the atomic bomb represents the ultimate realization of the first verse of the poem. It's the ultimate version, our version, of the sword and spear. It's up to you young people to finish the poem; to build the plowshare.

"You can't look back to old-time religion to see where you should go. You need to know the past to know where you are, but it can't show you the future and which way to go. Your mother and daddy are good people, but you can't direct your life by some idea just because they taught it to you. Test the ideas. Listen to new ones. Try them. 'By their fruits, ye shall know them.[15]'

"Neither of us have any idea where you'll be fifty years from now. One thing you should remember. One thing I didn't know and didn't do. Take some good friends with you. It's a hard balance to reach—running your life by your deep internal beliefs and having close friends—because they'll have their own agendas and priorities. You don't want to end up on a hilltop all by yourself."

His comments left me at a loss for words. He was looking at me intensely. I finally found a simple, true statement

"I won't ever forget you; how you taught my parents the things they needed to build a grocery business, to earn the money to send me to college, how you helped me learn about my family, your amazing story. I will try very hard to learn what parts of living are important, and I'll remember that there are no demons in the swamp. Oh yes, and I'll never judge people by just their names."

We got up and walked out together. He stayed beside me till the ground began to slope down.

"I envy you the things you'll know about the universe fifty years from now. Now hurry, or you'll be late to church."

"I'll come back to see you," I said.

"No. You have better things to do. 'Let the dead bury the dead[16].' Now go!"

I walked down the path maybe fifty yards, turned around, and waved. He waved back. I turned to the path again and walked on a bit. I felt uncertain about whether to turn and wave once more. I certainly didn't want to seem unfriendly, but would it just make him sad to drag out the goodbye? The idea of never coming back was making me very sad. While I walked on slowly trying to decide whether to turn around again, Mr. Tubalcaine called out a phrase, a Bible verse I had learned in Sunday school years earlier. I never imagined it would

---

[15] Matthew 7:16.

[16] Matthew: 8:22.

be said to me in such a personal way nor affect me so. He said in a loud, strong voice, not a yell, "Remember Lot's wife![17]"

I stopped in my tracks. The sentence was so short, so simple, and so unexpected, but I knew exactly what he meant. I threw my hand up and waved without turning even my head. And then I stepped on with no lingering uncertainty, and I didn't look back again.

I eventually achieved my childhood dream of being a scientist, and that brought me many new adventures of a different sort. I remembered the lessons I learned in the swamp and applied them in labs where, instead of fiery Theawatoosa, there is the glowing fire of electrical discharges. The Army Air Corps training program is no more, but NASA paid for my training through graduate school. Instead of hunting for marbles, I've searched for better understanding of the physical world. My domain expanded from the swamp to the world, and my coexplorers grew from Kavanaugh and the kids of Frog Level to include scientists from many nations. Despite all the changes, the lessons I learned in the swamp never lost their significance.

I also kept my word; I've never forgotten Mr. Tubalcaine, Frog Level, the amazing people who lived there, and the mysterious Sipsey Swamp.

---

[17] Luke 17:32. Said by Jesus in referring to the story in Genesis, Chapter 19. He uses the reference to tell his disciples to look to the future, not the past.

# About the Author

Wendell Wiggins grew up in Fayette, Alabama and learned to appreciate storytelling from his mother and grandmother. He attended The University of Alabama during the height of the Bear Bryant era and  then received a Ph. D in Physics from The Johns Hopkins University. He stayed on at Hopkins twelve years as a faculty member in Biophysics. Finally, determined to see the world outside the University while solving the oil shortage of the 1970s, he joined Gulf Research and Development in 1980, and later managed world-wide R&D for Western Geophysical, the world's largest oil-exploration service company at the time. He has published many technical articles on nuclear physics, electron microscopic imaging, and seismic imaging techniques; but this book presents his first nontechnical publication. Best-friend-since-1964, Joan, and their two very talented adult daughters made this journey possible and witnessed its accomplishments and foibles.

The author lives in eastern Pennsylvania on the banks of Appenzell Creek. This riparian atmosphere situated in the Appalachian Mountain chain, just as Frog Level is, serves as a surrogate of the Sipsey Swamp. The author ardently appreciates imagination, creativity, and innovation; so he tries his hand at woodworking, metalworking, kinetic sculpture, writing, cooking, building electronic gadgets, and whatever else strikes his fancy on any given day. Some of the goings-on at the author's home can be followed at http://www.froglevel.org.

LaVergne, TN USA
10 November 2009
163698LV00002B/9/P